ALSO BY ANNE RENWICK

THE SILVER SKULL

THE ELEMENTAL WEB CHRONICLES

BOOK 2

ANNE RENWICK

To my husband for indulging my love of castles.

Thank you to...

The Plotmonkeys. Thank you for all the laugh-until-we-cry moments, your many brilliant insights and all the love. Inspiration came from each of you.

Shaunee Cole, the opening scene.

Huntley Fitzpatrick, the stress baking.

Kristan Higgins, the closet.

Jennifer Iszkiewicz, the medicalese.

My brilliant editor, Sandra Sookoo.

Weiyi Zhao for adjusting Wei's English phrasing.

A German-speaking friend for catching the many errors of internet translation.

My sister and sister-in-law for their extreme fear of blood and needles.

My husband and my two boys.

My mom and dad.

Mr. Fox and his red pen.

CHAPTER ONE

London
January 1885

"SHALL WE MARRY, THEN?" In the back of his mind, Lord Ian Stanton, Earl of Rathsburn knew a better lead-in was expected, but he wasn't one for coy games. Far too much effort for too little gain. Time was wasting.

He rolled his shoulders and tipped his head from side to side, trying to shake the tension that spending hours in the presence of empty-headed debutants brought on. He'd had enough. Despite approaching the task with a ruthless efficiency, it had taken him two winter balls, three ice festivals and eight afternoon fireside teas to suss out an acceptable woman. Why did courtship need to be so tortuous?

Sustaining an artifice of charm for such extended periods of time required an exhausting marathon of frozen smiles and inane chatter all borne under a crushing weight of pointlessness. Love was not for him. He was done. This woman would do. There were twenty-eight other things he could have accomplished today. Yes, he'd counted.

Well, there was a point, he supposed. Money. The eventual production of an heir. He glanced at her. Try as he might, couldn't raise any enthusiasm for the attempt at the moment. For now, his immediate goal was to return to his laboratory, and to do that, he needed a wife who could infuse the family coffers.

The woman at his side fulfilled these most basic requirements and had willingly joined him on today's excursion.

For a hefty sum, one could take a young lady aloft for ten minutes in a private hot air balloon tethered to Grosvenor Bridge. He'd been assured that this particular diversion was the current coveted activity for a proposal. A certain path to garnering a swift answer in the affirmative. All advice that threatened to end in miserable failure.

"Excuse me?" Lady Katherine replied with an air of distraction.

High above the Thames, the various ribbons and flaps of the hot air balloon snapped and cracked in the wind that whipped about them. Perhaps she couldn't hear over the noise. He turned to face his future bride and raised his voice, enunciating each word. "Do. You. Want. To. Marry?" He paused at the confounded look on her face and clarified, "Me."

Lady Katherine was beautiful. At least by society's standards. Dark hair. Blue eyes. Slender. That was a slight disappointment. He'd always hoped for a well-endowed wife, but a well-endowed dowry would provide more lasting satisfaction. She—until this outing—had seemed content to snare a titled earl to form a superficial yet advantageous union for them both.

A tangled lock of hair blew across her face and stuck to the damp of her lips. Lips he supposed she'd expect him to kiss when—if—she agreed to his proposal. Lips that now pressed tightly together.

She turned her face away.

If it was sweet words and declarations of his undying love she wanted, he was bound to disappoint. Already he regretted attempting a romantic balloon ride. Clearly it hadn't worked.

He suppressed a sigh. Perhaps he'd been too blunt? It was evident he'd made a mistake. *Marrying* was a mistake, an irritating obligation he had no choice but to shoulder. With his father dead a full year, he'd run out of excuses. He'd tried to mourn—he had—but theirs had been a bitter relationship.

Dismissive of Ian's medical expertise, his father had welcomed a series of snake oil salesmen into their home, subjecting his sister to one ineffective—and often painful— treatment after another in desperate and misguided hopes of a cure. When the family coffers held nothing but cobwebs and dust, it had not distressed him in the least. At last, Father could no longer hire any more charlatans, and Ian could focus on devising a legitimate cure.

Tapping the edge of the balloon's basket with a finger, he watched the dark shadow of a pteryform glide above the

Thames while waiting for Lady Katherine's response. It was rare to see one ousted from its nest before nightfall. His gaze fell lower to the choppy, gray river water rushing beneath Grosvenor Bridge and, while he attempted patience, he counted the tentacled arms that gripped the central pier. Six. Another rubbery appendage lifted from the murky water. Seven. If he could see kraken from here, London river traffic had a serious problem brewing.

He pinched the bridge of his nose. With the cure for his sister within reach, he ought to be in his laboratory. Even if all he could do was observe while a visiting engineer from the Rankine Institute constructed the apparatus necessary to begin human trials.

But a memorandum from the Duke of Avesbury had landed upon his desk two months ago, instructing him that he was to use this lull to find a bride. The Queen, Ian was informed, viewed his earldom as his primary responsibility, not his research, and she was displeased with both his crumbling estate and his failure to produce an heir upon which to bestow his title. Her Majesty did not look fondly upon the other—distant—branch of his family. Employees of Lister Laboratories ignored the Queen and her minion, the Duke of Avesbury, only if they wished to lose their hard won position. *That* couldn't be allowed to happen.

Which brought him to, "Lady Katherine?" His patience was at an end. If she refused him, he wished to move with all due haste to the next woman on his list. He glanced at his pocket watch. Lady Adeline had hinted he would be welcome at today's calling hours.

"Marriage." She cleared her throat. "Yes, of course."

Was that an acceptance? Ignoring a faint sense of disappointment in her lack of enthusiasm—but to be fair, a passionless marriage was what he'd wanted—Ian reached for her, intending to perform the requisite embrace, but she stopped him with a palm to his chest and a quick shake of her head.

"Unfortunately, we must discuss this later," she said. "I foresee a slight problem."

"A problem?" Ian had been under the distinct impression that most young ladies—and their fathers—were desperate to snag the first titled gentleman who proposed.

"Yes. Flying directly at us." She pointed over his shoulder.

Ian spun about. Emerging from the low clouds that hung over the dirigible-studded London skyline was a man. His arms were strapped to an articulated wooden gliding apparatus covered in silver cloth, providing an impressive wing span with which to catch the upwelling air currents. His feet were hooked into a tail rudder, steering him on a course toward their balloon.

Extreme gliding sports in an urban environment drew those who sought the rush of adrenaline. Not only from placing their unequivocal trust in custom-built gliding equipment, but also from deliberately placing themselves in peril by dodging zeppelin balloons, tall buildings, bridge spans... normally nocturnal pteryformes. Or, for the truly insane, skimming above the kraken-infested Thames to land on the very edge of the river's bank.

"He'll realize his error momentarily," Ian predicted. That or they were about to witness tomorrow's newspaper headline. "But perhaps it's best we descend." He tugged on the balloon's tether, letting the man below know they wished to be reeled in.

The basket jerked downward—and the gliding man twitched his right wing, adjusting his trajectory accordingly.

It appeared they *did* have a problem.

Lady Katherine flapped a hand in distress, and Ian caught it, patting it to offer comfort as the passing pteryform dove, changing course to investigate this strange, winged human that dared make a bid to share its sky. At the last moment, the gliding man banked sharply to the left, narrowly avoiding a head-on collision with the flying creature.

"So close," she said, tugging her hand free. Her intense gaze followed the pteryform as its leathery wings carried its dark form off into the sulfurous haze that hung over London, and Ian was struck with the somewhat unsettling thought that his future wife had hoped the pteryform might knock the gliding man from the sky.

A grim thought, but perhaps she had reason, for the man banked again, stretching his arms backward and accelerated, dart-like, in their direction. Ian swore. Had the gliding man merely wished to chat, he could have sought an audience with him at any number of more traditional locations. Though Ian had been out of the field for nearly a year, someone must hold a deep-seated grudge against him. Why else approach when he was in such a vulnerable position?

Ian narrowed his eyes. The man's features were obscured by a leather flying cap and wide goggles. His body, however, was large and hulking. None of the resultant outcomes he could calculate ended well. He glanced down. At this rate, there was no hope they'd reach the relative safety of the bridge in time.

The pteryform reappeared, circling about, intent upon a closer look.

"It's no use," Lady Katherine said, throwing her hand up in the air, then slicing it sideways. "Better to take evasive measures while the pteryform distracts him."

"Agreed." Ian bent over and slid a dagger from his boot. "A hot air balloon ascends faster than a glider."

"I'll fire the burner."

He leaned out over the basket and sliced through the tether. But the balloon didn't rise, and he didn't hear the roar of flames. Ian turned to find Lady Katherine flipping the switch.

"It's useless! The flame has gone out!" she yelled as the pteryform swooped down toward their balloon, angling sharply in an attempt to grab the gliding man with its talons. It missed. There was the sound of cloth tearing, and Ian swore. A sharp claw on the tip of the creature's wing had caught the thin cloth and slashed a gaping hole in the balloon.

The rapid ascent he'd planned was now a rapid descent.

"Hang on!" he yelled, catching hold of the wicker edge moments before the gliding man slammed into the side of their basket, throwing them sideways.

Lady Katherine let out a piercing shriek as the basket tipped on its side, tumbling her perilously close to the edge. Instinct had him reaching for the most voluminous part of her. Her bustle made an ominous ripping sound, but the undergarment must have been tightly secured, for it held. Yet the cost of keeping her from pitching into the river below came at a price. His dagger was now in the hands—or tentacles—of the kraken.

And today he carried no extra weapons.

Ian dragged Lady Katherine to his side as the basket continued to lurch and career wildly in the wind. The balloon sank toward the river with undue speed, as if three men had landed on the basket, not one.

A hand gloved in articulated iron—sporting curved grappling hooks that protruded from each finger—appeared on the edge of the basket. Then another. With a mighty yank, the gliding man vaulted into their basket with such heft that one foot punched through the thick wooden flooring.

Lady Katherine cowered behind him.

"What do you want?" Ian demanded.

With the ease of movement that spoke of long practice, the gliding man unclasped a series of leather bands across his chest and shrugged the articulated wings from his shoulders, sending them plunging downward into the choppy waves of the Thames. He yanked off his goggles and fixed Ian with a piercing stare. One pale blue eye bulged as if something shoved it from the socket. A large, square jaw was covered with strange, knobby lumps that strained outward against the skin, threatening to break free.

Ian stared back with the certain knowledge that his greatest fear had come to pass.

In a low growl, the monster spoke. Whether he challenged him to a duel—or demanded a cure, Ian couldn't say. He hadn't spent much time studying German.

"*Nicht sprechen Deutsch*," Ian said. Or, rather, mangled.

The man snorted in derision. "You stupid English." He reached out. Metal hooks ripped through Ian's waistcoat and shirt, slicing through the skin of his chest as they curved into a tight grip. He dragged him close. "*Hören sie mir zu.* Listen."

Ian ignored the pain. "I'm listening. You'd best speak quickly. We're about to land in the Thames."

The monster didn't seem worried. "Your sister is at Burg Kerzen. You will come to Germany."

"My sister? In Germany?" No. He'd received a letter from her just last week. She was in warm, sunny Italy, safely tucked away in a nunnery, free from the rigors of daily life, safe from anything that might exacerbate her condition.

The monster nodded. "Yes. You come. Alone. To fix those like me. To make more who will not get sick. Or she will die."

"Who—"

"Brace." The monster said, and thrust him away to grip the side of the basket with his hooks.

Ian gathered Lady Katherine close. They were lucky. Rather than open water, the banks of the Thames rushed up at them. They hit ground with a hard, bone-jarring crash, and the basket toppled onto its side, dumping him and Lady

Katherine unceremoniously onto tidal mud strewn with rocks, rubbish and decaying kraken corpses.

As the balloon overhead deflated around them, Ian jumped to his feet and dragged Lady Katherine from the wreckage. Carrying her a safe distance from the water, he deposited her near a gawking crowd of onlookers and ran back.

There, still in the balloon's basket, lay the German monster, unconscious. Ian hooked his hands under the man's arms and pulled. And managed to move him not a single inch. He pulled harder. Nothing. It was as if the man was made from metal.

Which, in a way, Ian feared he was.

"Lord Rathsburn, please step aside," a familiar voice spoke. "We'll take care of this."

Glancing up, he found a number of official-looking men behind him. Queen's agents. The man who spoke was none other than Mr. Black, former mentor and colleague. Spy. Black rarely appeared publically in broad daylight, preferring to hug the shadows, hovering just out of reach.

Ian moved out of the way. A solitary man stood no chance of shifting the German. In the end it took six men to lift and carry the unconscious man onto a sleek, dark boat that waited at the river's edge. Braced on its bow and ostensibly targeting kraken, stood a man holding a sniper rifle. His presence also served to discourage curiosity.

"Your convenient proximity raises more questions than it answers," Ian said, tugging a handkerchief from his pocket and pressing it to the—thankfully shallow—gash upon his chest. The blood had already slowed, and the pain was tolerable. "Why have so many men watching me?"

"I don't suppose you'll believe it was purely for the spectacle of watching you tie yourself to a woman?" A corner of Black's mouth twitched. "Quite unusual, your courtship techniques, Rathsburn. The large German man landing upon your hot air balloon and the attacking pteryform were quite riveting."

"Glad to be of entertainment value," Ian snarled. "And, no, I don't believe you."

"Perhaps you should ask the duke directly," Black suggested. His gaze flicked to Ian's chest. "After you see to your ruined shirt."

"He'll not answer the questions I wish to ask," he growled.

"Take up a TTX pistol once more and he might."

Ian swore. "He let Warrick walk away. This is *his* fault."

Black gave him a dark glance. "You walked away as well." Ian opened his mouth to object, but the agent looked past him and lifted his chin. "I believe your lady is getting away."

Ian turned.

Lady Katherine, her dress ruined and her hat askew, climbed into a crank hack. She spared him little more than a disgusted glance before the vehicle jerked away.

"It would appear the wedding is off," Ian muttered. If it had ever been on. Given a decent marriage required a certain amount of loyalty, it seemed he'd dodged a bullet. But before he could even exhale in relief, dread wrapped cold fingers about his throat.

Caught in a tangle of conflicting thoughts and emotions, he looked back toward the Thames where the boat, its men and its cargo moved swiftly away, leaving him behind in what seemed to be his natural state: alone.

Even in a crowd.

CHAPTER TWO

L ADY OLIVIA RAVENSDALE's stomach churned as
Lord Rancide waggled his bushy eyebrows. She
glanced again at the half-closed parlor door and
shifted subtly onto the edge of her own seat. Recent trends
had hemlines rising, but the long skirts Mother forever
insisted upon had their advantages as well. Such as surrepti-
tiously readying one's feet for a mad dash across the parlor.

She'd changed her mind. Any old man would not do.
Particularly this one. He was still young enough to last
another decade. Perhaps more. There must be an alternative.
"I really don't think that's a proper activity for a young lady,
Lord Rancide." Under no circumstances would she... No.
Not even for England.

The paunchy, red-nosed marquis leaned forward on the
settee, leering at what he already assumed to be his property.
His eyes came to rest on her bosom and the edges of his lips
curved upward in a self-congratulatory, self-satisfied smile.

Her day dress covered her from wrist to throat, but it was exceptionally well tailored. With exactly this effect in mind. A valuable tool to employ as an element of distraction. If her recently increased proportions now strained the seams, well, she blamed cream cakes. And Emily.

Two months ago, news of her sister's elopement, detailed in that horrible gossip rag and picked over by all of *ton* society, had caused Lord Carlton Snyder to terminate their betrothal. Ever since, Mother's search for a new fiancé who wouldn't care if his bride was the brunt of society's current gossip had subjected her to increasingly intolerable individuals.

Olivia was, after all, a well-dowered daughter of the Duke of Avesbury. Certain gentlemen would overlook just about anything. She could have three eyes, a lantern jaw and a mechanical arm—and still such men would offer for her.

"Oh, come now. Can't we do away with all the missish protestations?" Lord Rancide patted his knee. "Come. Have a seat now. I'll give you a taste of the pleasures to come once we've married."

"I think not. I expect my mother to join us at any moment."

A blatant lie. In an attempt to cement a betrothal, Mother had taken to abandoning Olivia to her most recent male suitors, pretending to be overcome by agues, angina and aether fluxes.

Setting her empty tea cup upon the tea tray, Olivia shifted her weight onto one leg. Her ankle wobbled. *Cogs and punches!* Why had she worn shoes with heels? Still,

Lord Rancide was portly. She intended to be out the door before he could rise.

Just in case, she glanced down at RT—the roving table that held the afternoon tea—preparing her defense. To the untrained eye, the silver teapot would seem her best bet. It wasn't. From beneath the lacy tablecloth, a tiny metallic nose and wire whiskers peeked. Watson, her pet zoetomatic hedgehog was.

She snapped her fingers twice. Watson's nose extended into a long, thin rod. A faint hum indicated that the Markoid battery had engaged. Maybe it wouldn't be necessary.

Olivia sprang to her feet and darted toward the door. "Let me see what is keeping my mother."

But Lord Rancide was quicker than he looked. Damp fingers wrapped about her wrist, yanking her backward. Thrown off balance, Olivia wobbled on her heels and landed with a thump in his lap. His arm snaked about her waist, pressing her against his burgeoning girth. "Just like that, sweeting." Sloppy, wet lips squelched against her neck.

"Let me go!" Olivia twisted her face away from the foul odor of rotting teeth. "This is unseemly. I have *not* agreed to marry you." She pried at his arm, but he was stronger than looks alone would suggest.

RT whirled about, his brass bell clamoring in distress. The tea tray slipped from his surface with a clang and a clatter, spilling sugar, milk and Earl Grey all over the carpet. Watson backed up in alarm, dragging the snowy-white tablecloth with him into the mess.

Lord Rancide pulled away ever so slightly. "Stop this

nonsense. We both know I'm the best—and last—chance you have at marrying a title."

He'd brought it upon himself. "Watson," she snapped. "Engage."

On tiny, two-toed feet, the mechanical hedgehog rushed forward, ramming his galvanized steel nose into Lord Rancide's ankle.

There was a loud zap. Lord Rancide bolted upright, and Olivia took the opportunity to slam the flat of her palm upward into his nose. There was a satisfying crunch.

He howled, lifting both hands to cup his now bloody nose.

The door slammed open as Steam Mary burst into the room, steam billowing from beneath her skirts, whipping the coarse black cloth about her metal appendages. Behind her, a number of household steambots gathered in the doorway, all of them hissing and ringing and clanging their displeasure.

"Stand aside," Olivia instructed them. "Lord Rancide was just leaving."

Slowly, and with a reluctant creak of wheels, her loyal staff formed a narrow pathway to the front door.

Pressing a handkerchief to his nose, Lord Rancide stood. He yanked his waistcoat downward, smoothing the yellow satin over his rotund belly as he turned a dark eye on her. "*You* are unfit as a wife," he pronounced, then stormed from her house.

"I MUST SPEAK WITH FATHER," Olivia informed the steam butler, Burton, who rolled down the hallway behind her.

"I'm afraid he is not available at the moment." Burton's jaw creaked. He was an older model and forever in need of more oil.

The only household steambots that spoke—and their vocabulary was limited—were butlers. Theirs was a particularly ancient model, but Father refused to replace him. Olivia had done what she could, on the sly of course, but there were only so many commands his aging cipher cartridge was capable of reading.

Understanding Burton's need to fulfill his programming commands, she paused before Father's study rather than storming in. "Open the door, Burton."

"Impossible, my lady. His Grace left orders he was not to be disturbed."

Her eyes narrowed. "Did he?" Olivia tried the handle. The door refused to open. *Locked? The great and mighty duke hid from his daughter?* There was only one conclusion to draw. Father had *known* about Lord Rancide. Tacit agreement was still a form of assent. "Never mind," she said. "I'll open it myself."

Puffs of steam vented from Burton's ears. His fingers clenched and unclenched, his programming cards stuck in a feedback loop, one set of instructions demanding he always follow Lady Olivia's commands, the other insisting he never override those of his master, the duke.

Olivia reached into the bodice of her gown, slid two lock

picks free from her corset, and bent to the keyhole. A second later the lock snicked free, and she strode into Father's office.

He took one look at her and sighed, sinking backward into his chair behind the massive oak slab that was his desk. "What was wrong with *this* one?"

"What wasn't?"

"What are we going to do with you, Olivia?" He lifted a palm upward. "Lord Rancide was the last old, titled target who was willing..."

"Yes, it's clear Mother scraped the ooze from the bottom of the barrel." Was basic decency too much to ask?

"My sources informed me Lord Rancide was impotent," the duchess herself said as she swept into the room.

"They were wrong."

Father choked.

Mother waved away her complaint. "Nevertheless, this is unacceptable behavior, turning down suitor after suitor. There are no more suspect gentlemen above the age of sixty. We will have to look abroad."

Father cringed. "Olivia, enough with this determination to marry someone old enough to be *my* father."

"It is a critical consideration given our daughter's aspirations," Mother said. "If there are offspring, it will indefinitely delay her entry into fieldwork."

"Listen," Father said. "There's a delegation of Icelanders arriving in a month's time. Some are nobility. Let me see if—"

"Iceland." Mother raised her eyebrows at Olivia. "Foreign experience would be valuable."

"Not Iceland." Olivia lifted her chin. Then, considering

her present standing, adopted a more conciliatory tone. "Please, don't banish me to that icebox. All I want—"

"What now?" Mother huffed.

"No," Father rose and slapped a palm on the desk. "Enough. No more restrictions."

Swallowing a lump in her throat, one that felt the size of an entire cream cake, Olivia blurted, "Please, will you ask the Queen to waive the widow requirement?"

Father stiffened. Raking his hands into his hair, he pushed his palms together as if trying to keep his skull from shattering. "God, Olivia. You ask for the moon!"

"There's precedent." She looked pointedly at both of them.

"I entered the service by marrying your father." Mother's eyes were wide with horror. "Not by traipsing off into the countryside an unprotected innocent."

Father cringed.

"Absolutely not," Mother snapped. "The Queen will deny such a request."

"Why?" Olivia objected. "I've devoted myself to the Queen's service. I am the only societal liaison to hold a degree in programming from the Rankine Institute. I've completed every single task assigned to me."

"Except marriage," Mother pointed out.

"Not my fault."

"Your engagement to Lord Snyder was unreasonably protracted," Mother countered. "If you'd managed to lead him to the alter within a reasonable time frame, you would even now be making reports to the Queen."

She and Mother glared at each other.

"No," Father said. "I refuse to consider such an option. You will marry a designated target, or you will leave the Queen's service."

"But—"

"No." Father turned toward Mother. "Are any foreign targets acceptable?"

Mother tapped her lips. "Mmm."

Olivia fought the urge to slump. Nothing ever went according to her plans, no matter how much effort she expended. She'd played the role of brainless fool, agreeing with Carlton's every opinion, his every demand, and still it had not been enough. The freedoms afforded a married woman remained beyond her grasp. Perhaps it was time to give up.

Bed. That's where she wanted to be. Curtains pulled, under the covers, buried by soft, muffling feathers. Steambots would circle, bringing her endless cups of chocolate and cream cakes. Then, when all her gowns stopped fitting, she'd have an excuse to stay in bed all day. To see no one. To go nowhere.

"Italy," Father suggested. "Visit Aunt Judith."

"Aunt Judith!" Olivia's voice held a note of alarm. They would banish her? "But she's in Venice! It's far too dangerous."

Aunt Judith was a cryptobiologist studying the giant kraken that had devastated the city. There were reports that buildings fell almost daily as their sharp claws gouged away the pilings.

"Judith is in Rome for the winter." Father waved a hand dismissively. "Fulfilling academic teaching duties. Mother will accompany you."

Mother closed her eyes, reading down the list she held in her mind, men chosen for the secrets they might keep. "Baron Volscini," she announced. "Age eighty-three. Two previous wives. No issue. Likely sterile."

"Perfect." Father's voice sounded choked. "I have but one request. A bit of assistance on an unfolding situation. One small favor on behalf of Queen and country."

Olivia moaned. A catch? With Father there was always a catch, a price to be paid. Already his eyes had begun to sparkle with mischief.

"No," Mother said. "I object."

"She wishes to work in the field. Why not?"

"Because he is not suitable as a target," Mother answered.

"Agreed, but why not let her conduct a little surveillance en route?" Father lifted a shoulder. "She's trained all these years for it. Why not let her test her mettle?"

Mother's lips pressed together.

"I agree," Olivia said. Unsuitable meant young. Or smart. Maybe both. Perhaps Mother even thought him handsome enough to distract her from her mission. It didn't matter. Anything that Mother objected to held immediate appeal.

CHAPTER THREE

"WHERE IS THE GERMAN man who was brought in?" Ian demanded, glancing over the shoulder of the head nurse of Lister's secure hospital ward, searching the hallway. "I need to question him. Immediately."

She stared back at him over wire-rimmed glasses. "If you refer to patient SV140, the man involved in the balloon crash, he's no longer here."

Irritation festered. If Black thought he could keep him out of this... "Please clarify."

"SV140 was moved to the autopsy suite approximately thirty minutes ago."

Ian's eyebrows rose. Dead inside of an hour? He'd seen the rise and fall of the German's chest as the agents heaved him onto their shoulders. Of course, the tumors were massive and many, but if he'd survived this long... "Thank you, Nurse Quinn."

With a nod, he spun on his heel and headed for the ascension chamber. But when he reached it, as he lifted his hand to dial the code, he realized access would be denied. The combination was changed every month. He'd been gone two.

"Four. Six. Seven. Two," a familiar deep voice informed him.

He entered the sequence of numbers and the doors slid open. "I owe you for this, Thornton." A few minutes with the man's body was all Ian needed. Irrefutable evidence before he tore off to Germany.

"Black will be here shortly," Lord Thornton warned, following him into the chamber. Though they'd never worked together, the man was both a neurobiologist and a Queen's agent.

"I don't need your protection."

Thornton snorted. "I didn't offer it. I'm merely satisfying my own curiosity."

Ian tipped his head back, studying the grating that formed the ceiling of the ascension chamber as it lowered them deep into the ground. In truth, he was glad of the company. If anyone would understand his situation—betrayal, misuse of one's own inventions—Thornton would. Three months past, Thornton had been embroiled in a hunt for a foreign operative who had stolen his laboratory biotechnology.

The difference was that Ian knew who had stolen his research. Proving it, however, had been impossible. His detailed laboratory notebooks along with vials of mutated cells had disappeared with Warrick, and searching for the traitor had led to some dark corners and allegations from which there was no recovery. Accusing Lord Avesbury of complicity had been unwise. It had ended Ian's work in the field and nearly ended his career in research.

He had done his best to put the past behind him. Until today, when what he'd most feared had come to pass. His own work had hunted him down and presented an ultimatum.

Now his sister's life was on the line. Ian closed his eyes. Blood began to boil in his veins. All he'd ever wanted to do with his research was to find her a cure—and he was so close, so very close. Trust Warrick to throw a wrench into the gears. Again.

Warrick's betrayal had done more than damage Ian's reputation, it had ripped apart his family and shredded his sister Elizabeth's heart in the process. To think he'd almost called the man 'brother'. If only he could wrap his fingers about Warrick's throat and squeeze.

"When Warrick absconded with your work, the original cells showed promise *in vitro*, did they not?" Thornton asked, forcing Ian to set aside his anger and focus on the immediate situation.

"Yes," he answered, his voice tight. Inside their glass Petri dishes the first generation of mutated cells had shown every promise, but when transplanted into live hosts, into rats... He shook his head. "But the *in vivo* tests revealed that the immune system offered no resistance at all. The cells took over the bones. Osteosarcomas formed at unnatural rates." They'd aborted the trials, euthanizing the unfortunate research subjects.

"I understand Warrick believed the immune system of human subjects would react differently." He shook his head in disbelief. "Those in medical research should know better than to make such an assumption."

"He was utterly convinced," Ian confirmed. "Given the body in the morgue, he managed to persuade at least one German to risk his life to prove it." Pressing his lips into a tight line, he said nothing about the message, nothing about Elizabeth. She was all the family he had left. Nothing and no one would stop him.

"You followed protocol," Thornton stated. "Warrick is to blame for this. Not you."

Ian grunted.

"We need you back." Thornton's gaze was intense.

Ian shifted on his feet. Once he'd been a proud member of the Queen's agents, a member of the inner circle. He missed the camaraderie. "In the laboratory? Or the field?"

"Both. Either." A pained look crossed Thornton's face. "Any progress on the hunt for a bride? I only ask because I promised my wife."

"Don't." Ian grimaced. Of late every man and woman in love felt compelled to offer him their advice and assistance. "Just don't."

Thornton did anyway. "Should you have difficulty finding a bride amongst the debutants, my wife has offered to make introductions."

A strangled noise emerged from his throat. Though Lady

Thornton was both beautiful and brilliant, she was one of a kind. Thinking about what sort of woman she might drag up from inside the bowels of Lister Laboratories scared him. There were precious few females, and those he'd spied tended to scurry away under a direct gaze.

"Thank you, no. I'll muddle along on my own for a bit yet. Too soon to settle."

But he'd done exactly that, hadn't he? Proposing to a lady he barely knew. And that had gone so wonderfully. Nothing like a proposal that landed a man in the morgue.

The doors slid open, disgorging them into said facility where Mr. Hutton bent over a disfigured corpse stretched out upon a steel gurney. It rankled. His own technician allowed to remain behind in the laboratory while Ian himself —however temporarily—was banished.

The technician snapped to attention, his eyes wide with disbelief. "Lord Rathsburn!" He hastily dragged a white sheet over the disfigured face of the German.

Ian's eyes narrowed. "Is that SV140?"

Mr. Hutton gulped, then gave a stiff nod.

He took off his coat and rolled up his shirt sleeves and donned one of the many canvas aprons that hung from the wall pegs. "Let's begin."

"But... no... I mean," Mr. Hutton stuttered. "Mr. Black instructed me to allow no one to examine this corpse."

"Not even me?" Ian asked, reaching upward to flick on the overhead argon lamp. Brilliant white light shone down upon the body.

"Black is toying with you, Rathsburn," Thornton

concluded. "Giving you rope to hang yourself. Are you certain you do not wish to pursue official channels?"

"I am." With his sister in danger, every minute counted, and he would not allow politics to stand in the way of Elizabeth's safety. A coil of dread in his gut twisted every time thoughts of her situation rose to mind.

Ian pulled back the sheet. The German was huge. Well over six feet tall, he had the muscular build of a gladiator, one accustomed to regularly defeating lions. Blond and pale, he would have been the very model of Aryan perfection but for the ulcerating tumors that bulged beneath the skin of his jaw.

His own jaw clenched.

Warrick thought nothing of testing his hypotheses directly upon human subjects; he possessed not a shred of ethics. Before him lay the results of letting the man walk free, of allowing him to leave Britain's shores. Warrick should be rotting in a dank, dark prison at this very moment if not hung or shot for treason.

He pressed against one of the many lumps that protruded from the man's jaw. All three nodules were rock hard.

He palpated the man's upper arm. The man's deltoids, biceps and triceps were so thick that Ian had to dig his fingers into the musculature to feel for the tumors he was certain grew from the cortical surface of the humerus. There. He could feel them now. A number of them in varying sizes.

He pushed his fingers into the man's tree-trunk-sized thighs. Again he felt a number of tumors deep inside the tissue. A quick glance at the fingers and toes visually confirmed that several of those joints were also affected.

"As expected, a superficial examination shows an exceedingly proliferative osteoblastoma in an advanced state." A particularly horrible bone cancer. And in this case, a cancer made even worse by experimental manipulation of osteoprogenitor cells.

There was only one way to be certain.

He held out a hand. "Scalpel."

When nothing landed in it, he glanced up.

Mr. Hutton looked pained. "We should obtain clearance from Mr. Black first."

Ian made a sound of disgust and grabbed the scalpel himself. He sliced deftly through the pliant skin of the man's arm, above one particularly large malignancy that bulged outward between two muscles. He peeled back the skin and shoved his fingers inside the tissue, stretching and pulling and cutting to expose the surface of the bone.

Reaching up, Ian drew the argon lamp closer. The tumor was some two inches in diameter and protruded a good inch above what was left of normal humerus. The knotted lump of bone glistened a faint silver beneath the dark red periosteum, the connective tissue that supplied the bone with blood.

"I want to take a sample for confirmation. Pass the vibration knife." Ian hoped the tool was strong enough.

Mr. Hutton didn't move.

"If you're not up to the task, step back." Thornton

crossed the room to lift the device from the shelf. "No. Leave. I'll assist."

Mr. Hutton swallowed and backed away, exiting the room with haste the moment the ascension chamber arrived.

Ian lifted two pairs of safety goggles from a drawer and handed one across the body. "I should warn you, Thornton, if the antimony has been densely deposited, we might not be able to excise this tumor."

"Metal bones?"

"Metalloid."

He inserted a tissue spreader into the incision he'd made in the German's upper arm. Crank by crank the fissure widened until the tumor was fully exposed.

Thornton cocked an eyebrow, but asked no further questions.

Ian powered up the vibration knife. A loud mechanical buzz filled the air, making further conversation impossible. He pressed the knife against the relatively normal bone adjacent to the tumor. The knife passed though the white bone, then stalled. Ian pushed harder, but there was no give. The vibrational knife protested with an ominous groan.

He pulled the knife back, shifting to change the angle of the blade against the tumor, pushing with as much strength as he possessed. The knife sank into the bone, but only the slightest fraction. Any lingering doubts vanished.

This man was dead because of him, because of the research he'd initiated. His stomach clenched. How many more men faced the same fate?

Without warning, the knife surged forward. A shard of

the tumor broke free and flew into the air, skittering across the tiled floor. Ian set down the knife. With tweezers, he plucked the bone sample from the ground and carried it to the sink, rinsing its surface before sliding the sample into the chamber of the aetheroscope. He flipped a switch, waiting a moment for the gas to fill the chamber before peering through the lens at the tumor's magnified and illuminated surface.

"Mottled gray. Near complete replacement of normal bone minerals." Ian stepped back.

Thornton yanked off his goggles and peered through the eyepiece. "Impressive. You'll have Chemistry confirm its composition?"

That would be procedure, but... "To what end?" Ian had all the answers he needed. All the answers he could discover on British soil. Fix this? Unlikely. But he would have to try.

The door to the ascension chamber clanged open. Black stepped out.

Thornton drew out his pocket watch. "You're losing your touch. I expected you some fifteen minutes ago."

"Ready to take up your pistol again, Lord Rathsburn?" Black asked without a trace of humor on his face. He held out Ian's old weapon, one that fired cartridges of tetrodotoxin, TTX, a toxin gleaned from the muscles of pufferfish. One round to stun a man, two to drop him and a third to kill.

Ian's fingers twitched, but he kept his arm at his side. "No. Not unless the duke finally agrees to discuss shadow boards." He brushed past Black, jamming a finger into the call button of the ascension chamber.

"Perhaps you have heard, Thornton," Black said, the tone of his voice odd, "that the triumvirate negotiations with Germany and Russia concerning the Ottoman Uprisings are not proceeding well. That the Queen's agents are—at the moment—forbidden to cross the border into said country."

Ian froze.

Thornton's voice had a ring of the theatrical as he addressed his next words to Black. "You mean to say *we* are forbidden from investigating the origins of SV140?"

"So we are," Black said. "Such an action would end a career."

A familiar hollow feeling expanded in his chest. Despite their insistence that he could rejoin the Queen's agents with a simple apology to the duke, they felt no qualms using his civilian status to their advantage. "Are you telling me," Ian asked, irritated that they spoke around rather than to him, "that not a single thing is to be done?"

Silence was a loud answer.

Message received. Any actions he took to save his sister and stop Warrick would be unsanctioned and unsupported. He was on his own. But when had that ever stopped him?

Untethered, he was anything but adrift.

Time to go. He had a flight to catch.

CHAPTER FOUR

OLIVIA COULDN'T STOP smiling. She'd finally won herself a mission—even if she didn't know what it was yet. Not even the inescapable fact that Mother would be accompanying her as a chaperone was able to suppress the glee with which she threw herself into packing.

Time was short. The dirigible launched tomorrow at noon.

Chaos reigned. Her bed was strewn with gowns of all colors and fabrics. With combinations and corsets. Petticoats and stockings. Gloves and lace shawls. Scattered across the floor was an array of shoes. Her dressing table held a tangle of hairpins and ribbons, a profusion of perfumes and powders.

Steam Clara—her personal lady's maid—whirled about, folding and wrapping and packing while Mother sat by the fire, reading aloud facts about Baron Volscini—in Italian—

from a thick folder. No time like the present, Mother had announced, to begin adjusting to the language of her future husband.

"We must be mindful that word of our family scandal may have reached Italian ears," Mother said, setting the folder aside at last. "You must be on your best behavior. Ever deferential. No arguing or contradicting a gentleman. You must *not* discuss Babbage cards. Do not mention your degree from the Rankine Institute. No young lady is supposed to know a thing about programming. Baron Volscini is looking for a wife, not a difference engine. A pretty face will draw him close, but an empty head will keep him there."

"Yes, Mother. I know, Mother. I've been doing this for years, Mother."

As if she could even claim her engineering degree. Olivia had earned it via a correspondence program. Under the name of Oliver Bird. No women need apply to the Rankine Institute. She wished she could trumpet her accomplishments to the *haute ton*, watch their faces contort in shock and horror, but in the field of espionage appearances were everything, and her particular role required a certain amount of wool between the ears.

Mother's perpetual frown deepened. "This is not a game, Olivia."

She sighed. "I'm well aware, Mother."

In the midst of wrapping a purple, feathered bonnet, Steam Clara's jointed limbs froze, making odd grinding sounds as she struggled to move. Steam of frustration seeped upward from beneath her collar.

Olivia grabbed a screwdriver from her dressing table and rushed to the steambot's side, unbuttoning her uniform to expose the metal door in her chest. Opening it, she scanned the array of wires and gears before her. There. Nothing but a sticky valve. Easily fixed. The cipher cartridge, however, was cracked and needed to be replaced. Unfortunately, there was no time to sneak away to visit the scrapyard before their flight departed. She would have to wait until they reached Rome.

"Must you bring that old heap with us?" Mother snapped. "It's bad enough that your father insists upon retaining Burton. Let me purchase you a new steam lady's maid. Please."

"No thank you, Mother. I've made numerable and invaluable changes to her programming," she lied, using an eye dropper to drip oil into the valve. Certainly she'd modified Steam Clara more times than she could count. But invaluable? No. Steam Clara's presence merely comforted her; she was a mute friend to whom Olivia could speak freely. "I'll spare you the details."

A knock sounded on her door.

"Just a moment."

Olivia set Steam Clara to rights, then opened the door to find Burton, their steam butler, holding a silver salver. A letter rested upon it. With unladylike haste, she ripped it open and read the contents. All five words.

Nineteen hundred. Clockwork Corridor. Caravan.

There was no signature, but she recognized Mr. Black's spidery handwriting. She grinned widely. How exciting!

Father's top agent was to impart the details of her covert mission in a dark alley. Was it awful that she now wished for a dense, London pea-souper to complete the scene?

She glanced at the clock as she reached for a cloak. "I need to go."

Mother's back stiffened "Mr. Black?"

"Yes."

"I'll get my wrap." She began to rise.

"No, Mother," Olivia pleaded. *She had to go alone.* "Please? It's just Clockwork Corridor. You can't possibly think I need a chaperone in Mr. Black's presence."

Mother pursed her lips, always ready to ruin all the fun.

"It may take me some time," Olivia spoke quickly. "There are a number of items I need to acquire from Nicu Sindel, and we can't afford any friction between our families. Think of Emily."

Mention of the gypsy made Mother's lips curl with distaste. Not only did she thoroughly disapprove of Olivia's mechanical inclinations, she blamed Nicu's grandson for stealing away Emily, her youngest daughter. "Directly there and back," she ordered.

Some two hours later, Olivia's reticule bulged with a number of 'necessary' items. Unfortunately, though she'd rummaged in piles of antiquated 'junk', an additional cipher cartridge—model B257—could not be found. She had, however, managed to procure a backup power source for her pet zoetomatic hedgehog. Zapping Lord Rancide had all but drained his battery.

Nicu handed Watson back to her, shaking his head with a faint smile. "Clever," the old gypsy said.

Olivia beamed. It was strong praise from her mentor.

"Yet I dislike the darkness your mind must conjure that such a thing seems necessary. Remember where danger led your sisters and take every precaution. It is not safe to work with Mr. Black."

"How—?"

Nicu lifted his chin, and Olivia turned to find the man himself standing in the door of the caravan.

Mr. Black was dressed in a well-tailored, but plain, dark suit. Everything about him seemed dark. Dark hair, dark eyes, swarthy skin. Not quite a gentleman. In a crowd, he would fade into the background, but here, amidst his people, his presence commanded attention.

He muttered something.

Nicu snapped back a reply.

Though her Romani was a touch rusty, she caught the meaning. "Stop, you two." She turned to face Nicu. "No one is making me do anything. I *want* this assignment."

Nicu sighed, then his strong hands squeezed hers. "Be careful."

"Aren't I always?" she grumbled. Of late, such caution felt like a decided failing on her part. Weeks of hiding inside the family town home had her chafing for a touch of adventure.

She caught Mr. Black's midnight gaze. This assignment would finally allow her to prove her mettle. She would make certain of it. "Shall we go, Mr. Black?"

With a silent nod, Mr. Black held out his arm and escorted her down the stairs into the gas lit streets of Clockwork Corridor—toward her waiting carriage.

Olivia huffed in disappointment. She'd hoped to prowl the cobblestones committing pertinent facts to memory while sliding in and out of shadows. A carriage was just so... trite. Dragging her feet, she began, "Do you think we could—"

A man turned a corner and began walking in their direction.

With a hiss, Mr. Black yanked her into his arms, pulling her against his chest as he spun her around and pressed her back to the brick wall of a nearby building, folding them into a dark shadow. His hands slid up the sides of her face to press her forehead against his. She wrapped her arms about his waist. This was more what she'd had in mind.

"Don't move."

Her breath caught at the excitement. Her heart pounded. No, not at being embraced by this man. Mr. Black was a mentor of sorts. Ever since he'd been the one to oust her from her hiding spot in Father's study.

At first Olivia had been resentful. She'd enjoyed listening to Father and his men discuss secrets she barely understood. Yet instead of banishing her from the room, Mr. Black had suggested that the daughter of a duke, one with such devious talents and tendencies, might have use. So had begun her work with the Queen's agents. Only Father and Mother knew of her involvement. Her sisters and brother thought her a cotton-headed debutant bent on marrying a title and never thought to look closer. Nor had the rest of *ton* society.

"Who is he?" Olivia asked.

"Hush," Mr. Black ordered. "Embrace your role and observe."

Out of the corner of her eye, she watched the man approach. A brown paper-wrapped package was tucked under his arm, and he carried a metal case. Was it her imagination, or did a kind of fog escape its seam?

After several endless minutes, when the man was long past, Mr. Black released her.

"Was that—"

"Yes. The gentleman at the center of your assignment." Mr. Black all but shoved her upward and into her carriage. He climbed in behind her, took the seat opposite and yanked the curtains closed. "Ian Stanton, Lord Rathsburn. I don't believe he recognized me. Or saw your face."

She'd met the earl—once—at her sister's wedding. One of the many mad scientists from Lister University who'd attended. Though she'd spent the better part of the last two months reprogramming the kitchen staff, eavesdropping was in her nature, and she'd managed to keep abreast of society rumors. Lord Rathsburn had featured in many.

Olivia sighed, resigned. "And he's looking for a wife. What happened to Baron Volscini?"

"Lord Rathsburn is *not* your target." Mr. Black stared at her intensely. "Lady Avesbury expressly forbids it."

Forbid. She twisted her lips. Mother and her orders. Not that Olivia wanted a husband, particularly one so young and healthy. Rumor informed her that gentlemen wanted their wives at home and under their thumb. Tolerating that would be a trial, one she was only willing to endure for a brief period of time. She wished to be free to pursue her own interests, and the most expedient path toward that aim was widowhood. The sooner, the better.

"Use your... womanly charms if you must," Mr. Black instructed, "but only as a distraction to accomplish the mission. You are *not* to engage."

A shivery thrill ran down her back. At last she would be trusted to accomplish something important. She was to play a role, however small, in protecting Britannia's shores. A smug smile tugged at her lips. Whatever the task, she'd show Father that she was capable of independent fieldwork.

"Tell me," she said.

Mr. Black reached inside his coat pocket and withdrew a small, black case.

Olivia pressed a hand to her chest. "Oh, sir, I couldn't possibly," she teased.

Rolling his eyes, he tossed the case onto her lap where it landed in a puff of silk. "You are not for me, nor I for you."

"And why not?" She looked up at him from beneath her lashes. "I think we'd make a most effective team." It would save her from waiting any number of years to embrace widowhood. She could do worse than Mr. Black. Over time, they might even develop a kind of mutual affection beyond friendship.

"To begin with, the duchess would have me castrated."

Olivia gasped in mock horror. "Such words."

"You've heard worse." He waved at the box. "Open it."

She did. A glass vial filled with a clear viscous fluid lay beside four flat metallic discs the size of a half-pence on a bed of blue velvet. She lifted one and flipped a small switch on its edge. A tiny light flickered on, glowing a steady green. She glanced up, eyebrows raised.

"Acousticotransmitters. Listening devices. Powered by the energy emitted by degrading internal crystals. They have a three-mile radius and enough power to run for up to two weeks apiece. Lord Rathsburn will be traveling on the same airship as you and the duchess, en route to Rome. Your task is to enter his cabin and hide the acousticotransmitters inside his luggage."

"And the vial?"

"An adhesive. Designed to glue the acousticotransmitter in place and restore the lining of his valise."

"What then?" In her mind, Olivia was dressed entirely in black, her golden hair tucked beneath a watchman's cap as she slipped unseen down a dark hallway.

"Return to your rooms."

"That's all?" She frowned. "Aren't you going to tell me what Lord Rathsburn is suspected of?"

"Irrelevant." The tone of his voice told her there'd be no argument.

She snapped the case closed. "So I'm to conceal the devices and walk away."

"Most spy work is not exciting."

"No. Apparently it can also be insulting." Olivia

slumped back on the seat. "I thought I was to be trusted with an important task."

"It is." Mr. Black leaned forward and tapped the case. "It may not be the thrill you seek, but following Lord Rathsburn, listening to his conversations when he meets with foreigners, is critical. Lives depend upon what we will hear once he reaches his destination." He moved past her, pausing with a hand on the door handle. "Don't muck it up."

CHAPTER FIVE

THE STEAM TRAIN WHEEZED and coughed, belching one final black cloud into the dingy sky before jerking to a stop at the Dover station. Midst a sea of other passengers, Ian stepped from his private compartment onto the platform. A seething mass of rumpled voyagers swam past him, all calling for trolley services to collect their heaps of boxes, bags and trunks and drag them to various airships. Steambot porters rolled hither and yon, hissing and clanging as they attempted to meet travelers' demands.

He had no such need of assistance. Each hand held what appeared to be a simple valise. One was exactly that. The other, however, was a lead-lined, insulated and refrigerated case containing essential equipment and precious biochemicals. Materials he'd covertly appropriated from his laboratory before leaving Lister Laboratories.

Ian was good, but not that good. Not when the Queen's

agents were well aware of SV140 and his connection to his research. Yet not a single soul had stood guard at his laboratory. Or at any of the other exits. He'd been *allowed* to walk free.

Allowed to walk down Clockwork Corridor to purchase the mechanical parts he required. But not unobserved. Black had been there, wrapped around a woman in the shadows. He'd ignored them. It was all part of the ridiculous game they played.

They would not stop him, but neither would they assist him. Forbidden by the Queen to interfere with all things on German soil, her agents—Thornton and Black in particular—would simply turn a blind eye.

That was why Black had made but a token effort to reinstate him as an agent. He'd known Ian would refuse, that he would take it upon himself to hunt down Warrick and any other men responsible for creating the tumor-ridden monster with the dense, silver bones. Black wished to retain deniability.

He might not be an agent, but transporting experimental materials from Lister Laboratories across international borders without written permission constituted treason. Something he was certain both Britain and Germany would hold against him should it prove convenient. Particularly when they discovered he'd also made off with a certain as-yet unfinished piece of equipment designed by an engineer from the Rankine Institute.

Thinking of it falling into the hands of the Germans made his stomach churn, but thinking of his sister in their hands made him want to roll up his sleeves and raise his fists. He would do whatever was necessary to free her.

Everything short of handing over the new formula for the transforming reagent.

Ian scanned the crowds, looking for a familiar face. Or one that took far too much interest in his movements. Like a second skin, old habits slipped back in place without effort. Despite the dangers that awaited, this clear sense of direction was invigorating.

He'd told no one about this voyage, wiring ahead himself to arrange for his passage. Lady Katherine would not miss him, and there was no one else to take note of his absence beyond his colleagues who believed him to be on an indefinite leave of absence. Until today, he'd barely noticed how constricted his world had become.

Though there were now a number of Germans keen to spend time with him, ones desperate enough to kidnap his sister in order to hasten his arrival.

As soon as this was behind him, he needed to pay more attention to life outside the laboratory. He would begin by re-examining and revising his list of suitable brides. Domestic life would be more gratifying if he chose a wife whose company he enjoyed. One he *wanted* in his bed.

"Lord Rathsburn! Is that you?"

Ian closed his eyes a moment. Not missed, perhaps, but it seemed there was no escaping recognition. He took a deep breath and, forcing what he hoped was a pleasant expression upon his face, turned toward the source of the overly cheerful voice.

A young lady with a heart-shaped face beneath a tumble of golden ringlets smiled up at him. Dressed in a blindingly yellow gown embroidered with an array of bright flowers, she was nothing like the ladies he'd met of late. He would have remembered a woman who paired sunshine with seduction, wrapping the warmth of a sun-filled garden about a figure that promised a different kind of heat. Interest stirred. If he touched her, who would combust?

She looked familiar, but only vaguely. The gears in his mind turned furiously trying to place her.

"It *is* you," she said with shining eyes as she stepped close to place a hand on his arm.

"I'm sorry..." he began. He glanced about for a chaperone, but none hovered. Odd.

"We met at my sister's wedding?" The sparkle in her eyes dimmed. "To Lord Thornton?"

And then it came to him. A number of profane words rushed to mind, but he stopped them at his lips. "Ah, yes, of course, Lady Olivia."

Daughter of the Duke of Avesbury, of the man who was once his superior. Maintaining every outward appearance of a gentleman, Ian set down a valise to catch up her hand and brush his lips over the surface of her soft kid glove.

A coincidence? Unlikely. Alarm bells rang in his mind. In this case there was one possible explanation. He prayed it was so. "You must be embarking upon your honeymoon," he said. "I ought to address you as Lady Snyder. Allow me to wish you happy on your marriage."

Cheeks flushed, she glanced away. "I'm afraid not. Lord Snyder and I have parted ways."

Did one console or congratulate a woman for avoiding matrimony to a snake? He settled for a polite, "I'm sorry."

"Fear not. The experience has earned me a winter in Rome." She glanced at him from beneath a fringe of long eyelashes. A coy smile tipped up the corners of her mouth. "And one never knows where one might meet interesting people such as yourself."

Her gloved palm slid around his arm in a possessive move designed to warn other young women away. Lady Olivia Ravensdale was on the hunt for a husband. A failed engagement was considered a situation to be remedied at once. From the brilliant white smile she now wore, he surmised he had just become her latest target. To call the situation inconvenient was an understatement.

"Rome," he repeated flatly. "What a coincidence. That is also my destination."

Her smile widened.

"Olivia!" a woman with the voice of a harpy screeched.

The situation worsened. The Duchess of Avesbury. He was to be watched even aboard the airship, Lady Olivia no more than a convenient tool. Somehow, the duke knew, for he'd sprung the perfect trap. Ian could almost feel the steel teeth clamp down.

Lady Olivia winced. "Apologies in advance. My mother approaches, and I see you wear a sword upon your hip. Do say you will be my knight in shining armor and escort me aboard the airship." Her voice dropped to a whisper. "Please."

A knight? Though dueling remained illegal, in recent years a handful of gentlemen had taken to wearing swords, though few possessed the skills to wield the weapon. Most gentry considered it a boorish practice, one that ruined the lines of their clothing. Practicality governed Ian's attire for he was no knight-errant.

"Olivia!" the duchess bellowed, waving an orange parasol above her head as she bore down upon her daughter. Behind her a personal steambot pushed a cart piled high with no less than ten trunks and a dozen hatboxes. "Lord Rathsburn?" Chest heaving, the duchess pulled up short, her eyebrows soaring in a poor approximation of surprise. "Leaving behind London's young ladies?"

Ian bowed. "A visit to my sister, Your Grace. An attempt to lure her home to serve as my hostess. It seems my social graces require polishing if I'm to attract a bride."

"I'm not certain I approve of you using my daughter for practice." The duchess' eyes narrowed. "I heard about your ill-fated trip aloft."

"On the contrary," Lady Olivia objected. "We make the perfect pair. Both of us must hone our skills if we are to attract an acceptable spouse." He lifted his valise, and she yanked on his arm, dragging him toward the station's exit and away from her mother. "Go ahead, then. Compliment me."

Flirting. A skill he'd never cultivated, nor one that had yet been required of him in medical espionage. He preferred directness, but as there was no escape, it was time to change tactics.

Ian glanced at Lady Olivia, searching for something—anything—to comment upon. He swallowed. Hard. For his eyes caught upon a line of tiny pearl buttons that ran upward over the front of her form-fitting bodice, detouring quite some distance forward to accommodate the generous swell of her breasts, before continuing their march to her chin. Demure, yet so very tempting.

Yet even he was socially agile enough to know better than to comment upon her sumptuous bosom, especially in the presence of her mother. Instead, he fixed upon something safer: the decor of her voyaging bonnet. "The bird on your hat is quite..."

Bright? Fluffy? Large? He was hopeless. The right word escaped him.

"Dead?" She giggled. "Never mind. Scientists. Not a romantic notion in your minds." She glanced at him out of the corner of her eye. "Though my sister insists a man of medicine knows his anatomy."

He suppressed a grin and filed the comment away to hold over Thornton. "I do prefer directness."

Her head inclined. "Then you should employ that to your advantage. What is my most attractive feature?"

Another trap. He kept his gaze above her neck. "Your lips." He let his focus fall upon them. "They are a beautiful vermillion. And the peaks of your philtrum form an unusually lovely Cupid's bow."

"Philtrum," she repeated. Her smile grew wider. "Good,

Lord Stanton. Very good. I've no idea what that is, but you make it sound elegant." She winked. "Perhaps I shall reconsider my stance on physicians after all."

Ian tried to imagine himself standing before the duke, asking for his daughter's hand, and failed. He barked a laugh at the very absurdity and impossibility of such an event. Marrying the daughter of a powerful gentleman he'd once accused of aiding and abetting a criminal? It didn't bear consideration.

Lady Olivia came to a sudden halt outside the railroad station. Her enormous, ruffled reticule slammed against his patella, but before he could ask what she carted about, her face tipped upward to reveal a long, smooth neck. "Exquisite," she proclaimed.

He couldn't agree more. Trailing kisses, moving ever downward...

"Their sheer size." Her voice held a note of awe. "And number. All floating above us. Have you ever seen anything like it?"

"No." Neither her neck nor the airships.

A year ago, following the demise of Elizabeth's disastrous engagement, he'd escorted his sister here, to the ship that had carried her to far-away Italy. At the time, Captain Oglethorpe's Luxury Airways possessed but one airship, and they'd only just begun construction of the very first boarding tower.

Now there were five airship boarding towers, the last still under construction. Each tower reached some four stories into the sky. A sky darkened not only by the quantity of exhaust churned out by idling engines, but by the long shadows cast by the enormous, cigar-shaped, silver balloons of the luxury airliners that were currently docked, welcoming their passengers.

Prior to Captain Oglethorpe's enterprising investment, boarding towers were unheard of. Crews had climbed rope ladders. Gentry had stepped onto a ten-foot square platform, held tightly onto iron railings, and endured the unsettling sensation of being yanked in a series of jerks from the ground into the sky. On windy days, a lurching platform had caused many to lose their most recent meal over the railings.

But passengers of this luxury airline were no longer treated like cargo. Ladies and gentlemen now ascended the tower by way of a series of ramps, stopping along the way to take in the various spectacles presented for their amusement. Gentry were forever bored, and that was the attraction of this airline. It advertised glitz, glamor and gold plate, promising endless entertainment in the form of theater, banquets and masked balls from the moment a patron stepped inside the Oglethorpe gates. Though the gaudy, ostentatious, over-the-top decadence came at a hefty price, only one particular dirigible would pass near Germany's borders within the next week.

"Move along," the duchess commanded, swatting at his ankles with her parasol as the crowd surged around them. "I'm told one needs at least two hours to take in the sights on the way up."

Ian's heart sank. As much as he found himself enjoying Lady Olivia's proximity, in the back of his mind a loud clock ticked. There was much he needed to accomplish in preparation for his arrival in Germany. A thick bundle of papers filled half his valise. He had less than two days to learn everything he could about programming the device he'd appropriated. There were maps to study as well. He needed to plot a path to cross into Germany undetected, to slip past border control leaving no record of either his entry or his exit.

"Perhaps we ought take the loading platform?" he suggested. "It offers an unobstructed view of the cliffs and the ocean."

"I couldn't possibly." Lady Olivia blanched. "No. I'm so sorry, Lord Rathsburn. I'm terrified of heights."

Her mother sighed heavily. "It seems we must endure puppets, dancing monkeys, sword swallowers and whatever other nonsense awaits us."

Ian agreed with the sentiment. He glanced at the duchess and noted that her intense stare was focused not upon him, but the case he held. There would be no excusing himself for he was indeed being watched. Who had sent her. Black? Or the duke himself? Either way, the best thing to do was to cooperate. For now.

Glancing again at Lady Olivia's figure, his gaze traced the trail of vines as they twined over her hips and twisted across her bodice, highlighting one delightful convex curve after another. Curves he longed to take the measure of using the palms of his hands. There were worse ways to spend his time than gazing upon such splendor. Lord Snyder—who might have won the right to touch as well—was a fool. "Very well, Lady Olivia. Lead the way."

Two hours later, they at last reached the grand entrance hall of the airship's gondola. It dripped with decadence. Coffered ceilings painted with cherubs, dark wood-paneled walls hung with gold-framed mirrors, and a marble-tiled floor covered with thick-pile Oriental rugs.

But Lady Olivia refused to relinquish his arm. "I'll see you tonight at dinner?" Her bright, hopeful face suggested only his presence could keep the clouds away. "At the opening of ceremonies? It's supposed to be spectacular."

"I'm afraid I have a prior commitment," Ian begged off. His head pounded. There had indeed been dancing primates. Ones that accompanied an organ grinder with cymbals and bells. He had work, work which required a clear head, solitude and quiet. Elizabeth's life depended upon him arriving suitably prepared.

"Then you can't possibly miss tomorrow night's banquet." The duchess frowned.

"Mother's right." Lady Olivia fluttered her eyelashes. "Please say you'll come."

His hesitation caused her face to fall as if he'd kicked a puppy. Resistance began to crumble.

"I'll see to seating arrangements," the duchess threatened with a toothy smile. "Don't make me drag you from your rooms."

"I look forward to it," he capitulated. Since they were to play at courting, he held Lady Olivia's gaze a touch too long. The scowl on her mother's face was well worth the effort. Some new tricks were worth learning.

"I'll miss you," she whispered into his ear before disentangling herself from his arm.

"I will count the hours," he murmured in return, then bowed deeply and took his leave, surprised to realize he rather regretted that Lady Olivia was beyond his reach.

CHAPTER SIX

OLIVIA PRESSED THE open end of the drinking glass to the wall and her ear to its base. Silence. She even tried holding her breath but heard only the low thrum of the airship's engines that vibrated through the walls of the gondola.

Not a single noise.

"What is he doing in there?" she asked Steam Clara. "How can anyone bear to stay inside the same four walls hour after hour?"

Like a hydra, frustration of all kinds reared its heads. The voyage had begun with such promise. Lord Rathsburn's flirtations had sent even her hardened heart skittering sideways. He ought to be knocking on her door, begging entrance to her parlor and pleading with Mother to be allowed to escort her on a promenade about the high deck. Flirtation was not at the core of her assignment. It was merely a tool, a way to draw him out of his suite and away from his luggage.

A tool that had failed her. But why? She shook her head. The man was a mystery.

Steam Clara held up two ribbons. One blue, the other green.

"The blue, Steam Clara. It deepens the color of my eyes." Exhausted from hours of monitoring her silent neighbor, she closed said eyes and leaned her head back against the wall. "Is he in there?"

But the steambot didn't answer; her metal eyelids clicked open and closed in confusion.

Olivia didn't need an answer. She knew he was.

In nothing but her combinations and stockings, she slumped against the wall that divided her room from the suite in which one Lord Rathsburn was ensconced. She'd heard his heavy boots hit the floor soon after he'd entered. "It's been over thirty-six hours!"

What good was the convenient connecting door if the man never left his rooms? She glared at the box Mr. Black had given her, the one holding the acousticotransmitters.

Olivia spun a lock pick in her fingers. Would that she was a full agent. She'd caught Lord Rathsburn's glances at her chest, at her lips. If only she were an unchaperoned widow, she could combine work and pleasure, for her target did not have the pallid skin of a corpse from working too long in a windowless room. Nor did he have a hump on his back or a permanent squint.

Though Lord Rathsburn's attire was unfortunate, he was tall and broad-shouldered. The wind had blown back the edges of his great coat, and she'd glimpsed the black-satin waistcoat beneath, surprised to note it showcased a firm chest and a flat stomach. While the black cravat knotted tightly about a stiff collar seemed to emphasize a stuffy nature, his dark brown hair was overlong, waving gently to form the slightest curl about his collar. And wrapping her arm about his, beneath the layers of clothing, she'd felt inexplicable strength.

No, rather than being repulsed, Olivia was intrigued.

She'd enjoyed teasing a smile onto his too-serious face far more than she'd expected, enjoyed watching how his laugh transformed him into a different man. Most of all, she'd enjoyed being the focus of his attention. Months had passed since a man had last looked upon her with anything beyond lust—and never before with such intensity and focus.

Flirting shamelessly with the man as they climbed to the gondola, she'd managed to extract a number of anatomical compliments. She now knew Lord Rathsburn found the high placement of her zygomatic arches—cheekbones—pleasing and considered the gentle curve of her cervical vertebrae to be most elegant. Her neck, in other words.

She'd also confirmed exactly which piece of luggage held items of interest. The entire time he'd not once set down the silver case, the one she'd seen leaking fog on Clockwork Corridor. Though his eyes flashed at her compliments, his white-knuckled grip on its handle never relaxed. She knew, for she'd stared overmuch at his hands. To the point where she'd begun to fantasize about them, about what those fingers would feel like, stroking over her face, threading into her hair, catching the angle of her chin and pulling her close for a kiss.

Widowed agents had all the fun.

Olivia smiled, imagining herself in his bed even now, done with her task. For she'd overheard the female agents' whispers. She would have planted those acousticotransmitters while he slept from exhaustion, then returned to the warmth of his body, seeking yet more pleasure from those all too tempting lips. What it would feel like if he... well, she'd never know, would she?

She huffed in frustration.

Instead, she was stuck here, various body parts going numb from lack of movement while Mother gallivanted about the airship, enjoying all it had to offer. Her chaperone would be back soon, to escort her to the dining hall where more drastic steps would need to be taken.

Steam Clara flapped the blue ribbon.

"Very well, Steam Clara," she said, shoving away from the wall and pushing to her feet. "I suppose you're right. Best to start preparing for the banquet."

Boots first. Olivia eyed her new riveted, patent leather ankle boots longingly, but if—when—the distraction succeeded, she would need to shed her shoes quickly. Slip-on silk slippers would have to do.

Corset second. Always. For it contained her lock picks. She slid the curved hook she'd been toying with into the second left boning slot of her corset, then—out of long habit—checked each slot to ensure her set was complete. Then and only then did she wrap her corset about her torso and slide the metal posts of the busk into their corresponding steel eyes.

"Pull the laces extra tight," she instructed her lady's maid.

A low whistle from Steam Clara's release valve indicated that Olivia was reaching the limits to which silk and steel could cinch her waist.

"I don't care," she said, her voice breathless. "Tighter."

Not only was a tightly laced corset a necessity, given her recent overindulgences in cream cakes, but she also wished to showcase her female assets, to watch Lord Rathsburn struggle to keep his gaze above her neck, to render him speechless.

She should be concerned about how badly she wanted this particular gentleman to acknowledge his physical attraction to her beyond teasing her with obscure anatomical references negated by the wink that followed. Yet it was a part of the larger game. A man distracted by all things feminine missed much.

Steam Clara tied the corset laces off and helped Olivia into her cage bustle and a number of petticoats before slipping a low-cut blue silk gown over her head. As Steam Clara's articulated fingers threaded the blue velvet ribbon through Olivia's hair, braiding and twisting and pinning, Mother appeared in the doorway.

"Good." She nodded at the vast expanse of her daughter's exposed cleavage. "I see you're ready."

Olivia stood and ran her hands down the smooth silk sides of her bodice, reassuring herself that the seams still held, that they didn't strain overmuch the threads that bound them. She'd had nothing but clear broth since receiving her assignment, but two months of cream cakes could not be undone in two days. "How do I look?" she asked. Then wished she hadn't.

"Exactly as you are. A desperate woman on the hunt for a husband." Mother's brow furrowed. "Make certain you don't mistake Lord Rathsburn as an acceptable target."

She ignored the insult, opting instead for another attempt at extracting mission intelligence from Mother. "What, exactly, is in that case of his?"

"A medical device."

"That does...?"

"Not your concern, Olivia. You need only help track where it goes. Nothing more. You need not even do that if you'd care to leave the task to me." Mother glanced at the box Mr. Black had given Olivia and held out her hand.

"No." Absolutely not. There was no way she would give up her first chance to help collect intelligence, no matter how small. She crossed her arms and stepped in front of the box that rested on the dressing table. "You told me I needed to prove myself."

"You can prove yourself by marrying Baron Volscini." Mother's hand dropped. "You know the rules. You have until your twenty-fifth birthday. After that, targets will look past you. Don't scowl, you'll give your face premature lines."

Olivia marched past her. "I will complete this assignment. All you need to do is keep Lord Rathsburn occupied in the banquet hall."

"Oh, that won't be a problem. I arranged to have Lady Farrington seated at our table."

She froze. "I thought the intent of this trip was to set the past aside."

"A societal liaison does not set aside convenient tools," Mother stated. "Use her."

IAN WAS late to the table.

Steam footmen bearing platters of baked oysters wove through the banquet hall serving the first course. He'd abandoned all hope of teaching himself to program the osforare apparatus, making it halfway through the schematics before conceding defeat. Living systems were his forte, not machines. Learning to program the device would take months, not days. He hoped the rudimentary movements coded for by the handful of punch cards accompanying it would suffice.

Instead, he'd plotted his route into Germany, then turned his attention to a pitiably thin laboratory notebook generated by Mr. Hutton during the original—and failed— rat trials of modified osteoprogenitor cells. It was the only notebook not stolen by Warrick. The initial weeks of the study had been so promising... Then the rampant growth and spread of the immortalized cells had resulted in an aggressive bone cancer. There'd been no choice but to terminate the study.

It had been a year since that first study failed, and Ian

had made much progress using an entirely new technique; strengthening a man's bones without sending him careening toward an early death was now more than mere fantasy. Though not a procedure he would divulge to the Germans. They need only think he would do so long enough for him to secure his sister's freedom.

But the German's demands that he cure bone cancer? A task impossible to complete.

Submersed in the intricacies of bone tumor pathophysiology, Ian had lost all sense of time. If not for the sudden onset of a storm that pelted raindrops against his window, he might have missed the banquet altogether. And when Lady Farrington's presence registered, he nearly made his excuses. It spoke volumes that he'd rather contemplate the possible manner of a man's demise than spend several hours in her company. Self-proclaimed arbiter of all that was proper and right, the woman's acid words could etch metal.

But something about the way Lady Olivia perched upon her chair—her face pale and pinched, her lips pressed together as if she'd swallowed shards of glass—roused some innate protective instinct. She wasn't the lively, flirtatious woman he'd first met—and he was to be seated next to the reason why: Lady Farrington, a dried husk of an old, bitter woman.

Why did he feel such a need to watch those long eyelashes of Lady Olivia's lift, to catch her gaze and stare into her bright blue eyes? Eyes as windows to the soul. Rubbish. No, he merely wanted to ensure they weren't tear-filled. And if they were? What exactly could he do? It would be a dangerous thing to court the daughter of the Duke and Duchess of Avesbury. He'd insulted the duke, and the duchess' cold smile made it clear her invitation to the table was a farce designed to keep a suspect close. If Ian dared initiate anything with Lady Olivia beyond a light-hearted flirtation, he might mysteriously go missing in the night, never to be heard from again.

At last, she glanced up and Ian felt a strange frisson of recognition. There were no tears, but something else. Something indefinable in her eyes gave him the decided impression he'd not quite met the true Lady Olivia. His inquisitive nature aroused, it would be no easy task to walk away from this woman. Not that he had a choice. His fists clenched. Would the ramifications of Warrick's duplicitous dealings ever end?

"Ladies." He greeted each by name.

"Lord Rathsburn." Lady Farrington reached out, her fingers wrapping about his arm as a kraken grasped its prey and dragged him down into the seat beside her. "Do sit down and stop making a scene. Do you not possess a pocket watch?" She didn't pause for so much as a breath. "I was just congratulating Her Grace upon the advantageous matches two of her children have made while consoling her upon the loss of her youngest, Lady Emily."

A death in the family? He glanced at the two women—and his gaze nearly tripped and fell into the depths of Lady Olivia's exposed cleavage. No, they were decidedly not in mourning.

"Nonsense." The duke's wife waved off the meddling

woman's sympathies. "Emily merely ran away with the gypsies. What is distressing, however, is the way your grandson handled his engagement to my Olivia. Rather spineless of him to abandon a woman so clearly in need of support."

Lady Farrington's eyebrows arched. "I myself counseled him to terminate the entanglement. You've far too many family members pursuing alternative lifestyles. It speaks to mental instability. Why, even now you travel to visit Lady Judith Ravensdale..."

Ian looked up from his plate of oysters and leaned forward. "The cryptozoologist whose studies of the reproductive habits of the giant kraken were instrumental in informing London shipyards how to prevent future infestations from destroying their docks?"

"Yes indeed," the duchess said, her voice betraying a note of pride.

Lady Farrington inhaled sharply. "Well. That may be, but devoting one's life to studying such horrible water beasts..." She turned toward Lady Olivia, her face contorted with false concern. "You always struck me as the sensible member of the family, but rumors circulate that you've dabbled in programming household steambots. Do tell me you haven't been driven to," she lowered her voice, "scientific research."

Could it be? He stilled, awaiting her answer. As brilliance ran in her family's veins, it followed that she too was more than a pretty face. Yet Lady Olivia remained silent, her eyes empty of yesterday's spark.

"And why not?" Ian objected to the snub on her behalf. He hoped she traveled to Rome to do exactly that. "This ridiculous prejudice against dirtying one's hands in the direct pursuit of knowledge prevents numerous men—and women—from applying the many talents they have to offer."

All three women stared at him in wide-eyed horror.

"I'm afraid I have no interest in, or talent for, academic pursuits, Lord Rathsburn," Lady Olivia said quietly. Her eyes dropped to fix upon her plate as she poked a bivalve with the tines of her fork.

Lady Farrington's presence did have a way of ruining one's appetite.

"You would do well to take a greater interest in your appearance," Lady Farrington harrumphed, "lest you begin to gather dust upon the proverbial shelf. I advise you take many walks about the decks at a brisk pace and avoid sweets. A more slender and enticing figure might help a gentleman overcome any concerns of marrying into your family. Isn't that so, Lord Rathsburn?"

Lady Olivia laid her fork on the table and allowed the footman to carry her untouched plate away.

Enough. This entire conversation was evolving into one long, never-ending insult. "On the contrary," Ian said. "Most men find a woman with generous curves appealing. I find it abhorrent that women are forced to pick at their food. The preoccupation with corsets and the tendency to wear them tightly laced inhibits digestion, preventing food from passing through the alimentary canal in a normal fashion."

Lady Farrington gasped and pressed a hand to her mouth.

"Not an appropriate dinner topic, Lord Rathsburn," the duchess chided.

Blinking quickly to hold back tears, Lady Olivia pushed to her feet. "If you'll forgive me." But in making her escape, her chair tripped a passing steam footman bearing a large porcelain soup tureen.

The footman wobbled on its wheels, throwing its jointed arms into the air in a desperate attempt to right itself. For a moment, the soup tureen seemed to hang suspended above her. Ian reached for it, but his fist wrapped about nothing but air, a fraction of a second too late. The tureen tumbled, upending its bouillabaisse in a steaming cascade down Lady Olivia's skirts, turning her sky blue silk gown into the color of an angry rain cloud.

A flurry of activity followed wherein Lady Olivia burst into tears as steam footmen—bells ringing—rushed forth to blot her skirts. A multitude of faces turned to stare in horror.

"Are you...?" Ian began, pushing back from the table. Except she wasn't fine, and all he had to offer was a perfectly useless handkerchief.

"Please stay," she gasped. "Don't... I'll just..." Then she turned and ran from the room.

He moved to go after her.

The sharp hooks of Lady Farrington's tentacle-like fingers once again sank into his arm. "Sit down and let the girl go."

CHAPTER SEVEN

CLUTCHING HER RUINED skirts, Olivia ran through the gondola's hallways, past the curious stares of strangers. She paused only once, as she passed through the great entrance hall. The many mirrors that stretched from floor to ceiling beckoned. She *had* to look.

Cranks and springs! She was a mess.

Olivia blotted away crocodile tears and fought back a self-satisfied smile. Wet and crumpled skirts dragged the floor. A side seam in the bodice had pulled free. The silk dress was beyond hope, an unfortunate casualty in an otherwise beautifully executed public set down.

As was to be expected, the ever-acidic Lady Farrington had been unable to resist an opportunity to sit in judgment and pinpoint every inadequacy of her figure and her family. Olivia rather regretted meekly allowing that woman to use such ammunition, but the more one worked within the realm of truth, the more convincing the outcome.

A shame she'd not been able to smile and wink at Lord Rathsburn when his gaze had finally slid below her neck. She'd hoped to arrange for him to accompany her on a 'brisk walk about the deck' and expound upon the reasons men found her figure attractive.

But the soup course was the perfect exit strategy. She'd waited patiently until the steam footman was behind her, listening for the telling click of elbow gears. And then disaster spilled down upon her.

Her lips twitched as a smile threatened. Pressing a fist to her mouth, she feigned distress, then turned and resumed the race. For that's what it was. A race.

She had some two hours to complete her assigned task. Lord Rathsburn would not easily escape Lady Farrington or Mother. Still, that was where the uncertainty lay. The social behavior of scientists was unpredictable. She needed to hurry.

Olivia slammed the door behind her and fell against it, panting. Lord Rathsburn was correct; her corset was far too tight. "A stunning success, Steam Clara," she gasped, as her breaths slowed and adequate oxygen began to reach her brain.

Steam Clara held out Olivia's dressing gown, whirring and whistling in confusion when she waved the steambot away, kicked off her slippers and reached for her oversized reticule, shoving the box containing the acousticotransmitters inside.

"Later," she wheezed. "I need to go in now." She moved to the connecting door and set down her reticule. She did not wish to sacrifice a single minute. After the task was complete, there would be more than enough time to celebrate her success with a hot bath. "I'm fine, Steam Clara. Set to idle."

But her steam maid's various gears did not cease spinning, did not fall silent. Instead, her skirts billowed with steam and a warning bell began to ring. Of all times for a malfunction! She had to silence the steambot. Olivia tore through the steam maid's uniform and pried open the metal access door. She snapped the bell clapper free and yanked out the broken cipher cartridge.

Steam Clara sagged.

Mother would insist upon a replacement now, but the cipher cartridge held Steam Clara's programming cards, the essence of her personality. Olivia cracked open the cartridge and stuffed the cards inside her bodice. She'd think about how to fix this later, but somehow she would save her friend.

Ignoring the damp seeping through petticoats and combinations, she reached into her bodice and extracted two of her lock picks. Bending low, she set to work. A moment later, the lock popped open.

Olivia pulled Watson from her reticule, twitching his activation spine. He uncurled and leapt onto four silver feet. His green eyes blinked at her, awaiting instruction. "Prepare and assess."

A number of spines retracted and a multitude of oddly formed wire antennae extended to take their place.

With Watson ready, Olivia gingerly tested the handle.

The door swung open without resistance. There was no sudden buzz of electricity. No lights flashed. No whistles or sirens of any kind screamed.

She cracked the door open further, allowing him to waddle into position. First his jointed nose extended, sampling the chemical environment. Then he advanced into the room beyond the door, antennae quivering. Olivia waited, listening. There, a faint whistle signaling that all was clear.

Strange. She'd expected some kind of heightened security measure. Perhaps she'd grown far too accustomed to men —and women—not being at all what they seemed. Lord Rathsburn seemed a kind and honorable man, his conversation bluntly straightforward, his devotion to medical science unwavering. Unfortunately, Mr. Black seemed to possess a different perspective, and he was usually right.

She followed Watson, stepping into Lord Rathsburn's parlor. Gilded furniture, potted palms, a large mirror... all the expected items. She searched, but could find no personal possessions. Nor were there any in his dressing room or the valet's room. Not even an idling steam valet. The enormous suite appeared unoccupied.

Upon Watson's whistle, Olivia stepped into the man's bedchamber. At last, signs of habitation. A shaving kit and towel. A greatcoat flung across a chair. A large pile of type-written pages on his bedside table.

Her eyes narrowed, focusing upon the papers. Quickly, she flipped through the pages. It appeared to be the draft of an instruction manual for a medical device requiring

Babbage cards. Curious, but exploring the many facets of Lord Rathsburn's interests was not her goal. She needed to find his luggage.

She yanked open the drawers of his dresser. Every last one was empty. She bent over, ignoring the corset boning that pinched in numerous locations. Nor was there anything beneath his bed. She huffed in frustration. Where was his valise? That silver case?

Turning, her eyes came to rest upon a narrow door built into the wall's paneling. The escape hatch.

'Travel light' was one of Mr. Black's mottos, and if Mr. Black suspected Lord Rathsburn, duplicity was to be expected. Could it be he did not intend to remain aboard the airship? That Italy was not his true destination?

Olivia wrenched open the heavy door. Beneath the eerie glow of red emergency lights gleamed the iron catwalk leading to the dull gray metal hull of an escape dirigible. With Watson at her heels, she closed the door behind them and walked across the cold steel, approaching the entry hatch, certain she would find his possessions inside.

She did. There, in a corner, Lord Rathsburn's valise and the silver case. A smile curved her lips upward. Success.

Kneeling was an awkward procedure given the weight and volume of her skirts, especially considering the tightness with which her corset was laced and the heaviness of her bouillabaisse-soaked skirts. As always, she managed.

She cracked open Lord Rathsburn's valise, and the spicy scent of cloves met her nose. Inside were several clean shirts, a change of collar and cuffs, a cravat and waistcoat, and a single additional suit. A bare minimum of clothing.

Olivia pried free a discreet amount of the lining before tugging open her drawstring reticule and pulling forth the tube of adhesive and the first acousticotransmitter. She flipped the tiny lever to activate the device. Then, applying a drop of adhesive to its side, she secured the transmitter beneath the lining before gluing the lining itself back into place.

Closing the valise, she turned to the silver case. It was locked. Securely. She studied the lock. *This* was the kind of challenge she'd expected. A firkin cincture bolt. Far more stopping power than your average luggage case ought to require. The simple picks in her corset were not up to the task. But she had a tool that was.

"If you please, Watson, my special lock pick."

Several rows of Watson's spines retracted and a series of metal bands folded to stack one upon the other until an opening—large enough for a woman's hand—appeared in his lower back. Olivia reached in and extracted the cloth bundle that held Captain Jack's Tension Torque.

Such a handy device. The average lock could be opened with ease, but when someone had something truly valuable, only a fool trusted such a lock. Lord Rathsburn was no fool. This was a special lock that required a special key.

Or a special lock pick.

She inserted the hollow copper coil of the device into the key hole and depressed the plunger on the attached syringe, extruding a thick gel of alkylsorcin. She counted off the three seconds, then fiddled with the thumb wheel until a faint click sounded. With a twist of the wrist, Captain Jack's Tension Torque slid the bolt free.

Really, if Lord Rathsburn was going to survive selling secret British technology, he needed to invest in non-British security upgrades.

Olivia stowed the lock pick back inside Watson. "Close." His back snapped shut.

As she lifted the case's surprisingly thick and heavy metallic lid, a kind of cold fog pooled before pouring outward over the edges of the case. Her eyes grew wide as she looked upon a rack of vials filled with strange liquids. The contents swirled beneath the red glow of the emergency lights. There were a number of packets containing unlabeled powders and a medical device she hoped never to personally encounter as a patient.

Her hand shook as she lifted it gingerly from its padded housing, examining the contraption with horrified fascination. A number of fine silver springs were attached to a curved and jointed brass frame pierced with holes. Fixed to the end of each spring was a tiny gauge designed to indicate pressure of the long, steel needles that the thick, iron screw bar drove downward through the many piercings and, quite likely, into the patient.

The room spun as her stomach turned inside out. Swallowing hard, she returned the device to the case and took several slow, deep breaths. This—*this*—was why she avoided biotechnology espionage. The medical devices involved were inevitably sharp and glinting. This particular contraption looked as if it had been extracted from the jaws of a mechanical monster.

Yes, it was a personal failing, but one she didn't seem likely to overcome.

Olivia activated another transmitter and stuffed it deep beneath the padded lining of the case. She slammed the case shut and, blowing on the alkylsorcin to hasten its evaporation, reset the lock. She shoved herself back onto her feet.

That was all he'd carried aboard, but she had to be certain she'd located *all* of Lord Rathsburn's belongings.

She turned about, third transmitter in hand, scanning the cabin. Nothing but eight chairs bolted to the floor, security straps and a panel with levers, dials and a steering stick.

Perhaps something was stowed in the engine room? Gathering her skirts, Olivia stepped through a narrow doorway. A coal hopper, an engine and exhaust pipes running to an overhead vent. But no additional luggage.

There was, however, a storage compartment. She pulled it open and found a tall, narrow closet holding a number of strange leather straps with buckles, eight wool blankets, a flask of water, a rope and a flare. Rather meager emergency provisions.

Reflecting that the escape dirigible itself would need to be tracked, she activated and affixed the third transmitter to the inside edge of the storage compartment's doorway. No one would see it unless they climbed inside.

Climbed inside.

She stared at the nearly empty compartment.

She should leave. Slip back to her room and compose a

coded message reporting her task complete and warning Mr. Black that Lord Rathsburn's travel plans did not include Rome. That from all signs, his departure from the airship was imminent, and—given the airship's current location and the distance it could travel with the amassed coal—he would likely land in Germany. Another agent would then assume responsibility for discovering Lord Rathsburn's ultimate destination.

That last thought kept her feet rooted to the floor. Olivia didn't *want* to meekly hand off this assignment. Once he left the airship, the acousticotransmitters would quickly move out of range and, inside Germany's borders, the Queen's agents might never locate him. Those tubes and powders and that horrid contraption would fall into the hands of the enemy.

She could hide inside this compartment. Pretend to be an infatuated female desperate to find herself a titled husband by any means necessary. It fit with the public persona she'd spent years developing. Lord Rathsburn happened to be a very eligible, handsome and titled gentleman with whom she'd begun a social—and public— flirtation.

A parson's mousetrap sprung in the most unusual manner. She could easily cry off upon her 'rescue'. No one would expect her to marry a traitor.

Did she dare?

She was trained for this and fluent in German. But she was merely a social liaison, not technically allowed to work outside of sanctioned social events. Her heart pounded.

Mother would be furious, yet what kind of role model did she present, trapped within society's expectations? Perhaps she would do better to imitate Mr. Black's example. He broke rules with astonishing regularity and his career trajectory moved ever upward. The possibilities for advancement among the Queen's agents beckoned. Here was her chance to prove she had real value in the field. Behind enemy lines.

She would attach herself to Lord Rathsburn, force him to take her under his protection. The role would be no hardship. Besides, if she were 'ruined', Mother and Father might finally relent and allow her to move directly into field training without marrying. Mr. Black would champion her, wouldn't he? Perhaps not. He had been rather emphatic about *not* making Lord Rathsburn her own personal target.

The only other choice available to her was to marry the Italian. To become the third wife to an elderly man who had once worked against the British government. To what end? Merely to alter her name and divest herself of her virginity?

She jumped at a faint hiss, at the sound that accompanied the opening of the escape dirigible's door. Lord Rathsburn! She'd drastically underestimated his resistance to accepted social expectations, and therefore the time available to her.

It was now or never.

"Curl," she commanded Watson in a whispered voice. The hedgehog's spikes retracted as his head and feet tucked themselves inside the metal sphere of his body. Olivia scooped him up, holding him against her chest as she climbed inside the storage compartment and stuffed the volume of her damp skirts about her legs.

She reached out and caught the edge of the hatch door with her finger, easing it shut. There was a faint snick, and all was dark.

Not a moment too soon.

She listened as heavy footsteps paced outside the storage space. Her heart pounded against the corset's steel boning that dug into her chest as cold seeped into her stocking covered feet. Despite the dark, she closed her eyes. *Don't open the door. Don't open the door. Don't...*

Seconds felt like minutes. Minutes like hours. Her stomach rumbled reminding her that in feigning social trauma, she'd eaten not a single bite at the banquet. At last the engine room door slammed. There was a moment of silence, and then the engine roared to life.

A thrill shot through her limbs. It was done. After years of hard work and self-sacrifice, adventure awaited.

For better or for worse, where Lord Rathsburn went, she went.

CHAPTER EIGHT

I AN TOSSED HIS GREATCOAT across a passenger seat and settled into the pilot's chair. He flipped a series of switches and turned a row of knobs. Behind him, the escape dirigible's engine roared to life.

A fancy vessel, this. Fully automated, it needed no one to crank the engine and no one to shovel coal, time being a critical element when using an escape dirigible for its intended purpose.

His chair swiveled as he turned to his left, pushing a button to release additional hydrogen into the balloon's air cells. This would allow the dirigible to rise swiftly past the observation decks and out of sight above the great airship's own balloon. There would only be a thirty second window in which he risked discovery.

Once he cleared the Oglethorpe airliner, he needed to avoid detection for at least nine hours. By that point in time, he would be beyond the reach of any official French interference.

Ian hadn't planned on leaving the Oglethorpe for another six hours, preferring to minimize his time in the escape dirigible, but there'd been an odd light in the duchess' eyes. One that set his nerves on edge. Something was afoot.

Dread fell into his stomach, then surged upward to choke him. Had the duchess lured him from his rooms?

With haste, he'd returned to his suite and found... nothing. Nothing but an odd scent that hung in the air, one he couldn't quite place. Nothing but a bone-deep knowledge that someone had been in his room, knowledge that threw a wrench in his carefully arranged strategy. Simple surveillance was one thing, but to actively invade his space? That spoke of intent to thwart his plans.

He'd hastened to the escape dirigible, relieved to find his travel cases where he'd placed them, their contents undisturbed.

Black might unofficially endorse his efforts to track down Warrick, but that didn't mean the great duke himself was in agreement. The Duke of Avesbury might wish to see Ian stopped, and he had no intention of being forcibly returned to Britain and labeled a traitor. Not that the duchess was capable of stopping him, but on the chance there was another agent aboard planning to do just that, he'd decided to depart immediately.

His jaw clenched. He could not risk Elizabeth's health, her life. She was not safe in the hands of those hypertrophically-muscled, metalloid-reinforced German soldiers. All it took was a trip, a minor fall, and his sister would be bedridden for months. Active abuse at the hands of her captors would cause her permanent disability.

Ian reached forward and pulled the release cord. Above him, gears began to grind. Pulleys and cables and bearings moved. A torsion spring unwound, hoisting upward the large iron door built into the Oglethorpe's hull.

The vast night sky stretched before him. Buckling his seat's restraining bands, he made a final systems check. Normally, autopilot would be engaged, but his requirements of this flight were anything but standard procedure.

With a twist of a knob, he increased the torque of the engine and released the braking mechanism.

The dirigible shot forth from its launching tracks, slamming him backward into his seat. The moment the vessel was clear of the airship's hull, the additional hydrogen did exactly as planned, quickly lifting him above the Oglethorpe's strolling decks. In seconds, he cleared the airship's enormous balloon and nothing but dark sky and winking stars lay above him.

Free.

Upward momentum slowed and the dirigible began to make swift progress forward. He checked and readjusted navigation settings, then settled back in his chair and took a deep breath. For now, there was nothing to do but stare out the forward window and wait.

Waiting. Not something he did well.

He'd slept little these past few days. He needed rest, and past missions had taught him to grab precious sleep whenever he could. Ian unbuckled his restraints, swiveled in his chair to prop his feet upon the adjacent chair, and fell instantly asleep.

———⊱✦⊰———

A LOUD BANG WOKE HIM.

Ian sat up straight, dropping boots to the floor to stare at the engine room door.

Bang.

He turned to study the instrument panel. All dials and pressure gauges indicated the dirigible was operating within normal limits. A glance at his pocket watch informed him that several hours of the journey had passed. He looked up and out into a driving snowstorm. Perhaps flying debris had struck the dirigible?

Bang.

Soon, he would reach the German border. Of all times for something to go amiss...

Bang.

He swore. What was wrong? A bearing about to seize? A rod about to break? A piston requiring more lubrication? Or a backfiring spark plug? Ian shook his head. What good would it do him to diagnose the engine when there was no hope that he could repair it mid-flight? There were no tools on board. He'd checked.

More bangs sounded from the engine room, this time in rapid succession and without any kind of perceivable rhythm. And—he angled his head—an intermittent high pitched whine accompanied the noise. A decid-edly *un*mechanical sound, the tone and tenor of which exactly matched that of a hysterical female.

There was only one female with whom he'd recently tangled. Lady Olivia.

Cursing, he went to investigate.

Ian pulled open the door and glared at the engine, rather hoping he was wrong. But pistons churned, the drive wheel turned, and the axel to the propeller spun. The engine ran like... well, a well-oiled machine.

Another bang sounded beside him. "Help! Please help!" a voice cried from the storage compartment.

Bouillabaisse. A hint of vanilla and cinnamon. Ian swore again. *That* was the odd scent he'd detected in his bedcham-ber. All this time he'd been concerned about the mother, when he should have worried about the daughter.

Bang, bang. "Let me out!"

Unthinkable to leave the duke's daughter locked inside a storage compartment. What the hell was she doing in there? His hand hovered over the handle. Was it possible she worked for her father? Could she be an agent?

His mind rebelled at the thought. Surely the duke would never allow it. Nevertheless, he would tread carefully. For many reasons.

Bang. Bang. Bang.

Grumbling a few more choice curses under his breath, Ian yanked open the storage hatch door. A tangled mass of torn, damp silk and warm, soft woman tumbled out. He caught Lady Olivia—mostly—as she collapsed bonelessly to the ground. Lowering her the rest of the way, he crouched beside her.

She wrapped her arms about his neck and pressed her face to his chest, weeping. He patted her back. Then stopped. For the love of steam, who consoled a stowaway? He twisted his lips. Someone who stole dirigibles and flew them across enemy lines, apparently.

"Thank goodness you found me. I've been locked in there for hours," she sobbed into his neck, hauling in great gulps of air.

And whose fault is that? With great care, Ian grasped her shoulders and pushed her away. No more coddling the woman who was now his Great Huge Enormous Problem.

Lady Olivia wore the same low-cut gown he remembered from the banquet. Stained, tattered and torn, only a rag picker would find value in its remains. Her hair was now best described as a tangled rat's nest. Her eyes were red-rimmed, her nose was swollen and her full lips quivered.

An excellent actress. Any other man would have fallen for it, and even knowing her presence was no accident, he still felt an impulse to still that trembling with the press of his own lips. Did that make him a fool?

"Explain," he ordered, hardening his voice. Their eyes met and a faint blush rose to her cheekbones. Embarrassment? Or did she too fight a flare of attraction? He had to set aside this raw need that twisted inside of him. Logic needed to prevail.

She lifted a shaking hand to the side of her head. "When the dirigible launched, my head... it knocked against the wall, and everything," her breath shuddered, "everything went black. When I woke up..." She flinched. "There's no handle inside that compartment. I couldn't get out."

Ian tugged her hand away, gently pushed aside a few golden tangles and found a trace of blood from a small cut and a rather significant lump. Was it possible she told the truth? Did it matter? Truth or lie, her presence compromised his mission. "There's a medical kit in the front." He stood, dragging her to her feet and waving her through the engine room door into the cabin. He couldn't wait to hear her story. Truth or fiction, it would be telling.

On stockinged feet and wobbly legs, Lady Olivia stumbled forward. Her bodice gaped. Her stained and wrinkled skirts dragged at an odd angle, and her hair tumbled, one knotted curl at a time, over a very attractive bare neck.

Ian closed his eyes and ran a hand over his face. What the hell was he going to do with her? "Sit," he commanded, injecting a bit of ire into his voice. "Why are you on my dirigible?"

She sat. "I'm so sorry," she sniffled. "So very sorry. It was wrong of me to enter your rooms. I just..." Tears ran down her cheeks once more.

He ignored them, turning to yank the medical kit from the wall. He poured a good amount of isopropyl alcohol onto a gauze pad, pressed it against her head, and took a certain amount of satisfaction at the hiss of her indrawn breath as he wiped away a crust of dried blood.

She tipped her face upward to meet his gaze with wide and innocent blue eyes beneath damp lashes, but something about the set of her jaw—or was it the angle of her chin—gave her away.

It was clear that Lady Olivia expected him to play the gentleman, to excuse her bad behavior without comment, without reprimand. No doubt she counted upon it. Disappointment would be hers.

"I've no time for games, Lady Olivia." He scowled at her, narrowing his eyes. "No interest in crocodile tears and protestations. You have clearly targeted me." He watched closely as he posed his question. "Did the duke send you?"

"What?" She drew back, pressing a hand to her chest, blinking a touch too quickly. "No. He... My father—and mother—wish me to marry an Italian baron. Who is three times my age." Her voice dropped to a whisper. "I can't. I simply can't force myself to comply."

Ian crossed his arms and waited as she wiped away a few lingering tears.

"It was wrong of me. I apologize." She drew a deep, shuddering breath and looked away. "I simply hoped to escape. I thought—I hoped—you might take me with you. You *are* looking for a wife?"

A parson's mousetrap? So it seemed. Undesirable in the eyes of London society, she was being hauled away to marry in foreign lands. He bit back the harsh words he'd been about to utter. It was entirely possible she told the truth.

In which case Lady Olivia had made a drastic mistake and chosen the most unsuitable man possible to target.

He frowned as he took a long and hard look. She was not at her best, that was true. But she was beautiful. Blonde curls and blue eyes. A pert nose and pink cheeks. And his mind kept circling back to those tantalizing lips. Did they taste as sweet as they looked?

Though when standing she barely reached his chin, her curves were generous. The corset she wore struggled mightily to contain her breasts. His hands itched to curve beneath them and relieve the corset of its duty. His gaze moved lower. Or grip those wide hips and pull her tight against him.

Before the physical evidence of his interest became painfully clear, Ian turned away. How long had it been since he'd had a woman? Months? Too long, if he was considering such possibilities. "I am not in the position to offer for your hand, nor will I be forced to the altar," he said.

"But, everyone will know…"

She trailed off as he moved to stand before the console and waved a hand toward the forward window. The first pink glimmers of dawn illuminated the deep, dark forest that stretched out below them. To his relief, he saw no evidence of patrols.

"We're about to cross the German border," he said.

"What!" She wobbled to her feet and moved to stand beside him. "Germany! Why?" Her shock sounded genuine.

"Were you hoping for some quaint French village on the Côte d'Azur with a willing and ready priest?"

Her lips pressed together.

He stabbed his fingers into his hair. Time ran short. "No more games, Lady Olivia."

"Yes. The French have far better fashion sense."

His answering laugh was tinged with the absurd. Stuck in the German countryside with the daughter of the Duke of Avesbury. Either she had the worst instincts imaginable when choosing potential husbands, or she'd been sent to watch him. He was, as yet, unable to determine which. Unknown dangers lay ahead or he might have looked forward to teasing forth the truth.

Either way, he couldn't let her go. Without proper papers, she would not be able to legally return across the border. Invoking her father's name would do more harm than good; a particularly astute and enterprising border guard with political interests might recognize the duke's name. Lady Olivia Ravensdale would make a valuable prisoner.

And, of course, she knew where Ian was. Something as innocent as a telegram would reveal his whereabouts to her father, and the Queen would be informed. Nefarious activities would be presumed, cutting off all hope that he could quietly return home. He rubbed the back of his stiff neck. With two women now to protect instead of merely one, this voyage had grown infinitely more complex. Misgivings slithered down his spine.

"We haven't crossed the border yet," she said. "Take me back to the Oglethorpe." Her hands slid along the silk of her skirts, as if she might erase the many wrinkles. "I'll slip back into my room. We'll never speak of this again."

"I'm afraid we've traveled too far," he answered. Bad choices came with unpleasant consequences. Hers could well be deadly. "There's not enough fuel." Or time. "You'll have to come with me."

CHAPTER NINE

"Y OU WANT ME TO pretend to be what?" Olivia asked. Her slack jaw was no act. Lord Rathsburn had peeled off every last pretense of social veneer and tossed it to the wind. Though she should have guessed he would propose such an action from his earlier declaration at the banquet table. "I can't be your research assistant. I know nothing of biology."

Scientists. They were all mad. That much she knew. Still, she'd followed him, and therefore it fell upon her to bring him around to her point of view.

"I find it hard to believe that the sister of Lady Thornton can make such claims." Doubt laced his voice.

"My sister built some kind of clockwork spider contraption." She wiggled her fingers. Under no circumstances would she admit to playing any role—however small it had been—in the neurachnid's success. "It spins new nerves. *That* is the entirety of my medical knowledge."

Lord Rathsburn frowned. "Then I hope you're a quick study. We have about ninety minutes before we land." He reached inside his coat and, from a pocket, tugged forth a small notepad—its pages curled and worn—and the stub of a pencil. "I can teach you the basics, write down a few key phrases." He began to scratch away. "As to the rest, simply nod and agree with whatever I say."

Nodding and agreeing. Parroting and regurgitating. The very behaviors Lord Carlton Snyder had most admired in his future bride. She excelled at such performances. Except no one had ever asked her to play a role requiring her to project scientific intelligence. A confident medical research assistant? No. Not possible. Not if it required she interact with that vicious device. There was certain to be blood involved.

The parson's mousetrap, though tried and true, was also a bit stale and overused. Despite the unsettling feeling that it was only a matter of time before he would see through her carefully constructed façade, such a role was also her best chance of success. She pressed a hand to her throat. What other fiction had she to fall back upon?

He paused for a moment, tapping the pencil against his lips in thought as he stared at his scribbles. A wave of golden brown hair tumbled free across his furrowed brow, and she longed to reach out and brush it back into place.

Heat crept across her face. Not once in all the long months that she'd been Carlton's fiancée had she ever wished to touch him. Carlton had been a threat to national security, a snake in the grass to be monitored. A task. *Her* task. But as much as she wished to serve her country, marriage to such a man... well, it had been a relief when Emily's scandalous behavior became public knowledge.

"I'd do much better impersonating your *wife*," she said, desperate to re-direct Lord Rathsburn. Given how she'd thrown herself at him, the idea should have occurred to him on his own, but the annoying man didn't even look up from his notebook.

Where had she gone wrong?

He was attracted to her. Of that she was certain. A moment ago, his eyes had taken in her every feature, her every curve, and before he'd turned away, she'd seen desire flare in his eyes.

Yet without so much as a glance her direction, he dismissed her with a wave of his hand. "I disagree. I was instructed to come alone. I can argue that as my assistant, you are essential. As my wife, you simply become another potential hostage."

"*Another* hostage?" Olivia's eyebrows rose. A new complication. But that was to be expected when one made hasty decisions and assumptions. So Lord Rathsburn did not travel of his own volition. Good. She hated to think the man a willing traitor.

His lips pressed into a thin line. It was clear she was going to have to drag it out of him.

With a resigned sigh, Olivia crossed her arms and dropped all pretext of having cotton wool between her ears. "Fine. Tell me where we're going and why."

Lord Rathsburn looked up at her, his eyes narrowed, the

air between them charged with unspoken truths. *Cogs and pins*. He knew. Knew she wasn't entirely what she pretended to be, for he'd already expected her to know where and why.

How? Where had she gone wrong?

"To a castle in Germany to rescue my sister. They—whomever *they* are—somehow believe that I can correct a fundamental problem with an experimental cell line merely because they command me to do so. Because my sister Elizabeth is their prisoner, we will not disillusion them. Instead, we will reassure them that such a thing is possible. We will set up a make-shift laboratory and strive to convince them that we are making progress." He presented his plan as if there was no alternative. "In short, we will lie."

Olivia was still digesting his words when he ripped off a sheet of paper and handed it to her.

"I promise to explain the situation in greater detail. Soon. But time is short, and you have a great deal to memorize." He cleared his throat, a sound she recognized as a prelude to a lecture. "We study bone."

"We?"

"Do try to assume the persona, will you?" He exhaled a heavy sigh. "Recall your sister's mannerisms and words. Her drive for everything neurological. Adopt those behaviors, but incorporate these terms and phrases." He tapped pencil on paper. "Can you do that?"

The role of wife would have been preferable, but she had no intention of ending her days in a dungeon. So, until she collected more information and could judge the situation firsthand, she would accept his assessment. She nodded. "I'll do my best."

Standing beside her, he pointed to the first of many diagrams scribbled upon the paper. "Bone is a living tissue composed of both organic and inorganic substances."

"Organic?" she asked.

"Living," he answered through gritted teeth.

"Then inorganic is non-living?"

"Correct." His voice was tight. "There are two cell types you must remember. Osteoblasts and osteoclasts."

"Cells. The basic building blocks of all life forms." Yes, it seemed she had absorbed something from her sister's ramblings after all. "They are the organic part," she concluded, flashing him a pleased smile, quite proud that she followed.

But Lord Rathsburn's flat regard offered no praise. "Yes. Together these two cell types maintain bone homeostasis."

Homeostasis? Olivia frowned, but stayed silent.

"Osteoclasts break down bone tissue. Osteoblasts build it. Provided their activity balances each other—that they maintain homeostasis—the bone remains healthy."

That wasn't too hard. One kind built bone, the other destroyed it. "Go on," she said.

"Now for the inorganic portion." His finger moved down the page. "The non-living minerals, elements really, are calcium and phosphate. Together they form hydroxyapatite, a calcium phosphate mineral that composes seventy percent of our bone."

He was beginning to lose her. Thank goodness this was

all written down. It was going to take her at least five minutes to force her lips to pronounce the *hydroxy* word.

And Lord Rathsburn's finger was only halfway down the first page.

"Calcium phosphate is the predominant form of calcium found in the milk of all bovines."

"Bovines?"

"Cows."

"Why not simply say that to begin with?" she asked. Such a mouthful when a three-letter word would suffice.

"Because bovine is a more accurate term."

"Only if you're speaking to someone who also speaks medicalese."

"Medicalese?" His eyebrows rose.

It was Olivia's turn to sigh. "Two living cells, one to build, one to break down. Drink milk to maintain your minerals. Close enough?" she asked.

"To start."

Thus began a long-winded, overly detailed and tedious explanation of the intricacies of bone development and maintenance. In mere minutes, Olivia's eyes began to cross.

Any chance that she would be able to assemble such unfamiliar vocabulary into anything resembling an intelligible sentence was so remote as to be impossible. She would be caught in the lie and immediately be thrown into whatever prison they were keeping his sister. If she were going to accompany him, it was time to reconsider impersonating his wife regardless of the risk.

Verbal reasoning hadn't worked, but perhaps she could persuade him by other means.

Slowly, Olivia slid a stockinged foot across the floor until it bumped against his boot, then shifted her weight in his direction. Her skirts swayed, wrapping themselves about his leg. She leaned, and her bare shoulder skimmed the fine wool of his coat.

Oblivious, he kept talking.

Olivia leaned in closer, tilting her face as if to study the papers he held. Instead, she studied him. The faint shadow of a beard darkened his jaw. His lips were so expressive, so earnest and serious in their explanation. She longed to see him relaxed and smiling once again.

She pressed the side of her breast against his elbow. "Mmm," she murmured.

His breath caught ever so slightly, and she was almost certain he stumbled over a word. Alas, it wasn't one she could pronounce or define, so she couldn't be certain.

"Lord Rathsburn," she said, placing a hand lightly atop his. The fine, crisp hairs dusting the surface of his skin brushed her palm.

His words tripped and staggered to an uncertain halt.

Tipping her face upward, she stared into his bright, blue eyes and asked a question she knew would unbalance him. "I'm sorry, but I'm hopelessly lost. Is bone matrix organic or inorganic?"

He released the notebook pages into her hands and stepped back. Closing his eyes, he pinched the bridge of his nose. "The osteoblasts lay down the matrix so it is necessarily organic. I believe I mentioned that some ten minutes past."

"I believe I mentioned biology was not my forte some fifteen minutes past."

His lips twitched. "So you did."

"I do, however, have extensive experience in the role of fiancée. As newlyweds—"

"No." Lord Rathsburn snapped his fingers. "Lady Farrington mentioned you possess programming skills. Is this true?"

Every cell in her body let out a frustrated howl. *Wife!* she wanted to scream. But she had a part to play. She cast her eyes downward as if embarrassed. "I'm afraid it is. If you examine my reticule in the storage closet, you'll find proof."

Lord Rathsburn turned on his heel and marched into the engine room. The door to the storage hatch clicked open.

Olivia held her breath, afraid to move. If he discovered the acousticotransmitter...

But he didn't. He strode back holding her reticule. Already he'd yanked open its drawstring and was examining the contents. Thank goodness she'd had the foresight to hide evidence of her mission. Tucked safely behind the steel boning of her corset, the final as-yet unactivated transmitter seemed to burn.

"An assortment of unpunched paper, tin and copper cards." He placed the cards upon the dirigible console and reached back into the bag's depths. "A Franconian multi-punch?" He studied her with newfound interest. "Impressive, Lady Olivia. The only men I know who use the Franconian multipunch have quite advanced skills."

"If you consider punching recipes for the best cream cakes in London an advanced skill, then yes." Lord Rathsburn looked stricken. She shrugged. "Mother is prone to sinking spells. For years I've managed the household. Occasionally, I try my hand at improvements."

Watson emerged next from the depths of her bag. "A metal sphere." His eyebrows rose in question. Clearly the man was hoping for more than pastries.

"My pet hedgehog," she answered, smiling sweetly just to aggravate him. She held out a hand. "If you'll allow me to demonstrate?"

He dropped Watson into her waiting palm. In one smooth movement, she drew her other hand over his gleaming surface in a caress, and Watson uncurled, his spines emerging from the perforations in his many segments.

"Impressive craftsmanship," Lord Rathsburn observed.

"I cannot claim to have built him," she answered. "Only to have modified a childhood toy." Her finger triggered the mechanism that sent him into clockwork mode. In such a state his eyes would not glow, no probes could be engaged, nor could his secret compartment be opened. "Watson runs quite simple programs."

"Watson," he repeated.

She placed the hedgehog on the ground and issued a series of commands. "Spin." Watson spun in a circle. "Sit." Watson sat. "Beg." Watson straightened, balancing on his hind legs, front paws curled to his chest.

Tea cakes and animal tricks. How could he not see things from her perspective? She let the corners of her lips curve in a gentle, wifely manner.

"It'll have to do," Lord Rathsburn pronounced with resignation. "You will be my programmer."

"Programmer?" She echoed the word through clenched teeth.

"In the meager time left to us, our only hope is to have you speak intelligibly about Babbage cards and programming."

He crouched before his insulated case, unlocking it. Fog escaped. She watched, frozen in horror, as he carefully donned gloves and lifted the menacing device from its padding and turned toward her. With the twist of a knob, a set of copper punch cards slid from the contraption's interior.

With trembling fingers, she accepted the cards he held out, examining them closely. Better to stare at a pattern of punches than long, steel needles.

Or so she thought.

If she read the program correctly... The cabin seemed to tilt. Olivia lowered herself onto the nearest seat and made herself inquire. "Its function?"

"My early experiments, which the Germans have managed to reproduce, require that modified osteoprogenitor cells be inserted not via blood transfusion, but directly into bone marrow using a large bore needle."

She swallowed. The very mention of needles always made her ill. Her head felt buoyant.

Lord Rathsburn did not seem to notice her distress.

"This device, the osforare apparatus, is designed to take a different approach." Eyes gleaming, his voice grew animated as he pointed out specific features of the contraption. "After filling the glass reservoirs with transforming fluid, a small rotary motor punctures the skin and drives the needles through muscle to the very surface of the bone."

With each additional word, the buzzing in Olivia's ears grew louder. She clutched the edge of her seat. "Stop," she whispered. "Please. Stop."

But he didn't hear her.

"Pressure gauges provide feedback, slowing the needles' approach so that they barely pierce the periosteum, a thin membrane on the surface of bone, before injection..."

Her vision grayed at the edges. Then darkness closed in.

CHAPTER TEN

THERE WAS A CLATTER, and Ian glanced up. The copper punch cards he'd handed Lady Olivia lay scattered across the floor. The woman herself—her face pale and her eyes unfocused—swayed in her chair, looking as if she were about to join the cards. What on earth was wrong with her?

He caught her with his free arm as she slumped forward and lowered her to the floor. Setting aside the device, he pulled his greatcoat off the chair and used it to pad the floor beneath her head before returning the osforare apparatus and its punch cards to their case.

He sat down and stared at the beautiful woman who lay at his feet. Earlier, every time their eyes caught, Ian could swear he sensed a keen intelligence. But whenever he delved deeper, she quickly swept his attempt beneath the proverbial carpet with a flirtatious comment or a contrary observation. Never before had he met such a frustrating woman.

Whether she was brilliant or merely bright, he'd been mad to think he could teach her anything about bone biology in the space of one hour. Even a willing medical student would require more time to grasp the bare basics of bone physiology. Bone pathology and the intricacies of his research were far beyond her reach in the short time left to them.

He'd been encouraged by her pronouncement that she herself had designed and punched pastry recipes, but who did so using a Franconian multipunch? Then again, baking was a form of chemistry, was it not? Timing, temperature and precise measurements. If Olivia had managed to program a steambot to assemble cream cakes, then the delicacies of osteoblast transplantation ought to be within the realm of her programming skills.

Alas, she'd had a rather adverse reaction to his device.

A strong gust of wind tossed the dirigible, sending the hull into a chaotic rocking motion. Lady Olivia's eyelids fluttered open.

"Was it the needles?" he asked.

Her eyes closed again as she pressed her palm to her forehead. "Not entirely. You did mention blood."

This situation grew more absurd by the moment. She had tried to warn him. "I suppose that explains your aversion to men of medicine." What was he going to do with her?

Lady Olivia's lips curved in a smile, and her eyes slowly opened to catch his gaze. "I've recently reconsidered my stance." Her index finger lifted to trace the edge of her bodice, promising that she could be persuaded to do more than simply impersonate his wife, if only he would agree to her plan.

Given the jump in his pulse, Ian's heart clearly approved. He shifted uncomfortably upon his chair. Other parts of his anatomy agreed. He looked away. Now was not the time to allow instinct to overrule intellect. If she had any concept of how tempting the offer was, she would never relent. It would be wrong of him to yield. Very, very wrong. He needed focus, not distraction. She would be safer as his assistant in an entirely separate bedchamber.

On the other hand, if they were separated, he would not be able to protect her from other dangers. His eyebrows drew together. No. He shook his head. Her plan was untenable. As a wife she was merely another potential hostage, a tool to use against him. As his assistant, she would be by his side as he worked long hours.

Thud. Something struck the side of the gondola.

"What was that?" Lady Olivia's voice squeaked with panic as she pushed herself onto her elbows to stare out the window.

"Flying debris, most likely." Or so he hoped.

There was another loud thud. Ian turned. Not the best of sounds. They were in the middle of a driving snow storm some hundreds of feet from the ground, and their coal supplies were running low.

But as they stared, a small, round face appeared in the window of the dirigible's door. A girl with dark, wide-set and angular eyes grinned back at them. Black hair flew wildly about her face. She waved a greeting then gestured at the door, smacking it repeatedly.

"How is she—? We're still in the air!" Lady Olivia exclaimed.

In one smooth motion, Ian yanked open the door. Icy air whipped through the cabin as the child leapt inward, snow swirling about her feet. Behind her, a long rope stretched upward, its origin lost in the storm.

"Thank you much," the girl said. She unclipped the rope from her harness and casually tossed it back into the storm. Ian slammed the door closed.

He stared at her, struck dumb by her unexpected arrival.

"*NiHao*," the child greeted them in Chinese, bowing to each of them in turn. Though she wore a padded red silk jacket and pants, both elaborately embroidered with intertwined dragons, her feet were bare. "I am Wei. Sent to deliver you safely to Burg Kerzen."

Returning the bow, Ian said, "I am Lord Rathsburn. Pleased to make your acquaintance."

The girl laughed and her eyes sparkled. Another bright spot in all the dark surrounding the gloom of his voyage. Lady Olivia, he was surprised to realize, was the other.

"Burg Kerzen," Lady Olivia repeated, stumbling over her skirts as she rose. "Castle Kerzen. Our destination?"

The castle in which his sister was being held. Their approach had not only been noticed but anticipated. "It is," he said.

"We are close," Wei announced. "But have no docking

platform. The Roost it must be. It is not possible for dirigible landings. Even when weather clear. Which here seems almost never. I come to take you. Like harbor master." With another bow, the girl ran to the console. Ian followed, watching as she made a number of adjustments.

"The Roost?" he repeated.

Fingers flying over the dials, Wei explained, "A spire. A balcony with an iron railing. Count, he insists we call it so." Her voice sobered. "No one argues with Count." Wei nodded and locked in the new coordinates before turning to face them. "This weather needs lowering harnesses." To illustrate, she tugged on the leather straps wrapped about her own torso and between her legs. Then, eyeing them both as if assessing their attire and, finding it wanting, her mouth pulled once again into an adorable grin. "Saddle up!"

Ian had meant to find a field, to circle its perimeter while releasing hydrogen. Such a method of landing would have been rough in this weather, fraught with the likelihood of being smashed against a stand of trees. Best to let Wei guide them in.

Lady Olivia looked at him with panic in her eyes, and he realized dragging him level by level up Captain Oglethorpe's loading platform had not been—at least not entirely—a method of monopolizing his time and attention.

Afraid of blood, needles and heights. The statistical probability that she was a spy was low. Given what might await them at the bottom of the rope, he was no longer certain if that was a good thing.

He grabbed his greatcoat from the floor and strapped on

his sword before reaching out and catching Lady Olivia's hand. "Come. Safety harnesses are in the storage hatch." It wasn't lost on him that chivalry might severely handicap him in negotiations for his sister's release, but there was no abandoning Lady Olivia to her fate.

Eyes wide, she followed him into the engine room. "The girl, Wei, does she mean for us to..."

"Yes." He held out his greatcoat. "Put this on so that you don't catch a chill." She swallowed, but did as he asked. Ian lifted a harness from the storage hatch. "Slide your arms through here."

"I don't think I can—" she objected.

"Then don't think. Don't argue. Just do as I say. Soon, we'll be safe in a warm castle where you can use your many charms. It seems our host is a count." He pulled the belt tight across her chest, checking the buckle twice.

"You've done this before?" Her whole body trembled as he pulled her arms through the shoulder straps.

Yes. As required training for a field agent position. "It's a gear harness. A simple but effective method to lower oneself to the ground when inclement weather prevents a direct docking." He caught her gaze and gave her a reassuring nod. "Now, you'll have to forgive the over-familiarity of this next step. I assure you, it is necessary. Please spread your legs."

Her eyes widened. "My legs?"

Continuing as he'd begun, Ian gave her no time to object. He knelt, reached between her ankles and under her many petticoats to grasp the leather strap that hung behind her. He drew it upward, gathering those many petticoats between her thighs, and buckled it to the strap already secured about her chest. Her face burned a bright red.

Embarrassment was preferable to panic.

In moments, he had himself similarly outfitted. "Ready?" he asked.

"No."

"Excellent," he replied, grabbing her hand once more. "Let's go."

Wei nodded at them in approval. The girl was nothing if not efficient. A neat coil of rope lay beside the dirigible's door, secured to an iron beam with knots that would make any sailor proud. His valise and case were stowed inside a cargo net, ready to be lowered.

"Does lady have a trunk?" Wei asked, handing him two automated gear winches.

"No," he said. "There was a mishap at the launchpad. I'm afraid that is the entirety of our possessions."

"Good," Wei said. "Two minutes."

Ian clipped a winch to his harness, then turned back to Lady Olivia, clipping hers into place as well. Her breaths came in shallow pants. "Sit," he said, gently pushing on her shoulder. Her knees buckled, and she nearly fell into the chair. "Bend over, put your head between your knees."

"Can't," she exhaled. "Corset."

Ian swore. Women's undergarments were absurd. Still, he should have thought to loosen her laces. But to get to those laces... No, there was no time for it now. "Breathe slowly." He crouched beside her. "You *cannot* faint again." He did not wish to risk lowering a limp body in this weather to an unknown platform.

She nodded, making an effort to slow her breaths.

Behind him Wei opened the door. Cold, bracing air blew inward. His belongings scraped against the edge of the door-frame as she pushed them overboard. "Listen. We'll go down together. I'll clip my winch to the rope, and I'll clip yours directly above mine on the same rope. Climb on my back, like a child. Understand?"

"Yes," she whispered. Not a drop of blood remained in her face.

"Ready, sirs," Wei called.

"Use both your arms and your legs. Cling as tightly as you wish." Ian tugged Lady Olivia onto her feet and led her toward the open door.

Wei hurried over with a rope, expertly clipping Ian's automated gear winch in place and Lady Olivia's above his.

The wind howled into the cabin and the gondola swayed.

"I can't," Lady Olivia cried. She tried to back away.

Ian caught her in his arms, pinning her hands against his chest. Grasping her chin, he tipped her face upward, locking their gaze. "We need to go. Now. We're nearly out of fuel. Remaining aboard is not an option. I barely know you, Olivia, but I see untapped strength within. You can do this."

Impulse struck, and he bent, catching her lips with his. He meant it to be a brief, reassuring kiss. One that would distract her from their inevitable leap into a storm. But when she melted into him, when her lips parted as if on a plea, Ian found himself drawn deeper. Angling his mouth to hers, he tasted her. Salt from her tears and a faint hit of honey.

A frisson of recognition ran through his body.

"Aiyaaa!" cried Wei. "No time for this."

Or time to analyze his reaction. He pulled back and turned, dropping to a crouch. "Climb aboard, my lady."

Thighs and arms wrapped tightly about his waist and chest. Her face pressed into his neck.

Wei tossed the weighted rope out the door and waited. "Ready," she called when an answering tug came from below. "Gears set at two. Fast. But not too fast for the missus."

Wet tears slid across his neck and dripped behind his collar. "Here we go," he announced. Grasping hold of the winch's handle, he jumped before Lady Olivia could change her mind.

The wind howled about him, flinging icy needles of snow at his face and hands. The rope twisted and bowed as the geared hoist lowered them downward at a swift clip. In mere seconds he could see the outline of several castle spires. The one they slid toward, a cone-shaped cap set atop a circular tower, flew a red flag. From its side, a narrow balcony protruded beneath an arched window. Their rope disappeared inside.

"Hang on!" he yelled into the wind. Lady Olivia whimpered in his ear, but her grip tightened.

As Ian's boots hit the window casing, a sudden gust of wind slammed them into the stone wall of the tower, twisting the rope and throwing them back into the air. The automated gear winch continued to lower them—beyond the balcony.

Men yelled, and the rope tightened. Hands reached out, grabbing their arms, pulling them inside. At last, his feet mercifully landed on solid wooden flooring. Quickly, he released the clips binding them to the rope. Two burly men, those who had yanked them inside, threw the rope back outside and slammed the window shut against the storm.

"Good morning," a voice greeted them in perfect, unaccented English. From a narrow doorway on the other side of the circular room, a Chinese man stepped forward. His dark hair was pulled into a severe topknot. He wore a high-collared tunic cinched at the waist with a wide leather belt over dark trousers. Below his knees, tightly fitted boots gripped his legs. An embroidered overcloak with full sleeves hung from his shoulders. A curved sword strapped to his side was the only visible weapon, but Ian knew instinctively that more blades would be hidden in various locations about his person.

Likewise, the German guardsmen at the man's side also had various sheathed blades strapped to their sides. But no pistols.

Curious.

Lady Olivia slid from his back and moved to stand beside him. She glanced from the man to the guardsmen, and he noted the moment she observed the misshapen lumps upon their jaws. Her eyes widened as one of the guardsmen unconsciously rubbed a swelling tumor that had overtaken a finger joint on his right hand. Soon it would not bend.

Had he mentioned the tumors to her? No. She'd collapsed before he'd had the chance. Her gaze caught his, and ever so slightly, he nodded. She swallowed hard, absorbing the seriousness of the medical disaster. Two guardsmen at this point, but there would be many, many more.

With unsteady hands, she unbuckled her harness and let it fall to the ground. He followed suit.

"I am Zheng," the Chinaman said with a slight bow. "The count's huntsman."

Given the man presented no visible evidence of bone tumors, Ian surmised the man held a position of honor, one that lifted him above submitting to a mad scientist's experimentations. Ian bowed and stepped forward, but one of the two German guardsmen grasped his shoulder. "*Nein*."

The other pulled Lady Olivia from his side. She cried out in protest.

"Apologies, but it is necessary," Zheng said. "If you will spread your arms and legs, Lord Rathsburn, I'm afraid we must relieve you of your weapons."

With a show of reluctance, he did as requested. He'd expected this, but had hoped a blade or two might slip their notice.

They took his sword from him first. Then the German guardsmen extracted a knife from each of his boots, then yanked up the leg of his trousers to find the one strapped to his left thigh. Lady Olivia's stunned gaze raked over him, but the guardsmen had just begun. They found the one fastened at his ribs. The one tucked beneath his waistband at the small of his back. They even found the small knife built into the lapel of his waistcoat.

Satisfied, the German nodded and waved both him and Olivia forward as he lifted Ian's luggage.

"If you'll follow me," Zheng said. "The count awaits you in the great hall."

Ian held out his hand, motioning toward his case.

"*Nein,*" the guardsman said, narrowing his eyes and gripping the luggage more tightly. The other jerked his head in the direction of the door. It seemed they were to have a rear guard.

Like the gentleman he sometimes was, Ian held out his arm. Lady Olivia accepted, wrapping her arm about his and tipping her head up to search his face. *Who are you?* her wide eyes asked. He wished he knew the answer.

"Later," he whispered as they reached a narrow doorway.

Manners warred with instinct. Reluctantly, Ian motioned for Lady Olivia to precede him. The spiral staircase beyond the door would only accommodate one at a time. Silently, they followed Zheng down many stairs and through a tangle of disjointed, interconnecting hallways.

Finally, Zheng stopped before an enormous, carved wooden door. Its hinges objected with an ominous screech as he pulled upon an iron ring.

Together, he and Lady Olivia stepped back in time, into an ancient medieval hall with an enormous, unlit fireplace.

Dark beams coated with soot supported a ceiling that appeared to have once been richly decorated, but the pattern of intertwining vines and flowers painted onto the plaster was now largely lost to time and disrepair. Despite the snow storm, three tall, mullioned windows leaked a modicum of gray daylight into the room. Two brass chandeliers hung from a central beam. Though each fixture could have held twenty-four candles, only six burned. A single piece of furniture—an ornately carved chair—occupied the space.

A tall, broad-shouldered man with a thick, yet well-groomed beard rose from the throne and strode across the room, a fur-trimmed cape swirling about his legs. Ian guessed the man to be in his fourth decade. The count wore a close-fitted military coat of scarlet, his chest crossed with a dark blue sash. Everything else was decorated with gold. Golden epaulets, golden buttons, a golden belt and gold-edged collar and cuffs. Even the multitude of metals pinned to his chest—suspended by multicolored ribbons—were golden.

Pretentions to royalty.

Hopes of negotiating his sister's release faded in the face of such an autocratic and ostentatious display, leaving a bitter taste in the back of his throat.

Heels clicked as Zheng and the guardsmen snapped to attention. "Graf Otto von und zu Eberwin-Katzeneinbogen," Zheng announced. "You may address him as Count Eberwin."

Ian doubted he'd ever manage to address the count by his full title. After the slightest of hesitations, he forced himself to bow to the man who held his sister hostage. No need for open hostility; if the count equally despised Warrick, an alliance might be forged.

Olivia performed a deep and courtly curtsey, one worthy of Queen Victoria herself.

The count's gaze swept over her, taking in her bedraggled state with no more than a quirk of his eyebrows. "Herr Rathsburn," he growled, fixing Ian with a glare. "Already, we have problems. Although lovely beneath her rags, you bring an uninvited guest into my home."

With dread knotting his stomach, Ian performed an introduction. "To meet your demands, I require the help of my assistant—"

"Lady Olivia." She took a step forward before Ian could stop her. She curtsied once more. "Creator and programmer of the osforare apparatus, a device necessary to assess the malfunctioning cells of your men."

His shoulders relaxed. Not quite correct, but close enough. He'd been certain not a word of his discourse had lodged in her brain. He nodded agreement, grateful she had accepted the need for his protection. "A critical component of implementing a cure," he said, pausing for effect. "That is, if one can be developed."

Count Eberwin paced back and forth before her, drawing his thumb and forefinger over the length of his beard as he frowned. "I see. *Lady Olivia.*" He stopped directly in front of her. "Is that not the form of address the English use for an *unmarried* gentlewoman?"

"It is," she answered.

Ian detected the slightest tremor in her voice, and guilt elbowed him in the stomach for putting her in this position.

"Fräulein Olivia...?"

"Stonewythe, Olivia Stonewythe," she said, supplying a family name that would do nothing but chase its tail should the count choose to make inquiries.

Ian's opinion of her rose another notch. She knew labeling herself a Ravensdale would invariably connect her to the Duke of Avesbury, a man who antagonized the German Emperor Wilhelm the First at every opportunity.

But the moment Count Eberwin scooped up Lady Olivia's hand, pressing it between his palms, a new concern reared its ugly head. Ian did not care for the possessive light that blazed in the count's eyes as his gaze raked over her form, taking advantage of her ruined and gaping bodice to ogle her bosom.

He'd been wrong. She might not become a hostage, but Olivia's status as his assistant would not keep her safe from unwanted male attention. Ian's teeth began to grind. How far would the count press his advantage?

As far as was within his power. Any man who would subject his guards to experimental bone treatments and kidnap a helpless, sick woman in order to force a man to his will was unlikely to consider anyone's wishes but his own.

Ian stepped forward and wrapped his arm about Lady Olivia's waist, drawing her to his side. He'd not see her molested. "My lady forgets herself," he said. "Pardon her inaccuracy, we've only just married. She is now properly addressed as Lady Rathsburn. Your... invitation necessitated that we advance the date of our wedding so as to eliminate the requirement of a chaperone."

Annoyance twisted the count's lips. "I see. *Frau* Rathsburn." He dropped Olivia's hand. "A pity." He turned to a nearby guardsman and barked, "See my wife is informed that guests have arrived."

CHAPTER ELEVEN

T HE COUNT IS MARRIED?

Yes. And looking for a mistress. Olivia suppressed a shudder.

The moment Count Eberwin had turned his considering gaze upon her, fear and revulsion had slithered in, curling together in her stomach. Though she hated to admit it, Lord Rathsburn's assessment of the situation had the accuracy of a kraken sharpshooter standing on the gilded bow of the Queen's Royal Barge.

Shoving the visual memory of Lord Rathsburn's horrid medical contraption deep into the dark recesses of her skull, she'd claimed ownership well-knowing that professing to be a research assistant was something she'd pay dearly for when forced to confront the details of the device's mechanisms. What she hadn't expected was to draw the count's fierce attention.

He cut a handsome figure, Count Eberwin. Tall, dark

and fit. But the imperious man had a gnarled and malevolent mind. The bite of his gaze alone, promising midnight visits to her chamber, had shaken her. The manners he displayed were nothing but a thin veneer. Here, deep in the thick woods of Germany, the count might discard propriety at any moment without repercussions. Without a husband to claim her, no objections would be heeded if he chose to take her without consent.

Her heart had pounded against her chest. What nightmare had she jumped into by reinterpreting her orders, by placing herself in the field? She knew female field agents often took a man to their beds, exchanging pleasure for information. If the count found her physical charms appealing, she should view it as an opportunity to serve her country, but the thought of doing so with this particular man made her throat close in fear.

Until Lord Rathsburn's arm had wrapped about her waist, until he'd claimed her as his own, Olivia had forgotten to breathe.

With the bone-deep honor of a gentleman, Lord Rathsburn had set aside his own concerns, doing the very thing he'd most wished to avoid, and rescued the woman who had forced herself into his company.

She owed him, and would do her best to repay the favor by swallowing her fears and programming his contraption.

With a hard smile, the count turned away. "Zheng, if you will present Herr Rathsburn's luggage, we may begin."

Zheng stepped forward and set Lord Rathsburn's

luggage upon the floor. He flicked open the valise, dumping clothes at his feet.

A muscle jumped in Lord Rathsburn's jaw and his fingers tightened at her waist, but he stayed silent.

Zheng roughly tipped the case that held both the chemicals and the osforare apparatus onto its side, and Olivia flinched at the brutal disregard for her earlier words explaining the importance of the device they transported. He slid a dagger from his hip and pointed the tip at the firkin cincture bolt. Attempting to pry such a bolt with a knife would trigger a chemical fusion reaction, damaging the contents.

"Don't!" she yelled at the same time Lord Rathsburn called out, "Stop! The combination is four, seven, two, eight."

As Zheng opened the case holding both reagents and the osforare apparatus, he met her gaze with a blank stare over the cold fog that emerged. His move had been deliberate, a test to elicit information. How much had she given away?

"I hear we have guests, Otto." A woman swept into the room from a far entrance to lay her hand on the count's arm. "Are these the newlyweds?"

Guardsmen snapped to attention. Zheng slowly rose from his crouch.

The count grunted. "So they claim." He raised his voice. "My wife, Gräfin Katherine von und zu Eberwin-Katzeneinbogen."

Olivia resisted the impulse to squint. This woman—the countess—looked disturbingly familiar.

"Ian? Is that you?" The countess pressed a hand to her chest as she stepped forward into a beam of dusty light, and Olivia's heart stuttered.

Beside her, Lord Rathsburn tensed. It seemed he also knew this woman. Given that he made no move to greet her, Olivia concluded not all was sunshine and roses between them. His face an unreadable mask, Lord Rathsburn bowed. "May I present my wife, Lady Olivia Rathsburn."

The countess turned her attention toward Olivia, yet no flicker of recognition crossed her face. Thank goodness. She did, however, lift her chin ever so slightly that she might emphasize her superiority by looking down her nose upon this inconvenient wife.

Olivia curtsied. "Countess."

The countess swept up her hands with her own. "How wonderful to have another English lady present in our castle. You must call me Katherine, and I shall call you Olivia." She winked at Lord Rathsburn. "Your husband and I once shared a most memorable experience."

A wink? Really? In front of the bride? *That* spoke volumes. The feverish burn of jealousy and dislike crept across her skin. She ought to be disappointed with herself. Such uncontrolled and inappropriate upwellings of emotion might be convincing, but they were not promising for a career in the field. Katherine was tall, elegant and well-dressed. Everything she was not. Her only claim to status involved invoking her father's name, and *that* she could not do. Not here.

"Did you?" Olivia straightened her spine—it would not

do to let any weakness show—and returned the woman's false smile. She pulled her hands free and wrapped them about Lord Rathsburn's arm with a tight grip, staking her claim. At least those ingrained aspects of her training held true. She had spent numerous years learning to feign love and loyalty. Protecting her target was merely professional instinct. Lord Rathsburn was her husband now—if only her pretend husband—and a bride would not tolerate another woman attempting to steal away her groom's attentions.

She glanced at him and noted a dark stain high upon his cheeks. At least her *husband* did not recall this past event with fondness. *My husband.* Ian. She needed to remember to call him that. Even in her mind, if they were to maintain this charade. She prayed his history with the countess wasn't recent. The count didn't seem the forgiving type.

"You forget yourself, Katherine," the count boomed. "They have arrived at my behest to solve the problems of the silver skeletons."

"Did The Doktor not puzzle out the problem while I was away?" Katherine pouted, but she retreated meekly to her husband's side. "I miss Berlin, and I miss Augusta. You know Wilhelm won't allow us to visit again until this matter is resolved."

Olivia's chest tightened in dismay. Did Katherine refer with ostentatious familiarity to the wife of the German Emperor, Wilhelm the First? If so, this situation she'd inserted herself into was no trifling matter. Whatever Ian had discovered, created... if the emperor was the driving force behind this failing project, they were in trouble. As in likely-to-end-their-days-in-whatever-passed-for-a-dungeon-in-this-castle trouble.

"Did your recent visit not console you?" The count patted her hand absently. "Soon, *liebling*. Herr Rathsburn and his wife will fix this small inconvenience, and I will see you and your many pretty dresses returned to Berlin."

"Small?" Ian unleashed his tongue at last. "How long do your guardsmen survive once bone replacement is complete? Years of military exercises and training so that your guardsmen may gain what? A few months of unbreakable bone?"

"Enough!" the count barked. "Your complaints are irrelevant. You will fix it." He snapped his fingers. "Zheng, search for hidden tracers."

Zheng nodded and crouched once again before Ian's luggage. From one of the many loops on his wide leather belt, he pulled a silver-capped glass tube. Shards of various opaque crystalline material filled the cylinder.

Nuts and rivets. Where had he managed to secure an efflux detector?

Fear pricked at her spine. Was the crystal decay signal strong enough to detect if the acousticotransmitter had not been activated? Ian glanced down at her with a furrowed brow, and she realized she'd forgotten to breathe. Olivia forced her lungs to take careful, shallow breaths.

Zheng waved the glass cylinder over Ian's valise, then over his silver case. Both times, the crystals emitted a weak, pulsing yellow light. "Evidence of bioluminescent decay. A weak yet nearly undetectable source of power." He turned toward the count. "It is as you surmised. Not only do the Queen's agents suspect Herr Rathsburn's defection, they have taken steps to tag him, no doubt in hopes of locating his ultimate destination."

Ian frowned.

"Find them," the count ordered.

This time, Zheng moved the crystal-filled tube *slowly* over the scattered contents of Ian's valise. When the crystals began to glow a deep gold, he paused to push his fingers against the lining and—with the quick slash of his knife—drew forth a small, metallic device to hold it in the air. Its tiny light pulsed a faint green.

There was a hiss of indrawn breath from the count.

Olivia did her best to blink in surprise. The device, designed by her brother-in-law, was brilliant. A mechanical refinement of the middle and the inner ear, it was originally implanted directly into the skulls of the Queen's agents. This particular version was modified for extracranial use. An extremely useful tool. Until, of course, it was found.

"A transmitter of sorts," Zheng announced.

He pulled a screwdriver from his belt and pried away the copper housing to reveal fine wires, three strange, misshapen lumps and a tiny, golden, coiled tube. What he couldn't see, what was visible only beneath a specialized aetheric microscope, were thousands of gold microfilaments spiraling inside that tube.

She held her breath. If German engineers were provided the chance to analyze the acousticotransmitter, to reverse engineer it...

Everyone had turned to stare at Ian. Olivia too arranged her features to project confusion.

"I had nothing to do with this." He held up his hands. "I did as you asked."

The count snorted. "You did not come alone. How can I be certain you do not still attempt to work with these agents? Perhaps you hope they might assist you in freeing your sister." His countenance darkened. "Such will not be the case." The count turned to Zheng. "Give the device to me."

Zheng dropped the acousticotransmitter into the count's outstretched palm. He took a long look, then tossed the device to the floor, grinding it under his heel as if it were a poisonous insect.

"Find the others," he ordered Zheng.

Seconds later, the strange crystals flashed gold once more. Zheng found the second device buried beneath the padding that cradled the osforare apparatus. It too met its end beneath the count's heel.

"Hold out your arms. Spread your legs apart," Zheng commanded Ian.

His jaw clenched, but he did as requested. The cylinder remained clear.

Zheng turned to Olivia. "Frau Rathsburn?"

Though Olivia did not hesitate to comply, her skin felt cold, her heart pounded and she was certain someone would detect the slight tremor in her outstretched hands. Fortune favored her, and the cylinder remained clear.

She exhaled slowly, trying to disguise the fact that she'd been holding her breath again. Ian caught her hand in his and gave it a reassuring squeeze. She looked upward to smile gently in gratitude, as would a dutiful wife, and caught a flash of something in his eyes. He knew. Suspicion of her motives for sneaking aboard the escape dirigible had crept into his mind. She would have to dispel them before they became lodged too firmly.

"Excellent." The count clapped his hands together. "Now that outside interference is no longer an immediate concern, we may proceed. Zheng, if you will escort Herr Rathsburn to the laboratory." The count turned to his wife. "*Liebling*, see to Frau Rathsburn." He waved his hand at Olivia's sagging gown. "It seems there was a mishap with her luggage."

"This project is of the utmost importance," Olivia objected, willing to pad about longer on cold, stockinged feet if it meant she remained at Ian's side. "My attire can wait."

"Nonsense," Katherine answered, bringing with her the faint scent of jasmine as she threaded her arm through Olivia's, tugging her away from Ian and leading her from the room. "Your husband will need time to renew old acquaintances with Doktor Warrick and consult upon recent developments in his work. Besides, dinner is at eight, and we will need much time to determine which of my gowns might be adjusted to fit your more... generous proportions."

Olivia ignored the veiled insult, looking over shoulder at Ian. "But I need to—"

"Go, darling. I'll see that our workspace is set up properly." His face was stoic and unreadable. "I want a few words alone with *Mr.* Warrick. Count Eberwin, perhaps I might visit my sister first?"

"*Nein.* You will see her tonight at dinner," the count said. "Not before."

"You must tell me all about this unusual courtship of yours. A physician courting a programmer," Katherine prattled on as if Ian had not spoken. "I want to know *everything*. For we are to become the closest of friends."

Though it ought to have felt like a reprieve—Olivia did not look forward to confronting the mechanics of the osforare apparatus—the smile the countess turned upon her did not reach her eyes. It was probably a trick of the light, but her teeth appeared somewhat pointy.

CHAPTER TWELVE

I AN WATCHED AS HIS now-married almost-fiancée dragged his self-proclaimed, pretend wife from the great hall. Both women, it seemed, lived double lives. In the space of mere days, his life had twisted itself into a Gordian Knot. Alas, there was no simple way to solve the many problems strewn before him.

Had Lady Katherine, more appropriately known as Countess Eberwin, wanted him here in Burg Kerzen from the beginning, to cure the cancerous nature of Warrick's modified bone marrow transplants? Possibly. Yet the count knew nothing of her recent voyage to London. At the time his guardsman had landed on their balloon to deliver his summons, he'd thought she was in Berlin. Hell, it was even possible she worked for the Queen. What game did Katherine play?

He cursed Black's name. Had the man known who Katherine was and simply withheld the information from him, preferring to send him in blind to enhance the authenticity of his story? If so, he looked forward to their next meeting when he would greet the spy with a swift uppercut.

Olivia. She was the greater mystery. Until she'd called out in horror when Zheng pointed his knife at the firkin cincture bolt, he'd dismissed every suspicion that she could be an actual agent. Fearful of blood and needles, afraid of heights. She was *ton*. A beautiful, privileged flirt in search of a titled husband. He'd been so certain the duke would never place his daughter in harm's way. But now? He had to admit to the possibility. He was almost certain she herself had planted those acousticotransmitters.

Impressive.

She was bright, with a memory like a steel trap, and read punched Babbage cards as if they were pages in a book. What other as yet undiscovered skills might she possess? His gut informed him that he'd only peeled back the first of many layers.

At least she seemed to be on his side. For now.

Until a year ago his work had been beneath the notice of emperors and queens, of foreign and domestic agents. If not for the immediate threat to his sister, he might even have been flattered at all the sudden attention.

Presently, however, he deeply resented that his own government viewed his activities in a suspicious light. That they would attempt to listen to his conversations, to hone in on his location. That he wasn't worthy of their confidence. Or help. Not if such assistance might lead to a breakdown in international negotiations. The thought ignited a slow angry burn deep in his chest.

"Doktor Warrick awaits you in the laboratory," the count bellowed as he turned and strode from the room.

Zheng waved at Ian's case. "Bring the device."

"Warrick is not a physician," Ian said, carefully restoring the osforare apparatus to its padding.

"It is what the count desires to call him. *That* is what matters. And The Doktor is in charge of this project."

"For now." He would not allow that man to ruin any more lives.

A long corridor, many doorways and several spiral staircases later, they finally arrived at a cavernous tomb at the base of the castle. Zheng motioned him inside. As Ian started down stone steps worn smooth by the passage of time and thousands of feet, the thick wooden door slammed behind him. A key turned in the lock.

He eyed the vast, windowless chamber before him.

Three walls were constructed of stone and mortar. The fourth wall and the floor, if they could be termed such, consisted of the very bedrock upon which rested the foundation of Burg Kerzen. The room was cool and damp. Stacked floor to ceiling, wine barrels lined the space and exuded the pleasant, and somehow calming, scent of oak.

Torches of the medieval variety—sticks wrapped in rags and dipped in kerosene—had been thrust into wrought iron sconces embedded in the stone walls, though the darkness in the far reaches of the room swallowed up most of this ancient light.

In the corner of the room nearest the door, bright argon lamps blazed over a surprisingly modern and well-equipped space dedicated to bone research. It seemed the wine cellar was to be his laboratory. He saw but one research impediment: Warrick.

This flaw rose from a stool and spread his arms wide. "Every modern laboratory convenience you could wish for will be provided. Except, of course, a copy of the key that keeps us here." Warrick lifted an empty beaker from a nearby table and flourished a barrel spigot. "I am consoled by the abundance of ready wine. Do you prefer red or white?"

Ian ignored him, stepping past the man as if he did not exist, and set his insulated case upon the floor. Prisoner or not, Warrick had taken the first steps that led to this fate whereupon a mad scientist found himself employed by a power hungry despot. It was enough that Ian didn't kill him on first sight; indulging Warrick's pretense of bonhomie was out of the question.

A battery-powered cell culture incubator sat on the floor beside a long workbench. Ian crouched before it, swinging open the door. Inside, some twenty Petri dishes filled with blood-red media glistened in the damp heat. With closer examination, he was certain they would prove to be a line of deadly osteoblast progenitor cells.

"What countermeasures have you employed in an attempt to remedy the progression to osteoblastoma?" he asked Warrick. Ian left the door ajar, knowingly exposing Warrick's cells to airborne infectious agents. It was a test.

Did Warrick himself believe in his work enough to protect his cells?

"Until the count gives me a direct order, I'll not be sharing any confidential research information with you," Warrick snapped, firmly closing the incubator's door. "It's taken me over a year to progress to this point."

So Warrick had a solution in mind, if not one in fact.

Once, this man had courted his sister, had once begged for her hand on bended knee. At the time his future was bright. Now, his eyes were sunken and hollow, speaking of long hours fruitlessly searching for a remedy. It burned like acid upon his skin that he himself had been the one to introduce this monster to Elizabeth.

He shrugged, as if Warrick's progress didn't matter. It didn't. Not if he could lay hands upon his sister and escape this castle. Escape. Would he also have to rescue Olivia? Or would she provide assistance? "At some point the count will order you to work with me," he said. "Though I very much doubt I'll be able to find a cure. You've certainly managed to make a mess of things. Self-perpetuating, and therefore cancerous cells, are not the answer."

Warrick crossed his arms. "And how do you propose to work with cells that will not renew themselves?"

"Working directly with the cells in tissue culture is the wrong approach. You've been exiled from Lister University for over a year. Much progress has been made. None of which I intend to share with you."

Progress, but only in treating rats, his mind grumbled.

But Warrick stiffened at his pronouncement and that, for now, counted as a minor victory.

Given a choice, Ian would chain Warrick to one of those many iron rings bolted to the stone walls and leave him there to rot. Except he couldn't. He needed a competent laboratory assistant. Allowing Warrick to work at his side would take the pressure off Olivia, leaving her free to work on the osforare apparatus alone, where her talent lay, rather than forcing her to pretend to skills she did not possess. Skills that would be very difficult to fake and might ultimately hinder his work.

Warrick huffed.

Ian turned to the workbench.

On its surface gleamed an aetheric vacuum-chambered microscope—the latest model that touted enhanced resolution. Beside it was a fuge. A case containing needles and syringes. Rocking platforms, scales, a hot plate and ring stand. Above the bench were shelves that held a variety of glassware: Erlenmeyer flasks, beakers, titration equipment, bulbed pipettes. And Petri dishes—stacks and stacks of them.

A wooden cabinet at the far end of the workbench held jars and bottles and boxes filled with all manner of chemicals in both liquid and powder form. Labels had been carefully written and pasted to each. Unfortunately, the labels were all in German. Some, those with Latin or Greek names or the few that bore their chemical symbols were decipherable, but others...

"Can I assume your German approaches fluency?" Ian asked.

"It does."

"When you are done pouting about my arrival, made necessary by both your incompetence and betrayal, please turn your hand to relabeling all these chemical supplies in English."

"If you think I'm going to take orders from you," Warrick's voice grew strident, "slide into past patterns—"

"*That* is exactly what I think." Ian closed the cabinet and turned on his heel. "Don't pretend to be dense. Do you think I'm here voluntarily? My sister's life has been threatened." Lacking a blade, he pointed a finger at Warrick. "Don't think for a moment that I don't hold you responsible for her situation."

Warrick sputtered.

"The count thinks you incompetent, no matter his show of loyalty by keeping you alive," Ian continued. "I've been tasked with both curing your victims and providing an alternative therapy that will accomplish the same result in a nonlethal manner."

"Victims!" Warrick's face was red.

"I see no cages, empty or otherwise." Ian swung an upturned hand about. "I doubt very much that there is an animal facility tucked at the far end of this chamber behind the barrels." His voice took a hard edge as suppressed rage made his body vibrate. "You broke protocol, experimenting directly upon humans. How many graves have you filled this past year?" Nothing would satisfy him more than to add Warrick to that number.

"Boys who desire nothing so much as to become

guardsmen are readily supplied," Warrick said. "But there are rats about if you wish to chase one down."

"More than one," Ian said. "We'll need about fifty to start."

Warrick gaped.

A blatant lie, that arbitrary number. If necessary, he needed but one rat to demonstrate the effectiveness of the transforming agent he'd developed this past year, one rat who would have the strongest *healthy* femur in the castle, one rat to prove to the count that he could do as promised.

With luck, such a demonstration would never become necessary. In the meantime, he would enjoy watching Warrick hunt rats.

But first, Ian needed to know what the other man had done to make his cells so extremely malignant. "Concerning the *research* you've conducted this past year, where is your laboratory notebook?"

"There is no notebook," Warrick sneered. "I see no reason to lay my work out in logical order. What would my life be worth if my research was so easily reproducible?"

From the moment students stepped into a laboratory at Lister University, it was drilled into them that they must make daily—even hourly—entries into a notebook detailing their thoughts, their procedures, their discoveries. If another scientist could not reproduce the work, what value had any discoveries made?

Though there was a certain sense of logic to Warrick's defense, Ian trusted him about as much as he would a gear missing a tooth, and the lack of a comprehensive, detailed laboratory notebook triggered a rather loud alarm. "You must have something in the way of notes," he glowered.

Warrick's lips twisted into an approximation of a smile. "Not a single blasted page."

Impossible. Ian refused to accept Warrick's statement as truth. Blood pressure rising to critical levels, he turned his back on its cause and arranged a number of unusual ingredients upon the surface of the workbench. Warrick would assume they were vital to his breakthrough, a new method to coat bones in antimony, rendering them unbreakable without condemning the recipient of the treatment to an abbreviated lifespan with a most gruesome and painful end.

He tugged a packet of powder from his case, the one labeled simply with an "X" and measured out exactly one gram of dehydrated crystals. Pulling a bottle labeled "water" from the cabinet—his German could manage that at least— he poured the powder into the flask, added a measured amount of water and swirled the contents, watching as the reconstituted chemicals took on a rusty red color.

This powder was purely for effect, composed of chemicals that produced a spectacle of color to draw the eye. He wouldn't flaunt the *true* transformative powder before his enemies. A foreign scientist would need advanced skills and a sophisticated laboratory to analyze and tease apart the many chemical and biological components of that powder. Still, it could be done. *That* powder, carefully packaged and sewn into the lining of his waistcoat, was out of view from those who would force him to betray his country, his Queen, his sister. Himself.

As expected, Warrick leaned in, peering over his shoulder. "You cannot convince me that the osteoblasts can be transformed *in situ*. To inject them directly with that fluid would require—"

"Open the case," Ian interrupted.

Warrick did so. The sneer fell from his face.

"Not at all impossible," Ian said. "Not with Rankine Institute engineers close at hand. Do not presume to tell me what is or isn't possible. You, now isolated from all work conducted at Lister, a solitary scientist—to use the term loosely—housed in a cavern beneath a castle falling into ruin. The antiquated conditions under which you work hamper your progress. Could you find no one sane to fund your treasonous work?"

"I have made numerous advances. There is a way to stop the cells from multiplying. You should not have abandoned your original supposition that—" Warrick inhaled sharply.

"How?" Ian demanded. "If so, why has it not been deployed?"

"No. I will not allow you to badger me into revealing my plans. Keep your secrets. Perhaps they will save you."

Warrick lied. He was certain of it. There was no known method to cure cancer of the bone. Yet with so many lives at risk, he could not afford to ignore the man's boast. If he could not be goaded into sharing his so-called advances, Ian was certain he could convince the count to compel him to produce his research notes. In the meantime...

"I also require antimony," Ian said. Perhaps ignoring

Warrick would loosen his tongue. The man did love to brag. "I did not see it in the supply cabinet. Where is it?"

"Zheng supplies it. On an as-needed basis."

Realization struck. China was the leading supplier of antimony. That Zheng and the count worked so closely together... He frowned.

Warrick nodded. "Now you understand why Zheng is in the count's pocket. If the Germans manage to develop an unbreakable soldier, Zheng stands to make millions. He's not simply a mercenary chemical peddler, his family owns and operates an antimony mine."

"I will speak to him." Ian opened the cell incubator, removed one of Warrick's Petri dishes, and filled a large bore syringe with both fluid and cells. "Time to study the destruction your cells have wrought. We've no time to waste. Fetch me a rat."

Warrick stood, arms crossed, a belligerent look upon his face.

"Go!" Ian snapped. "Or I will tell the count you refused to assist. That should make for interesting conversation about the dinner table this evening."

Minutes later, Warrick dropped a vehemently objecting feral rat inside a makeshift cage upon the laboratory bench top. "Catch the next forty-nine yourself. I am done working for the day." He snatched up an empty flask and a barrel spigot—and disappeared into the gloom between the stacks of wine barrels.

A certain grim satisfaction surged through him at Warrick's hot-headed abandonment. Would the count's temper flare upon learning his cherished "doktor" refused to assist? Ian contemplated the rat before him. Until he'd assessed his sister's situation, he would make every appearance of cooperation, beginning with a thorough assessment of Warrick's so-called progress.

CHAPTER THIRTEEN

THE GUARDSMAN IN front of Olivia finally stopped climbing yet another twisting flight of worn stone stairs—to the relief of her poor, constricted lungs and frozen feet—and set Ian's valise down before a wooden door to fumble an iron key from his pocket. That was when she noticed this particular man's hands. "Your fingers." She pressed a shaking hand to her mouth, then pointed at the lumps protruding from his knuckles, the reason they were here. His joints barely flexed. "Do they hurt? Are you in pain?"

Behind her, Katherine's breath caught. Had the woman thought she wouldn't notice?

"Pain?" The guardsman scoffed. "A soldier accepts pain. What he does not accept is death. You will fix."

Fix. Yes, that was what she and Ian were here to do, fix the tumors she'd already noticed upon the jaws and fingers of a number of guardsmen. Presumably such growths affected bones in other locations, locations a physician and his assistant would inspect. There was no escaping total immersion into the medical field. Biology lessons concerning bone growth and development would continue and, as they veered to the pathological, would grow more morbid.

Her stomach curdled.

Lifting the valise, the guardsman led them into a room. The castle was in bad repair. It was cold and drafty and—from what she'd glimpsed so far—poorly furnished. This bedchamber she and Ian were to share was no different.

Though a generous size, Olivia suspected that—were she to yell—her voice would echo off the bare stone walls. A minimum of furniture occupied the space, and the bed took center stage. Heavy, green brocade curtains fell from a carved wooden canopy supported by four sturdy posts. The mattress itself rested upon a platform so high that three wooden steps had been built to allow a person to climb inside. Inside. For the bed seemed to be its own room.

Aside from a simple writing desk and chair, seating in the room was limited to a stone bench built into the wall beneath a tall window, their sole source of light. Currently of the gray and dim variety. A number of its panes were broken, rags thrust into the cracks the chosen method of repair.

An insert in the old fireplace across from the bed was the only visible attempt at modernization—a carbonite steel stove optimized for burning coal, though why one would bother in the middle of a forest... She crossed to hold her hands above the vent, scooting her frozen feet as close as possible. The heat emitted was meager and, given the paltry ration of coal in a scuttle, there wasn't much hope of raising the temperature of the room above bearable.

"*Sie können jetzt gehen*," Katherine informed the guardsman. *You can go now.* She held out her hand.

He frowned and shook his head, refusing to drop the key into her waiting palm. "*Ich warte draußen.*" *I wait outside.*

Interesting.

Olivia gave no indication that she understood their exchange. Had the count instructed his guardsmen that his countess was not to be trusted? Lady Katherine, as she'd been known once, had been the most selfish debutant of Olivia's first Season. She'd ruined a number of young girls' marital prospects that year. Including Olivia's.

At her debut ball, Katherine had swept in, uninvited, turning all male heads in her direction. A number of targets invited expressly for Olivia's perusal had failed to take interest in the duke's daughter, favoring instead the tall, raven-haired beauty.

Mother had been furious.

But Katherine had a proclivity for luring eligible men into gardens—and of turning down their subsequent proposals. One day, she'd simply disappeared. Her parents, thin-lipped and rigid, had faded from society, leaving the *ton* to embellish upon a variety of rumors.

Olivia allowed herself a small smirk for now she knew the truth of Katherine's fate. Forced marriage to an impoverished German count, life in an ancient fortress deep in the primeval forest. After all the hopes and dreams she'd ruined, it was hard to dredge up much sympathy. She frowned.

Though her husband was a kidnapper and a philanderer. No one deserved that.

The door closed behind the guardsman and, nose wrinkled, Katherine turned her attention to Olivia's attire. "Take off that coat. Let's see if the blue silk can be rescued."

Silently, Olivia slipped Ian's woolen greatcoat from her shoulders and draped it over the chair. She had no desire to become fast friends with this woman. Every moment spent alone in Katherine's presence was a threat to her cover. Any second the countess might recall her true identity.

"Turn around." Katherine twirled her finger in the air, clucking her tongue. "It's hopeless. Whatever happened?"

Olivia spun. "An unfortunate accident and an unanticipated early departure." Best to stick as close to the truth as possible. "There was no time even to change. My husband suspected he was being watched."

And he'd been right. She only hoped Zheng's detection of the acousticotransmitters hadn't led Ian to the conclusion that *she* was the one who had been tasked with surveillance. Given the man's intelligence, it was a rather feeble hope. Should she be worried that a small part of her wanted to drop all pretense in his company?

"My red gown will fit without alterations," Katherine pronounced. "I will have it—and its matching slippers—sent to you. Along with my white, silk nightgown. It is the only one fit for a new bride. It is thin, but..." she tipped her head as if amused, "it will help you cope with the cold."

Olivia frowned.

"By drawing your husband close, of course." Her laugh

held a note of ridicule that pricked at Olivia's skin. "Have you not yet shared a bed?"

"Of course," Olivia said, her face hot. Would he kiss her again? She hoped so, for she'd been too terrified to soak in the marvelous sensation of his lips pressed to hers. Her eyes darted to the massive bed. Did she dare encourage further explorations? Desperate to steer the conversation elsewhere, she continued, "I only wondered about a bath. But, this castle, it seems its distance from civilization must make modernization... difficult."

"This drafty old heap needs repairs that would empty the count's coffers. Better to let it crumble." Katherine waved a hand dismissively. "I will see if hot water can be managed. In the meantime, do make use of the wash basin. Facilities are, regrettably, primitive."

Katherine opened the door and leapt backward, barely managing to avoid collision with a mechanical maid who careened forward into the room bearing a tray. Steam rose from a large bowl. Beside it rested a loaf of dark, brown bread. Olivia's stomach growled in a most unladylike manner, reminding her that it had been nearly a day since she'd last eaten.

"And the steam staff is in an equal state of decay. Rusty beasts, all of them." With a huff, Katherine exited the chamber, slamming the door behind her.

The aged steambot lurched about the room like a spider with multi-hinged legs—a necessity when one lived in a castle with no ascension chambers and only spiral staircases connecting one floor to another—but its steps were so uncertain and unbalanced that a good portion of the soup spilled over the edge of the bowl, soaking the bottom half of the bread with broth.

Desperate to save what was left, Olivia rushed forward and snatched the tray from the steambot's arms to set it down upon the window seat. Ignoring hunger pangs, she turned to study the steam maid and considered the unlikely solution that presented itself. Where better to secrete an acoustico-transmitter than inside a household steambot, one that moved about the castle and was in frequent contact with its inhabitants?

She pressed a hand to her chest. The glass and crystal wand Zheng had waved over her clothing wasn't able to detect an inactive, non-transmitting device. But she couldn't keep the device behind her corset. Not when a thin, silk nightgown threatened.

Plans. It was time to form one.

By now, Mother would have alerted Father as to her disappearance. Agents would be deployed to locate her. The sooner this acousticotransmitter was activated, the sooner help would arrive. Mr. Black would be angry that she required rescuing, yet he would also be proud. If not for her actions, the acousticotransmitters would all be destroyed, and the Queen's agents would know nothing of the bitter enemy that inhabited this castle.

She called out, "*Stillgestanden!*" *Stand still!*

The steambot staggered to a halt.

Careful contemplation of the steam made led her to the conclusion that it was of a similar age to Steam Clara. Therefore, it should contain an equivalent cipher cartridge. She could slip in a few of her steam maid's Babbage cards. "I hearby dub thee Matilda," she said aloud, and her voice did indeed echo.

Olivia blew on her stiff knuckles, flexed them against the cold and set to work aware that at any moment the door could open again, summoning Steam Matilda back to the kitchens. She reached behind the edge of her corset, drawing forth one of its steel stays—the one that concealed a warded pick.

Aural chambers were a challenge to open—even with the proper tool—but they were on level with the human mouth and sufficiently removed from noisy internal mechanisms. The perfect place to conceal an activated acoustico-transmitter.

Flipping the switch to the "on" position and adding a touch of remaining adhesive, Olivia managed it inside of two minutes. A new record.

She tucked away her pick with a self-satisfied smile. Provided Zheng did not march about the castle waving his crystal wand over the steambots, it should escape discovery. Once Mr. Black was within range, he was certain to pick up various bits of conversation. She hoped some of it would be useful. At the very least, it would lead him to her.

Now to make Steam Matilda her very own personal castle steam servant. Lifting the simple black gown that covered the steambot's iron framework, Olivia set about accessing the cipher cartridge. She fanned through the programming cards, tugging some out to replace them with Steam Clara's commands.

Worried about Steam Matilda's overall condition and the not unlikely possibility that her mechanics could fail at any moment, perhaps ending her in a dusty broom closet, Olivia focused her attention upon making minor adjustments to various components of the steambot, both internal and external.

With a hairpin, a dull pencil and the flat end of a spoon at her disposal, there was only so much she could do, but as she wiped gear grease from her hands on the hem of her ruined skirt some time later, Steam Matilda walked without the slightest wobble. Even a solid shove against her shoulders failed to topple the steam maid. "Stop fussing with the innards of the steambots, Olivia." She planted hands on her hips and pitched her voice to match the tone Mother always used. "Such talents will never serve your purposes."

Ha!

With the exhilaration of a task well done, Olivia at last sat and turned her attention to the tray devouring the—now cold—watery broth and hard, brown bread. Amazing how hunger could make the worst food taste better than any confection served at a proper English tea.

A sudden blast of icy cold air blew into the room, howling its displeasure. One of the rags stuffed into the window pane had fallen free. Shivering, she moved to replace it when a small, pale hand stretched inward and caught the latch. Olivia gasped as the window swung inward and Wei appeared in its frame.

Olivia reached for the child. "Nuts and rivets, get in here before you fall to your death."

But the girl quickly hopped past her outstretched arms to the floor. "I don't fall," Wei declared. "Almost never. But that is the why of wings." The girl spun and pointed over her shoulder to her back. Strapped to her torso was a folded contraption built of wood and canvas and metal hinges. "The stone of castle big and lumpy. Many hand holds. Toe holds. I climb around mostly."

"In snow storms?" Olivia gaped.

Wei shrugged. "I'm strong. Not so hard." The girl waved at the rag in Olivia's hand. "Why you wait? Is cold. Close window. Stuff it back in."

Olivia jammed the damp rag back into the broken glass, then turned back to her unexpected guest who now stood with her hands outstretched above the iron stove.

"Quite the talented explorer, aren't you?" she observed. "Swinging from ropes. Rock climbing. Flying."

"Gliding," Wei corrected, but her eyes gleamed with pride. "Only go down. But is fun."

"Fun?" She lifted her eyebrows. "Scary seems a better term."

Wei shrugged. "Zheng, my uncle, is traveling chemical man. We live on airship. I learn as safety precaution."

Zheng was her uncle? Olivia would need to guard her words. "There's another airship here?"

"*Sky Dragon*," Wei said. "Uncle commands. I come to your airship from *Sky Dragon*. You see by river when snow stops."

147

Ah. Though she'd been panicked at the time, it made sense that a rope hanging in the air must be attached to something. That something was, in this case, a Chinese dirigible. "*Sky Dragon*. I like that name. Are your parents aboard?"

"No parents. Not since I was—" Wei held out a hand at knee height. "I grow up traveling with Uncle." She unbuttoned her padded jacket and reached inside. "Think you want this."

"My reticule!" Olivia exclaimed as the girl pulled forth the ruffled, oversized item. "Thank you ever so much!" She dropped the bag upon the desk and looked inside, grinning widely. Her tools. Her punch cards. Captain Jack's Tension Torque. And her friend, Watson. She'd thought them lost to her.

"I no tell anyone about bag." Wei tipped her head. "Or metal animal. Uncle has stone heart. Would order guardsmen to take toy if they know. One took my bird. Returned broken." She tugged a tiny mechanical nightingale from her coat pocket. Thin sheets of copper shaped like feathers fluttered and jointed copper cylinders formed feet to grip Wei's finger. As she gently stroked its head, the bird's tiny beak opened and closed. "It not fly now."

"Let me see." Cupping the zoetomatic bird in her hand, Olivia carefully lifted its wing. She opened the small panel, studying the beautiful craftsmanship of the toy's inner workings. "It's nothing but a stripped gear. I think I have..." She dug into the bottom of her reticule and produced a gear of comparable size.

A few minutes later the little brown bird fluttered about the room.

Wei clapped her hands with glee. "Thank you!" She pointed at Watson. "You show me how yours works?"

"I will." Olivia was glad of the distraction and grateful to the girl for returning Watson along with her tools and cards. She put the mechanical hedgehog through all its paces, teaching Wei simple commands and delighting in her excitement at the metal animal's antics. As a grand finale, she sent Watson rolling across the floor to disappear beneath the bed.

All was brought to an abrupt end by a knock at the door.

Wei's eyes grew round. She whistled, calling the nightingale to her outstretched finger. "I must go," she said, tucking the bird into a pocket before rushing to the window and throwing it wide. She buckled a wooden strut to each wrist and climbed upon the window seat.

The knock came again.

Outside the storm had finally died down, leaving a blanket of snow covering the ground, the trees. Likely the stone sides of the castle were icy or wet or both. "This can't be safe," Olivia objected, stashing her reticule beneath the bed. "You can hide here, under the bed with Watson."

"No worry. Easy. Watch." Flashing her a quick grin, Wei jumped with her arms held wide. Without hesitation, without fear.

Heart pounding, Olivia ran to the window. Though icy wind lashed at her skin, she ignored her stomach's queasy protest and leaned out the window, unable to look away. Canvas wings unfurled, spreading wide upon the jointed wooden frame, and caught the wind. First Wei flew in wide circles, then in ever smaller ones, spiraling down to a river that wound its way around the castle and through a small village. People on the streets and paths paused to look upward, to stare at her descent. A moment later, Wei landed upon the deck of the oddest—and most beautiful—airship Olivia had ever laid eyes upon. Strange, to see an airship floating upon water and not upon air.

Its balloon took the form of a dragon, long and sinuous. At one end was the face with wild eyes and snarling teeth. Red scales began at the head and traced down the spine to the very tip of the pointed tail, which snapped in the wind as if annoyed with the unsettled weather. Four clawed feet reached down to grip iron fastenings bolted to the deck. And the gondola, both boat and airship it seemed, was built of golden wood that gleamed in the sun.

Zheng might be the girl's uncle, but she couldn't help but think Wei might prove a most useful ally. Perhaps she might know of a way to send a message over the mountains through the snow-dusted forest and across the border into France.

CHAPTER FOURTEEN

I AN ARRIVED TO FIND his *wife* wringing out a wet cloth as she crouched before a bucket of steaming water in a state of undress. Her gown lay in a heap upon the floor, her ruined silk stockings beside it. The smell of bouillabaisse hung in the air.

"You must be cold," he said, stating the obvious. Despite the warm water, the simple fact of evaporation and a drafty room had set Olivia's teeth chattering.

She glanced up. "Very," she said through purple-tinged lips. "Alas, this is what passes for a bath in Burg Kerzen."

No private space was allotted to them, and she made no apology for her near-nakedness. Amazingly comfortable in her own skin for a young lady of the *ton*, she did what she must. Practicality. It was what he had sought in a woman— and had seemingly found.

At the base of his spine, desire stirred. He took in the delicate turn of her bare ankles and toes, the fine lace that edged her combinations and the pale blue satin of her corset. It was laced far too tightly, but still, the primitive portion of his brainstem approved.

"Let me see what I can do to warm the room." He crossed to the stove inset within a large, medieval fireplace. Most of the heat it generated flew straight up the chimney, a simple fact of physics that the small amount of coal provided would be unable to overcome. Nevertheless, he opened the stove's door and dutifully shoveled coal in a futile attempt to do so.

Behind him, a splash echoed. Olivia continuing her ablutions. To be a drop of water sliding across her smooth skin, disappearing behind her corset as it dove into her tight-laced cleavage. His fingers longed to trace its damp path. Given the temperature in this room, by morning that water would form a thin layer of ice in that bucket.

By morning. After a night in that great bed. Even fully clothed, she was going to end up huddled against his side, a distraction of the highest magnitude. There was nowhere else for him to sleep. The floor, the window seat, all out of the question if he wished to be alert and focused and not frozen in the laboratory. Not to mention they needed to maintain an illusion of marriage. There would be no keeping her at an arm's length with both the count and the countess watching.

Ian slammed the stove door shut and turned about, watching. Lust battled with amusement as Olivia wrestled a padded petticoat free from what he supposed was a steam valet. Not that he'd trust it to tie his cravat. To say its many arms seemed uncoordinated was a kindness. Buttons and boots seemed beyond its capabilities. She tugged the petticoat over her head—sending tangled, golden curls cascading—and tied it about her waist with fumbling fingers stiff from the cold.

He ought to offer to help. A husband would. Except he wasn't. Yet with that fiction presented to the count, they needed to be comfortable—physically—in each other's presence. Within reason. He *was* a gentleman, and he would not take advantage by forcing himself upon her.

Ian stood immobile, staring at her enticing form as she struggled to free a silk shawl from the valet. Was it possible? Could she be a spy? If so, who had sent her and why? Did it even matter? Eventually the count would insist upon a demonstration of the osforare apparatus, and he needed her skills if there were to be any hope of carrying that off. What training did she have—if any? Would she be an asset or burden when the time came to attempt escape? Time to set about discovering her secrets.

So when Olivia hurried to the low stool beside the iron stove and began tugging hairpins free to run her fingers through the tangled mess of her hair, he snatched a brush clipped to the steam valet's side and followed. At last, a way to touch her that wouldn't—for the most part—cross the line.

"Let me." He brandished the brush.

Her hands stilled as she caught his eyes. "You needn't. I can manage."

"There's no need to manage when you have a husband at hand." He tugged a pin from her hair, threading the lock of gold silk that fell into his hand through his fingers. If she were truly his wife, he would thread his fingers into those locks and draw her face close for another taste of her full, sweet lips. The temptation was nearly overwhelming. He cleared his throat. "We must be convincing."

"Convincing? That doesn't explain the kiss you gave me on the dirigible." She glanced at him from beneath long lashes. The corner of her mouth curved upward. "Or is that how you treat all your laboratory assistants?"

He refused to apologize. "I was trying to distract you," he insisted. Only partly true. Never before had he lectured with a woman's breast pressed to his arm. He'd had the devil of a time focusing. "I don't recall you objecting."

"True." She let her shawl slip to bare a smooth shoulder. "Nor will I object now, even in the privacy of our own chamber. Tell me, Ian, how much further can I persuade you to take this charade?"

A clear invitation. Or was it a test? Either way, he could no more resist than any other man. His gaze slipped downward, taking in her generous bosom which swelled above the tightly laced undergarment. Behind the satin of her corset, her nipples pebbled. His own body responded. With enthusiasm.

At least they would not have to feign mutual attraction. *Aether.* Sleeping beside her would be pure torture. If he slept at all, it would be a miracle.

Time to quell his desire, to remember his goal. "Consummation is not required. We are already working together. You need not be *that* dedicated to your work."

"Work?" She blinked.

Though she was the very picture of innocence, her spine stiffened. "As an agent," he stated bluntly. Until she'd called out in horror when Zheng pointed his knife at the firkin cincture bolt, he'd dismissed every suspicion that she could be an actual agent. But now? He had to explore the possibility. "*You* planted those acousticotransmitters."

"Acousti..." she trailed off. "The contraptions Zheng stomped upon? I've never seen them before." Olivia bit her lip. "But I can see how you'd be concerned. Listening devices... do you suspect... does someone have reason to spy upon you?"

"Come now. Theft of an escape dirigible. My sister held hostage. The small arsenal they removed from my person. Armed escort through the castle. Experimental devices and potions coveted by our country's enemy." Ian shook his head slowly as he spoke. "Playing dumb does not become you, and as you clearly possess much programming skill—"

"Merely a skill I acquired to better manage a large household," Olivia objected, her voice a touch strangled. "*All* my family's steam servants run like clockwork."

She pulled the shawl back over her shoulders, tying it in a firm knot across her chest and obscuring the stunning view. Offer retracted. It was better this way. He couldn't possibly accept. On the off chance he made it back to Britain in one piece, her father would see him dismembered and fed, limb by limb, to the river kraken.

He was a fool to think she would confide in him. Why should she? He ran a hand down the side of his face, over

155

rough stubble. He was in possession of dangerous materials, illegally transported. Loyal to Queen and country, she would refuse to tip her hand.

"Very well, we will play this your way," he said. "Turn around. I've a sister, remember. I know how to brush hair, and you need to warm your hands. They're nearly blue."

After a moment's hesitation, she turned and held her palms out toward the stove. "Tell me about her, your sister."

Trust. To win her to his side, he needed to give her reason to trust him. Women liked words. Emotions. He knew this. Yet until this very moment, he'd had little incentive to provide them. If ever there was a time to share a family tragedy, this was it. Time to open a vein.

He pulled a hairpin free, then another, collecting them in a small pile and delaying the moment as his chest grew tight. Never before had he shared how his story made him *feel*. How to explain? He took a deep breath and started with the bare facts. "Her name is Elizabeth." His fingers began to move over her hair, working free the many knotted braids and twists. "And my only sibling. All those who came between us died in the cradle. I myself put my mother in her grave."

Olivia sucked a breath. "No. Never say that. Mothers die in childbirth all the time. It's never the baby's fault."

"That may be, but my father disagreed. My mother was not up to the task of bearing children, but she insisted and in the end it killed her. In my father's eyes, his heir and only son stole his one true love from him." His gut twisted, but he forced the words past his lips. "As a child, my existence was ignored. Every moment of his life was dedicated to curing my sister of the disease that took my mother. He invited one silver-tongued, snake oil doctor after another into our home with their crackpot cures. At best, their treatments did nothing." He swallowed the rusty nails that had lodged in his throat. "Sometimes they were pure torture."

Those screams would haunt him forever. It had been a relief when the family coffers were empty and the charlatans' visits ceased.

"Is this why you became a physician?" Her voice was gentle.

"I believed it the only path to winning his regard." Had his father ever looked upon him with pride? "Though I never did. He's been dead a year, and still I feel the need to set things right, not only to cure my sister, but to earn his approval."

She lifted an arm, catching one of his hands in hers. "This illness in your family has something to do with bone?"

Her soft hand fell away, and he resumed his work upon the tangles in her hair. "At least one family member is afflicted in every generation. My grandfather. My mother. My sister."

"A family curse?"

The vacuous debutant was back. His story must have struck a nerve for now she was trying to push him away with nonsense. He wouldn't allow it. Though this Olivia might be fun to flirt with, his glimpses of the competent and accomplished woman that lay beneath intrigued him far more.

"You're no fool, Olivia. I wish you'd stop trying to play the ingénue."

"Fine." She huffed. "Explain to me in exacting detail what plagues your family."

A minor victory, but it was the first crack in her shell, one he would pry at until he exposed the truth. "They all possessed—possess—brittle bones, a congenital disorder, one they were born with. Do you remember those cells I spoke of, the ones in charge of creating new bone?"

"Osteoblasts?"

"Yes." His spirits lifted. She might yet make a convincing research assistant. "Elizabeth's osteoblasts are dysfunctional," he said. "The matrix, the living material that they create is malformed. Calcium and phosphate cannot bind to it correctly. As a result, her bones are brittle and easily broken."

"Easily?" Concern laced her voice. "Then your mother..."

"A broken pelvis during delivery. A severed artery. She bled to death."

"I'm so sorry," Olivia said, her voice soothing.

Though he'd achieved his goal, Ian found himself sharing a long-buried memory. "It's a cruel disease, everything seems normal until the simplest of accidents occurs." The knots in her hair loosened. "One of my earliest memories is of a simple walk along a path in the woods. I was running ahead when I heard Elizabeth cry out. The path was smooth, but for a single tree root. Her slipper caught, and she tripped and fell. That simple fall, one that might have not even caused so much as a bruise in another?" Ian's throat closed at the awful memory. "It broke her leg. My sister couldn't leave her bed for months."

"How dreadful!" Olivia exclaimed.

"Many more years and many more bone fractures, and each brought their own special form of misery." Ian's hands moved steadily as lock after lock of hair fell upon her shoulders, her curls smooth and silken once more. "So perhaps now you might understand why a gentleman would dirty his hands in the field of medicine?"

"I suppose," she conceded. "Yet after all these years, you're no closer to a cure."

Now the question arose: did he trust her? Not entirely. Not yet.

"I have every expectation of arriving at one," he hedged, setting the brush aside. He had every reason to believe his transforming serum would succeed. Months had passed and the rats were healthy and hale. The board of directors had approved his petition to move on to human experimentation, using volunteers fully appraised of the risks, of course. "But, no, at the moment I have nothing to offer my sister."

Risking the life of his only living relative was not an option until he was absolutely certain.

"Who is this Doktor Warrick, what is his connection?" Olivia asked, gathering her hair into a simple knot at the base of her neck and stabbing the hairpins back into place.

"He is *not* a physician," Ian answered, his nostrils flaring. One year of medical school did not qualify him to lay claim to such a title. "He is the man who stole my original—and faulty—work. He sold it and himself to Count Eberwin, no doubt hoping to disappear before the inevitable and deadly side-effects appeared."

"Those lumps and bumps?" She shuddered. "They're deadly?"

"Indications of advanced osteosarcoma—bone cancer. By the time the tumors are visible beneath the skin, death is imminent. I've nothing to offer at the moment but false hope."

"Nothing?" She twisted on the stool to look up at him, distress etched upon the delicate features of her face.

"The cells Warrick engineered were specifically designed to avoid the body's natural defense mechanisms. That is what allows them to multiply, to spread and invade, to become cancerous. They have no 'off' switch that I know of. Yet."

"Is it painful?" she asked.

"Very."

"And you're certain there's no way to save them, to cure these guardsmen? Not even with that device?" Olivia stood and began to pace before the fireplace rubbing her hands together. As suspected, the stove insert provided little warmth.

"The osforare apparatus. I—*we*—will certainly try. Warrick claims to have improved upon my original cell line. He also claims to have a cure under development. I've no idea what—if any—progress he's made as he's kept no record of his work, no laboratory notebook."

Olivia brightened. "If we can win him over…"

"Don't." Ian shook his head. "Don't even try. He's not to be trusted. Warrick thinks only of himself. I doubt he has the slightest inkling of how to help those men. The moment he injected those unfortunate guardsmen with his cells, he condemned them to die." Warrick had dangled the possibility of a cure before him, and guilt for his part in their creation wouldn't allow him to flee, not without first attempting to save the guardsmen. "Still, I have set up a number of experiments to see if I might stop the cancer."

"A number of experiments... in which, as your assistant, I will be involved." All the blood drained from Olivia's face.

"How on earth do you manage it?" he asked, incredulous.

"Manage what?"

"Aren't spies forever being fired upon by any number of dangerous weapons? Not to mention knives, daggers... and blades too numerous to mention."

"I. Am. Not. A. Spy." She glared at him, a flush of anger returning color to her cheeks. "How many more times must you hear me say it?"

"Until I believe it." He leaned backward against the stone wall. "What bothers you most about my work, the blood? Or the needles?"

"Both. And the pain." She pinched her lips together. "There's always so much pain involved. Your device, my sister's. Every item emerging from a physician's black leather bag appears an instrument of torture to be inflicted upon a helpless, trusting individual who is in search of nothing but relief."

"I see." Ian gave a clipped nod. "How, then, do you fare with surprise attacks and self-defense?"

Her eyes flashed, then narrowed. "I've no experience with which to judge. Unlike *you* with your hidden arsenal of knives, I do not moonlight as a spy."

"Well, that experience might arrive sooner than later. Keep in mind that the only person keeping us alive is that megalomaniac, Count Eberwin. Should something not go his way, he won't hesitate to use my wife against me to pursue his delusions of building a stronger—unbreakable—race of soldiers."

She nodded. "So that he will find favor in the eyes of Kaiser Wilhelm II and be allowed to return—along with his wife, Countess Katherine—to Berlin."

"Exactly." Finally. What a relief that she'd stopped playing the simple miss.

Olivia tipped her head. "And who is she to you, the countess?"

"No one." Too long out of the field, he'd hidden his surprise poorly.

Her lips pursed and her eyes narrowed.

Ian sighed. "A brief acquaintance during a transportation mishap. The countess alludes to more than she ought."

Katherine hid more than she revealed. Why else pursue a path toward bigamy? Not that he was about to share his suspicions with Olivia. Not yet. At the moment the countess' own agenda aligned with the count's. Until that changed, he would present Katherine with every reason to allow his pretense of a marriage with Olivia to stand.

"Perhaps." Olivia smiled too sweetly. "Time runs short. I ought to dress for dinner, and you need to attend to your own appearance. You wouldn't want to disappoint the count or *countess*."

"Jealousy," Ian agreed, "is an excellent reaction to the countess' insinuations. A perfect excuse for any awkwardness between us." He couldn't resist needling her. "But a bit of advice? The key to a successful cover is to maintain a consistent personality. As you have claimed the role of programmer *and* snagged yourself a husband, it's time to jettison the feather-brained act."

Crossing the room, she jabbed a finger in his chest. "Fine." Her eyes blazed. "But the outcome of such jealousy is also a quarrel between newlyweds."

CHAPTER FIFTEEN

Olivia ignored Ian's proffered arm, brushing by him with her nose in the air. She strode down the hallway behind the guardsman sent to escort them to dinner. To think her *husband* had the nerve to accuse her of being a spy, matched only by his audacity in telling her how she ought to execute her duties. Maintain a consistent role, indeed! She would maintain the role. She would channel her anger at herself—for underestimating his ability to think while staring at her chest—and use it to play the jealous wife in a snit.

Easier to be angry at him than to reveal the bone-deep sadness his childhood story elicited. How awful to grow up under such a dark cloud, to feel obligated to pursue a career in research and medicine. What might he have done with his life otherwise?

No. She pushed her concern aside. He was a grown man and suspected of nefarious intent by her government. She could not allow sympathy to cloud her opinion of his activities here in Germany. For the moment, Ian had done nothing traitorous beyond carrying a few potions and that osforare device across international borders. He might claim he was loyal to Queen and country, but she'd seen how the pain and suffering of a sibling could cloud a person's judgment. Her own sisters had made several questionable decisions while pursuing a treatment for her brother.

What might Ian be prepared to do in order to set his sister free?

Her stomach growled, so empty it had tied itself into a knot. Anger combined with hunger was dangerous. Perhaps she wasn't thinking clearly anymore. Thirty-six hours of nothing more than broth and a single roll of soggy bread. She held great hopes for a heavy German meal—sauerbraten, strudel, kuchen—at least this once while the count and countess still pretended that she and Ian were "honored guests".

For that reason alone, she tried her hardest not to burst into the great hall at a dead run in hopes of finding a feast laid out upon groaning boards.

She was certainly dressed for a banquet, trussed up in a blood-red, bustled skirt and laced into a red-embroidered and glass-beaded gold bodice. Though the sleeves stretched to her wrists, the neckline was cut low. A row of red, knife-pleated ruffles fanned upward from its edge, highlighting her generous feminine assets.

Katherine knew how to attract the hungry gaze of a man, and Olivia had the distinct impression she'd been dressed not for her own husband's approval, but for that of Count Eberwin's. With Ian nearby, and provided she could blunt her hunger with something thicker than bouillabaisse, she would endure the count's leer.

To her great disappointment, the long banquet table was devoid of food.

"*Frau* Rathsburn!" Count Eberwin strode across the room in red and gold military splendor to grasp her hand in his. He bent low, breaking all manner of protocol to press his lips to bare skin. Gloves had not been among the items provided by the steam valet. The count straightened, taking in her appearance with hungry eyes, and the countess, who stood behind him, smirked.

Ian was already across the room. He'd cast aside all manners to reach for the hands of a tall, thin woman who must be Lady Elizabeth. She was garbed entirely in a gown of pure white that covered her from to wrists to chin, leaving exposed only the creamy oval of her face. Purple half-moons underscored pale blue eyes that sparked with hope at her brother's approach—even as she glanced warily at the glowering man beside her and cringed as Ian lifted her hand.

"What is the meaning of this?" he demanded.

A silver cuff encircled Lady Elizabeth's wrist. The man at her side wore a matching cuff—complete with switch and dial—and broke into a nasty smile as Ian glared. This would be the hated Warrick, the man who peddled defective biotechnology to Britain's enemy.

The edges of the silver cuff glowed an eerie blue. Olivia's eyes widened. An axon thrall band? If Lady Elizabeth tried to pull away from Warrick, the resultant electric arc would send a bolt of electricity traveling up her arm straight to her spine, forcing her into submission. How could such a woman, who resembled nothing so much as a ghost, be considered a flight risk?

No, she realized, not Lady Elizabeth. Ian was the risk. All those weapons he'd carried were the mark of a man prepared to do violence to protect those he loved. A primitive thrill shot through her even though he was decidedly not hers.

"Ian," Lady Elizabeth's voice held a note of warning. "It is a special night. In honor of your arrival and," she caught Olivia's eyes and smiled, "your recent marriage, the count has graciously permitted me to join you."

In other words, now was not the time to cause a scene.

A vein throbbed on the side of Ian's temple. He ground his teeth, such that his molars nearly cracked with the effort of not rounding upon on the count and howling his displeasure. But with Zheng standing nearby and a cancer-ridden guardsman positioned at every door, each with his hand upon a sword, there was no choice but to cooperate with this parody of a dinner party.

"Are you well?" Ian asked through gritted teeth.

"For the moment," his sister replied.

With a final lewd glance at her bosom, the count wrapped Olivia's arm about his and drew her forward. "I don't believe you've met Doktor Warrick or his fiancée, *Fräulein* Elizabeth."

"Fiancée?" Olivia's gaze flicked to Ian's. A muscle jumped at his jaw.

"Your husband will have informed you otherwise," the count said. "Yet I happen to agree with Doktor Warrick. His country did him a great wrong. *Fräulein* Elizabeth has no need to fear her future husband. His entire life is devoted to finding her a cure. Besides," the count sniffed, "I find it a grave miscarriage of justice that the British allow a woman to cry off with no consequences, while a man may be sued for breach of promise."

"You would force Lady Elizabeth into marriage?" Olivia asked the count. Of course he would. She glanced around the room. Was anyone present here voluntarily?

The look that crossed Ian's face would have frozen the Thames. "I'll not allow it."

"Force? Allow?" The count's head shook slowly back and forth. "*Nein*. Not into marriage. I *will* insist she make reparations for the damage done to Doktor Warrick's reputation. If—when *Fräulein* Elizabeth is cured, she still finds marriage to him undesirable, I will allow her to dissolve their connection."

"Let's be clear," Ian spat. "By reparations, you mean my sister is to serve as an unwilling research subject, an experimental hostage."

"She will be cured," the count insisted. "Now, take your seats." He pulled out a high-backed chair, waving to indicate that Olivia should sit at his right hand.

Vibrating with anger, Ian lowered himself into a chair

beside her. Across the table from them sat Lady Elizabeth and Warrick. The countess perched at the far end.

"Let's begin." Katherine clapped her hands and called, "Hanover! The wine!"

There was a low whistle, then with much clicking and clacking and hissing, a tripod butler lurched forward from behind a carved wooden screen. One of his three wheels wobbled making his rapid progress unsteady and uncertain. As the steam butler bore down upon them, his single eye blinked in a frantic and irregular pattern, suggesting a number of internal loose wires and an improperly calibrated pacing unit. Like Steam Matilda, the butler was a relic of a generation past, sorely in need of updates or outright replacement.

Her stomach rumbled, complaining at the steam servant's slow progress as he dispensed a generous amount of wine to each guest. At long last he wheeled away.

"A toast." The count raised his glass. Everyone followed suit, some more grudgingly than others. "To scientific progress."

The wine was heavenly, a rich Bordeaux, and Olivia drank more than she ought. Anything to sooth the gnawing ache in her abdomen.

Hanover returned, this time clutching an enormous silver urn to his chest. His other arm now ended in a ladle attachment, and she watched with alarm as the steam butler slopped a pink, silver, and spotted gelatinous goo into their bowls, making her think imminent starvation might be a more appealing prospect. Task complete, Hanover careened back behind the screen.

She stared at viscous... soup? And began to recall soggy brown bread with great fondness. With regret and dread, she lifted her spoon.

"Wait!" The count held up a hand. "Send in the girl."

Wei stepped from behind the screen and moved to stand beside the count. Though dressed in a beautifully embroidered silk dress with a high Mandarin collar, her wide eyes were glazed, and her face was tight with fear.

"We begin the meal with the ceremonial first taste." The count picked up a spoon and lifted a sample of the glutinous material to Wei's lips. "Open," he commanded.

Olivia's stomach twisted with a growing sense of unease. Surely this was mere formality, the count acting as if he were king of his castle.

Wei's lips parted only slightly and Zheng—standing guard behind the count—slid his sword from its sheath, ready to prod his niece into obedience. A tear ran down her cheek, but her mouth opened, and the count inserted the utensil. Wei closed her mouth, and after a second, swallowed.

"What—?" Ian began, but was cut off by a raised hand.

"One minute." The count tugged a pocket watch from his waistcoat, counting down the time.

Did the count fear someone might try to poison him? She took a deep breath, ready to protest, but across the table Lady Elizabeth's eyes were wide, and she was slowly shaking her head.

"Otto," the countess said. "Really, is this demonstration necessary? The cook assured me it has already been tested."

"It is tradition," the count replied. After a long, steady look at Wei, he snapped the face of his pocket watch closed. "Excellent. Dismissed." He waved the pale girl away. "We may proceed." Picking up knife and fork, he wasted no time in enjoying this...?

Olivia lifted her own flatware, gently nudging the rubbery item that curled tightly upon her plate. It flipped, and—the light was dim—were those suckers? She cut a tiny portion from the tip and lifted it.

"Jellied kraken, a local delicacy from the Rhine, *Frau* Rathsburn," the count announced. "The sharp claws and poison glands have been removed so as to assure safety. Nonetheless, precautions must always be taken to ensure the cook didn't accidentally pierce the poison sac."

Setting down her fork, Olivia lifted her wine glass and took a long, steady swallow.

The count waved at her plate. "You *must* try it."

Her throat constricted. "Poison glands? I wasn't aware river kraken were poisonous. My aunt—"

"Those in the Thames are not," Ian interrupted, fixing her with a pointed stare.

Olivia replaced her wine glass. A misstep, referencing her aunt. There could be only so many female cryptobiologists who studied kraken.

"Yes, like many things German, our kraken too are deadly." The count's eyes were still upon her. Steady. Waiting.

His tight smile a reminder that everyone in this room was subject to his whims.

She lifted her fork again, abandoning a childish plan to cut the tentacle into tiny pieces and move them about the plate until the next course arrived. She took a deep breath, put the slimy morsel in her mouth, then swallowed, nearly gagging as it slid part way down her throat. And stuck.

Dropping her fork, she reached out and grabbing her wine glass to gulp down the remaining contents.

The count bellowed a dark laugh. "Ah, perhaps you will prefer the next course, *knödel* made from black potato and stuffed with shredded wild boar."

"Black potato?" More potentially deadly food items?

Already, Hanover was at her elbow, pouring more wine. The liquid splashed and overflowed her glass, but he also lifted away her plate. Grateful, she tried to ignore his increasingly jerky movements as he rolled about the table.

She lifted the glass to her lips. Ian caught her eyes and frowned. She looked away.

"The black potato is a marriage of an arbuscular mycorrhizas fungi with a common potato," Warrick proclaimed in a tone she recognized: lecture mode. "A plant-fungi symbiotic union that restores nutrients to the soil as it grows such that the Germans have no further need to fear famine, nor to let a field lie fallow."

By the end of that lengthy sentence, Olivia had again drained her glass. That was a decided mistake; her head felt... floaty. She set the glass down. No more.

Warrick launched into something more concerning

onions. This variety was purple. But she was distracted by the count's steady gaze. Which had come to fall—surprise, surprise—upon her bosom. The countess smirked.

Forget consistency. There was no need to feign jealousy or some lover's tiff. No need to manufacture more drama for there was already enough tension in the room to set everyone at each other's throats at the slightest provocation. Olivia knew when to keep her mouth tightly shut.

And so she lifted her wine glass instead.

CHAPTER SIXTEEN

HIS WIFE GUZZLED wine under the count's appreciative and overly familiar gaze. As the count ogled, a smoldering sensation built deep in his chest, as if a sleeping dragon awakened to find a gold coin missing from his hoard. In a premeditated move, Katherine had loaned Olivia an exceptionally revealing gown. To distract her husband? To prick Ian's ire? Both, he suspected.

He cleared his throat. Loudly. "It is British tradition for a woman to wait until she has produced both an heir and a spare before conducting an illicit liaison. You'll need to wait a few years, Count Eberwin."

All conversation stopped.

Had he a knife, Ian would have been tempted to aim for the count's throat and put an end to this madness, but he'd only been provided a fork and a spoon. Every muscle in his body tensed. Eyes could be removed with a spoon.

But no. It would solve nothing. Too many in this room would stop him. Still, he saw no reason to act the gentleman. The food was inedible, the company unbearable, and he could no longer tolerate the count's lustful glances at Olivia's chest.

He dropped his fork with a clatter and tossed his napkin on the table and stood.

Several guardsmen about the room slid knives from sheaths.

Ignoring them all, he addressed the count. "What is the point of forcing us to share a meal together? We are not friends, not guests. Three of us are prisoners. Your guardsmen are dying. Yet you force us to cease working so that we may engage in pointless social charades."

"Scientists." Count Eberwin sighed. "Such little regard for manners. I'd hoped your status as an earl might restore some dignity to the profession, but alas." With one last longing glance at Olivia's bosom, the count leaned back in his chair. "If you could view my goals in a different light, we might be partners. Sit down and hear me out."

The wobbly steam butler rolled back into the room, this time with a tray balanced upon metal fingers. It began slapping down a most disgusting, steaming pile of black hash upon their plates. He supposed this was the infamous black *knödel*.

"Partners," Ian sneered, reluctantly taking his seat. "Germany is an enemy of Britain. How could we be partners?"

"Even now our two countries' ambassadors meet."

Katherine spoke from the distant end of the table. "Allegiances change."

"Do they, *Countess*? Which country is it that you support?" *For the moment.* With that stray thought, Ian realized that it needn't be either Germany or England. With new awareness, he studied her face more closely and... No, there were no telling features. She could be loyal to any number of countries.

"Why that of my husband, of course." Her mouth drew into a knowing smile. "Though my heart will always hold England near and dear."

The count set down his fork. "Zheng recognizes the value in aligning China's interests with that of Germany. When this project succeeds, he will win both fortune and favor with emperors, both his and mine. Doktor Warrick's own country dismissed him, but with my patronage, he continues his work here in Germany. Why not join us?"

"I have no cause to abandon my country," Ian said.

The count's eyebrows drew together. "Your queen has forced you from your laboratory, away from your passion, and by now she will suspect treason. Your estate is in shambles, in need of a great infusion of funds, but you chose to marry whom?" He barked a laugh. "A research assistant?"

Ian stared. Loathing rose like bile from his gut. "I am only suspected of treason because *Warrick* betrayed his country and *you* kidnapped my sister."

"But of course." His eyebrows lifted in haughty disdain. "Time is limited. Persuasion was necessary." He leaned back in his chair and steepled his fingers across his chest. "Now that you are here, I hope you will allow me to make you happy, but if you refuse to cooperate, there are many avenues of enticement I intend to pursue," the count's gaze flickered again to Olivia's bosom, this time with a pointed message, "many of which will make me a very happy man."

Ian wanted to throttle him and Olivia who, sipping her third glass of wine, watched the exchange as if she were at a cricket match. No experienced agent would overindulge while in such a precarious position. With all the guards lining the room, the situation could easily turn ugly.

The count leaned forward and tapped a finger on the table. "Solve my problem. Build me an indestructible army, and I will see you established in Berlin—in a laboratory at the prestigious Friedrich-Wilhelms-Universität—where you will be allowed to poke and prod at any anatomical curiosity your heart desires."

"What assurances do I have that you, an egotistical, maniacal despot, can accomplish such a thing?" Ian sneered. "From the primitive, downright antediluvian appearance of your castle, your family has been out of political favor for generations. For all I know, you will squander any such army attempting to storm the Berliner Stadtschloss and die before you cross its threshold."

The count slammed his hands down upon the table. The dinnerware and all its guests, who had grown silent and wary during their exchange, jumped. "This time and this time only, I will not kill you for your insults. However, should you address me in that manner again—"

Olivia screamed.

All eyes followed the point of her finger. Gleaming kitchen knives attached to the steam butler's arms waved wildly in the air as it pitched across the great hall on a direct course for the count.

Chaos erupted.

Guardsmen drew their swords, but Zheng moved with blinding speed. With a loud cry, he leapt forward wielding his curved blade and lopped off the butler's head with one blow.

Valve oil spurted from Hanover's severed neck as some internal pump continued to churn away. Hot steam hissed from several damaged valves, one of which happened to be on level with the count's face.

Howling in pain, the count shoved away from the table with such force that his chair toppled backward. Warrick, sycophant that he was, jumped to his feet and rushed to the count's side, dragging Elizabeth with him in an attempt to press a napkin against the man's cheek, all the while shouting at a guardsman to bring ice.

His sister screamed as blue electricity arced. The smell of burned flesh met his nose at the very moment Elizabeth's eyes rolled backward. With surprising agility, Olivia flung herself between his sister and the floor, cushioning her fall.

"Warrick!" Ian yelled, running to his sister's side. "Fix the damn dial, you bastard."

Olivia had pried the wrist band free by the time he crouched beside Elizabeth, and her convulsions had stopped. He put a hand to her chest. Still breathing. Checked her pulse. Thready, but regular. He shoved aside the ruffled lace at her wrist and grimaced. First degree burns.

Elizabeth's eyes flickered open. "I think it's broken," she whispered. "My wrist."

He lifted her arm, but Warrick slapped away his hand. "She's mine now."

"Boys," Olivia chided, helping Elizabeth to sit up. "Fighting over her will worsen her injury."

They both ignored her.

"You take poor care of whom you claim to love," Ian snapped, turning on Warrick. "That convulsion, that fall could have broken more than her wrist. What were you thinking? An axon thrall band?"

Ripping the master control band from his arm, Warrick slammed it down upon the table. "It would not have been necessary had you not poisoned her mind against me."

"Necessary!" Ian yelled. "In the presence of twelve guardsmen and Zheng? You vastly overestimate my abilities."

"Step aside, Lord Rathsburn." Katherine crossed the room to stand beside the count. "Doktor Warrick will see Lady Elizabeth's bones set."

Ian growled. A vein pulsed at his temple. He'd not broken a dozen rules to reach his sister only to be brushed aside when she needed him.

"I'll be fine," Elizabeth whispered. "It's but a minor break. Warrick is competent enough. You'll cause more problems if you insist upon setting my wrist yourself. Look around, Ian. *This* is not the time to stir up trouble. *Please*."

He glanced up. All eyes were upon him. Zheng adjusted the angle of his sword and his eyes flashed, daring him to contradict the countess' words. Twelve guardsmen held knives at the ready.

Elizabeth was right. The situation had degenerated past repair. Though his body—his fists—shook with the need to lay Warrick flat on his back, doing so would only cause the count to tighten security. "Very well," he conceded.

In deference to his sister's wishes and the inevitable trouble that would ensue, he forced himself to rise slowly and hold his tongue. He caught Olivia by the elbow as she struggled to stand, steadying her as she tripped on the train of her dress.

"Thank you," she slurred and fell against him, her body soft and warm.

"Guards," the count bellowed. "Take the prisoners to their assorted cells."

As four guardsmen bore his sister away—Warrick in their wake—Ian scooped Olivia into his arms and exited the room at the point of Zheng's blade.

<hr />

HE DEPOSITED his drunk wife on her feet.

No.

His *pretend* wife.

But he was right about the drunk.

"What the hell were you thinking, drinking half a bottle of wine in the space of two courses?" he yelled. It was enough that he now had to worry about Elizabeth's broken wrist in the care of Warrick.

"Nothing else to eat..." she slurred, wobbling as she turned about on her too-high heels to face him. "I'm not drunk."

"You are. Drunk enough to smile at Count Eberwin."

It had been a defining moment. Never before had he felt such an upwelling of insane jealousy, of irrational possessiveness. Acting the possessive husband had not taken the slightest effort. She was his. At least for the duration of their time in Germany.

"I wasn't smiling," she said. "I was trying not to laugh. At him." She stepped forward and jabbed at his chest. "And I didn't see *you* eating any poisonous, jellied kraken, taking the chance that a sharp barb might get caught in *your* throat." Olivia spun away. She staggered to the bed, steadying herself by clutching the bedpost. "Two glasses of wine were a necessary coping measure."

"Three." He pinched the bridge of his nose.

Thud. He looked up. Her ruined bodice sparkled upon the floor. He stared as she unfastened the hooks of the skirt, the ties of the petticoat, and let it all slide to the floor. She kicked them away and bent over, reaching for her shoes... and presenting him with a most enticing view of her rump.

Approving, his shaft rose to attention even as his brain vetoed the thought. What was wrong with him? He was angry. They faced a life and death situation. His sister was injured. Why was he lusting after this woman? This very beautiful, if frustrating and exasperating woman.

"I thought it added a certain verisimilitude to my role," she said, her tongue tripping over the long word. Her shoes made an odd clang as she kicked them beneath the bed. "Bride in a snit when confronted by her husband's former paramour."

"She's not... I didn't... we were never romantically involved." Not really. He might have proposed to Katherine, but they'd never shared so much as a kiss, thank the aether. Though if not for the attack upon their balloon... How had Olivia managed to make this about him? Time for the voice of reason. "Something like this can't happen again. You agreed to *help*. If it's too much, play ill. Confine yourself to this bed for the duration."

This task he'd undertaken was beginning to look impossible. He raked a hand through his hair. How was he—unassisted—to stop Warrick, free his sister, and return both Olivia to her father and the osforare apparatus to his laboratory?

Somehow he would manage. There was little choice.

Olivia swayed as she turned around. "You're right. I'm sorry. Alcohol consumption in the presence of the enemy..." Her eyes met his. She clamped her mouth shut.

"You *are* a spy," he accused. An incompetent spy, perhaps, but any help was preferable to none at all.

"No. I only want to be." She flapped a hand in the air. "But I think one is about. A spy, that is." Olivia giggled. "To be able to say the butler did it..." She shook her head. "Such a middling assassination attempt. A corroded tripod butler wielding kitchen knives..."

Ian tipped his head. "Could you have done better?"

"Of course!" Her eyes grew wide. "Not that I would. Kill someone. Or try to do so."

"Who—if anyone—in the room do you think would want to attack the count?"

She fell silent as her face contorted in an effort to concentrate, trying to pluck a coherent thought from the alcoholic pickle she'd made of her brain. "I think... What if Hanover wasn't meant to succeed?" She reached deep into her bodice and dragged forth a metal cartridge. "Can you pry the lid free? My fingers aren't quite so... nimble."

"How?" He gaped. She was intoxicated. "Is that from—?"

"Hanover." She flapped her fingers at the cartridge. "Everyone was yelling. He just lay there on the floor, his chest cavity cracked. I thought... I wondered... who was trying to kill who. So I... Just pass me the cards."

"The steam butler was clearly after the count," Ian said, handing her the stack of yellowed, dog-eared punch cards.

"Was he?" With the palm of her hand she spread them out upon the desk where a single tallow candle burned and bent over them, reading the pattern of holes. "Crude. Though no surprise here. He's a Model 2A Grefenshaus. Some twelve years old. Daily commands: polishing silver, selecting wine, dinner at eight... Wait. There it is."

"What?" Ian asked, bending closer. "Can you truly determine who punched a card by looking at it?"

"Not without a sample identified as their work." She studied the card, then held it out to him. "Look."

"Same kind of paper," he observed, turning it over in his hand. "Only in pristine condition."

"Exactly. A series of commands instructing Hanover to kill 'the Chinaman'. The butler wasn't attempting to kill the count, but Zheng."

"Katherine is no doubt behind this," Ian said. "She's the only one with unimpeded access to the steam staff and, married to the count, a simple knife to his throat while he slept would make her a widow."

Her mouth fell open. "That's a gruesome view of marriage."

"A pragmatic one, steeped in historical tradition. But why kill Zheng? He provides the antimony. Without him, there can be no unbreakable army. Perhaps she was testing Zheng's loyalty? That corroded, old steam butler was bound to fail."

Nodding, she swayed forward and caught herself by grabbing the lapels of his coat. "I agree. But what if she deemed either outcome acceptable?" She lowered her forehead to rest against his chest. "I do not believe you. I think you were once lovers. Katherine clearly mourns the loss of your affections. I think she aspires to widowhood."

He agreed. Just not with the countess' motivations. Katherine was playing her own game, yes, but Ian sincerely doubted her motivations were amorous. "We weren't lovers and never will be."

"She is so beautiful." Both of Olivia's hands now gripped his coat. "So very tall and regal. And I'm... not." She sniffled.

ANNE RENWICK

Oh, no. No, no, no. Was his mock wife about to cry because she believed he lusted after another woman? The excessive wine had made her maudlin. "Stop," he said. "You are far more beautiful than her."

"Really?" She looked up. A stray tear ran down her cheek.

He sighed. Words. She wanted words. Romantic ones. Strangely, he felt an urge to provide them. "Were you not listening to my many compliments when we boarded the airship?"

"Silliness to pass the time." She waved a hand.

"Not silliness."

"But earlier, I offered you..." Her face flushed. "Everything. You turned me down."

"And before that, I kissed you."

"So you did." She shifted closer and tipped her face upward. Her blue eyes caught his. "So which is it, husband? Attraction or revulsion?"

He brushed away the tear, then trailed a finger down the side of her face, tracing the edge of her jaw until his finger slid beneath the tip of her chin. "You captivate me, Olivia. With an allure beyond having curves in all the right places. I've yet to meet a woman with such complexity."

She blinked. "Is that a good thing?"

"It is." Except it wasn't. It was going to take every ounce of his self-restraint not to respond to her unpracticed advances.

Her eyes fluttered closed. "Then might we try a kiss again now that I'm not terrified of plunging to my death?"

So tempting, those soft, full lips. But he was a gentleman, and she was drunk. His hands moved to press against the satin and steel of her narrow, corseted waist. Gently, he turned her around, directing her toward the bed. "Another time. The only thing you're fit for at the moment is sleep."

CHAPTER SEVENTEEN

OLIVIA DREAMED SHE was in the kitchen, standing before a toasty oven. She reached out and pressed her hand against the delicious heat, sliding her palm over its hard surface. The stove grabbed her wrist.

"Olivia," the stove said. "Wake up."

Her eyes flew open. "Ian," she breathed. He was stretched out beside her on the bed—beneath the covers—one arm about her waist.

Half undressed, she was curled against him, her head on his shoulder, one leg draped over his. He held her hand pressed to his chest. His warm, hard chest. Never had she been so cozy and comfortable and... humiliated.

Wine. There had been much wine and no food. No *edible* food.

She groaned and tried to snatch back her hand, but he held tight. She lifted her head. "What did I say?"

The corners of his lips twitched. "What do you remember? Anything?"

Her face grew hot as memories of the night before flooded back. She'd all but stripped in front of him, suggested he was the motive behind attempted murder... and thrown herself at him, begging for a kiss.

He'd turned her down.

But he hadn't slept on the floor. That had to be a good sign. On the other hand, where else would he sleep? They were supposed to be married. Anyone with a key could march into their room at any moment, and appearances must be maintained.

A rush of guilt chilled her. "I remember that I was slow to catch your sister as she fell. I'm so sorry."

"The break was minor, and Warrick *is* capable enough." The admission came through tight lips. "Though I will double check his work."

"He has the eyes of a basilisk," she said. "No wonder you don't trust him."

There was venom in his answering laugh. "You don't know the half of it."

"I should. Your wife would know. Tell me, how is it that your sister came to be engaged to such a man?" Any man who would force a woman to his will using axon thrall bands didn't deserve a wife, he deserved a prison cell. It pleased her that even in a muddled state, she'd managed to smuggle the bands away, to kick them beneath their bed. The minute an opportunity presented itself, she would secrete them inside Watson.

Ian's eyes met hers. "Not everyone considers a man of medicine a social pariah."

"I didn't say..." Olivia sighed. "I did. I'm sorry. If it's any consolation, I'm becoming rather fond of one physician in particular."

"Then put your head down." Tension melted from his face. "It's a long tale."

Lowering her head again to his shoulder, she curled back into his warmth. There were, it seemed, to be some benefits to her temporary marriage. She'd have to be careful not to become too accustomed, but she would not argue if Ian wished to hold her close. It was the oddest sensation to feel so secure.

"Once, Warrick was a student at the Lister University School of Medicine. I became his mentor when he asked to join my laboratory, to work upon my research project. He was a bright young mind. We became friends. One summer, he came to visit me—all the way to the wilds of Yorkshire—at my crumbling, country estate."

Crumbling? That would explain rumors of the heiress hunt that had reached her ears. "Where he met Elizabeth."

"It seemed like love at first sight," Ian said. "And he offered for her hand. Before Warrick, she had no prospects, no hope of a family, and she begged for my blessing. I hesitated."

"As would any caring brother. Her condition..."

"She was of age. If she insisted upon marrying, who better to look after and care for her than another scientist, a future physician?" His fingers tightened upon her wrist, and his voice grew resentful. "Except Warrick wasn't courting her. He was courting her condition. Who she was as a person didn't matter."

Olivia knew the feeling. She too had been viewed merely as a prize, a means to an end. "How could you know?"

"I didn't. Not at first. Our research had become his obsession. He found her mutation fascinating and was convinced a cure was possible. If they married, Warrick would have the legal right to—"

"No." Olivia gasped. "You can't mean... He wouldn't..." They had to save Elizabeth from marriage to such a monster.

"I do." His hand slid over the back of her hand, and his fingers threaded through hers. "When a project has merit, when it has shown potential to effect a cure, it is protocol to conduct the first *in vivo*—in a living animal—study upon rodents. We proceeded, but our cells quickly grew out of control. The rats were riddled with tumors. Somewhere, our work had taken a wrong turn."

The poor creatures. She curled her fingers, holding tightly. There was comfort in touch. "Continue."

"Warrick insisted our work was valid, that a human's immune system could control the cell growth. But to perform such a test would break every last rule and regulation set in place by oversight committees at Lister Laboratories."

She stiffened. "He didn't!"

"Not on British soil," Ian answered. "While looking for a particular data set, flipping through his laboratory notebook, I came across a research proposal addressed to a group identified only as CEAP. With this group's approval and funding, Warrick proposed to test the cells in humans. A perfect first candidate, he argued, would be a woman suffering from osteogenesis imperfecta."

"Elizabeth." Olivia lifted her head and stared into Ian's eyes.

He nodded, his eyes haunted. "If her bones could be made indestructible, he argued, think what the cells might accomplish within the ranks of the British military."

"Unbreakable soldiers," Olivia said. "Such as the count's guardsmen."

"I confronted Warrick." His arm, strong and muscled, tightened about her waist. "He didn't even bother to deny my accusations, answering only that his project was supported unconditionally by a shadow board within Lister University."

"A shadow board? You think CEAP and this shadow board are the same thing?"

"I do."

Something cold trickled into her stomach. She'd heard that term before, shadow boards. In her own home. Listening at doors, one rarely heard anything good. A lesson learned at the tender age of eleven.

Unable to sleep and annoyed with her nursemaid for taking away her book, Olivia had slid silently from her room and tip-toed down the grand stairway. She'd slipped, unseen, into Father's library and pulled the largest book she could reach from the shelves, a volume written by Charles Babbage. Secreting herself on a window seat behind heavy curtains, she'd read by the light of a small, bioluminescent torch, secure in the knowledge that her nursemaid would never find her. Later, when the meeting convened at midnight in the library, no one thought to look behind the curtains.

Listening to the words of men who visited Father in the dark of night had become a habit, and quite some time had passed before she'd been caught. Enough so that she knew too much. With reluctance tinged with pride, Father had brought her into his fold. If he'd thought to stop her eaves-dropping, he'd failed. At some point, she'd overheard a discussion concerning shadow boards, a group of scientific-minded gentlemen who worked together to bypass official protocols. One such board aimed to study individuals in possession of unusual traits or abilities: The Committee for the Exploration of Anthropomorphic Peculiarities—CEAP.

It fit. Who else would be interested in a human with bones that could not be broken?

Her heart stopped a moment, then began again, galloping like a clockwork horse whose springs had been wound too tight. She swallowed. Could Father be involved with Warrick? No. Her mind rebelled at the idea. Absolutely not. Neither he nor Ian would betray their country in such a manner.

On the other hand, Ian had stolen equipment from a laboratory and transported it to Germany. Technically, that was treason.

How to label this shade of gray?

"I found no evidence of such a board, no matter how I

searched, no matter who I questioned. Warrick disappeared along with the cells. Scandal erupted. An internal investigation was conducted. My laboratory was turned upside down in a hunt for evidence of intent. They found nothing. In the end, I had to take responsibility." Ian paused. His next words were grim. "They *were* my cells."

"You are not to blame for Warrick's actions." She squeezed his hand. Not to blame, but she understood his guilt. His work had inspired and motivated Warrick's actions, and such vile research had to be terminated.

"I was responsible for his oversight and on that regard, I failed." Ian turned his head on the pillow and looked directly into her eyes. His next words came slowly, heavy with the weight of implication. "Your father himself accepted my resignation."

Her breath caught. That meant... he was—or had been— a Queen's agent. It explained much. "For my father?" she asked, doing her best to project ignorance. She might have agreed not to conceal her intelligence from Ian, but she wasn't yet convinced she ought to reveal her place within the organization. "How? You work at Lister University."

Dawn had arrived, and Ian lifted her hand so it caught the light pouring in through the windows. His fingertips brushed across the odd calluses and scars she'd acquired fiddling with steambot mechanics, punching tin and copper cards, picking locks. "Do you remember telling me you were a spy?"

"I did no such thing!" She was nearly certain.

She tried to pull away, but his arm held fast about her

waist, keeping her pressed against him. It seemed there would be no escaping him or the topic under discussion.

"True. You said you *wished* you were. A spy. Why would a pretty, young woman like you want to be a spy?" He was smiling now, a deliberate attempt to lighten the dark mood while still hunting for information.

Pretty. But not beautiful. Or, it seemed, kissable. Yet he'd shared so much, he deserved a measure of honesty in return.

"Do you know how tedious it is to be a respectable young lady of the *ton*? The hours wasted shopping. The days spent at endless teas, balls and garden parties. The years spent behaving impeccably. All in search of a husband." Olivia huffed. "Only to lose the one thing you thought you'd secured at last."

"You never did mention why Lord Snyder abandoned you." His breath was warm on her hair. Why, then, did it make her shiver? Especially when every inch of her skin burned for his touch.

"He did not wish a wife tainted by family scandal."

"Family scandal?" he scoffed. "Your sister married an earl. Your brother, the daughter of a viscount."

"You pay no attention to *ton* gossip, do you? My youngest sister, Emily, ran off with her gypsy lover." Beneath her cheek smooth linen and hard muscle shifted as Ian's chest rumbled in her ear. Laughter. He thought the impropriety amusing? "It's not funny," she protested. "Her behavior reflected upon me, and no gentleman wants to marry a woman who won't conform to the expectations of society."

"Are you trying to tell me you wish to live a conventional life?"

Olivia pressed her lips together and stayed silent. How was it he so easily saw through her pretenses? One by one he stripped them away.

"Exactly. So perhaps he had good cause," Ian pointed out. "You too are a rebel, teaching yourself difference engine programming."

True. Mollified, she allowed herself a smile. "And robotic engineering skills," she bragged, tempted for the first time to reveal her degree from the Rankine Institute. "Among other things. Can you blame me for wishing to have the opportunity to put such skills to use?"

"So you're not a spy," Ian concluded. "You're simply an unusually talented young woman whose father took advantage of her, tasking her with planting acousticotransmitters in the luggage of an unmarried gentleman while she conveniently traveled aboard the same airship."

"Yes." *Close enough.* No need for him to know all her secrets.

Casually, Ian's thumb began to trace a path back and forth across the base of her palm. Her breath caught as his touch ignited a low flame beneath her skin, one that flared hotter with each sweep. Not that he noticed.

"What did he promise you in return?"

Several heartbeats later she lifted her gaze to his. *What could it hurt?* "A chance to find an Italian husband." His thumb now stroked the sensitive inside of her wrist, making a clear and logical mind nearly impossible to maintain.

"You sound disinclined to matrimony," he said, studying her as if she were a puzzle he was determined to solve.

She was. Or, at least, she had been. Why could Lord Ian Stanton, Earl of Rathsburn not have been her assigned target? "A duke's daughter has little choice."

"Is that why you locked yourself in my storage closet?" His mouth was inches from hers.

Behind her lock pick-lined corset, her heart tripped, recovered, then picked up its pace. "A decision I soon came to regret."

"I'm sorry I'm not the gentleman you believed me to be." His fingers stilled.

No. She didn't want this moment to end. She closed her eyes and clarified. "I regret the location and the circumstances, but not the man." She tipped her face upward and let her lips part slightly. There could be no clearer invitation.

"I'm glad to hear that," he said, but there was nothing tender left in his voice. Instead, it grew rough and caustic. "Because you'll need to kiss me."

CHAPTER EIGHTEEN

"Need to..." Bewilderment tinged her voice but there was no time to explain. "I don't see how—"

Tugging on her wrist, he pulled her against his body, crushing her generous breasts to his chest. He kissed the soft skin of her neck just below her ear and whispered, "Someone has cracked the door open and is watching."

She stilled, but attraction still sparked between them. The pulse at her neck fluttered. Her eyes were dilated. Her cheeks flamed. A most gratifying response to his demand, but considering the implications was for later. For now, they must act.

Ian caught her face in his hands, brushed both thumbs along her cheekbones. "Don't look. There is much doubt as to the truth of our relationship. Give them something to whisper about. Kiss me."

"Pull the bed curtain," she breathed. "Let them use their

imagination." Wiggling, she lifted an arm to do exactly that, but he caught her hand, pressing a kiss to her palm before moving it to his shoulder.

Seconds ago she'd been all but begging for a kiss, and now she resisted? A woman was entitled to change her mind. He wouldn't force her, but neither was she pulling away. Perhaps it was the audience.

"You are missing the point entirely." He slipped his fingers into twists of soft, golden hair that had tumbled free again as she slept. Cupping her head, he turned her face away from the door and nibbled on her earlobe.

"Explain," she gasped. Her fingers dug into his shoulder.

Desire, pure and simple. She craved his touch as much as he craved hers. Lust exploded through him and blood rushed to his groin, refusing to concede that this was all an act, doomed to end in nothing but frustration.

Struggling to keep his kisses gentle, he brushed his mouth along her jaw as he spoke, moving ever closer to those full lips he'd tasted all too briefly aboard the dirigible. "The count knows much about me," he whispered. "He knows nothing about you. Our marriage was unexpected and sudden. He will have doubts. Perhaps he suspects an alliance rather than a marriage. I would not want him to suspect a spy in his midst."

"I'm not," her objection came on a whimper, "a spy."

"He likely requires proof." He reached down and slid her thigh suggestively across his own before pressing a kiss to the hollow of her throat. She smelled sweet, like caramelized sugar. "An enthusiastic kiss from my new bride—when we think ourselves alone and unobserved—would help substantiate our claim."

Olivia pulled away and looked down at him, her dark blue eyes wide. Tangled curls framed her face. He couldn't imagine a more beautiful sight. Save, perhaps, one in which her lips were swollen from his kisses. He was enjoying this far too much when he should be worried that the band of his iron self-control had snapped.

"I... I..." She stuttered, then the words came out in a soft rush. "I've never kissed a man before you. If a convincing performance is required, you'd best provide firm direction and stage whispers."

Never?

Before he could respond, she dipped her head. Soft and tentative, her lips skimmed over his mouth, as if searching for the perfect fit. A new surge of heat shot through his body in response to her uncertain explorations and dragged forth a tortured groan.

She hesitated. "Did I...?"

"More." He tugged her face back toward his own, brushing his thumb across her lips and hooking it in the corner of her mouth. "Open for me, let me in."

Her lips parted with a shaky breath, and he tipped her face, capturing their soft sweetness with his own lips. When she melted into him, when her heart pounded in time with his, he deepened their kiss, sliding his tongue into her mouth, tasting, teasing. As he ran his hand down her side, past her narrow waist to trace the generous curve of her hip, to cup her round buttocks, it took every ounce of control he had to remind himself that this was all for show.

For her enthusiastic response made it all too easy to believe what they shared was real. If only she was his bride in truth, if only they were truly alone and on their honeymoon, he would roll her over and introduce her to the many pleasures of his lips, tongue and teeth, beginning with those taut nipples that peeked from beneath the edge of her corset. If only.

But she was an innocent. A duke's daughter.

Not mine.

Sensing his hesitation, she pulled away, her eyes hazy with desire. "Do they still watch?"

"I don't know," he rasped. "A blatant look would reveal our game." Pushing his hand against her corseted waist, he shifted her back onto the mattress, away from his throbbing arousal. Ian dragged in a breath and forced the words past his lips. "Loosen my cravat. Tug it from my neck and toss it to the floor. Unbutton my waistcoat. As you do, sneak a glance at the door."

Her long, clever fingers made short work of his cravat before working their tortuous way down his chest, button by button. When she tipped her face downward and pressed a kiss to the skin of his neck, he moaned as pleasure became frustration. Want and need fused leaving him rock hard.

Warm lips brushed over his earlobe. "Still there," she whispered in his ear. "It's a guardsman, the pervert." His self-control—stretched to the limit—almost snapped at the erotic promise of her next words. "Time, perhaps, for a bit more drama?"

They had to stop.

Yet greedy, he caught her mouth once more for a final kiss. "He's seen as much as I intend to allow," he whispered several long moments later. "But if you'll voice an objection to the open curtains, we could provide quite an entertaining performance backstage."

"Oh?" Her lips curved in a conspiratorial grin.

Ian threw back the covers and sat up, pushing her back onto the mattress. He raised his voice. "On your knees, wife. This corset must go."

A look of panic crossed her face.

"I'll only loosen the ties," he murmured, skimming his palm over its satin surface, his hand stopping beneath her breast. "It's a wonder you can breathe at all wearing this torture device."

Turning, she pushed onto her knees to present her back to him. "Sweet torture, I've been told," she said, lifting her hair to provide him better access, "for those who look upon its accomplishments."

If she were his—he dragged his index finger down the nape of her neck—he would kill any man with the effrontery to talk to her in such a manner. "Play your role," he grumbled under his breath as his fingers fumbled with her laces. This torment needed to end.

"As you wish." She smiled coyly over her shoulder and raised her own voice. "Ian! Anyone could walk in at any moment."

A sharp tug closed the curtains. Dark, gray light engulfed them. Suppressing primal instinct, he dropped her laces, dragged in a deep, steadying breath and moved away.

"Now what?" she breathed.

"On your hands and knees," he whispered, forcing a mischievous grin onto his face and ignoring the ache in his groin. Humor. That would diffuse the sexual tension that still arced between them. He demonstrated. "Bounce. Rock. Thrash. Gasp and moan with pleasure, for I am a fantastic lover."

She grinned back. "Such arrogant male pride." But she followed suit, matching him cry for cry. The ropes beneath the feather mattress creaked, and the wood frame shook as they nearly brought the bed canopy down upon them.

After an acceptable length of time—he wouldn't have his endurance criticized—Ian groaned loudly. Then whispered under his breath. "Now cry, scream—whatever—but bring it to a fever pitch. Stop abruptly and drag me down onto the bed with you." And she did so with such enthusiasm that when they collapsed onto the mattress, the guardsman would be forced to report that the couple did indeed enjoy robust marital relations.

A minute later, he peeked from behind the bed curtains. The door to their chamber was firmly closed.

As they lay there, shoulder to shoulder, he smiled broadly, unable to recall the last time he'd enjoyed himself so thoroughly—if, perhaps, incompletely. He turned his head to stare at his wife. Her hair spread across the pillow, her cheeks rosy, her lips swollen. Except for the fact that she still wore her undergarments, Olivia was the very image of a well-bedded bride.

His body thrummed with longing. What would she say if he offered marriage in truth? He looked away. Innocent. Duke's daughter. *Not mine.*

But she could be, a contrary and persistent corner of his mind insisted.

"I find it hard to believe," he began by way of self-reprimand, "that a young woman of your beauty has never been kissed."

"Oh, but I have now," Olivia corrected him. "Quite well. I assure you playing the role of your wife is not at all a hardship."

Ian's heart gave a great thud. Lower parts of his anatomy were still quite hard, and her voice fairly purred with an invitation to resume their earlier activities. But it would be nothing but an exercise in frustration. He kept his eyes firmly fixed on the canopy above him.

"I am rapidly revising my opinion on certain aspects of wedlock," she continued.

"I can't offer for your hand," he began with regret. "Circumstances—"

"Oh, I know," Olivia cut him off. "By now you're wanted for treason, and Father would never consent. Yet seeing as how both our reputations are compromised..." She rolled onto her side and slid her hand beneath his open waistcoat, pressing her palm to his chest, holding his gaze the entire time.

"Olivia," he injected warning into his voice, "this is not a harmless diversion."

"I can feel your heart pound," she said. Her fingers skimmed downward over his stomach. "The tension in your muscles." She tugged the linen of his shirt free from his waistband. "And earlier, I felt—"

He caught her wrist before she touched definitive evidence of his body's enthusiasm for her proposal. "Stop. You deserve a husband, not more scandal."

She yanked back her hand and huffed. "Lord Rancide offered for my hand—"

"Lord Rancide? The man is—" An ancient, syphilitic rake. "How could your father even consider such a match?" He bristled at the very idea of such a degenerate being allowed to touch her.

"I agree. Much as Lord Rancide made the notion of becoming a young widow appealing, I declined. Father then decided it best that I allow the gossip in London to die down. Hence my proposed destination."

"Until you made the mistake of pursuing me," Ian finished. "Let's hope it's not a fatal one."

A sharp reminder of their situation. Of his inability to offer her any kind of future. Save one that threatened to end badly. He had no business thinking anything of her other than to provide for her safety. But to do so, he needed her help.

"You're right. We ought to focus on the problem at hand." Olivia slid from the bed, snatching up a shawl. With her corset looser, her hips swayed in a most alluring fashion as she made her way across the room to the washstand. Bravely, she broke through the ice and splashed water over her face.

Ian followed her out into the sub-arctic temperatures that lay beyond the bed curtains, the cold a welcome antidote to his libido. "We need to find a way to escape this castle."

"Before Warrick experiments upon your sister," she agreed. "And that device must be returned to British soil while you still have hope of a pardon." She dried her face with a towel. "Wei visited me. Here, in our room, when we were separated. She came through the window to deliver my reticule."

"The window?" He listened to a tale of rock climbing and canvas wings. Did the girl have no fears?

"Perhaps Wei might send a message for us. It's clear she has no love for her uncle."

"No." Ian shook his head. "We must exit Germany as we arrived. Without any of our countrymen knowing we crossed its border." But first he needed to discover where his sister was being held.

His sister. He closed his eyes. There was much to discuss, much to plan. Even with such threats hanging over their heads, he'd found himself enjoying Olivia's company while Elizabeth endured Warrick's ministrations. Never before had a woman distracted him so. Her appeal was an inescapable magnetic field, not that he had any desire to resist its pull.

ANNE RENWICK

"What of the guardsmen?" she asked. "Is there any hope for them?"

"Unlikely. Osteosarcoma is not, to my knowledge, treatable, though I intend to try. Warrick did hint at a possible cure. If we can discover what he is about, perhaps we can help the guardsmen. In the meantime, while we search for a way to leave this crumbling pile of rocks that passes for a castle, we must convince the count that we are following his orders."

"The osforare apparatus." Her voice was tense.

"Yes. If we're to succeed, you will need to work at my side." He paused. "Your fear of blood, of needles and pain..." Her back stiffened. "I'm sorry, but we must discuss it."

Placing a hand atop the table to steady herself as she turned, she lifted a bloodless face to meet his gaze. "There's not much hope, I'm afraid. Ever since I found my brother broken and bleeding upon the ground, watched what he went through in an attempt to piece him back together..."

Her brother's legs, broken during a tragic fall. He'd heard the story, seen the contraption her sister Amanda had created to restore her brother's ability to walk. A distressing process to witness even for the most unshakeable of surgeons. It explained her fear of heights and blood.

"My process is nowhere as invasive," he promised. He used needles, not knives. "And we will apply anesthesia to dampen any pain." He reached out a hand to steady her when she swayed. "There is a way to overcome hemophobia, but it will take practice."

CHAPTER NINETEEN

"PRACTICE." That didn't sound promising. Already her head wobbled upon her shoulders. Though she'd rather enjoyed "practicing" at being his wife, there was no choice but to move on to blood. And needles.

Ian took her hand and led her to the stool beside the stove. "Let's see if there's any hope of heat."

A few smoldering embers allowed themselves to be coaxed back to life, but even as flames danced before her, cold seeped deeper into her skin. "Perhaps I ought to sit upon the floor?"

"A logical precaution." His voice held all the emotion of an executioner.

Lowering herself to the floor, she buried her face in her hands. "Your bedside manner needs much work," she groaned.

He crouched before her and tucked a lock her hair

behind her ear. "You seemed to be enjoying my bedside manner earlier."

Out of the corner of her eye, she saw it again, that wicked grin she'd first teased out of him at the start of their voyage. It wouldn't last long. It never did. After all, their situation was far too serious—but that smile transformed his face from serious scientist to heartbreaking rake.

Her heart stumbled, then picked up its pace. Why did she feel such a strong attachment to this man when all he'd done was kiss her senseless?

Fanning the attraction that sparked between them was a dangerous proposition.

Understanding dawned. This was why female field agents were all widows. Prior experience with men must allow them to keep their wits about them. To seduce a man, yet not hand over their hearts. To maintain focus at all times.

For she had not wanted Ian to stop. If his hands gripping her waist atop layers of silk and steel could kindle such desire, what would it feel like to have them touch her bare skin?

Ian pulled her hands from her flaming face. "There. See? Already the blood has returned to your face. Arousal is one way to raise blood pressure."

"Not nice. You turned me down," she reminded him. "I only wanted to suggest an alliance with... certain benefits."

"Not nice, perhaps." His dark eyes flashed. "Yet enjoyable. I'll not deny my attraction, Olivia. You're a captivating woman. I want you. A bit too much. But you deserve better, and I'll not ruin you."

Ruin? An interesting concept among the *ton.* Men placed such value on a woman's virginity. It was, in her line of work, a considerable asset for a young female societal liaison to be able to present herself as unspoiled by a man's touch. All the better to draw a target's attention. Given the men she'd been tasked with enticing, that had been a factor in her favor.

But now? Ian's flirtations, his kisses, convinced her she was missing something wonderful. "I've been gone from the airship for over two days," she countered. "The damage to my reputation is already done."

That last part was a lie. Her parents would be furious, but Mother would have concocted a likely excuse. For if the truth were discovered, the gossip would never die down, and Father would have no choice but to send her into premature retirement. Still, unless she could complete this self-appointed mission with honor, they would never trust her with a mission again.

If she could help prevent an army of unbreakable German soldiers from threatening Britain's shore, she might —*might*—be able to salvage this situation. Perhaps the Queen herself might be moved to intercede on her behalf. And Ian's.

"Perhaps." Ian abruptly rose, his smile gone. "I think, for now, that we had best focus on the present situation and revisit such... societal concerns should we manage to leave this castle alive."

It was becoming harder and harder to think of him as a target. But he *was* both an unauthorized and a forbidden target. A scientist and a former agent who—rightly—suspected her motives.

He was also a man.

In this their mutual attraction would work to her advantage. It had already sparked a protective instinct to keep her close, to keep her safe. She would return the favor for it was impossible to think of him as a traitor. He was a man placed in a difficult situation, a nearly impossible situation, and she would do her best to see him—and his sister—safe.

Yet they could be in this castle together for days, weeks—maybe even months—before help arrived. They could end up spending a lot of time together in that bed. Flirting she knew, but anything beyond? All her life she'd been carefully chaperoned and steered in the direction of distasteful gentlemen. For the first time Olivia wanted... more. And it was almost within reach.

Cogs and gears. What was wrong with her? Being alone with this man clouded her mind. The door could open at any moment. It was time to prepare for the tasks that lay in her immediate future, for a day of distasteful laboratory and medical procedures. If there was to be any hope of her becoming a full-fledged Queen's agent, it was time to confront her greatest weakness.

"Very well," she agreed. "You said there is a cure for my blood phobia. Lest you plan to kiss me each time I grow faint, I assume there is another method to raise my blood pressure?"

"There is." He shoved the last of their allotted coal into the stove. "Your reaction is not uncommon, quite understandable. Though there are psychological reasons for your fear, the solution I offer is based on simple biological facts."

Good. The last thing Olivia wanted to examine in excruciating detail was the day her brother had plummeted from a balcony, nearly ending his life. She knew the basis for her phobias. Her sisters had overcome their issues by joining forces to invent a cure. They'd fixed Ned. Amanda had even caught a spy in the process. But what had Olivia accomplished with all her training and skills? Not a single thing.

That needed to change. Immediately.

"When you see or think of blood, your unconscious mind feels threatened and decides that the blood might very well be your own. A sudden and significant fall in your blood pressure causes you to faint, dropping you to the ground— the safest position for a bleeding individual—thus ensuring sufficient blood flow continues to your brain."

As Ian spoke, his tone changed, reminding Olivia of the times her sister had attempted to lecture her on basic scientific principles. She tried not to grind her teeth. "That seems reasonable."

"Not if the blood is not your own." He began to pace. "If you are, in fact, uninjured, then fainting places you at the mercy of your environment, one you can no longer control. I need to be able to depend upon you. There will be needles. Then there will be blood."

She swallowed convulsively. "That word..."

"The trick is to increase your blood pressure, something that can be done by tensing and squeezing your muscles, preferably the larger ones, whenever you start to feel weak."

He stopped pacing, all his intensity focused into his gaze. "Try it now. Make fists. Tense your arms. Your calves, thighs and buttocks."

What a marvel that he could say such words aloud, casually and without innuendo. The embarrassment of this situation alone sent her blood pressure soaring, but she did as he asked.

"Good. Like that. Now hold for ten seconds." He waited. "Then relax for twenty seconds. Repeat."

She huffed. "If it is as simple as that—"

"Not simple, Olivia. Because now comes the difficult part." He crossed the room to snatch two pillows from the bed and returned to drop them on either side of her. "I need you to make the osforare apparatus fully operational. The count is likely to demand a demonstration. So I am going to describe what it is and what it's supposed to do in great detail."

All those needles. Her head spun.

"Look at me." He snapped his fingers. "Focus. If you faint, we'll repeat this again and again and again..."

She lifted her chin and clenched her fists. "Just get on with it."

He nodded. "Originally, we thought to provide Elizabeth with a definitive cure, to fix all two hundred and eight bones of her body. To do so, we set about altering osteoprogenitor cells. Unfortunately, years of work demonstrated—in rats— that if one attempts to manipulate those cells residing within the marrow of the bone, cancer is the final and fatal outcome."

"As Warrick demonstrated in humans," she said.

"The man's ethics are all but nonexistent. Avoid him." Slicing a hand through the air, Ian began to pace again. "So I changed tactics. Elizabeth's bones break easily. The bones of those individuals who guard the Queen's safety and welfare are frequently broken. Therefore, rather than attempt to remodel the entire skeletal system, I decided to focus upon the break itself, to create mature, differentiated cells that would replicate quickly, but only for a short, defined period of time. They rapidly repair the break, then die. But because they have such an ephemeral lifespan, they must be delivered directly to the location in which they are required."

"And the osforare apparatus is the means by which you propose to deliver them." Her stomach threatened mutiny.

"Yes. The apparatus is built primarily of a new chromium alloyed steel designed to resist corrosion. A metal alloy that is both strong and light and easily cleaned." He paused a moment, judging her reaction. "The many joints the osforare apparatus possesses allow it to wrap about or fold over the skin and muscle that covers nearly every bone in the human body."

She breathed in, she breathed out.

"The apparatus is an experimental device."

"You've never used it before?" Her jaw unhinged.

Pain flashed across his face. "I snatched it away from my laboratory while it was still under construction. It's not even complete. Its punch cards are little more than hypothetical programs. Making it fully functional is a task that now falls to you."

She stared at him. Helping him to perfect and deploy an experimental medical device on foreign soil on behalf of foreign soldiers would also make her guilty of treason. As her presence was unauthorized, any missteps on her part would come with more severe punishments. Did she dare assist? "Are the cells themselves fully functional?" she asked, not certain if she wished to hear an affirmative or negative answer.

"They are, but..." Ian pressed a thumb to his lips.

"Rats?" she guessed.

"Yes. I have proven the concept in rodents, but not humans. The Queen decided that while the Rankine engineer constructed the device, my time and attention was better directed elsewhere."

"Marriage?"

He glanced at her sharply.

Shrugging a shoulder, she offered no apology. "Every single unmarried lady of the *ton*—and every mama—is aware of your recent social activities."

"Are they? Most debutants made their excuses and sought the retiring room upon my approach." His tight voice told her he'd not been immune to the sting of rejection.

"Consider your chosen profession."

"And the disaster that is my estate," Ian snapped. "Yes, it was strongly suggested that I turn my attention to marriage and the need for a male heir." His eyes bored into her. "You are, Olivia, one of only two women to actively vie for my attention in that regard."

"I don't recall suggesting actual marriage," she said,

meeting his steely gaze. "Nor offering to provide an heir. But out of curiosity, who was the other woman?" The countess flashed to mind, but Olivia pushed the ludicrous thought away. Katherine had married last Season.

His eyes flashed as he turned away. "I can generate those mature cells here—in human form—but only as a last resort. Regardless, the osforare apparatus must function. Once clamped about the injured bone, tension springs will uncoil. Multiple needles will simultaneously pierce skin, muscle and connective tissue en route to bone. Blood vessels will be compromised. There will be leakage."

Cold sweat broke out over Olivia's skin. Suppressing a moan, she clenched every muscle in her legs. In her arms.

"The program, using a feedback loop, must ensure that the springs do not drive the hollow points into the bone itself. Rather, the needles must rest gently upon the surface of the bone where a thin tissue, the periosteum, resides. It is there that my modified *human* osteoblasts will be created and begin their work."

Olivia's vision grayed about the edges, and it flitted through her mind that there would—necessarily—be more "practice." She chose the left pillow.

CHAPTER TWENTY

I AN SCOOPED OLIVIA from the floor and regretted that smelling salts were not among the contents of his medical supplies, when he heard the snick of a key in the lock.

"Wake up." He patted her cheek. "We have company."

Olivia groaned.

The door swung open and in rolled a steam maid carrying breakfast—clear broth and brown bread—and the steam valet bearing yet another gown for Olivia.

The guardsman standing at the threshold looked uncomfortable. "Is she ill? Or," he cleared his throat and lowered his voice to a hoarse whisper, "perhaps with child?"

Ian sighed. "We've been married but two days."

"Not everyone waits for the wedding," Olivia needled.

The guardsman's face reddened.

"Overacting," he muttered into her hair.

In retaliation, she nuzzled his neck.

He might have set her down upon her own two feet a bit too forcibly. Not that she seemed to care. Pressing a hand to her *empty* stomach, Olivia fell upon the tray of food as if she'd not eaten in days. Which, Ian reflected, was a distinct possibility.

"Dress quickly," the guardsmen urged them. "You are to visit *Fräulein* Elizabeth."

At last. After the previous night's events he'd worried the count might refuse him the right to visit his sister. He ran a hand over the stubble upon his face, regretting the loss of his razor as he walked to the wash stand.

As he tied his cravat, Ian caught the reflection of the guardsman in the mirror. Unobserved, his stoic expression had fallen away. The man looked as if someone had shoved needles beneath his fingernails. Did he worry about the lumps upon his jaw? Or did the man regret something else? Was Ian's reunion with his sister to be overcast with new threats and demands?

Together, they stepped out the door. Olivia walked before him, following the guardsman who led them through the maze of interconnected rooms, corridors and stairs, this time toward a distant corner of the uppermost reaches of the castle. With each step, dread coiled tighter in his gut. It wasn't lost on him that Katherine had loaned his wife a sapphire blue gown much like the one she'd worn the day he'd proposed. He expected he was to read between the many ruffles, but whatever message the countess intended to send was lost upon him. Regardless, it didn't bode well.

The cry of a terrified woman echoed down the long stone

hallway, yanking him from the quagmire of his thoughts. A cry he recognized.

"Elizabeth!" Ian pushed past Olivia and the guardsmen, following the sound of plaintive whimpers. Slamming the door open against the stone walls, he burst into the room rushing past a number of staring faces, focused entirely upon his sister.

"Halt!" A guardsman's arm shot out, wrapping about Ian's neck as he lunged forward, forcibly stopping him from approaching his sister.

Behind him, Olivia gasped.

A portion of the turret had been sectioned off into an alcove, one fitted with iron bars and a stout metal door. Inside, his sister lay on her stomach, stretched out upon a narrow bed. Her ankles were bound by thick rope to the footboard, her wrists—one in a plaster cast—to the headboard. Two thin linen sheets were draped over her body, parted in the middle to expose the bare flesh of the posterior curve of her hip.

Warrick stood beside her, wearing a long, rubber apron.

"Please, John," Elizabeth cried. "Don't do this!"

The sharp scent of ethanol met Ian's nose as Warrick wiped the patch of bare skin with disinfectant.

Bone marrow could be obtained from a number of locations in the human skeleton, but the flare of the hip, the iliac crest, was the location of a large volume of bone marrow—an ideal location from which to harvest marrow cells. He'd executed the painful procedure himself on a number of patients suffering from different blood disorders. But Ian had obtained consent—and had acted in an effort to understand disease origin and implement an effective treatment.

There was no consent here. And the equipment spread out across a metal tray suggested that more was about to occur than a mere sampling of his sister's defective bone marrow cells.

His fingers found the ulnar collateral ligament of the guardsman's elbow joint. He shifted his grip infinitesimally and dug into the nearby ulnar nerve. The guard released him with a howl of pain.

"Don't!" He ran to the prison cell, yanking on the iron bars that prevented him from reaching his sister's side, hoping the stone and mortar would crumble like the rest of this cursed castle. But the bars refused to shift. Reaching between them, he snagged Warrick's sleeve, wrenching him backward against the bars and away from his sister. "First do no harm," Ian hissed into his ear. A central tenant of the physician's oath. One that was drilled into the minds of every medical student ever to attend Lister University.

Warrick turned toward him with hard eyes. "A pledge I never took. Or have you forgotten?" He tore free of Ian's fingers and stepped out of reach. "The procedure *will* succeed."

"Ian?" his sister whimpered, twisting against her restraints to face him.

"I'm here, Elizabeth." He kept his voice as calm as possible considering he wanted to murder the man he'd once thought of as a brother. "You promise much, Warrick, but deliver very little."

"Do you mean to inform me, *Herr* Rathsburn," Count Eberwin's voice boomed, reminding him that there were others present, "that *you* can deliver what Doktor Warrick cannot?"

Turning his head, Ian glared at the count. At his side stood the ever-present Zheng. The Chinaman's hand shifted, and the sharp blade of his curved sword flashed in warning. Ever so subtly, his head tipped.

He followed Zheng's direction and swore. Katherine held a strange two-pronged device against Olivia's neck. Coils of wire protruded from the side of the device, curling downward to a power source. A voltaic prod, an instrument designed to deliver bolts of painful electricity.

Katherine's gaze met his. "My husband favors all things sharp. Me, I find other tools more captivating. The last person who opposed my husband? The electrical shock nearly stopped his heart." Her gaze raked down Olivia's form. "Though well-padded, your wife is considerably smaller."

Olivia jerked and whimpered as the voltaic prod dug deeper into her flesh. This was a dangerous game. He considered the odds. How much was the count depending upon him to fix his guardsmen, to design and build him stronger ones?

"You wouldn't dare," Ian countered, not taking his eyes off of Katherine. "Without my expertise and cooperation, this project is doomed to failure." She frowned, and he shifted his gaze to the count. "I've seen the end result of *Doktor* Warrick's work. It's not encouraging. How much time and money have you wasted on his effort?" He shook his head slowly. "A poor return on your investment." He paused. "No. I consider my sister, my wife and myself safe. Quite simply, you need me."

"You are, of course, correct," the count agreed. "Doktor Warrick, your past successes keep you alive. Nevertheless, as *Herr* Rathsburn points out, you have completed only half of the task set before you. Strengthen their bones, that you have done." The count narrowed his eyes. "Yet as the months pass, my guardsmen fall ill. They sicken. They die without honor."

"I've done my best," Warrick countered.

"And it has not been enough," Count Eberwin answered. "Which is why I arranged for *Herr* Rathsburn to join us at Burg Kerzen. After today's procedure, you will continue to work with him—and his wife—in the laboratory. I expect to see progress. My men need a cure, and they need it now." The count waved in Elizabeth's direction. "Proceed."

"No!" Ian's entire body vibrated with the effort it took not to throw himself at the count. He fought hard to keep panic from his voice. "Wait! Warrick has refused to let me examine his work. There are certain to be problems with his process."

Warrick's brow furrowed. The man's greatest fault was pride.

"There likely are," the count said. "You will fix them. I am providing motivation." His lips curved upward and an unholy light appeared in his eyes. "And if this vial of cells fails your sister, your wife will serve as her replacement. Time runs short."

He heard the sharp intake of Olivia's breath. The hard steel teeth of reality bit down. His sister was beyond his reach, and he could offer Olivia no reassurance that she would not be next. Clenched muscles shook with suppressed frustration, but he was no match against the weapons Zheng and Katherine wielded.

The count waved at Warrick. "Proceed."

As Warrick turned back to Elizabeth she cried, "No, John. You don't need to do this. I'll marry you. Just let me go."

"Stop, and I will permit it," Ian offered, despite the bile that rose to his throat at the thought of calling this man kin.

Warrick hesitated.

"Do it. Now!" the count barked.

Lifting a scalpel, Warrick made a small incision through the skin above Elizabeth's hip. He then inserted a large bore needle of a syringe through the cut. Ian watched helplessly as Elizabeth cried out in pain while Warrick twisted and pushed, forcing the sharp tip through the cortical layer of bone. Tears ran down her cheek in a torrent. Warrick pulled back on the plunger drawing a sample of bone marrow into the body of the syringe. With a twist, he separated the body of the syringe from the needle and set it aside.

Warrick lifted another syringe from the metal tray upon the bedside table. As he turned, Ian caught sight of the cloudy liquid inside the body of the syringe. His heart began to pound. These were the same cells that were killing the count's guardsmen, men who were far, far stronger and healthier than Elizabeth.

Cells that owed their existence to his initial work. Cells that had left British shores because of his inability to see the narcissistic light in Warrick's eyes, because Ian had blindly followed protocol. Valuable time had been wasted waiting for the Queen's agents to capture and detain the rogue scientist. He should have shot Warrick and dragged him directly to Newgate when he'd had the chance.

"Don't." Ian gripped the iron bars, his knuckles white. He wanted to howl, to scream, to *do* something, anything to stop this nightmare. But he was utterly powerless. Keeping his voice calm and rational took every ounce of control he possessed. "Modifying the osteoblast progenitor cells found in the marrow doesn't work. Their undifferentiated state is what causes the cells to grow out of control, to form tumors."

Determination wavering under the assault of Ian's words, Warrick paused.

"If you care at all for my sister, you won't sentence her to certain death."

The count growled.

Still Ian pressed onward. "The new procedure is to modify mature osteoblasts directly, to transform fully differentiated cells of the periosteum at targeted locations."

Warrick turned toward him. "You mean to address each bone individually?"

"Yes," Ian said. "Painful and tedious, I know, but it is the only way to ensure the patient survives." He reached through the bars, holding his palm upward and lowered his voice. "Give those cells to me. I'll destroy them. We'll begin again."

"Silence him," the count ordered.

Katherine swung the voltaic prod in Ian's direction and before he could yank his arm from between the bars, the pointed metal probes pierced the skin of his upper arm like a hot iron poker and every muscle went rigid. All motor control fled. As the floor rushed up to meet him and the probes pulled away, his body grew limp. Then his head hit the ground and darkness swallowed him whole.

OLIVIA RUSHED to Ian's side, grateful to see the gentle rise and fall of his chest. Falling to the ground beside him in a puff of silk, she pulled his head into her lap and pressed a hand to its side. Already a nasty lump formed on his temple.

Never before had she witnessed such horrors. A frail, young woman tied to a rough bed, subjected to a painful medical procedure that was likely a death sentence. The same threat now hanging over her own head. Sharp prods shoved into Ian's shoulder generating an electrical pulse strong enough to drop a six-foot man.

What had she gotten herself into?

She turned her face upward toward the count, her eyes wide and glistening with unshed tears that were far from fake. Warrick had yet to complete the procedure, but if he continued they would be trapped. If there was even the slightest chance that he had developed a way to keep his cells under control, Ian would refuse to flee the castle without discovering it. As would she.

"Please stop this," she pleaded, her throat thick with concern. Too much was happening too fast. She needed to buy them time. Time for the Queen's agents to mount a search, time for them to locate the acousticotransmitter's signal. "Please don't do this. Warrick's procedure won't work. But with the modifications my husband has made, your goal can be achieved. Our new device, the osforare apparatus, is nearly ready. We need but a few weeks."

"Weeks," the count replied, his voice flat and his eyes cold. "You dare ask for *weeks*?"

Olivia swallowed and nodded. "Scientific progress is by its very nature slow and tedious. To expect instant results is insanity." The moment she spoke, she realized her mistake. Unwise to suggest the count had a mental disorder... But it was too late, the damage was done.

"Insane?" the count repeated, stepping closer. "My men have but weeks—days—to live and you think me *insane* for demanding fast results? Your husband—you—have had years to perfect this procedure. It is my sound opinion that scientists spend far too much time performing unnecessary tests on rodents. Rats and humans do not appear at all similar to me. Indeed, with the slightest of motivations, Doktor Warrick was able to generate an unbreakable soldier for me within months."

"With deadly consequences." Must she state the obvious?

"Which you will solve. Quickly. Lest your fate be the

same as the *fräulein's.*" The count's head snapped up. "Now, Doktor Warrick, or your life is forfeit."

Elizabeth broke into loud sobs.

Olivia pressed her lips together, willing herself not to cry out as Warrick completed the procedure by shoving the plunger of the syringe home, claiming yet another life in this mad count's bid to produce a race of unbreakable soldiers.

CHAPTER TWENTY-ONE

T HE DINGY, DANK dungeon the cancer-ridden guardsman marched Olivia into should not have surprised her. The laboratory space of mad scientists never came equipped with windows. Her own sister had set up research space in the back half of a chicken coop. In comparison, a wine cellar was a step up.

The door closed behind her and a key turned once more, leaving her alone in a vast room filled with wine casks, miscellaneous laboratory equipment and her thoughts. Disturbing, unwelcome thoughts.

She wrapped her arms across her chest, rubbing her shoulders against the dank chill emanating from the stone walls, but nothing could ease the cold knot that twisted low in her stomach.

A plan. They needed a plan. She began to pace. First they needed to gain the count's trust. As much as she detested the notion, she was going to have to fashion herself into a biologist, into Ian's laboratory assistant. They were going to have to produce measurable results in record time.

From what she could piece together from his instruction, her brief observation of the osforare apparatus, and the words he'd thrown at Warrick, it seemed that transforming the entire skeleton—hundreds of bones—was an impossibility. She spun on her heel. Well, not impossible, exactly, but Warrick's method ended in certain death.

Ian possessed the ability to create a different kind of cell that could transform bones, one or two at a time—a lengthy procedure—but only with the assistance of the osforare apparatus, a device which still needed to be completed before its programming card could be adjusted and refined to deliver these cells to the surface of the bone.

With all those sharp needles, there was going to be blood. More blood than the simple incision she'd just witnessed. Black spots appeared in her vision and her steps faltered. She put a hand out, steadying herself against the wall. She took a deep breath and focused on contracting her muscles. There was no choice. She had to move past this irrational fear.

So. Create a new kind of altered cell. Make the osforare apparatus function. And the last and most significant hurdle, find a way to kill Warrick's cells, the ones that multiplied without restriction, forming those horrible tumors that protruded from so many of the guardsmen's hands and faces.

Warrick's claim that he could stop the growth of cancerous cells would need to be investigated. She pursed her lips. If he truly possessed the means to cure the count's guardsmen, why had he not yet implemented it? The man seemed to make a habit of practicing shoddy medicine while making unsupportable claims.

Nonetheless, Warrick's assertion would have to be investigated because the moment those cells he'd injected Elizabeth with were rendered harmless—or the moment they held the cure in their hands—the three of them could escape, treasonous scientific equipment in hand.

Help might come. Or it might not. Best to plan on its absence.

Which was why Olivia had taken care to count every stair and every turn, forming a mental map of the castle. With lock picks in hand and Watson at her feet, she could have them free in moments. The greatest challenge would be avoiding the guardsmen.

Unless.

She recalled the small arsenal removed from Ian's person upon docking and wondered at the possibility of finding him a serviceable weapon. The Queen's agents were all well-trained and quite capable of improvising...

⟶⟶◈⟵⟵

THE MOMENT IAN REGAINED CONSCIOUSNESS, Zheng forced him to his feet at sword point. Behind the bars lay the sleeping form of his sister, unbound and tucked beneath a thin wool blanket. The count and countess along with their guardsmen were gone. As was Warrick.

And Olivia. An icicle pierced his heart at the thought of her coming to harm.

"What have you done with my wife?" he demanded. Speaking made his head throb. "I need her."

He was surprised to find he meant it. Though her loyalty lay with Queen and country, Olivia was the only sane, able-bodied ally he had in this pile of rocks. He hoped her programming skills were as good as she claimed, for they needed to work closely and quickly together if they were going to survive.

"*I* have done nothing to your lovely *wife*." Zheng scoffed. "The count ordered her to the laboratory. Business concerns compel me to insist you join her without delay."

The room tilted, and he reached for the iron bars to steady himself. He pressed his fingers against a large, painful lump on his head and prayed he hadn't sustained a concussion. "Might I have a moment to speak with my sister?"

"A moment," Zheng replied, but made no move to step away. It seemed their moment was not to be private.

"Elizabeth," Ian called.

His sister's eyes fluttered open, and she pushed herself onto her elbows. Her face was pale and drawn. His stomach twisted in despair. If those cells could drop a hulking guardsman, he didn't hold much hope that his sister's weakened immune system would be able to fight off cancer long.

"You shouldn't have come, Ian." Hand pressed to her hip, she rose, limping to the iron bars. "Bringing your bride! Whatever were you thinking? And why is it you never mentioned her in your letters?"

"Never mentioned?" Zheng stepped forward, taking far too much interest in his sister's words.

"As if I would abandon you," Ian said. "And Olivia..." His sister waited, her eyes wide and sparkling. For years now, she'd nagged him to take a wife, build a family. No doubt she expected an impressive tale, one full of stolen moments, heartfelt declarations and a romantic hot-air balloon proposal.

She wasn't going to get one.

But, as it was safer for everyone if his sister believed the lie, Ian inhaled deeply and, ignoring his pounding head, attempted to provide a convincing story.

"Ours was a whirlwind romance." Wasn't that how they were always described? "And a forbidden one." That part was true. "Romantic liaisons with staff members are prohibited. I've a new treatment device, one so complicated it requires an engineer to program it. Olivia was the engineer assigned to my project."

"The Rankine Institute allowed a woman to enroll?"

Lister University School of Medicine had opened their doors to women last year. He'd assumed the engineering school had as well, but perhaps not. "The circumstances of her employment are complicated. When she learned of your plight, she refused to be left behind. We—er—eloped."

There. All of it true. Nearly. Well, some of it.

Zheng grunted. Approval or disapproval, Ian couldn't tell.

"Smart and necessary to your research." Elizabeth's eyes narrowed. "Do not tell me you married her for *me*?"

Trust his sister to question the façade. Ian summoned indignation. "Not at all!" He'd "married" Olivia to save her from the count, but there was convincing to accomplish. "From the moment we met, Olivia made me feel... alive. I wanted her and no other."

His heart gave a great thump as Ian realized he'd presented his sister with a singular truth. He couldn't recall the last time a woman had occupied such a large portion of his conscious thoughts. Despite Elizabeth's condition, despite the nearly insurmountable difficulties they faced, he looked forward to being the sole focus of Olivia's attention. His face grew hot. Even if it took every last ounce of gentlemanly willpower to turn down her intoxicating offer. She was a temptress, a lady and probably a spy.

"Enough about me." Ian reached through the bars, caught Elizabeth's hand and slipped his fingers around to her wrist. Her pulse beat steadily if weakly. "How long have you been here?"

"A week?" Elizabeth tipped her head. "Perhaps more."

Zheng prodded him with the sharp tip of his blade. "Say goodbye. There is work to be done."

Ian ignored him. "Is this the first time you've been experimented upon?"

She nodded, then drew in a shaky breath. "Don't help them, Ian. My life is not worth the devastation the count would unleash."

"He has no choice," Zheng barked.

"Keep up your strength," Ian said. "Watch for signs your

body is rejecting the cells. Chills. Body aches. Nausea. Pain or swelling. I want details."

"Very well."

"Enough!" Zheng shoved the sword point into Ian's shoulder, breaking skin and drawing blood. Pain bloomed.

Ian stepped and spun, slamming Zheng's sword arm into the iron bars. Elizabeth screamed and stumbled backward.

But his only advantage had been surprise. Without so much as a stick with which to defend himself, the upper hand fell to Zheng, who blocked his next move. A second later, Ian froze as the sharp edge of the curved blade cut into his throat.

"Enough!" No spite laced Zheng's voice. Merely a hint of amusement. "Now. Through the door and down the stairs. Doktor Warrick awaits you in the laboratory. With your wife."

THE HINGES of the laboratory door creaked.

Olivia quickly shoved the various scraps of metal and sharp rocks she held beneath an empty wine barrel. She hadn't found much. The most promising implement lay in plain sight, an iron auger, a corkscrew that someone had been using to tap into the count's wine supply. Given it lay next to a wine-stained beaker, it wasn't hard to guess that that someone had been Warrick, the very man who now stepped into the laboratory with the countess upon his arm.

"Ah, Countess, it seems Lady Rathsburn shares my fondness for your wine." Warrick crossed the room and held out his hand. "Time for a new cask. Red or white, my lady?"

"Neither." Olivia's fingers tensed about the auger, but it was bad form to injure a man who might yet be useful. "How can you sample wines while your fiancée languishes in a cage? Perhaps it would be more appropriate to explain this supposed cure you've developed, *Mr.* Warrick."

How could he care so little for Elizabeth as a person, preying upon her hopes and dreams of a family to ensnare her into a marriage where she would serve as his personal laboratory rat?

It struck her like a cane behind the knees. She too was equally awful. She had detested Carlton, yet planned to marry him, to bear his children, to manage his home all the while reporting his every action to the Crown. Yes, he was a traitor, but did that alone justify her actions? Could she have taken such steps without eventually coming to detest herself?

Katherine's laugh brought her back to the moment at hand and reminded her now was not the time for self-doubt. "For all her lush beauty and golden locks, it seems Olivia is as intensely focused and relentlessly driven as her *husband.*"

"Beauty, you say?" Warrick narrowed his eyes and pursed his lips as he raked his gaze over her from head to toe. He clearly found her wanting.

She returned the favor, raising her eyebrows as she paused to take in the lack of a cravat, the fraying cuffs of his shirtsleeves and the buttons of his waistcoat that strained against a burgeoning waistline. It only made his lips curve in smug acknowledgement of her notice.

"Red it is." He plucked the auger from her fingers and strolled off into the stacks of barrels, leaving the two women alone.

"I have to admit, the low cut of my blue silk was a poor choice on my part for today's activities," Katherine said conversationally. "Perhaps something more demure tomorrow?"

She wanted to discuss fashion? Now? After casually electrocuting a man whose bed she'd once shared? "Why are you involved?" Olivia lifted her chin and took a step forward. "What do you stand to gain by watching Germany invade British shores? Your family lives in London."

"Do they?" Her voice was cold. "I should still claim them after they forced me to wed Count Eberwin? No, Lady Olivia *Ravensdale*, my loyalty is to myself. Remember that."

Olivia's mouth fell open. This woman was not at all who she seemed.

"Yes, I know well who you were. And perhaps are still." Katherine moved to close the gap between them, looking down her nose. "Though I very much doubt your marriage *and* your skills, I have every desire to see Lord Rathsburn's laboratory endeavors succeed. See that you make yourself useful."

"Olivia!" Ian called from the doorway.

"How timely." With an evil gleam in her eyes, Katherine faced him. "Our brilliant scientist arrives. Feeling... inspired?"

Concern burning in his eyes, he stalked past her to

Olivia's side, catching her hand and lifting it to his mouth to kiss her knuckles. "I was so worried."

A lump formed in her throat. How was it possible that he'd come to care about her in such a short time? She gingerly touched the nasty lump that had formed at his temple. "As was I."

"Leave," he snapped at Katherine. "We have work. Your presence accomplishes nothing but to waste my time."

Warrick reappeared, a flask filled with red wine in hand. Smug smile firmly in place, he crossed to the countess' side. Lines had been drawn. "Don't let our presence disturb you," he said. "We but wish to observe the count's newest protégé. And his assistant, of course."

Olivia was done with these two. She tugged Ian in the direction of the laboratory space. "If they will not assist, let them watch. We need to work. I didn't want to start without you." She hoped he heard the underlying cry for help in her words. He needed to orient her, and quickly.

"Of course." Ian too turned his back on Katherine and Warrick and escorted her to a long, waist-high table that stood beneath overly bright lamps. Aside from a single rat in a cage, it was covered in glassware and rubber tubing and all manner of disconcerting steel items that she could not begin to name. Save the syringe. That horrid device would haunt her nightmares for years to come. Tensing every muscle, she forced down her revulsion.

"I thought we might set you up here," he said, "in proximity to this odd collection of batteries."

A thousand or more tiny, sealed copper canisters were

lined up like an army of miniature soldiers across the back of the table. Wires protruded from their tops, coiling and twisting upward, connecting with the overhead lights and various pieces of equipment.

"Gantz batteries!" Olivia was desperate to lay claim to any expertise she could for the tiny hairs on the back of her neck stood on high alert under Katherine's scrutiny; any misstep on her part could have fatal—or worse—consequences. "The Hungarians recently developed them to install inside steambots. Except, can they correctly be termed steambots if they require neither coal nor steam to function? Batterybots?" She looked at Ian with wide eyes, suddenly aware she was overplaying her role as a technician, but she couldn't seem to help herself. "The Gantz battery is rumored to provide enough power to allow a bot to function uninterrupted for some twenty days. Days!"

"Is that so?" he said calmly as he stretched out a padded cloth. "Then one Gantz battery should easily generate enough voltage to drive the electromagnetic osforare apparatus motor. I expect you'll need to modulate capacitance and resistance."

The silver case of nightmares rested upon the counter. Time to release the fanged contraption from its prison.

Ian cleared his throat. He was looking at her expectantly, his eyebrows drawn together. "Ready?" he whispered.

She nodded, and he opened it with a flourish to reveal the osforare apparatus. Glass vials, India rubber tubing, wires, brass hinges, an iron framework. Horrid steel needles. She tensed every muscle in her body and counted to ten, then forced herself to relax. "It seems to have survived the journey relatively intact," she pronounced.

Careful to avoid its many teeth, Ian lifted the device from its padded velvet case onto the table before her, positioning it so that she could easily reach the card-reading cartridge.

Katherine and Warrick drew closer, peering at the contraption as torchlight flickered in the reflection of its many sharp needles. Though black spots dotted her vision, Olivia congratulated herself upon remaining upright. Fainting at this juncture would plant seeds of doubt in their minds. It was unprofessional, and she could not afford to have doubt cast upon her story or her abilities.

"I thought we might remove the needles for now," he said. "They require sterilization, and we wouldn't want to inadvertently snap any while making modifications."

Thank the aether. Olivia made herself busy, arranging the punch cards beside it in meticulous order. Anything to avoid looking directly at the apparatus.

Warrick inserted himself between them. "This is how you propose to deliver what exactly?" He lifted a finger and reached out to touch the device. "It looks... painful."

"No more than a bone marrow core." Ian swatted his hand aside. "Do not touch. You will not be involved in this aspect of my work." He slanted his head sideways. "Unless you wish to volunteer as a test subject?"

"How droll." Though Warrick's lips curled, there was worry in his eyes. Served him right.

"Then step aside." Ian's fingers flew over the osforare

apparatus, unscrewing knobs and plucking out its sharp needles. "My wife has much work to do."

"Come, Doktor Warrick," Katherine commanded. "I grow bored. There are other matters that require your attention. Something copper if I recall correctly? Lord Rathsburn, let us know when you require a test subject. An aspiring guardsman will be delivered."

The door banged shut and the key turned. Unsteady, Olivia sank onto a stool. She took a deep breath and wiped her damp palms upon her skirts. It was time to turn herself into that expert. "So these cells of Warrick's will heal broken bones. That I understand. But how is it that they make the bone *stronger*?"

"Antimony." Ian lifted a small glass vial from a wooden rack. At the vial's rounded bottom rested a small amount of a silvery, white powder. "A poison in larger amounts, this element is key. It crumbles easily, but when it replaces the phosphate found in bone, when it combines with calcium, it forms a biological alloy that is four times heavier and at least four times stronger than normal bone."

Her mind spun, but latched on to one particular word. "Wait. Poison?"

"Yes." Rubbing the back of his neck, he began to pace. His voice shook with agitation. "Those cells you witnessed Warrick injecting into Elizabeth's hip? They will migrate into every bone, demanding antimony at levels that would kill an untreated individual."

Needy cells. Not only were the guardsmen—and Elizabeth—doomed to develop bone cancer, in the meantime they would be chemically dependent upon whomever controlled the supply of antimony. "And if she fails to receive it?"

"The cells will scavenge phosphate from any source they can." Eyes glazed and distant, his hand waved in the air as if the answer ought to be obvious. "Hypophosphotemia would result."

"There you go with those impossible words again," she said. "I believe we've had this conversation."

"Low phosphate levels," he said. "Leading to mental confusion, muscle weakness and ultimately kidney failure. Should anyone withhold antimony from Elizabeth, she will die within a matter of days." He rolled the vial between his fingers, his face drawn and tense.

Die. Too many lives were on the line. She looked at the small amount allotted to them. "Is it rare, antimony?"

"For our purposes, yes. Zheng, I've learned, is in possession of an antimony mine. He closely monitors and rations all antimony usage. No doubt he aims to become the principal supplier to the Kaiser's unbreakable army."

A profitable endeavor to control the substance that kept an army alive.

The count and his countess. Warrick and Zheng. Alliances constantly shifting as they all struggled to win at this morally reprehensible game. Time to control that which they could. "So. Cure your sister and the guardsmen. Plot an escape."

"And prepare to demonstrate my device as if we plan to commit treason," Ian finished. His expression was pinched, but he'd carried that contraption away from British shores knowing he might well be forced to use it.

This was not at all an assignment a Queen's agent would undertake. "It won't come to that, will it?" she asked.

"I desperately hope it will not."

But with their backs against a wall...

"Well then." Surviving this "adventure" was priority number one, and working on the device would buy them more time to plot an escape, more time for Mr. Black and his men to track them down. A demonstration was one thing, but pains must be taken to ensure technique was never placed into their enemy's hands. Olivia rose to her feet, surprised to find she did not feel the least bit weak. Instead, she felt the urge to do something, anything. And to do it now. "My skills are yours to employ. Show me how this contraption works."

CHAPTER TWENTY-TWO

A CONFUSION OF QUESTIONS churned through Ian's mind. Had Olivia been sent to stop him? Help him? Did he protect her with this sham marriage —or was it the other way around? He wouldn't put it past Black to send such an unlikely reinforcement. If such was the case, the man deserved both a sharp uppercut to the chin, followed by a warm pat on the back.

As she worked, he took a long hard look at her. Blonde ringlets had pulled from the twist of hair at the base of her skull to curl against her cheeks. He had the absurd idea to reach out and give one a tug, just to see if it bounced. So very beautiful and feminine. Most men would look no further than the surface. Lord knew he hadn't.

Kissing her this morning had been as much about satisfying a deep, nagging urge as it had been about establishing their cover. Though rather than satisfaction, he'd found only frustration. The first man to kiss her. Him. Though he couldn't seem to stop turning that particular piece of information over in his mind, he'd now glimpsed what lay beneath Olivia's façade. Loyalty. Vulnerability. A keen intelligence. Thank goodness for that.

"This program card is but a raw prototype," she said, examining the pattern of punch holes beneath the argon light. "There are a number of discrepancies. You say it's never been tested?"

There was much she wasn't telling him, but even if she'd been sent to stop him, to return him to British shores, it was clear that she would not do so without first attempting to save his sister. She would work to save even the lives of the count's guardsmen.

For now, he would place his trust in her—though he fully intended to insist upon detailed answers to his earlier questions. He was certain she worked for the Crown, but perhaps she didn't answer to her father. Perhaps she answered to Black.

"Ian!" Olivia waved the paper card before his eyes. "There is no telling how long the count and his minions will leave us undisturbed. Explain to me, in painstaking detail, exactly how you expect this device to function."

She was right.

Though he had every intention of departing before it became necessary, the count was bound to insist upon a demonstration. He pressed a palm against his chest, against the packet secreted within his waistcoat and prayed it wouldn't come to that.

"The osforare apparatus has never been utilized," he

admitted. "Though nearing completion, it was still being constructed when I... appropriated it."

"Stole it," she corrected.

Ian lifted a shoulder. "I had assistance. Your own brother-in-law looked the other way."

"Did he?" Her voice was disinterested, but her fingers tightened on the punch card.

Interesting.

"Have you ever worked with him, Lord Thornton?"

"I attempted to, but he was largely unconcerned with the finer points of ice sculpture even though it was his own wedding." She peered down at a card, pencil in hand, ready to transform mathematical operations into a pattern of holes.

"I wager he drives your father mad." Would she elaborate?

But she didn't bite. "May we discuss my relatives another time?" She tapped her fingernail on the Babbage card. "We need to focus."

"Fine." He tugged the leather gloves from his hands and pointed. "Pressure sensitivity of these spring mechanisms is the greatest concern. The transformative liquid needs to be deposited precisely beneath the periosteum."

"A density occlusion shift algorithm might be the answer." She scratched a few notations on a nearby sheet of scrap paper. "Go on."

Ian spoke at great length, marveling at her ability to rapidly internalize both vocabulary and concepts. Occasionally, he lifted the pencil from her hand to sketch a diagram to further clarify his words or to point out particular features built into the apparatus. If his fingers brushed over the surface of her skin as he did so, it was entirely accidental. Her breath hitched at the lightest of touches, but even more satisfying? She didn't pull away.

At last she looked up, eyes sparkling. "I think I've got it." She tucked the pencil behind her ear and began to gather up the papers strewn across the workbench. "I'll work with this card stock for now, but the apparatus is constructed to accept a two-by-three copper punch card. A sturdier material will better withstand frequent usage." Her face paled and her hands began to shake. "Frequent. Will I be required to operate the device?"

"Yes." Ian reached out to steady her hand. "I will assist. We will run our first trials without the needles."

"Trials. The count will pluck some poor soul from the nearby village." She shook her head. "This is wrong, Ian. We can't experiment upon a perfectly healthy young man."

"I do not intend to do so. The fluid I intend to use will contain none of the transformative ingredient. His treatment will be a sham. Painful—there is no way to avoid that—but harmless." He dropped his hand and stepped away.

"But the count demands evidence. He is bound to discover our duplicity."

"Early trials often fail." He had no intention of remaining in Germany any longer than absolutely necessary, but... "If it becomes unavoidable, we do have one willing human volunteer. Me."

Her eyes widened. "Are you so very confident in your scientific advances?"

"I am." He didn't relish the idea of allowing those needles to pierce his skin, but he would not subject anyone but himself to the first real test. "In the meantime, I will try to direct the count's attention to curing his guardsmen."

Olivia took a deep breath, then nodded. "It's a plan. I don't like it, but at least nobody else is harmed. For now."

"For now," he agreed.

She set down her stack of notes. "Before I begin to punch bits from cards, even paper ones, I need to understand how the osforare apparatus bends, how it moves, how it conforms to different parts of the body."

"Then allow me to provide an anatomy lesson." He pulled his coat from his shoulders, unfastened his cuff and began to roll up his sleeve. A blush rose to her cheeks—such seductive innocence. He was surprised to hear his next words emerge as a hoarse whisper. "In which the student is invited to touch."

"Oh?" She stepped closer to brush a fingertip over the surface of his skin. "Just your arm?" she teased, then glanced at him from beneath long lashes. "If I'm to appear competent, I must be far more familiar with male anatomy and expanses of bare flesh. Arms, legs, back, hips."

Blood rushed away from his brain, finding itself needed elsewhere as his groin tightened and stirred with interest, remembering all too well the enthusiasm she'd poured into their morning charade. They were alone now, unwatched, and he wanted her as much as she seemed to want him.

"If that is what you want." How far would she take this game? How far would he? Blood pounded in his veins, and the air was thick with hunger. "We should progress with care and intention. With the knowledge that what is done cannot be undone." He wasn't certain if he spoke to remind her or himself.

She nodded and tipped her face upward.

He let his gaze fall to her lips, but only for a moment. "We will begin with my arm." Ian turned back to the osforare apparatus and, lowering himself to a stool, stretched his arm beneath its curved frame. "Let me show you how this works."

"Tease," she whispered.

His answering laugh was soft. Ignoring the electricity arcing between them, he demonstrated how the various joints, levers, and screws could be adjusted to conform to any given surface, then held still as she tailored them to fit his forearm.

As she leaned forward ever so slightly to bend the apparatus about his limb, he took in the view presented to him. The bodice she wore was supportive and uplifting. To the point of creating the illusion that her breasts were moments from breaking free. When she shifted, they surged forward. Perhaps it was not an illusion after all. A man could hope.

Resisting the impulse to tug at his suddenly too-tight collar, he concentrated upon bringing his respiratory rate back under control.

An effort that failed the moment she adjusted a screw and whispered, her lips mere inches from his ear, "Like what you see?"

Caught. A gentleman would apologize. But a lady

wouldn't have asked. A corner of his mouth turned up as he tore his eyes away and forced them to look upward. "Guilty as charged."

She flipped a lever that clamped steel bars about his wrist, then another lever to lock the device about his arm below his elbow. "You are the first man to admit as much aloud. Today is certainly a day for firsts."

How could such a flirtatious young lady—one who had been engaged!—have no knowledge of her physical attractions? "Whatever did you see in Lord Snyder to recommend him as a husband?" he asked. "He shared no kisses. No compliments. Did his eyes never stray beneath your chin?"

"Never. He was ever the gentleman." Her hand stilled, and she twisted her lips. "Do you mean to categorize the act of staring at a woman's chest to be paying her a compliment?"

"No," he backpedaled, sensing he was in hot water. "Not exactly."

"I find it curious." Her voice was light and flirtatious as her fingers deftly worked the leather buckles, yanking the bands tighter than strictly necessary. "Tell me, what, exactly, is going through a man's mind as you stare?"

Her fingers brushed the surface of his arm, sending bolts of electricity through his body as she adjusted a number of parallel spring tension rods to align several metal bars parallel to his ulna.

He ran his free hand over his eyes. "This conversation surpasses anything remotely appropriate."

"Our entire situation is inappropriate." She tightened a

series of screws above his radius. His entire arm was now encapsulated in several pounds of metal. "But I wish to know."

He ought to refuse.

"A scientist at a loss for words?" she mocked. "Can you not manage to verbally convey the attraction of my bosom?" Seemingly unaffected, Olivia lifted a tension gauge and began to take spring pressure readings, carefully recording the numbers into a notebook.

A choked laugh emerged from his throat.

Her hand stilled as her eyes met his. "Come now, what is it about these two mounds of flesh that appeals to you so much?"

Resistance snapped.

"Very well. Step closer." With his free hand, he caught her hip, urging her closer until she stood between his knees, her chest at eye level. "Men are physical creatures," he began, wishing he dared pull her closer still to press her against his hard length. "Often words fail us."

She scoffed. "You love to lecture."

"That may be. But we *are* in a laboratory. Perhaps a bit of hands on demonstration? A bit of experimentation?" He looked into her eyes and waited. He would not touch her without permission. "Unless you are adverse."

"Not at all."

Thank God.

He ran his hand up the side of her rib cage, stopping as the edge of his thumb brushed against the side of her breast.

"A man tends to become non-verbal when confronted by such opportunity."

"Try." From the look on her face, retreat would not be permitted.

"What do I think?" His gaze drifted downward. "At first, my attention is caught by tantalizing slopes and peaks, by promises hidden in their curves and shadows. Generally, at this point, I would tear my eyes free and force my mind elsewhere."

"But?"

"But, upon the rare occasion that I am permitted to look, I begin to think about touching." He ran his thumb across the silk of her bodice, over the generous swell.

She leaned into his touch.

Encouraged, he continued. "I wonder what their soft weight might feel like in my palms." He slid his hand to cup her breast, lifting it. "And then I think about doing this." He stroked his thumb across the silk over her taut nipple.

Her breath caught. A most beautiful, satisfying sound. With blood rushing away from his brain, it was a moment before he could speak again.

"I begin to anticipate further what sounds you might make." He lifted his hand, drawing the tips of his fingers over the swell of her breast, until they rested lightly at the edge of her bodice. He ran his fingers back and forth over lace ruffles that barely concealed the rosy edge of her areola.

His gaze lifted. Olivia's eyes were dark with desire. The pulse at her throat throbbed. Desire growled, threatening to chase away rationality.

"By the time my mind has drifted this far into a fantasy of thought, I'm imagining the expression upon your face should I reach behind, dip my fingers where they ought not be." He matched his actions to his words. "To pinch this tight peak between my fingertips."

With the tiniest of gasps, her back arched pressing her breast into his palm. Her eyes drifted shut, waiting.

But he'd already taken this too far. He willed himself to stop, willed the throbbing in his groin to subside. Slowly, deliberately, he withdrew his hand from beneath the row of ruffles. "And that, dearest pretend wife, is all your pretend husband is prepared to explain or demonstrate." His body knew that for the lie it was, but his mind demanded time to untangle a knot of conflicting desires.

"All?" Her eyes, hazy with desire, opened. "I rather like your approach to laboratory experimentation." She dragged in a deep breath. "Perhaps another time I can convince you otherwise... for I've many more unanswered questions."

CHAPTER TWENTY-THREE

Q<small>UESTIONS.</small>

Another day had passed with no answers. A string of equations wrapped their way down the page before her, but still she'd not arrived at a solution that would allow her to control the negative feed-back governor with a simple punch card. Were her skills up to the task?

Olivia glanced at Ian. Deep in concentration, alternately peering through an aetheroscope and pouring over pages of Warrick's spidery notations, he took no notice of her. He'd avoided her gaze since yesterday's... encounter. It was quite deliberate, this avoidance, as if he wished to snuff the spark of attraction that kept flaring to life between them. Perhaps it was for the best.

Never let your heart rule your head.

How many times had she heard that phrase recited? With good reason. For her head had certainly been turned by a particularly handsome, young earl. She was forgetting herself, her mission. Mr. Black would chide her. Track Lord Rathsburn. That she'd done. The next logical step would be to keep the osforare apparatus inoperational and out of enemy hands. Yet she'd been working diligently to perfect its operation. Elizabeth's presence was an unforeseen complication; one she couldn't dismiss. If not for her, Olivia would even now be slipping from the castle and heading for the border on foot, the device securely in her possession.

As an agent, she was floundering. She had a sneaking suspicion that a field agent would prioritize national security and the return of the device over the health and well-being of a woman she barely knew, but she couldn't bring herself to abandon Elizabeth.

As a societal liaison... well, she wasn't after marriage. Not a real one.

Never mind that her thoughts kept straying back to that enormous bed. By the time the guardsman escorted them to their frigid bed chamber last night, her fingers were so frozen, Ian had needed to assist her with the laces of her gown. While he himself undressed, she'd tapped a faint rhythm on the floor, calling Watson forth and secreting the axon thrall bands within him. Perhaps the device might prove useful. It was another secret to keep from Ian, but at least it was a gratifying one. Warrick would not be able to use them to bind Lady Elizabeth to him again.

She slid beneath the bedclothes with every intention of picking up where they'd left off in the laboratory. But when Ian reached for her, tugged her to his side, his hard angles and planes a pleasure to lean against, she was too exhausted to attempt a seduction. As a wondrous heat and a curious sensation of security enveloped her, she'd fallen into a deep sleep.

A new day brought a new—thankfully woolen and high-necked—dress, a brief conversation with Steam Matilda when she delivered yet more broth and hard bread, and a return to the wine cellar where Ian resumed his research, answering her questions in a brisk voice, all business.

Hours later, eyes bleary with fatigue and fingers cramped with cold, Olivia rubbed the back of her neck. Time for a break. Time to reconsider her course of action. She stood and began to pace, blowing on her stiff knuckles, flexing them against the cold, as if preparing to pick a lock.

Lock.

The lock that kept them in this wine cellar taunted her. She hated being confined, and it was ancient, easily cracked. More a suggestion she remain in the laboratory than an actual impediment to her escape. What if there was no cure for Elizabeth, for the guardsmen? The longer they labored in this prison, the sicker Ian's sister would become. Might her best chance of survival lie in London where an entire team of scientists could focus upon a cure?

She glanced again at Ian. He was so certain of his path. But locked here midst the wine, they knew nothing of the intrigue that swirled about the castle. Time to reconnoiter. She'd slip out for a bit, creep down a hall or two. Climb a spiral staircase or three, pay a visit to Lady Elizabeth. The woman who was at the center of this dilemma might well possess critical insight.

Olivia would only be gone a short while, no reason for anyone but Ian—and perhaps not even him—to notice her absence.

Sliding a lock pick from her corset, she opened the door. A guardsman lay unconscious on the floor of the hallway. Sick? She closed the door quietly behind her and pressed a hand to his chest. It did not rise or fall. So young, barely a man, and yet he was dead, another victim of those horrible cells.

A deep sorrow swelled in her chest, but there was nothing she could do for him. Better to move onward, to work to put an end to such future atrocities.

Heart pounding, she slid through the hallways, pausing to listen at half-open doorways. Only once did a guardsman approach. She held her breath, certain she was about to be discovered behind the suit of armor—which provided rather poor concealment—but his glazed eyes stared at his shuffling feet, and he moved as if his every joint throbbed. Her chest tightened. Sentenced to an early death by impatient, immoral men.

Halfway to the turret room, the clanking of Steam Matilda's spider-like legs met her ears. Olivia froze. Then ever so carefully, peeked around the corner.

A tea tray. Despite the fear that banded her chest, her stomach growled. Loudly.

"Halt," she called in German. Steam Matilda stopped. Such a delicate porcelain tea service must belong to the countess. Did she dare divert the steamboat, deprive Katherine her small luxury?

Olivia's stomach growled again. "To the tower. To Lady Elizabeth," she ordered, crossing her fingers that her programming would override that of the countess'.

With creaking joints, Steam Matilda turned and altered course. Olivia followed. At the turret room's door, the posted guard straightened at her approach, his hand falling to the hilt of his blade.

But a meek woman was rarely seen as a threat. She directed her gaze to his boots. "Sent by countess," she said, deliberately mangling her German. "My guard... too much pain," she waved at the spiral staircase behind her. "He waits below."

A slight hesitation. A grumble. But with stiff fingers, he unlocked the door.

Olivia followed Steam Matilda into the small turret room. "Good afternoon, Lady Elizabeth." The guardsman locked her in.

No fire burned in the grate, and with every gust of wind, panes of glass rattled in their casement. At least the voltaic prod was gone, no bizarre medical equipment was in evidence, and Lady Elizabeth was dressed and seated in a chair. The thick wool blanket wrapped about her shoulders slid to the floor as she stood, mouth agape. "How—"

"I came alone." Olivia poured a cup of hot tea and handed it to Lady Elizabeth through the iron bars that separated them. Her cheeks were a healthy pink, not flushed with fever. *Thank the aether.* After that horrible procedure... "The door to the laboratory was unlocked," she said, spinning the tale she would stick to, "and I rather thought we should speak."

"Please, call me Elizabeth. We are, after all, sisters. I am so pleased that Ian has finally married." She tipped her head and regarded Olivia with a touch of suspicion. "I have to admit the announcement rather took me by surprise."

Though it pricked her conscience to let that fiction stand, it was all that stood between her and the count's unwanted advances. "As it will my own parents when we return." She thought of Ian's delightful kisses and hoped she glowed with starry-eyed delight as she lied. "We eloped, saying our vows aboard the airship. Though this isn't the honeymoon I would have chosen, your rescue was paramount." She poured her own cup of tea, wrapping her chilled fingers around its heavenly warmth. She closed her eyes and sighed. "This castle is so very, very cold. I rather expect I shall be made to regret stealing the countess' afternoon tea, so we ought to make the best of it before we are found. Cream cakes?"

Elizabeth accepted the delicacy with a twist of her lips. "The cook means well, but she's a simple village woman and terrified of the rusty, old steambots. Nearly everything emerges from the kitchen raw in the center or baked into a brick."

Olivia tasted the cream cake. "A bit short on sugar, but otherwise consistent with my recipe."

"*Your* recipe?" Elizabeth looked at the steambot doubtfully, but took a bite, humming in delight. "Oh, it's wonderful."

"Steam Matilda brought me a tray my first evening and, well..." It was no secret that her presence was tolerated at Burg Kerzen for her programming skills. "I've talent with mechanical household staff. I dismantled her, polished her various parts and pieces, reassembled her. And, having sampled what passes here for brown bread, I may have slipped a baking program into her card reader while I worked. If I could only spend a few hours in the kitchens..."

They shared a smile.

Elizabeth set down her tea cup. "What are the plans to remove me from this prison?"

"*That* is what I wish to discuss," she began. "As yet, there are none." Elizabeth's face fell. "The cell transplant you received altered Ian's plans. I left your brother pouring over Warrick's scribblings, trying to discover if his boasts are fact or fiction. If he finds any glimmer that Warrick's words are more than a brave-faced lie..."

"My brother will refuse to leave without that information," Elizabeth finished. "John Warrick is a madman."

"Even the rantings of a lunatic sometimes contain core truths, and his work has not been entirely unsuccessful. Think a moment. Has he mentioned anything about your future, about how your treatment might proceed? Odd words, scientific jargon?"

"No." Elizabeth blinked, then reached to a small bedside table. "But he did give me this. He called it a promise stone. It's strange. Watch." She tapped the gray metallic lump against an iron bar. It stuck.

"A magnet?" Olivia frowned. Perhaps Warrick's words

about a cure *were* nothing but braggadocio in the face of Ian's arrival and the count's threats.

"What it might have to do with my condition, I've no idea." Elizabeth tugged it free and dropped the smooth nugget into Olivia's hand. "Keep it. Give it to Ian and see what he makes of it."

She slid the odd stone into her pocket. "What do *you* want to do?"

"I don't want to die here in this awful castle, behind bars." Elizabeth closed her eyes. "If there's no cure, I want to return home. Six months." She swallowed. "That's time enough for one more English spring."

Olivia nodded, then eyed the lock that held the iron door closed. Another basic, rudimentary lock. It would take her mere seconds to open. The tools in her corset would suffice, but two women brazenly exiting this chamber wouldn't make it far. First they needed a plan.

"Have you met Wei?" Elizabeth asked.

"She visited you here?" Olivia's heart gave a great thud at the thought of the girl climbing seven stories up the side of the castle wall, of her gliding down *seven stories*.

"Before your arrival, she offered to free me."

Her heart stopped even as her lungs demanded more air. "She has suggested you jump from the window and glide to freedom. But your... condition. You could easily break several bones." Ian would refuse.

"Not once Warrick's cells lodge themselves in my bones. Soon I will be unbreakable," Elizabeth reminded her. "Alas, there is the matter of my prison and the question of where I would go once—if—I reach the forest floor."

Biting her tongue against the temptation to reveal any more of her skills, Olivia walked to the small window in the far wall. She lifted the latch and swung the casement inward. Cold air blasted into the chamber as she leaned outward. Overhead, a dark shadow passed. Odd to see a pteryform circling in broad daylight. But the wildlife was none of her concern. The distance to the ground concerned her much more. Far, far below, like a tiny toy boat, the *Sky Dragon* floated in the river. Her heart thudded against her breastbone in terror at Wei's acrobatics.

She pressed a hand to her heart. "Pistons and pipes."

"I am in complete sympathy," Elizabeth said. "If only she could bring the airship to my window instead."

Olivia wiped her damp palms over her skirts and turned to face Elizabeth. "If it came to it, if I could find a key, would you? Jump and glide? Are you strong enough? Brave enough?"

"Stark, raving mad enough?" Elizabeth finished with determination, wrapping her hands about the iron bars. "I just might be. Just enough."

CHAPTER TWENTY-FOUR

IAN CRUMPLED THE page of notes he held. He stared at the closed laboratory door, his mind unwilling to believe his eyes. With movements that spoke of considerable practice, Olivia had slid a lock pick from her bodice and slipped through the cellar door in a matter of seconds. Was she mad?

Though he'd done his best to focus on the work before him, his unruly mind kept drifting back to her cry of pleasure as he'd slipped his fingers beneath the edge of her corset. It had taken every ounce of willpower he possessed not to rip the apparatus from his arm and drag her into a shadowy corner of the wine cellar to finish what they'd started.

Maybe *then* he could once again think clearly.

For as she'd worked at the table behind him bending over the osforare apparatus and its cards, his imagination had spun every sigh of frustration at her calculations, every rustle of her gown as she shifted positon upon her stool into unsated yearnings, and he'd slowly begun to go insane.

So when she'd stood, he'd held his breath, refusing to turn about yet hoping to feel her touch on his arm.

But she'd uttered not a word. And then she was gone. It shouldn't surprise him. Sneaking about was the skill that had landed her in his escape dirigible. Any moment now, he expected a guardsman to toss her back into the room. She'd mentioned plotting an escape, but the door to the wine cellar had been locked, a guard posted directly outside.

He pressed the base of his hand to his forehead. He should have known. Upon discovering his stowaway, he'd assumed she'd coaxed a porter into allowing her entry to his suite aboard the Oglethorpe airship, but...

Crossing to the door, he tried the handle. Unlocked. The door bumped into something soft but solid. A guardsman lay prone on the floor. No pulse. Had Olivia...? Unlikely. There was no sign of a struggle. Likely bone cancer had claimed yet another life. Still, he couldn't discount the possibility.

Where had she gone? He had to find her before someone else did. He slipped down the hallway.

A voice. Hers. But speaking in German. As he'd suspected, she used her soft curves to obscure more than a penchant for programming. He'd been a fool to underestimate her. He was about to glance around the corner when he heard the unmistakable sounds of boots aimed in his direction.

Moving quickly, he ran, ducking into the nearest room— the kitchens. A cast iron range crammed into an enormous old hearth. A long and scarred wooden table covered in various cooking implements. And a variety of rusty steam-bots struggling to make the next meal. The cook looked up from the thick lump of dough in her hands. "*Herr* Raths-burn," she whispered. Then her wary gaze moved past his shoulder.

A low-pitched laugh full of dark amusement met his ear. "Slipped your guard, have you? Abandoned your *wife*? How convenient," the countess purred. "Though I've just returned from a ride, any excuse to take the air with a hand-some gentleman. Cook, do let my husband know tea shall be delayed."

Caught.

Ian turned and inclined his head. "Katherine."

She sauntered forward slapping a riding crop upon her gloved hand. Only then did he note her attire. Her bodice was cut for ease of movement and beneath a split skirt, she wore leather leggings and riding boots. Aviator goggles hung about her neck, her dark hair was tightly braided.

Aviator goggles?

"If you'll come with me," Katherine pointed her crop at the kitchen door, one that lead to the castle courtyard. "I've a proposal to make." Her eyes flashed. "Of an entirely different nature."

He thought of Olivia wandering through the castle. Any attempt to follow her now would only expose her to danger and—suspicion reared its head to remind him—she seemed to know what she was about. Better to drag answers from her later, in a more secluded, private location.

If Katherine was about to tip her cards, he couldn't afford to miss the chance to see what hand she held. With grim reluctance, he followed her into the cold winter afternoon. She raised her arm overhead, flexing her wrist so that the flat of her palm faced upward. The dark shadow of a pteryform blotted out the weak sun as it plummeted to the ground and landed, its sharp talons clicking on the cobblestones as it crouched low. Ian gaped while Katherine climbed onto the beast's back, settled into a saddle strapped to its back and took up the reins.

"Meet Sofia," she said.

He recalled the odd flapping of her hands aboard the balloon over the Thames, the day he attempted to propose. Not fear at the approach of the gliding man, but hand signals to the pteryform. All that time she'd kept her beast close by—an attempt to prevent the count from contacting him.

A tame pteryform. Britain might have more to worry about than the theft of his research. He swore. He'd been such a blind fool.

"Come. Meet the others." She held out a hand. "See for yourself that *my* project enjoys more success."

A mixture of awe and revulsion washed over him as he climbed astride. The creature ran, leaping into the air, half-flying, half-clawing its way up the castle walls in a terrifying, near vertical takeoff. Without stirrups or reins of his own, he was forced to wrap his arms about Lady Katherine's waist to keep from falling off.

With a final kick, the beast launched them into the air. Beneath him, the pteryform's back was hard and rigid, shell-like. Ian's legs, tightly gripping the animal's neck and shoulders, informed him that the rest of its hide was equally solid and unyielding. Yet its leathery wings beat with supple power.

He was no cryptozoologist, but insofar as he was aware, pteryformes were no more than winged lizards. Accidental air collisions with dirigibles often dropped them from night skies. Yet none of those towed by crank carts from London's streets had possessed any kind of natural body armor.

Had Katherine ridden this creature from London all the way to Germany? A direct flight would certainly explain how she'd managed to arrive before him. Though he'd known she must be a foreign agent from the minute she'd been introduced as the countess, without a network to consult he had no idea—yet—for which government she worked. Her lack of empathy for Elizabeth's state suggested it wasn't his own. Or did she hate all other women on principle?

They soared over the castle, the icy wind biting into his skin and tearing at his clothes as the pteryform slowly widened its circles. Beneath him passed the castle's walls and gates, a road that twisted down into the sparsely populated village to cross a river flowing swiftly with the melting snow. The few streets that led beyond the village wound their way into a vast expanse of woods that climbed ever upward into the surrounding hills.

Though escape by foot appeared impossible, Ian committed the view to memory, mapping out the route he would take the moment he could free his sister from her cage.

Here and there, tendrils of smoke stretched upward from the blanket of trees into the sky, suggesting that the forest was not uninhabited. As the pteryform circled again, Ian caught sight of a clearing, of wagons drawn together to form a half circle about a central campfire. Gypsies.

Black sometimes traveled as one of them. Though the Queen had forbidden border crossings, might Ian's disappearance have forced her to make a single exception? Had Black managed to track the acousticotransmitters before they were destroyed? Was it possible he camped there now, eyes trained on the castle walls? If so, how long did Ian have before he interfered?

As they reached the distant crest of a hilltop, the winged reptile began to descend, dropping steadily toward a thick stand of coniferous trees. At the last possible moment, the creature folded its eight-foot wingspan, and gravity took over. The landing was bone-jarring, dropping them into a clearing beside a small, squatting hut. Four additional pteryformes were chained to nearby trees. The beast they rode tossed its head back, screeching a greeting that the others returned. A young man, their apparent caretaker, fell to the ground upon his knees, his head bowed.

"Meet my dowry," Katherine said, ignoring the caretaker. "Otto believes them a gift of the Kaiser, a reward for taking on the difficult daughter of a German spy raised in London. It is near enough to the truth." She swung her leg from the creature's neck and slid to the ground. An order barked at the boy in German sent him disappearing into the hut.

"The perfect transport for men who lumber about with

metallic skeletons," Ian said. Their situation was more dire than he'd thought. "Only five?"

"They will breed, come spring," she answered. "But what good are my steeds without riders? Warrick's cursed project has consumed my husband's funds, and we've nothing to show for it yet but deformed and dying guardsmen."

Ian wrinkled his nose. Without the wind whipping about, a vile smell amassed. The beasts reeked, a sour smell bringing to mind burnt hair and rotten eggs. "You seemed confident of his success earlier."

"He might yet redeem himself, but his methods are slow, awkward and ponderous. If you were to offer me a more appealing alternative," she waved at the pteryformes, "you could take his place."

Not a chance. "You don't intend to remain in Germany?"

"No longer than I must." She stroked the crest extending from the pteryform's skull. The beast hissed, but otherwise ignored her.

So the pteryformes weren't quite tame. He glanced at Katherine. Neither was she.

And to think he'd proposed.

Though he hesitated to ally himself with her, one did not turn down a possible escape plan out of hand. If there was any chance of steering these pteryformes toward home... "Am I meant to infer you offer me safe passage? If so, where? Austria? Hungary?" Certainly not England.

"Further still," she said. "Russia. The count overstates his influence upon the Kaiser. You were right to doubt his offer of a position in Berlin. I, however, am already authorized to offer you your own laboratory among the Kadskoye scientists."

Ian kept his face impassive. The rumored Russian biological research facility, location unknown. Whispers of great technological advances occasionally reached Lister Laboratories. Such as the existence of an armored mammoth.

Exactly how much influence did she wield, a women sent to work with—marry—the likes of Count Eberwin? "I don't think I'd care to live in Siberia," he ventured.

Katherine's boots crunched upon the snow as she stepped closer, until her face was inches from his. "You will learn its location upon your arrival, not before. So you are aware, I extend the offer to both you and your so-called wife." She toyed with a button upon his coat. "I had great plans for us. Imagine my disappointment when my fiancé married another. While I know the game we play, I am not convinced Olivia does."

Ian stepped back. "Bigamy doesn't suit me."

She let go of the button, flashing him a smile. "How unfortunate. I do like to keep men scattered about in castles and manors. Sometimes I even tuck them away in secret laboratories."

Ian rather believed she did. "Anyone I know?" How many were enemies of Britain? Did any work within its borders?

She laughed. "Come with me, and I'll tell you."

The young man returned, a sack in one hand, a terrified, flapping chicken in the other. He tossed the bird upward, and the beast they'd ridden snapped it out of the air with a razor sharp beak, scissoring the screaming animal in two.

So the beasts were useful for more than mere transportation. No doubt one of the reasons Katherine felt safe bringing him here alone. If he lunged for her, would he lose an arm?

She gave the man further orders in German. He handed her the sack before running, slipping and sliding upon the icy path, back into the hut.

"What of my sister?"

"Think of me as recruiter of talent," she said, waving her hand dismissively. "Sadly, Elizabeth has none. Olivia, on the other hand, has value beyond her programming skills."

He swore.

"Yes, exactly. I know who she is. We met at her debut. The Duke of Avesbury himself bowed over my hand at her ball." She pressed a hand to his arm. "It gave me great pleasure to steal his daughter's targets."

"Targets?"

"Interesting." Katherine's eyebrows lifted. "You don't know. Perhaps you are one."

Suspicion wormed its way deeper into his mind, but Ian stayed silent. He would take up the topic with Olivia directly.

"Regardless, I offer you a choice. Stay and labor tirelessly for the count in his austere laboratory. Enough of Otto's wealth remains that you may expect supplies to last through summer. Or leave and avail yourself of the vast resources made available to the personnel of Kadskoye. Either way, know that in the end, I will have what I want."

Ian did not intend to avail himself of either option, but until an alternative presented itself... "Although your offer is intriguing, I will not leave without my sister."

"This again." Katherine sighed. "Are you not even curious? Look before you at the creatures we have altered." She reached into the sack and pulled forth a yellow lump. "Sulfur, I am told, is a key component of keratin."

"A protein found in horns and hooves."

"And skin." She tossed the sulfur crystal to the pteryform, who swallowed it whole. The young man, now back at her side, handed her a... flamethrower? "Much like you seek to modify human bones, your potential scientific comrades have discovered a way to modify the skin of a pteryform. Provide them with enough sulfur in their diet and..."

She lifted the flamethrower and pulled the trigger. Flames roared forth. Ian took a healthy number of steps backward as she pointed the blaze at the beast's chest. The pteryform reared on its hind feet, spreading its wings and throwing back its head to bare its chest to the flames. Katherine stepped forward and methodically swept the creature's torso from sternum to pelvis.

When the roar ceased, she turned to him. "I'm told it catalyzes a sulfur-mediated cross-reaction of the modified keratin in her scales. All that is needed to develop a natural protection, resistant to almost every weapon." She tipped her head. "And the man who developed this process, he specifically asked for you. So. Will you come?"

Irritation pricked his skin. How had reports of his research reached Siberia? "Not without my sister."

Katherine swore in Russian, then shoved the flamethrower back into the arms of the young man. "Time to face reality, Ian. Elizabeth's days are numbered. Warrick is not half the scientist you are."

Only a truly horrible woman could think flattery made up for blithely predicting his sister's death. "You doubt his cure then?"

"I'd be a fool not to." She paced in a circle, then threw up her hands. "Fine. Elizabeth can come upon one condition. You must prove to me—here, in Germany—that *your* bone treatment works."

They'd not be traveling anywhere with a Russian spy, but if it bought her cooperation, he could pretend to acquiesce to her plans. "Bone remineralization takes time."

"Take all you require."

Ian stared at her. "You intend to toss aside Warrick the moment you're sure of his replacement."

Her eyes narrowed. "Think what you will of me, but I am tasked with recruiting talent. I will not abandon him if he is worth something."

"And my sister is not." It grew harder to keep the tone of his voice steady and even.

"Now you understand."

Katherine possessed no empathy. None. Anger swelled in his chest. "I will not leave here until I have exhausted every possibility of finding her a cure."

She crossed her arms. "I may give you no choice."

"Then you will not have recruited anything, for I will refuse to work." Under no circumstances could he let Katherine move them all to Russia. To travel there was to disappear forever.

They glared at each other until Katherine threw her hands in the air. "Fine. He builds a solution."

Builds? "I need details." Hope rekindled. He'd been certain Warrick lied.

"I am no scientist. I care only if it works... or if it does not. The count, he is not a patient man. Doktor Warrick's time grows short. Much of his work is now concentrated at the mill."

"The mill?"

"Yes," she answered. "The grist mill at the river's edge."

"And?"

She shrugged. "He builds a prototype."

"A prototype of what?"

"What do I care?" Katherine waved a hand in the air. "He promises it will stop the cancer." She stepped closer. "I prefer the disease never starts. Can your treatment promise that?"

"It can." In rats. Probably in humans. But testing that was the last thing he intended to do outside of Britain. "Take me to the mill."

"Ha! Take yourself to the mill. I have my role to play, and it does not include any overt interference in my husband's work. You managed to escape today. Do so again. So long as your sister remains locked in her tower, I can count upon your return to the castle." Katherine leaned close and lowered her voice. "For if you whisper of our negotiations to the count, I *will* reveal your wife's parentage. My husband has exerted such restraint during your visit. It would be a shame for her to be introduced to his collection of knives."

Every muscle in his body tensed. He couldn't allow that to happen. Sneaky she might be, but he very much doubted Olivia had been trained to withstand torture.

CHAPTER TWENTY-FIVE

T HE DOOR TO THE turret room slammed open. Zheng stared at her with dark, cold eyes. "I warned the count you would be trouble."

"The door was unlocked," Olivia protested. A slight tremor shook her voice. She'd known she would likely be caught, but had hoped for a somewhat sympathetic guardsman. Zheng's cold-blooded stare unnerved her. Still, she turned her back on him, as an innocent would, reaching to close the window with a shaking hand—and gasped. "Is that..." She spun back. "Someone is riding a pteryform!"

"The countess," Zheng informed her. "A common sight. Yet not your concern. A guardsman is dead, and your husband is missing. *This* should concern you. Where is he?"

Ian must have seen her leave. By now, he could be anywhere. Except he wouldn't leave his sister behind. "That man in the hall was already dead. Lord Rathsburn is not responsible. If you wish to cast blame, blame Warrick."

"Please," Elizabeth called. "She's hurt no one."

"Out," Zheng ordered. "You go to the count."

The count? She swallowed. The man was unstable and without Ian by her side... "That's not necessary. I need to return to the laboratory. I only came here to collect medical data from—"

Zheng reached out with strong fingers and gripped her arm, half-dragging her from the room, and marched her through the corridors of the castle. They passed many ill guardsmen whose eyes followed her with a mixture of hope and despair. She was to be reprimanded by the count, by a man who thought nothing of forcing potential poison down a child's throat? A chill slid down her spine.

They came to a sudden stop. "You stay where you are placed. Next time, there will be no leniency." Zheng swung a door open and thrust her roughly into a room.

Olivia stumbled forward and came face to face with the terrifying tusks of an enormous wild boar. She let out a yelp of terror and leapt away, colliding with Count Eberwin.

The count caught her about the waist with an amused laugh. "Impressive, is he not?"

She gulped. It was a stuffed boar. A well-preserved hunting trophy. "Very life-like," she agreed.

The count's regal military dress was gone, replaced by brown breeches and tall, black leather boots. From his shoulders hung a brown, double-breasted jacket with tarnished brass buttons and dark, Loden lapels. Hunting attire.

She tried to step away, but he moved a hand to the small of her back, guiding her deeper into the dim room. "Welcome to my *Jagdzimmer*. Each member of my collection was brought down by traditional hunting methods, those which require skill and training. Nothing so prosaic as a rifle."

Gaping, she took in the variety of animals whose heads adorned the walls. A warthog. A pteryform. Moose and deer. Something she thought might be a wildebeest, and a number of other horned and hoofed creatures she could not put a name to. Overhead, candles flickered in a chandelier constructed of horns. A rack of swords and crossbows stood beside the fire.

Death glorified by a man who reveled in the thrill of the hunt.

With lead in her stomach, she turned to face him. "Your trophy room is densely and exotically... populated, *Graf* Eberwin-Katzeneinbogen." Flattery, she hoped, would get her everywhere.

"I rarely miss my mark." He rocked back on his heels, chest puffed and eyes gleaming. "It is one of the many reasons I adore life here at Burg Kerzen. So many wild beasts prowling the woods. One doesn't need to venture far at all in order to hone one's skills."

"So it seems."

"You must wonder, *Frau* Rathsburn, why I bring you to this room." He lifted her hand and, wrapping it about his arm, drew her further into the room, toward the large, central fireplace where a fire blazed.

Stretched out before the hearth was a long, canvas-wrapped lump. A dark pool of liquid stained the fabric. The canvas... its shape...

Count Eberwin snapped his fingers and Zheng strode forth, reaching for the canvas, yanking, lifting. A man's body spilled forth, an arrow protruding from his chest, blood staining his shirt. But his face—her heart climbed into her throat—his face was that of a monster. Raw, oozing lumps covered his jaw.

Gravity lost its meaning and the room tipped. She fisted her free hand. Open. Shut. She tensed her thighs. Her arms. Tensed every single muscle. Slowly, the room wobbled back onto its axis.

The count nudged the body with the toe of his boot. "Of late, it seems I hunt more men than beasts. As the cancer spreads, the pain eats into their bodies. Some die writhing upon their cots. Some take their own lives. Some, they go mad. They run. And we must hunt them down."

"Must?"

"It is a merciful thing, to kill a once loyal guardsman, to end his pain. And I can't have my secret reaching the next village. Not when success is in reach." His lips twisted into something approximating a smile as he looked down at her. "I fear you and I got off to a bad beginning, *Frau* Rathsburn. Please, sit." He waved to a chair.

It was not a request. Olivia obeyed.

The count sat across from her upon a settee and crossed his legs as if a body lying upon the floor was an everyday occurrence. She felt hot. Then cold. Perhaps it was. "Why did you leave the laboratory?" He tapped a finger upon the arm of his chair.

Terror ran across her skin like a many-legged insect, and

she tensed, waiting for it to bite. "The door was unlocked, and I thought to evaluate *Fräulein* Elizabeth's medical condition."

"Doktor Warrick is monitoring her." The count frowned. "He will report any changes in her condition to your husband. I cannot allow my guests—which we both understand to mean prisoners, do we not, *Frau* Rathsburn?" She gave a sharp nod. "I cannot allow guests to wander the castle unaccompanied, no matter their *stated* intentions."

"Understood." She kept her voice steady and controlled as she met his eyes. Better to look at the count than at the dead guardsman.

His expression grew fierce as he leaned closer. "You are here to work. Your husband is to focus upon a cure for my men. Your task is to make that device of his operational. I *will* have guardsmen with silver skeletons. At any cost."

She recalled his threat to see her implanted with Warrick's deadly cells and her heart gave a great thud of terror. Time to plan for the possibility that escape might prove impossible. "Doktor Warrick has been uncooperative, and our research progresses at a snail's pace without his assistance. Might I beg for more time, Count Eberwin?"

"Beg?" His gaze swept over her, lingering with interest upon her breasts for a moment before he gripped her chin between his fingers and tipped her face upward. "I like the sound of that. You on your knees before me."

His breath was hot and moist. She closed her eyes as a wave of revulsion overtook her. Every fiber of her being wished to jerk away. "I wasn't offering..." She trailed off, not wishing to hasten her—or Ian's—demise.

"No? A shame." He dropped her chin. "Let me know if you change your mind. I might just accept."

"Darling!" Katherine strode into the room, her cheeks pink and her hair wind-blown. She tossed a leather jacket, gloves and a riding crop into Zheng's arms before seating herself upon the settee beside the count. She pecked his bearded cheek with a kiss. "I see you had a successful hunt."

Olivia's eyes widened. He'd shot his own guardsman while mounted upon a... "Both of you ride upon pteryformes?"

"Much superior to horses," the count replied. He squeezed his wife's knee. "My bride promised me a good ride, and she has delivered. In more ways than one."

"Hush. She's but a newlywed." Katherine slapped her husband playfully. "I'm so sorry to be late to tea, but look who I found wandering our halls." Her hand waved at the chair beside Olivia. "Do join us, Lord Rathsburn."

With a dark look that promised Olivia much later grief, Ian stalked across the room and sat. "Are we to pretend to manners again? In the presence of a murdered man lying in an ever-expanding pool of blood?"

Olivia pressed a hand to her throat. "Ian," she hissed in warning. The count and countess were twisted in ways she barely understood, but even she knew they ought not insult those who held all the blades.

"Yes, how obtuse to point out such an obvious threat." Katherine heaved a sigh. "Scientists. Is it any wonder they're social outcasts?" She glanced about. "Where is that artifact of a steambot?

"I'm afraid your tea service has gone astray, *leibling.*" The count fixed Olivia with a stare that pierced her skull. "As did our guests. *Frau* Rathsburn was discovered in the turret room." He rose to his feet. Hands behind his back, he moved to study the array of weapons mounted upon his wall. "We were discussing the future consequences of such wanderings." He lifted a spear. "Any progress to report, *Herr* Rathsburn?"

"None. Warrick is exceptionally disorganized and refuses to answer my questions. He prefers to consume your wine rather than assist me in the laboratory. In fact," Ian crossed his arms, his voice accusative, "the last I saw him, he was flouncing off to see about a copper delivery."

Katherine narrowed her eyes at Ian as something ominous passed between them. "I left Doktor Warrick tending to the guardsmen in the barracks before my ride."

What had Olivia missed in the short time they'd been separated?

"Zheng," the count barked. "Deliver these two back to the laboratory, then locate and impress upon Doktor Warrick —forcefully—the necessity of his cooperation."

CHAPTER TWENTY-SIX

OLIVIA STOMPED ACROSS the wine cellar to the corner laboratory. The count's indecent offer rang in her head. All her training to become a societal liaison was a resounding success. She attracted only men with prurient desires. She glanced at Ian. Decent, honorable gentlemen weren't interested. Her mistake to hope otherwise.

But now was not the time to wallow in self-pity; threats had a way of generating inspiration, one of which had struck. Snatching up a pencil, she scribbled out a critical insight. *That* was the right equation. She reached for the Franconian multipunch she'd smuggled to the laboratory beneath her skirts. Moments later she held a series of cards that would allow for a smooth insertion of the needles.

Ian appeared at her elbow, and she caught a whiff of the jasmine perfume favored by Katherine. Her heart ached, but she refused to acknowledge the irrational flare of jealousy that made her stomach burn. "Impressive," he commented, bending over her work.

Once such recognition would have made her beam with pride. Today she rather felt like smacking him. For challenging the count. For not immediately launching into an account of his time with the countess. She didn't look up. "I need your arm."

Without hesitation, Ian unfastened his cuff and rolled up his sleeve. "My sister?"

"Elizabeth is fine." She flipped a series of levers, locking the device into place. "The metal framework positions the injectors, but the program controls their descent. To test the response of the pressure sensors, the injectors should release fluid—water—when they encounter resistance from your skin."

"Fine?" Impatience roughened his voice. "That's all you have to report?"

So *he* need not elaborate, but *she* was expected to detail her time away from him? Unfair. "Our visit lasted mere minutes. We shared a cup of tea. I inquired as to her health." Olivia didn't mention the contemplated escape plan. He was certain to object. Elizabeth would consult Wei about the particulars, and only then would Olivia inform him of their plans. "We discussed Warrick."

Shifting impatiently on his feet, Ian pressed for more information. "And?"

"He gave her a promise stone. This." She pulled the smooth lump from her pocket and dropped it into his free hand.

Ian turned the gray stone over in his palm. He stuck it to the incubator's metal door. "Magnetite. A magnetic mineral."

"Does it mean anything to you?"

"No." But he slid it into his pocket.

Olivia could feel his questioning gaze on her as she flipped a switch. Good. Let him wonder what she left out. The small motor of the device began to hum. "If this works, there will be no avoiding the needles. I cannot program the hydraulics until they are in place."

"You seem rather... steady, considering the topic." He chose his words carefully. Too carefully.

"I am annoyed." She planted her hands on her hips. "My blood pressure is elevated."

"As is mine."

She pursed her lips and narrowed her eyes.

Nostrils flaring, he leaned forward. "Fine. Directness it is. Look me in the eye, Olivia, and explain. Picking a lock? Waltzing from the laboratory over a dead body? Skulking about speaking to guardsmen? *In German.*"

"Father insisted all his children speak German, the language of Britain's sworn enemy. Now hold still," she snapped, refusing to meet his eyes, refusing to relent until he shared whatever had passed between him and Katherine. "I don't need additional variables."

"German. The better to spy upon Britain's enemies?"

What could it hurt, a small boast? "I speak French and Icelandic as well. A little Russian."

"A very agent-like answer, which is to say, not really an

answer at all. Not that it explains the lock picking." He reached for her chin, but she stepped back and glared at him. She'd had enough of such treatment.

Gears turned, silently and smoothly, gradually encasing Ian's forearm in a copper and steel cage. The pressure sensors leaked fluid as they bit into his arm, stopping just as they threatened to break skin. A twinge of guilt niggled; there would be bruises, but his arm was locked in place. What better time to begin an interrogation?

"You smell of Katherine's perfume," she accused. "Explain that."

He flipped a lever. The injector released with a slow hiss. "You're jealous." He sounded surprised. "Why?" Lever by lever, he set his arm free.

"Perhaps it's all a part of my act. I *am* supposed to be your wife." This argument was ridiculous. They weren't married. He'd made her no vows. Why then could she not let the matter drop? "What brought the two of you so close today? Don't bother denying it. I've heard enough stories, endured her allusions to your past along with her appreciative glances at your backside."

His ears burned red, but he refused to bite. "Why did you not tell me that you knew her?"

"Also not an answer." Olivia crossed her arms. They were getting nowhere. Grudgingly, she informed him, "Lady Katherine and I were never formally introduced."

"Yet she attended your debut?" Ian's eyebrows flew upward.

"Uninvited, yes. She rather ruined the event. If not for

her I would..." *Be married to a traitor. Perhaps widowed.* All true, but not the reason for her anger. Her frustration. She stared into Ian's brilliant, blue eyes. For the first time, she wanted a man for himself, not simply to complete an assigned task, to move another rung higher toward her goal. Sharing secrets and desires had twisted her feelings into something new, into something she didn't recognize.

"Your insinuations are unfounded," he said, shaking his head. "I—"

She didn't want to know; it would hurt too much. Olivia turned and stalked away. It was darker midst the wine barrels and easier to hide the tears that welled in her eyes. How stupid of her to let emotions rule her behavior. She'd been warned—again and again—never to let the heart grow fond.

His footsteps followed. "Olivia, wait." He caught her by the hips and spun her around. "Before we met, I proposed to Katherine. A misguided attempt to fulfill an obligation the Queen forced upon me to marry, to produce an heir. But there is nothing between us. There never was and never will be. Not only is she married, she's a Russian spy."

Blinking at the onslaught of unexpected information, she repeated, "A spy?"

He nodded and a flood of words rushed forth. Her jaw dropped as he spoke of tame pteryformes with reinforced hides and an offer to emigrate east. Her stomach flipped. Why did every escape scenario involve aerial acrobatics?

"Did you not inform me that China is the leading producer of antimony?" she asked, recalling the murderously coded punch card slipped into the butler's daily schedule of commands. "If so, why attempt to kill Zheng? Why not also invite him to Russia?"

"Russia possesses antimony, but has yet to fully develop its mines. A resource they would expand if they possessed the ability to quietly generate their own elementally enhanced soldiers."

"And no one would be the wiser until they marched upon their enemy."

"Exactly." His voice grew harder as if his words twisted with steel wire. "Now. What did Katherine do to you? Steal away your suitors?"

An entire failed Season explained so simply. Katherine a spy. The countess had indeed stolen her suitors. Or, rather, targets. Close enough. "Yes."

"Good. For as much as you hate to think of me with her, I hate to think of you with another man." His hands still at her hips, Ian backed her against the stacks of wine barrels as he stared into her eyes. "I never wanted to touch her. But you," his voice grew rough, making her entire body hum with awareness, "you drive me insane."

Flames flickered behind his eyes. With a little fanning, could she set him ablaze?

Always her targets' physical interest in her had been something to be manipulated and endured. But with Ian... Finally, Olivia understood what made otherwise intelligent young women follow gentlemen out on balconies, down stairs and under the shelter of a private arbor, risking both their reputations and their futures. She shouldn't act on these feelings. She knew that. Yet after breaking so many unwritten rules, why not overstep a few more?

A thrill ran over her skin, and a deep hunger settled low in her belly. Lifting a hand to his cravat, she tugged his mouth close. "How fortunate for you, then, that you are my first... instructor," she whispered. "And know that I very much enjoyed yesterday's practical, hands-on tutorial even if we reached no definitive conclusion."

Ian dropped his gaze to her lips.

"Might I persuade you to offer another private lesson?" Heat flooded her as she dragged her hands down his chest and slipped her fingers beneath the edge of his waistband. She shocked herself with her boldness. "A more *advanced* lesson?"

His laugh was low and dark, but he didn't pull away. "You won't give up, will you?"

"Do you want me to?" She brushed her thumb against the topmost button of his trousers.

"No." Dipping his head, he caught her lips with his own, and for a moment she forgot to breathe. He pulled away. "But I want something in return."

"And what is that?" She freed the button.

"You claim not to be a spy." His fingers fell on the tiny jet buttons beneath her chin, unfastening one after the other, moving steadily downward. "Yet neither are you a civilian. Explain." He paused. "Or shall we cancel today's class?"

No. Not that. Anything but that. "I'm not a field agent," she breathed. "I am—was—a societal liaison."

The last button popped loose, and he pushed her bodice

apart. He yanked her corset downward, spilling her breasts free. "Beautiful," he said, lifting a finger to trace their swell. "What—exactly—is a societal liaison?" He cupped the weight of one breast and ran his thumb across her nipple, scraping it with the tip of his nail.

She gasped as the thrill of his touch shot through her entire body, then regrouped, gathering in a tight knot of need between her thighs. "An innocent young woman who marries whomever the Queen chooses." Arching her back, she pressed her breast fully into his warm hand, demanding more. "Marries a gentleman whose activities are suspect."

"A target. Such as Lord Snyder?" He bent his head low, the slight stubble of his chin rasping against her skin as he nibbled the sensitive tip. "Answer me, Olivia." The hot wet of his mouth engulfed her nipple, sucking it deep into his mouth.

"Yes!" Warmth flooded her sex and left her mewling. *Aether.* She clawed at the buttons of his waistcoat, needing to feel more of him. The heat of his bare chest against her own, its crisp hairs brushing over her skin. Increasingly desperate fingers hurried down the row of buttons before greedily applying themselves to those of his shirtsleeves.

He caught her wrists. "And you were to...?"

"Flirt, marry, take control of the household. Keep my mouth shut and my eyes and ears open. Report any and all suspicious behavior to my superiors."

Dark eyes looked down at her, waiting.

She whimpered. What more did he want? "A societal

liaison is not field trained. I've no ability to fly a dirigible, steer a submersible. Slip about in any manner of disguise. I've never used a pistol, a sword—or any knife, save those found in a kitchen." Not for lack of trying, but no amount of badgering agents had convinced them to train her in even the most basic of techniques.

He released her wrists. "Am I your new target?"

Not a question she wanted to answer. She parted the linen, exposing hard planes of skin and muscle to view, humming in appreciation. "My education seems to have stalled." With a single finger, she traced the hair of his chest as it narrowed over his stomach to disappear behind the edge of his unbuttoned waistband. "I do so wonder where this directs my attention." Sliding her hand beneath the material, she cupped his long, thick—and very hard—length. "*This* is supposed to fit inside me?"

HE GROANED, but caught her wrist and twisted away. "No. It's not." No matter how much he wanted her. "That is a far more advanced lesson than I am prepared to offer."

Standing there in the shadows, her bodice gaping open to expose the smooth skin of her generous breasts and their rosy nipples to the flickering light of the torches, she was his every fantasy. He swallowed and leashed the primitive beast that had roared its approval the moment she'd touched him. Conscious choices needed to be made, and logic needed to prevail.

She raised her eyebrows. "I begin to doubt the qualifications of my tutor."

Ian almost laughed. "In your enthusiasm, you rush past several important steps."

"Oh?"

"If you will stop trying to divert my attention..." He stabbed his fingers into her hair and pulled her close, kissing her deeply, tasting tea and sugar on her lips. Stepping forward, he crushed her against the stacked barrels, reveling in the feel of her taut nipples against the rough hairs covering his chest. Only when her heart pounded next to his, did he drag his mouth away to stare down into her dark, unfocused eyes. "Am I your new target?" he repeated. He hated using her—their—desire against her, but he wanted answers.

She huffed in frustration, digging her fingernails into the muscles of his back. "No. I mean, yes."

"Which is it, Olivia?" Her nibbled her neck and her knees sagged. "Did Mr. Black send you? Was that you in the alleyway?"

"Yes. I was only to plant the devices in your luggage. But you were about to leave. It was the perfect chance to prove my worth as a field agent without first having to take a husband..."

Curious. He dropped his hands to her sides and gathered the wool of her skirts and petticoats in his hands, drawing their hems upward—and found no other undergarments between them and her stockings. Lust knocked reason aside and growled low in his throat. His hands swept over the firm, round swells of her buttocks, and catching her beneath her thighs, he lifted her as he pressed his straining shaft against her center. *Sweet torture.*

"Ian!" Her hips flexed. "Please. Don't stop."

He froze. Didn't dare move. He was too close to the edge, too close to taking her here, now, against this very wine cask, but he suspected she was a virgin. And he had more questions to ask. He inhaled deeply, willing control, forcing his body to cooperate. A question—and perhaps her answer—might dampen his lust. "Do you have an assigned target?" he asked between gritted teeth.

"I do. In Rome."

"Who?" Olivia as someone else's wife. The thought didn't sit well.

"Can we not talk of this later?" she pleaded, squirming against him.

"No." He shifted and dropped one of her legs, letting that foot touch the floor. He trailed a finger up her soft, smooth inner thigh, his gaze locked with hers. When he reached the apex of her thighs, he found her hot and wet. For him. God, he wanted inside her. Now. Instead, he slipped a single finger along her damp folds. "Tell me who, or I'll stop."

Her nails dug into his shoulders. "Bastard."

"Such language." What he wouldn't do to hear her scream in pleasure. But he stilled his hand.

"A Baron Volscini," she gasped. "He is old, nearly eighty. Widowhood is a requirement for a woman to work in the field, but I don't want him. I *want* you. I *want* this." She pressed against his hand.

"Of your own free will."

"Yes!" Frustration laced her voice.

"No more lies, no more attempts to manipulate me?" To survive, they needed to cooperate, to work together.

Lifting her eyes to his, she whispered, "Only if you promise the same."

"Done."

"Then no more."

Ian heard the truth in her words and knew she was doing nothing more than trying to direct her own fate. As was he. Together, they had a chance of escape, of a future they controlled. Did he dare hope?

Enough. This lesson had become all too serious. He bent his head low and his lips brushed across hers, tender and sweet. When he pulled back, he let a naughty grin tug at his lips. "Then it's time to bring this lesson to an explosive climax." He pressed the pad of his thumb against her swollen center and stroked a slow, circular pattern. "What would you have me do, Olivia? Kiss your full lips? Tease your stunning breasts, or should I concentrate all my attention here, between your legs where your body is hot and begging for my attention?"

"God, Ian." Her hands wrapped around his neck. "I can't think. I can barely stand."

"Choose." He gritted his teeth.

"Between," she gasped. "But more. I need..."

He slid his finger deeper into her tight channel, working her. "Better?"

Face contorted in frustrated pleasure, her hips bucked against his hand. "No. Still... empty."

So perfect. His body ached for release as he slid a second finger inside, stretching her, filling her. He wanted her to the point of mindless insanity, but as her eyes fell closed on a groan, he vowed her first time would not be here, in a cellar.

Instead he would taste her, feel her come apart in his mouth. With one hand he pinned her hips against the barrel as he lowered himself to his knees. Tossing her leg over his shoulder, he clamped his mouth against her hot, wet center and teased her with his tongue, with his lips—all while plunging his fingers deep inside her.

"Oh!" she cried out, arching her neck, tipping her head backward against a wooden cask as the room turned upside-down. Shockwaves of new, spectacular sensations rolled over her as he licked and—she gasped—sucked. His fingers withdrew and plunged again. "Oh, yes. That. *That!*" It was almost too much.

Heart pounding, lungs gasping, and skin burning hot, a fever consumed her, one that was increasingly demanding release. She strained against him shamelessly, burying her fingers in his hair. "Ian, I—"

Something snapped and she came apart beneath his mouth, his hand. She bucked, crying out as her climax tore through her, spreading outward in waves, leaving her limp and drained.

Carefully, he lowered her onto the floor beside him and

wrapped an arm about her, pulling her tight to his side as he drew deep, ragged breaths.

"Mmm," she hummed against his bare chest. "That was wonderful." Far, far better than she'd dared hope or imagine, because it was Ian, a man she *wanted* to touch her. She looked up into his tense face. Instinctually, she knew his body was tense with unmet need. Reaching for the buttons at his waist, she purred, "It's only fair we both finish."

He caught her hand. "No." There was no heat left in his eyes.

"But." After such intimacy, how could he—

"Look." He pointed. "We're not alone."

A tiny, brown bird fluttered above them. A nightingale.

CHAPTER TWENTY-SEVEN

OLIVIA YANKED HER corset upward, her fingers flying over the buttons of her bodice. "Hurry," she said. "Make yourself presentable. That's Wei's toy nightingale. She must be nearby."

Ian turned his attention to his own buttons, willing his arousal to subside. Overhead, the clockwork bird fluttered, flipping and flapping in circles.

"Is it safe?" a small voice sounded from the dark, cavernous space where wine casks were stacked to the ceiling.

This child had the worst timing, but if she could get in, perhaps there was also a way out.

He stood, the ground not feeling quite stable beneath his feet despite its flagstones. Was this what it felt like when a woman threatened to steal a piece of your heart? He'd lost all awareness of anything but how Olivia felt, how she sounded, smelled, tasted. Ian held out a hand, pulling her to her feet and against his chest wishing there was more time to explore her soft curves, for her to explore him. *Later.* "I still have more questions." He kept his voice low as he stroked the back of his finger over her still-flushed cheek. "And you've promised not to lie."

"I've not much more to tell you." She glanced at him from beneath lowered eyelashes, and a faint blush rose to her cheeks. "But if you'd like to question me again later..."

He laughed into her hair. He'd like to do so much more. She'd driven him close to the edge as she fell apart beneath his hand, his mouth. Next time he doubted he'd have the willpower to stop her wandering hands. Even now, it took effort to let go as Olivia pulled away, smoothing her skirts as she moved back into the pool of light.

"It's safe," she called to Wei. Metal grated against stone as Olivia stretched out a finger and the bird fluttered downward, perching upon it and cocking its tiny head.

"I'll add an ability to charm mechanical animals to your list of skills." So many talents all hidden from view. What would he discover next?

"It's built of tin, silk and paper mâché," she said. "Wei brought it to me broken. I fixed it. A worn gear was the difficulty, an easy enough repair." The bird hopped from her finger, launching itself back into the air.

Wei, her face streaked with dirt, danced into the bright circle of light cast by the argon lamps. She stretched out a hand, and the nightingale alighted. With great care, she tucked the bird inside her pocket and studied the collection of scientific equipment before her with wide eyes. She pointed at the osforare apparatus. "Does it bite?"

"It does." Olivia pulled a cobweb from the girl's hair. "It's not safe, Wei, creeping about the castle."

"True. But a man sends me." Wei's expression grew serious. "His name is... Dark."

"Black?" he asked.

"Yes. That." Wei nodded. "He say he found your airship."

Olivia caught his hand, squeezing it with delight. "Help has arrived."

That hadn't taken long. Black must have been called in the moment Olivia turned up missing. Ian swore and shook her hand free. "He's not supposed to be here. Interference could ruin everything."

Would Black be here if the duke's daughter hadn't stowed away? Perhaps. He *had* sent her to plant those acousticotransmitters. Yet even if he'd only arrived to escort Olivia safely home, Black didn't leave a task half-finished. He wouldn't agree to leave him behind unless he'd repossessed both the transforming biochemicals and the osforare apparatus. But Ian couldn't let those leave his possession as a cure alone would not satisfy the count. Furthermore, if Olivia and the device disappeared, he would lose Katherine's limited support and the count would know enemy agents had infiltrated his village. With increased security, he and Elizabeth might never escape.

"No help." Wei shook her head. "He hurt bad. Snuck too close to countess' leather birds. One bite his leg."

"Oh no!" Olivia's hand flew to her mouth.

The image of a chicken and a sharp beak flashed through Ian's mind. He'd not wish that end on anyone. "How bad?"

"Stephan—countess' leather bird stable boy—and I take him to gypsies. They say he will walk again." Wei frowned. "He grumbles much and tries to stand too soon. So I come with message." She straightened and pulled back her shoulders. "Black heard your airship, but already too late. *Sky Dragon* captain stripped much from inside and drained aether. Black sent gypsies to buy it as scrap and drag to other side of mountain. He try to make it fly again. Says everyone need to leave. Lady, husband, sister."

"Did Black say that?" His lips twitched. "Use the word husband?"

"I say. He laughed."

Olivia flushed bright red.

Ian was a dead man. Condemned by a single word. *Husband.* But the term had grown on him. As had a certain sense of possessiveness...

"I thought maybe you tunnel out, like rats." Wei twisted her lips into a frown. "But pipe too narrow. You get stuck."

He crouched before Wei. "Tell Black we cannot leave, not yet. Not before we visit the mill."

"The mill?" Olivia asked.

"Something the countess let slip. Warrick's so-called cure apparently lies in the grist mill."

"I help," Wei announced. "I have perfect distractions. Slip us pass the guardsmen. We go darkest hours before dawn. Three strikes of the clock. Back before sun rises."

"It's not safe," Olivia said. Lines furrowed her brow. It was much to ask of a child. "Perhaps if we formally request the count for an escort—"

"No." Ian shook his head. "Warrick and Katherine are hiding this from him, from Zheng. There might be reason. We do this covertly. With Wei's assistance. Then—after—she can carry news directly to Black."

Olivia frowned. "You will end with an arrow in your back. The count did offer to grant us more time if I..." She swallowed, dragged in a deep breath and—with a soft whisper—threw herself on the sword instead. "If I agreed to grant him certain personal favors."

In his bed? The question must have registered on his face, for she nodded. "No. Unacceptable." Ian caught Wei's small hand and walked her back to the drainage pipe. "Go. Stay safe. I will question Warrick and learn all I can before our trip." He lowered the metal grate to the floor and strode back to Olivia to cup her skull. "Understand this. I don't care that it might work. My *wife* will not play the whore. You are mine and mine alone."

His kiss was hard, almost punishing, yet she leaned into him, matching every thrust of his tongue with her own. He had to force himself to pull away.

"Yours," she breathed. "I like the sound of that."

Ian stared at her swollen lips and something feral inside him stirred. He shoved it back inside its cage. "Something to consider another time. Right now, I need to insist upon some answers." He dropped his hands and strode up the stairs to the cellar door. Pounding on its ancient boards, he yelled, "Open the door! I demand to speak with Warrick."

Zheng slammed open the door. "Stop your infernal noise. He's on his way."

They glared at each other, jaws tightly clenched.

Several long, tense moments later two guardsmen marched Warrick through the door. Only then did Ian redirect his gaze. "About time. We have much to discuss."

"Do we?" Warrick sauntered past, managing a tight nod to Olivia as he snagged a beaker from the workbench and strolled to a nearby barrel. With the turn of a spigot, he decanted fifty centiliters into his makeshift glass and tossed it back. "Riesling," he said. "A nice apple undertone, but I believe it's spent too much time in that oak barrel. Good of me to liberate it. Sure you don't want any?"

Ian snatched the glassware from his hand and threw it to the ground. It shattered upon the stone floor. "Time runs out for both of us. I could save you. Why will you not work with me?"

"I wondered when you'd finally snap. So calm. So collected. Always in the right." Warrick leaned back against the workbench, his elbows propped upon its surface. "Why? Because it amuses me to see you in such an impossible situation. Your research and reputation are in ruins, you have no answers, no possibility of escape. To top it all off, your bride is your Achilles heel. Turnabout is a sweet, sweet thing to witness."

"Turnabout?" *What the hell is he talking about?*

"Yes. Turnabout. I loved Elizabeth. Despite appearances, I still do." Warrick's mouth flattened. "A year ago, my life was stolen from me. If your bride is snatched from your arms as was mine, then I shall consider it a boon."

"Unlike you, I would do anything to keep Olivia safe. Imprisonment and experimentation?" Ian sneered. "Not the best method to win a woman's esteem. Whatever happened, you brought it upon yourself."

"Perhaps. But your own father, the great seventh Earl of Rathsburn, agreed with my methods. Your slow, methodical work exasperated him. Years of schooling, years of research and still no cure. When I proposed we present my research to the Committee for the Exploration of Anthropomorphic Peculiarities and suggest Elizabeth as a candidate for treatment, he agreed."

Olivia gasped. So she knew far more than she'd admitted. No more lies, they'd agreed, but it seemed they'd yet to share all their secrets.

Betrayed by his own father. Was it possible? Pain stabbed through him as he remembered the constant missives, how Father's inquiries into the progress of his work had increased in frequency following Elizabeth's engagement. And then the letters had simply stopped. His own father had lost faith in him? Grasped at Warrick's offer instead? Possible.

No. Probable. Father was often sick that last year, and a man who once seized upon the promises made by every charlatan to arrive with a black doctor's bag in hand... "You took advantage of a sick, old man," Ian accused. "Of a man you proposed to call family."

"*Because* I care for Elizabeth. Your research proceeds at a snail's pace. Your father knew he was dying and wanted to see his daughter cured. *I* don't want my wife terrified to bear children, and time runs out for her. Already it may be too late." Warrick's nostrils flared. "I was thrilled when the committee accepted my proposal and offered generous funding. We were slated to begin as soon as the wedding took place. Until you ruined everything."

Ian sliced a hand through the air. "By bringing your unethical behavior to light, I saved her."

"And lost your father," Warrick snapped back. "That too you brought upon yourself."

Ice shot down his spine. "Explain."

"I had no choice. When you denounced me to the Duke of Avesbury, your sister broke our engagement, and your father wanted to step forward and reveal all. Had he named the members of CEAP, my life would have been forfeit. Loose ends had to be tied up and quickly."

Ian clenched his fists and gave Warrick one last chance to save himself. "Loose ends?"

Warrick smirked and turned over one palm. "Was it lung fever?" Then the other. "Or antimony poisoning? The two so closely resemble each other."

With a roar, Ian surged forward, grabbing him about the throat, pinning him to the stone wall. "Murderer! You deserve to die."

Zheng shouted a warning and Ian loosened his grip. Slightly. Enough to allow a bare minimum of blood flow to the man's brain.

"Possibly. But you need me." Warrick laughed darkly. "Your refusal to break rules is rigid and naïve. It leaves you... vulnerable. The committee wanted nothing to do with you. Even your father-in-law had been left in the dark. Not a very trusting man, is he?"

Ian growled.

"Oh, yes," Warrick breathed. "I know exactly who Olivia is. It makes my work here that much more poignant. Tell me, how much longer before the Queen's agents arrive?"

"I do not work for him."

Not anymore. Not since the duke had attributed Warrick's illicit research to him, flinging allegations of wrongdoing without first verifying the source. Ian had dropped his TTX pistol on the man's desk, turned his back, and left. No one had ever dared do such a thing. The duke had been furious, and Ian had nearly lost his position at Lister that day.

Later, there had been apologies, but no explanations. It was too little, too late.

"Are you so certain?" Warrick taunted. "The Duke of Avesbury rarely draws clear boundaries. If you work for Lister Laboratories, you work for him."

Manipulated by him would be a more accurate assessment. "Give me a reason not to kill you."

"Were you not listening? Though Elizabeth's mind was poisoned against me, I vowed to see her cured. My cells *will* save her."

Ian tamped down the simmering rage that threatened to boil over and shoved Warrick away from him. The man was talking, and that meant he would live. For now. "This cure you purport to design, what has it to do with copper and magnetite?"

Warrick's eyes widened. "How—? Who told you?"

"So confident you are in your patronage, yet a conversation with the countess indicates her loyalties, were I to demonstrate a better method to make a man's bones silver, could easily lie elsewhere."

"The countess' loyalties lie with her husband," Zheng barked, striding forward. "Here. In Germany."

"Do they?" Warrick sneered. "As do yours? A Chinese chemical peddler who overreaches, styling himself a warrior as he tries to climb the rungs of society's ladder. *You* believe in loyalty? I doubt it. The minute I succeed you'll want the biotechnology for your own Emperor. Would he not reward you generously for an army of soldiers with uncleavable silver skulls?"

The metal of Zheng's sword sang as he drew the curved blade from its sheath. "I will have the truth now. If the countess is not loyal to Germany, then who?"

Warrick lifted his hands in the air. "No need to overreact, simply make me a better offer."

"Who?" Zheng took a step forward.

"The countess claims my work for the tsar." Warrick backed away, his eyes wild. "But my work, it's all in my head. You *need* me alive."

"Yet now two men wish you dead." Zheng spit on the ground. "The count has ordered me to *insist* that you share all details of your research with Lord Rathsburn." He pointed his sword at Warrick. "Ask your questions, Lord Rathsburn. The doktor will answer them or I will recommend to the count that he turn him loose so that he might hunt him from the sky."

"What?" Warrick cried. His face turned ashen.

"I've seen the results of the count's last hunting expedition with my own eyes," Ian said. "Rather gruesome. I suggest you cooperate. Now, how can these cancerous bone cells be stopped?"

"By making them grow even faster," Warrick spat out.

"He speaks nonsense." Zheng's blade sliced through in the air.

Behind him, Olivia whimpered. She was right to be worried; a promise of death glinted in Zheng's eyes. "Perhaps not. Let him continue." He wrapped his hand around the barrel auger Warrick had used to tap into the count's wine supply. It was the only metal tool available with any hope of deflecting Zheng's sword.

"Rapid proliferation enlists certain internal cellular mechanisms," Warrick blubbered. "Cells destined to become cancerous can be induced to accumulate a certain toxin and self-destruct."

At last, answers! "What toxin?" Ian demanded. "Respond to what?"

"A cure is possible," Warrick insisted. "It *can* be done, but the minute I tell you how, I'm a dead man."

Entirely possible. If Ian had the answers to save Elizabeth, he would find it difficult to mourn the man's demise. He turned back to Zheng. "Warrick claims he has not kept a written record of his work. I don't believe it. Perhaps you might persuade him to produce his research notes?"

"Perhaps a little bloodletting." Zheng eyed the sharp edge of his blade. "Pain has a way of loosening tongues. Not to mention wolves have such an excellent sense of smell, and the count would enjoy the added challenge of racing against the wolves in an attempt to bring you down."

Warrick's eyes bulged from their sockets. He turned and walked down the narrow path between the wine casks, all but disappearing into the shadows. Wrenching free a barrel lid, he reached inside and dragged forth a handful of loose paper before striding back into their brightly lit corner and dropping the disorganized pile on the workbench. "A puzzle to wrap your mind about."

Ian set down the augur and lifted one sheet of paper, then another. Words were scrawled in every direction. Nothing was dated. Or numbered. A chaotic pile of notes that looked to be written by a mad scientist. It would take days, possibly weeks, to sort through such scribblings. Still, as he flipped through the notations, he saw flashes of brilliance behind the disorder.

Olivia appeared at his elbow, lifting a piece of paper covered in equations. "A Harald-Fletcher formula!" Wide-eyed, she turned to face Warrick. "Can you explain why you think cyclic loading stimulates cell growth?"

"Can I?" From the sound of Warrick's voice, he was back to being recalcitrant.

"Do you have what you need?" Zheng asked.

"I think I just might," Ian said, turning a sheet of paper

sideways. "It appears he was using Mendeleev's periodic table to—"

Olivia screamed and Warrick let out a cry of protest.

Zheng advanced on Warrick, spinning the curved blade in his hand, angling it so the cutting edge aligned with Warrick's neck.

"No!" Ian cried, grabbing the iron barrel auger from the benchtop, lunging between the two men, lifting the augur. The steel sword clanged against the wrought iron cork screw, ripping the tool from his hand. But though he had succeeded in deflecting the blow, he'd not prevented the blade from meeting flesh.

Warrick fell screaming, clutching his arm as blood poured from a deep gash.

"How dare you interfere!" Zheng bellowed.

"He still has information I *need*!" Ian yelled back. He turned back toward Warrick. The wound was deep. The blood was bright red. Ian yanked his cravat from his neck, crouched beside Warrick, and began to apply a tourniquet. "If you care for Elizabeth, now is the time for you to tell me how to save her."

"Toxin in... my coat." Warrick's eyes were glassy, and he gasped for air. "Feed her toxin. Then... the cells... need oscillating m—"

A blade whistled past Ian's eyes. There was a sickening crunch, and Ian stared at a knife protruding from Warrick's chest. Zheng's blade had passed straight through his heart.

He stood, spinning toward Zheng with both hands

clenched into fists. "You bastard! You just signed my sister's death warrant."

Zheng pointed his sword at Ian. "The man was a traitor. You have what you need. I do us all a favor. And do not think to challenge me again, Lord Rathsburn. Next time, I will cleave your hand from its arm."

CHAPTER TWENTY-EIGHT

I F THE GUARDSMEN who escorted them to their room looked a bit panicked, they had good reason. *"Können Sie uns retten?"* one man, his jaw painfully swollen, rasped in German. *Can you save us?*

She caught up his hand and stared at his knobby joints. She couldn't lie. "I don't know," she answered in German. Could she leave behind so many young men, condemn them to death if an answer was in reach? No. "But we will do our best."

"Gunther," the other guardsman barked. "Do not consort with the prisoners."

Any hope that she might convince them to let her walk free in the early hours of the morning evaporated like a drop of water on a hot iron skillet.

The door closed. A key turned.

Setting the armful of scrawled notations he carried onto the desk, Ian crossed the cavernous tomb of their bedchamber to stand at the window and stare through its leaded glass panes. She set down the case holding the osforare apparatus and followed, moving silently to his side. In the far distance a pteryform soared beneath a full moon. She squinted. Did Katherine ride upon its back?

Tempted though she was to admit to her possession—or rather—that Steam Matilda housed an active acousticotransmitter, given Ian's reaction to Mr. Black's presence in the forest, she didn't dare confess. Besides, now was not the time. Warrick had all but admitted to murdering Ian's father to save his own hide. She would offer whatever comfort he'd accept.

"I'm so sorry, Ian." She laid an unsteady hand on his shoulder.

And then his arms were around her waist, pulling her close. She lay her head against his chest and listened to his heart beat as he dragged in a long, ragged breath, struggling for control. They stood together wrapped in silence. For a brief moment, the harsh world about them faded.

All too soon, Ian set her aside. His eyes were tired and tense. "Tell me what you know of this committee, of CEAP."

Given Warrick's revelations, he deserved to know. She swallowed hard, then nodded. "This past fall, while listening at doors, I overheard my father discussing something preposterous with one of his men. He ordered an agent north, to investigate the possibility of selkies on the Scottish shore."

Ian scoffed. "Seals who can shed their skins and take the form of a woman?"

"Such is the myth. From what I could gather, there are

members of our government who believe that myths and fairy tales conceal core truths. They have formed a shadow board, side-stepping rules and regulations of all kinds in an attempt to discover their underlying biological facts."

"They're interested in more than simple facts," Ian said. "It would seem they also strive to create new myths. Men with unbreakable silver bones would easily weave into the fabric of legend." He paused. "I've known the duke to bypass the law before."

"Father would, but only in the most honorable of ways. He wouldn't support men who would willfully harm other humans, no matter what peculiarities or talents they might possess."

"Are you so certain?" Ian asked, his eyes haunted.

"I've no evidence." She caught Ian's eye. Would he believe her? Trust was a fragile thing between them. "But we will ask him when we return."

"I asked once," Ian said. "He refused to acknowledge the existence of shadow boards. He will not answer questions."

"He will answer mine."

Ian stared at her for a long minute, then nodded.

Thoughts of returning to London called to mind Mr. Black, who even now lurked in the German forest, ready to assist their escape. Yet they could not turn tail and run, not until they'd exhausted all possibilities of finding a cure.

"Warrick spoke of rapid growth and the accumulation of toxins. What was it that he whispered as..." As his own blood pooled about him. A horrible death, but one such agents must witness with regularity. Olivia closed her eyes. Perhaps she was not cut out to work in the field after all. "I saw you reach beneath his coat."

Ian pulled a vial of powder from a pocket. "This."

"Antimony?" The moonlight gave the powder a silver cast.

"It can't be antimony. The color is a shade different. Without access to a laboratory, I can't be certain, but I believe it may be arsenic."

"Arsenic!"

"A certain poison. But what if it could be delivered directly to the cancerous cells?" He began to pace. "Warrick told me to feed this to Elizabeth and then to induce rapid cell growth. With his last breath, he told me the cells needed something that oscillated." Ian ran a hand through his hair. "But Zheng's blade cut him off before he could finish."

Olivia forced her mind back to her correspondence coursework. "Oscillating. To move back and forth between two things. Could he have been referring to different forms of energy? Or perhaps he alluded to alternating current, electricity that is constantly changing directions because the voltage follows a sine wave oscillation?"

Ian's steps slowed as understanding dawned. "Does the Rankine Institute even accept females?"

"They do not." A smile curved her lips. "They did, however, grant one Oliver Bird a degree in engineering."

He yanked her against him. "I should have guessed." Warm lips pressed to hers and her pulse jumped, but as quickly as it began, the kiss ended. "Your talents are wasted as a mere societal liaison." He drew her across the room to the desk. "Time to comb through Warrick's notes. I will attempt to unravel the biology behind his claims, but I will need the critical eye of an engineer to decipher this bewildering tangle of equations."

As she'd been forbidden to reveal her engineering skills, not once had anyone ever praised her degree. Father considered it an unnecessary waste of time. Other agents, he'd insisted, would analyze any data she collected. Whereas Mother worried her daughter's over-educated mind might dissuade would-be suitors. A certain lightness filled her chest as Olivia lifted a sheet of paper.

Warrick's penmanship bore much resemblance to chicken scratch. She turned the page sideways, attempting to read the notations beneath the faint moonlight that filtered through the window. "We're going to end up blind."

Ian's laugh was bitter. "Very probably." He reached into his pocket again and withdrew a decilamp. "The other item I found in Warrick's coat pocket." He shook the device to activate the bioluminescent bacteria within. "Perhaps it will help."

Long minutes passed as they peered at page after page in the blue-green light. Then, there it was. A seemingly arbitrary note scrawled by Warrick.

"Have you heard of Wolff's Law?" Olivia asked.

"Of course. Julius Wolff is a German surgeon who works in Berlin. He studies bone remodeling, how increased forces upon bones strengthen them by stimulating osteoprogenitor cells to differentiate into osteoblasts. Why, what did you find?"

"A reference to cyclic loading," Olivia said, passing Ian the sheet of paper and pointing to a paragraph scribbled in the corner of the page. "Forces applied in differing directions." She looked up at him. "That's an oscillation."

"That's it!" He snapped his fingers. "It has to be. Warrick found a way to induce extremely rapid growth by stimulating the differentiation of his precursor cells into bone-producing cells. If the dividing cells could be induced to uptake a toxin at a rapid rate—"

"It would kill them," Olivia finished.

A wide grin transformed Ian's face. "That must be what's in the mill house, a device to stimulate bone growth."

"Built out of copper," Olivia agreed.

He tossed the page aside and dragged her into his arms. "What would I have done without you?"

IAN POURED the chaos of his emotions into their kiss. Relief. Exhilaration. Wonder. Admiration. Rising desire.

Olivia's lips parted in encouragement. She wrapped her arms about his neck, holding him close as he spun her about, walking forward until her back pressed against the bedpost.

Breasts crushed to his chest, he held her there, looking down into her eyes as her heart pounded, as her breath came in gasps. He worked hard to rein in his desire, to remind himself of all the reasons he should take this no further.

No other woman he'd ever met compared. Lock-picking, eavesdropping, stealth programming of household steambots.

Not once had he thought to list them as qualifications for a wife. She complicated his life in a way he would not have chosen, but also in a way it seemed he could not do without. With her, he could see a future. One in which he didn't spend every waking hour locked inside his research laboratory. He could envision a home. Children.

He'd meant to wait. To court her, to win her hand, to marry her first. But with Warrick dead and fire burning in Zheng's eyes, it wouldn't be long before the count learned of Katherine's betrayal. Then, he too would lose his temper. Would the desire to command an unbreakable army still be strong enough to rein in the count's anger? Ian lowered his forehead to hers. What if this moment was all the time they would ever have together?

"Don't stop," she breathed. "Don't tell me you can't. Or won't. Please don't be a gentleman tonight." As she spoke, her fingers moved quickly over the buttons of his waistcoat, his shirt. "I want to feel your skin against mine, Ian. I've never wanted anything so much. Please. Take me to bed."

The last of his willpower crumbled. She was a woman who knew her own mind, who knew what she wanted. His fingers plucked at the buttons of her bodice, pushed the material free from her shoulders, down her arms to the floor. Her skirts, petticoats followed. As her chest rose and fell erratically, he twisted a golden curl about his finger,

"When we return home," he whispered, refusing to speak of any other possibility, "I will offer for you." Not because of some strict moral code, but because he could no longer imagine not having her at his side. Always.

"You can try." Olivia turned her back to him, lifting the tangle of her hair from the nape of her neck.

"Will you say yes?" Heart racing, he loosened the laces of her corset.

"Convince me I should," she teased.

The corset fell to the ground. The thin chemise she'd worn followed, leaving nothing beneath his hand but smooth skin.

Running his fingers down the knobs of her spine, he skimmed his hands outward over the flare of her generous hips, upward to the narrow indentation of her waist, then forward over her ribs until he cupped the full roundness of her breasts.

He nibbled at her neck as he pinched her nipples, drawing forth the most gratifying gasps and moans. Her head fell backward onto his shoulder with a cry, fuel to the fire that burned within him. One hand toyed with her breast while he slid the other down to the soft curls between her thighs and found her already damp and ready.

He was lost.

THE HARD LENGTH of Ian's arousal pressed against her buttocks. Though his touch clouded her mind with pleasure, she clung to her resolve. She wanted all of him. Now.

"You wear far too much clothing," she said, turning in his arms. His eyes smoldered as she stepped backward, climbing into the enormous bed. "Coming?"

Ian's answer was to tug off his shoes. Her lips parted to give voice to another comment but—as he shoved his trousers from his lean hips—her mouth went dry. His bare form was perfection. Wide, muscular shoulders narrowed inward to his waist. Below, his thick erection jutted, and her breath caught as she thought of him fitting inside her.

Their eyes locked. His gaze was liquid heat.

"Like what you see?" His voice was rough.

"Very much." Her heart pounded, sending fire through her veins. "Come closer, though, so I might touch."

He bent to grab something from his travel case, then climbed onto the thick feather mattress and yanked the bed curtains closed, plunging them into near darkness.

Olivia shivered at the cold air that drifted over her exposed skin. Then shivered again in anticipation as he pushed her backward onto the pillows, trailing kisses along her jaw and neck. She arched her back, brushing her nipples against his chest. Sensation exploded inside her. "This is much, much better." She ran her hands over his firm shoulders, down the cords of his muscled back, exploring his hard shape even as she urged him closer. "Ask me anything, Ian," she said. "There's nothing I could refuse you right now."

"Later," he laughed against her skin. The roughness of his unshaven cheeks scraping over her burning skin sent electric jolts of pleasure coursing through her body. "I've other uses for my mouth at the moment." Then his mouth was indeed too busy. It was everywhere—neck, breasts, hips, stomach.

"Oh! Yes! There!" she cried as his lips fell upon the aching center between her legs.

Long minutes later, he twined his fingers in her unbound hair, cradling the back of her head and dragging her face to his. His mouth covered hers with a groan, demanding she open to him. His tongue slid against hers, twisting and twining, hot and erotic. As he thrust his tongue, mimicking what was to come, damp warmth pooled between her legs.

She wrapped her hands about his biceps while he braced himself above her, as his knees nudged her legs apart. His weight settled at her core, and she pushed upward, moaning as the hard column of his need pressed against the soft wetness of hers.

"I want you. All of you." Every nerve ending of her body hummed.

"Patience," he murmured, and reached between them, his thumb circling at her center, drawing low cries from her throat and a new flood of heat.

"Please," she begged. "Now."

He shifted. Paper tore and she knew he covered himself with a sheath. Then she felt him at her entrance. Slowly, he eased inside. There was some pain, a dull burn. But certainly there was far more pleasure to come.

"Hurry." Olivia lifted her hips.

"I'm trying not to—"

Grabbing his hips, she pulled. Deep and tight, he filled her, and she cried out at the marvelous sensation of being stretched so completely.

"You'll be the death of me, Olivia," Ian growled through gritted teeth. "Are you—"

Dragging her nails up his back, she whispered, "I'm fine. Better than fine. Please don't stop."

Ian pulled away, then eased back into her again.

"Mmm. That's nice," she murmured. Though not quite what she'd hoped. She shifted, squirming against him, struggling to find the right kind of friction.

"Only nice?"

"I rather enjoyed your entrance."

He groaned, then leaned forward and kissed her. "Perhaps this?" He withdrew, then thrust into her, deeply.

"Oh!" She gasped. "Yes, that! Again!"

Again and again he drove into her. Flexing her hips with each plunge, the sensation multiplied and built to dizzying heights. This joining of bodies, it was far, far more than anything she could have imagined, so much more than the pleasures he'd shown her hours before.

"More!" she cried.

Bracing himself on his knees, Ian reached beneath her buttocks, pulling her against him. Deeper. Faster.

She met him, thrust for thrust, keening as something inside her coiled tighter as it crept closer and closer to a hot and feverish edge... then leapt over with a roar. She cried his name as a blaze of sublime pleasure enveloped her. "Ian!"

Once, twice more he ground into her, shouting as his own climax overtook him.

"Olivia." His breath rasped in her ear as he collapsed

onto her. She wrapped her arms about him, welcoming the heavy weight. "You are an incredible woman."

"And you *are* a fantastic lover." She smiled against his skin.

"Husband."

Closing her eyes, she laughed, low and husky. "For a pretend husband, the pretend wedding night was quite wonderful." She was already looking forward to tomorrow evening, scheming how she might entice Ian into a little naughty behavior in the laboratory.

How strange that she should feel her safest and most cherished while stretched out, naked, beneath a man willing to commit treason to save those he loved. That she herself had had to break any number of rules and regulations, fleeing into enemy territory on what amounted to little more than a selfish whim, to feel so...

Dear God, she was in danger of falling in love. With the most perfect, yet worst man she possibly could. A biologist. A former Queen's agent. A suspected traitor.

"I was serious." He pressed a kiss to her forehead. "About asking for your hand, Olivia. I want you to be my wife in truth. Will you marry me?"

She looked up at him, shocked her instinct was to answer yes. She opened her mouth. Closed it. A tendril of worry twined about her chest. "This thing between us, Ian, it's not a trap. I don't expect an offer of marriage. I've made certain promises. I have responsibilities, commitments I need to honor."

"Yes, of course." He rolled away, taking his warmth with

him, to stare upward at the bed canopy. He ran a hand over the rough stubble of his beard. "Your Italian baron."

It surprised her just how badly she wanted to wipe the disappointment from his face by agreeing to be his wife. Giving up marriage to an elderly Italian baron would be no hardship, but he was her assigned target. If she accepted Ian's offer, an unapproved marital alliance, would the Queen dismiss her from her service? She bit her bottom lip, fighting the sinking sensation that she was not cut out for a life of intrigue... "Let me think about it."

CHAPTER TWENTY-NINE

OUTSIDE THE WIND blew and the window rattled as they dressed in silence. Without a word, Ian helped tighten Olivia's corset strings. What more was there to say on the topic of marriage? She wouldn't be here with him in Germany but for her drive, her ambition, her desire to serve Queen and country, to be more than a mere wife. What had he to offer but an empty title and a crumbling estate? Villainous foreign operatives pursued him at every turn, his sister faced a gruesome end and, should they survive their sojourn in Germany, he faced a charge of treason.

He let out a hollow laugh. At her questioning glance, he tried to unbend, to focus on tonight's mission. "How did you reach my sister, the turret room, undetected? Fortune was on your side when you left the laboratory—"

"I do not consider the untimely death of a guardsman good luck," she protested.

"Of course, but two guardsmen now stand guard at our door. We won't make it past the threshold."

"It is a problem," she agreed. "Our first day here, I adjusted Steam Matilda's programming cards, altered her loyalty. When I encountered her in the hall, a few short commands redirected her to the turret room. The guardsman at Elizabeth's door believed my escort in too much pain to climb the stairs and allowed me entrance without a single question."

"*You* stole the countess' tea?" Ian lifted his eyebrows. Both a brave and ill-advised ploy.

"I did." She beamed with pride. "Steam servants move freely where humans can't. It is always wise to recruit them to collect information. In short, I possess unparalleled eavesdropping skills." Her eyes saddened. "A useful skill for a societal liaison committed to ruining her husband's life."

With her programming expertise, Olivia would place every mechanical household servant under her thumb. All manner of technology could be concealed inside an innocent steambot, from maids to roving tables to the lowly roto-sweeps. An unsuspecting yet traitorous husband would be under constant surveillance.

What a waste of such intelligence and ambition.

Wait.

"Eavesdropping? Olivia, have you done something to this steam servant that you've neglected to mention?" *Of course she had.*

She turned reaching for her shawl, and when she

answered, her voice was tight. "Nothing that will assist us in tonight's exit from the castle."

"Olivia—"

But again the wind blew and the window rattled—this time with an accompanying rhythmic tap.

"She's here!" Olivia rushed to the window, throwing the casement wide, letting in both a blast of icy wind and a grinning Wei.

Wei, dressed entirely in black and wearing wings, tossed a sack to the floor, and hopped down from the window sill into their bedchamber. "Look what Mr. Black give me!" she exclaimed, holding aloft an acousticotransmitter.

Olivia tried to grab the item from Wei, but Ian was closer. And faster. He snatched the device from the girl's hand. A rough, solid substance coated its surface as if it had been— "You planted a listening device on my dirigible?"

"Yes! Is how Mr. Black *heard* ship!" Wei bounced on her toes, pleased as punch, pointing to the small green light that pulsed.

With a fingernail, Ian flicked the switch and the light blinked off. He stared at Olivia. "Were you going to tell me? Are there other acousticotransmitters you've failed to mention? Perhaps one inside the steambot?"

"Please, it needs to be on." She reached for the device.

"Why?" He moved his hand behind his back. He lifted his eyebrows. And waited. "Black knows we're here."

Wei glanced between the two of them, and her smile faded.

"He should be allowed to listen," Olivia said, planting her hands on her hips. "We need his help. It is the only way we will be able to return safely to England."

"He's injured and the dirigible is not airworthy." He shook his head. "Even if we discover Warrick's device in working order, we won't be able to leave for days, possibly weeks. We need to conserve its power."

"If Mr. Black listens, he can better provide for all contingencies," she protested. "Assess the situation."

"Assess my loyalty?" He shoved the acousticotransmitter into his coat pocket and forced himself to hold her gaze. Certainly they'd enjoyed themselves in that bed, but had she climbed into it with ulterior motives? His stomach clenched.

"Your loyalty is not under question. I will attest to it."

"Will you?"

Her eyebrows drew together. "How can you even ask? Do you think I would—" She glanced at Wei and dropped her voice. "I would not... align myself with you otherwise?"

They'd *aligned* rather nicely. He struggled to dampen his emotions. "No? *Agents* are known to play all angles. Above. Beneath."

Her face turned beet red. "I told you, I'm not that kind of agent!"

"Ooo." Wei whistled through her teeth. "Lady a spy?"

Olivia snapped her jaw shut and pressed a hand to her mouth.

Ian swore. The last thing he needed was yet another complication.

"No worry," Wei said, holding up her hands. "I not tell. But I come."

"Come?" he asked.

"Come to England."

"Why?" Olivia asked. "Why would you want to come with us?"

Wei crossed her arms. "Zheng is my uncle. I do not like."

"She will be your responsibility," he warned, "when they throw me in prison."

"If," Olivia objected. "Either way, I will see to her education." She pulled her shoulders back and straightened her spine, daring him to object.

He admired that, her refusal to acquiesce to society's expectations. There was much about her to admire, even if he did want to shake her until all her secrets rattled free.

"I *am* agent enough to know we need to develop an escape plan that does not rely upon coincidence and convenience. One we can implement at a moment's notice should the count decide we are an impediment to be jettisoned." She turned to Wei. "Did you speak with Elizabeth?"

Wei nodded. Excitement lit up her eyes again. "Germany, it not safe for you. I will help. I build three wings like this, only bigger." She turned around, pointing over her shoulder. "For lady. For gentleman. For princess in tower. It will carry you far, far into the woods. Then, you run."

Olivia placed a hand Wei's shoulder. "Thank you."

"Fly?" She'd nearly fainted when asked to exit the escape dirigible by rope. "Are you suggesting we fly from this room?"

"No," Olivia said. "I believe she is suggesting we glide."

"Are you both mad?" he bellowed. "Elizabeth may think the cells have strengthened her skeleton, but they've had less than forty-eight hours to alter the mineral content of her bone."

Seven bones in each ankle. Nineteen bones in each foot. Any or all could break upon landing. If she tripped... A cold sweat broke out beneath his collar at the idea of strapping such gear onto his fragile sister's back. He turned upon Olivia. She, on the other hand.... Well, he no longer knew *what* to worry about. She'd seemed genuinely terrified of heights when they'd leapt from the escape dirigible, but now she was willing to leap from this castle window with no safety harness, no rope, no assistance? No practice? Could she work up enough nerve to jump?

"How many times have you worn wings?" he challenged.

"About as many times as I have been imprisoned in a castle," Olivia snapped. "But I'm willing to try. When it's time to make our final exit, if we're to have any hope of outrunning the count, his guardsmen or Zheng, we need an escape plan, a way for all three of us to exit quickly and travel well beyond the village."

They glared at each other a long moment.

"We'll discuss this later," he stated.

"At length." She offered him a false smile. "But we have much to accomplish tonight. Show her the vial."

Ian pulled the toxin from his pocket. "These Chinese characters, can you read them?"

Wei took the vial and her eyes grew round. "Is poison

called *shen*. Kill rats on airship. Medicine for blood disease. And British ladies use for making face white."

It was all the confirmation he needed. "Gray arsenic. Rapidly oxidized to form arsenous oxide. A classic skin purifier and poison." He snapped his fingers. "Warrick designed his cells to uptake both antimony and arsenic. If the patient consumes antimony, his bones harden. Then, at the first sign of osteoblastoma, a cure could be effected by forcing rapid bone growth and providing the cells with arsenic instead."

"Causing the cells to accumulate the poison and self-destruct." Olivia jumped to her feet. "We need to see what's inside that mill. Now."

There was a hiss, a whoosh. A sharp intake of air. Wei plucked a dart from her chest and stared at it in amazement before staggering backward. With a cry, Olivia rushed to her side, catching the girl as her wings clattered and tore against the stone wall.

"Brilliant deductions, all of them," a familiar voice said behind them. "But we must prepare for departure. Please, gather your belongings."

Ian didn't need to turn. "Good evening, Countess."

Olivia looked up, her face pale. "What have you done?"

"Distractions must be removed. She'll be fine," Katherine said. "Eventually."

Olivia pulled Wei into her lap, and Ian knelt, pressing a hand to the girl's chest. It still rose and fell, but slowly and shallowly. He'd used this weapon before, but never upon a child. Wei would survive, but at half the size of an adult, a second dart would kill her.

"How did you obtain this weapon?" he asked, knowing full well Black had been the last to possess this TTX pistol.

"That man, the one who attended the balloon crash, he followed you here. He dared approach my children." Katherine narrowed her eyes and aimed the purloined weapon at his chest. "You betrayed me, Ian." Her voice grew colder. "Even now my husband and Zheng hunt for me. Time to depart. If you cooperate, I will allow Lady Elizabeth to accompany us."

Hands in the air, Ian rose. He also shifted closer to the washstand. "No. Not yet. I need to investigate the mill and Warrick's cure."

"Warrick is dead." She waved at the desk. "You have his notes. It is enough."

He held firm. "First I visit the mill."

"A tiresome refrain." Katherine sighed heavily. "No. I will not risk losing you. You will hide elsewhere in the castle until it is time for our extraction." The countess turned her attention to Olivia. "Step away from the child. We must leave now. Come without resistance, and I will let the girl live. Gather your belongings, the device and whatever you require to ensure it functions."

With the faintest of movements, the slightest tip of his head, he informed Olivia of his plans.

Olivia answered with an equally imperceptible nod. She snapped her fingers twice and whistled. Making a faint humming sound, her hedgehog trundled out from beneath the bed. A long, thin rod extended from his nose. Her mechanical hedgehog was more than a simple toy. At the very least, it was a distraction.

"What is this?" Katherine stepped backward. "Order it to stop."

"But I require his contents to program the osforare apparatus," Olivia objected, gently lowering Wei's head to the floor.

Ian reached for the porcelain ewer, wrapping his hand about the pitcher's handle.

"Watson, engage," Olivia ordered.

The metal beast scampered toward Katherine. She leapt backward. It missed.

Ian didn't. He brought the ceramic pitcher down upon the side of her head, against her temple, and she slumped. The TTX pistol clattered to the ground. He kicked it aside. "Olivia, help me tie her ankles and wrists."

"Pistons and steam," she muttered. "Electrocuting her would have been immensely satisfying, but perhaps we might still have that chance—for I've a better option than tearing strips from her petticoats. Watson, come."

Whirring with satisfaction, her zoetomatic waddled across the floor to bump against her leather-laced ankle. She scooped it from the floor, running a hand over the surface of its spines, then tapped out a code on the zoetomatic's spines and the curved, interlocking sections of its back retracted to reveal a hollow interior.

"Think of him as a mobile reticule." She reached inside to extract an axon thrall band and its master cuff, ones he'd last seen fastened about his sister's wrists. He gaped as she tossed back the hem of Katherine's skirt and locked a band about her ankle. She clamped the master band about the leg of the bed, locked it, then activated it with a twist of her fingers. "We hide her underneath." She tore a strip from the countess' petticoat. "A gag as well, in case she decides to yell, though she's rather made enemies of everyone inside the castle."

"I'll add sleight of hand and enemy immobilization to your growing list of skills. Might I find you've any other useful items inside Watson?" Did he dare hope for a weapon or two?

"A rather... advanced lock pick," she answered. "A device to call upon should we encounter a particularly difficult lock, such as the firkin cincture bolt."

He lifted his eyebrows, about to press further when Katherine moaned. Instead, he placed the osforare apparatus case onto the desk. Setting aside the device, he began to disassemble the container, revealing hidden compartments that concealed tubes, powder packets, glass vials, needles. And a steel syringe.

"Cogs and gears," Olivia said. "I never thought..."

"To look beyond the first layer?" A satisfied smile tugged at his lips. "Neither did the count's guardsmen. They were far too concerned about the blades I carried, about the acousticotransmitters you planted." He stuffed most of the items into his pockets, then picked up a vial and the syringe.

"What is that?"

"This is crinlozyme." He tapped the glass and metal tube, squirting out a small amount of the drug to eliminate bubbles. "A second layer of imprisonment. The drug will immobilize her for up to twenty-four hours, unless the antidote is applied."

Katherine's eyes flew open.

"It will not kill you," he spoke to the countess. "But as I mentioned, we must visit the mill. We'll save *questions* for later."

If he intended to make a serious offer for Olivia's hand, he'd need to do more than return her safely to the duke. He needed to make amends, such as providing the location of Kadskoye, the secret Russian biotechnology facility.

"*Nyet*. You will learn nothing," she spat.

"I will learn everything." He grabbed the hem of her sleeve, tearing it upward to her elbow. He wrapped the strip of petticoat about her arm and felt for a vein, then slid the needle in and pushed the plunger home.

"You won't get away with this," Katherine slurred. Her eyelids drooped.

"Won't I?" He wrenched the ring of keys from her belt and handed it to Olivia. "Not that I doubt your abilities, but these will speed us on our way."

While Olivia pried free the end of the bed, Ian stuffed a wad of silk into Katherine's mouth, securing it with a strip of petticoat. Just in case. Nearly a year had passed since he'd last replenished his supplies, and he couldn't be certain of the drug's potency.

He searched her body, relieving her of a variety of many razor-sharp and useful blades. A scrap of paper fell to the ground. A note. Scrawled in Cyrillic. "Olivia," he called. "Do you read, as well as speak, Russian?"

"Of course. Why?"

He handed her the note.

She translated. *"Vorontsky en route. Eliminate test subject. Secure scientist, additional guest and materials. Prepare for flyby boarding at The Roost."*

So much for her promise of including Elizabeth.

"Flyby?" Olivia asked.

"Typically, it involves boarding a dirigible by rope. The reverse of our entry into this castle, except the dirigible does not stop. The opportunity to board is a finite window, dependent upon the speed of the airship and the length of rope available."

Her eyebrows drew together. "Or perhaps she means to leave by pteryform?"

"It would redefine the term 'flyby'."

"And when she's not there?"

"They keep going," he said. "Depending upon the value they place upon her, upon this biotechnology, agents may or may not be sent to look for her."

"Screws and shafts," she grumbled, as they grabbed the unconscious countess beneath her arms and dragged her to the foot of the great bed, prying off the end panel to shove and push Katherine into decades of accumulated dust and grime. "This is one of the most satisfying moments of the entire mission."

"Oh?" Ian pressed the panel back into place. "I rather enjoyed spending time atop the mattress."

Olivia's face burst into flame.

"Time for a trip to town." They would revisit the subject of marriage later. "Can you carry the osforare apparatus?" He eyeballed her large reticule. "The situation here appears to be deteriorating, and there is the faintest chance we might be unable to return." In which case he wanted the device with him.

"The seams might rip." She grabbed a thick woolen stocking and began to wrap the apparatus. "But if it keeps you from a charge of treason..."

Treason was the least of his worries now. If the duke learned Ian had deflowered his daughter, he'd be drawn and quartered.

He grabbed the TTX pistol—two darts remained—and eased the door open. Two guards lay unconscious upon the ground, TTX darts protruding from their thighs. It seemed Katherine had also taken possession of Black's small arsenal of pufferfish poison, clearing a path for her escape.

But perhaps not theirs.

Shoving Wei's torn wings from her shoulders, he scooped her up and handed Olivia the girl's sack. "The hall is empty but..."

Ruffled reticule hanging from her elbow, Olivia crouched beside him. The hedgehog had curled itself into a metal ball. "Watch."

She rolled Watson down the hallway. Three yards out, he sprang to his feet, spines at the ready. The creature scurried nimbly to the turn of the hall, whistled twice, then scampered onward. "All clear," she whispered and stepped into the corridor.

He shifted Wei's weight to his shoulder and followed. Surprising, the allies one sometimes made. A child. A mechanical toy. A woman who was not-quite-a-spy.

One who had inserted herself into his life, filling a gaping hole he'd not known existed.

CHAPTER THIRTY

THE CASTLE HALLS were littered with the guardsmen Katherine had incapacitated, and they had almost reached the kitchens when Watson returned to bump against Olivia's ankle. She glanced down in time to see him blink twice before curling into a ball and retracting his spines.

"Someone's approaching," she hissed, scooping him up and shoving him into her reticule.

"I've only two darts left," Ian warned. "Be prepared to run." Drawing his pistol, he whipped about the corner and dropped the patrolling pair of guardsmen.

One managed a strangled cry for help. "*Hilfe!*" *Help!*

German echoed down the hallway as she leapt over the prone bodies of the two guardsmen to follow Ian into the kitchens. Heart pounding, she ran into the room, past Steam Matilda kneading a lump of dark brown bread upon a scarred wooden table, and darted through the door to the courtyard.

Ian pulled her to his side and closed the kitchen door while clutching a sharp knife, courtesy of the countess' personal weaponry. Olivia prayed hand-to-hand combat wouldn't be necessary.

The wall at her back was bone-chillingly cold, and the glacial wind scoured her face and clawed at her skirts. At some point, the sun must have shone, for the snow upon the courtyard's cobblestones had melted, leaving behind frozen puddles and icy mud.

The drawstring of her reticule bit into the skin of her forearm. Watson, the osforare apparatus and all the punch cards and tools made the bag unwieldy and impractical. Next time, she would design a purse with a shoulder strap. *Next time?* She'd gone mad.

There was a shout of alarm, but the door stayed shut. Perhaps the guardsmen were too preoccupied—or sick—to follow the trail of fallen men and reach the rather obvious conclusion. Either way, lingering was a bad idea. Soon logic would return and compel the guardsmen to search the courtyard.

Wei stirred against Ian's shoulder. "Down," she said, struggling in Ian's arms. "My bag. Need the... sticks."

He slid the knife back into its sheath and lowered the girl onto unsteady feet. "Take a moment. Find your feet. That was a dosage meant for a grown man."

Wei's answering smile was dazzling. "I tough to kill."

The girl hopped back and forth, from one foot to the

other, testing her legs. Satisfied, she reached into her sack and pulled out two long, paper tubes painted red. Sharp sticks protruded from their ends. All had long... fuses?

"Rockets?" Despite the danger, Ian grinned like a Cheshire cat.

"Yes! Distraction." Wei pulled another item from her sack. "And matches! Come, we move fast."

Hugging the shadows, Ian and Wei set off down the stone stairs, stopping to peek around corners. Careful of her footing, Olivia followed, listening as they discussed the best strategy for employing the rocket.

Ian lifted a fist into the air.

They froze. Olivia held her breath, doing her best to become one with the shadows as a patrol of guardsmen passed not three feet from where they stood.

Several heartbeats later, Ian lowered his arm and pointed.

Wei nodded, and he jammed the end of a sharp stick into the hard-packed ground, pointing the tip of the rocket away from the castle gates. Wei lifted a match.

Looking over his shoulder at Olivia, he whispered, "Be ready to run."

She tightened her hands on her reticule.

With a flash of igniting phosphorus and sulfur, Wei lit the fuse.

He and Wei scuttled backward, away from the rocket, grinning at each other with childish enthusiasm, giving her a fleeting vision of what it might be like to marry such a man. To raise a family. Anything but dull. Her heart ached, yearning for a love that could no longer be denied.

A whoosh and the rocket was gone. A trail of smoke led into the air, but try as she might, Olivia could not follow the rocket's path.

There was a loud bang, and thousands upon thousands of lights flashed, forming a bright starburst in the still-dark sky. Guardsmen yelled and ran for the ramparts, gathering behind the castle walls, crouching, conferring. For not a single one possessed a pistol. A few brave souls peeked above the wall, searching for the as-yet unseen enemy.

Ian grabbed her hand and tugged her forward. In the commotion, no one noticed the three of them running for the castle gates.

Not one sentry stood before the gate. The count's guardsmen were strong, perhaps, but not disciplined or well-trained. She slammed into the rough, wooden gate, her reticule knocking against the wood, and ran her palms over its surface, searching in the dark for the cool steel of the lock. Though her heart pounded, the lock—large and old—presented no challenge. The pick caught, and the lock fell open with a soft *thunk*. She nodded to Wei.

Wei lit a second rocket and, as a succession of bangs resulted in yet further chaos at the castle walls, Ian shoved the gate outward.

They hurried down the muddy road that curved around behind the castle's base, leading ever downward. At last the road reached the winding, cobblestone streets of the village where tall, half-timbered houses stood shoulder to shoulder, rising upward, overhanging the streets and providing an illusion of protection.

Wei led them toward a stone bridge that arched over a river swollen by the melting snow. On the far bank, water diverted into a wooden trough poured and splashed onto a water wheel's slats, spinning it at a furious pace. Beside the water chute loomed a squat building of rough plaster and exposed wooden framing. Its windows were securely boarded.

The mill. Almost there.

Olivia stepped onto the bridge, veering to avoid a lone, drunken man crossing in the other direction while staring at the sky in bewilderment—but his shoulder slammed into hers, throwing her sideways.

"*Tut mir leid,*" he murmured. *I'm sorry.* He caught her elbow, steadying her.

"*Mir geht es gut,*" she answered. *I'm fine.*

But he didn't let go.

She looked up. His face was half-shrouded by a dark, woolen hood. But not shrouded enough. It took every ounce of self-control she had not to react. He gave her a sharp nod, then slid his hand down her arm and pressed a piece of paper into hers before limping onward. Hurrying, she stuffed the note into her bodice and caught up to Ian who waited beside a narrow path.

"What happened?" he asked.

"Nothing." Her chest tightened at the lie, but she curled her hand tightly about the paper. "A drunk staggered into me. I'm fine." She'd promised him no secrets, but that was before Ian had all but forbidden her contact with Mr. Black.

"Come!" Wei beckoned from beside the spinning water wheel.

Ian waved her ahead, and Olivia stepped onto the narrow path that led to the mill house. One glance at the door told her the building housed something of value.

"A Kreuger-Schalterhammer lock," she whispered on an exhale. Impressive. "Forty-seven pins and a level containing a liquid mercury trigger." Captain Jack could manage forty-six.

"Is that complicated?" Ian asked.

"Yes. It's a significant investment in a lock for such an old building." Impossible if one wasn't a well-versed sneak thief with the latest advancement in technology available. "But nothing I can't handle. Hold this." She shoved her reticule into his arms and dug deep. Extracting Watson, she tapped his spines. "I can't do this with picks alone." She reached into Watson's back and retrieved a tube of alkisorcyn and—

"Captain Jack's Tension Torque," Ian said.

As a former Queen's agent, he would be versed in its use and an excellent assistant. "We use both this and my picks. I'm going to need your help." *Even then...* Olivia rolled her shoulders. This was no time for self-doubt. She placed the zoetomatic upon the ground. "Tremor mode," she ordered. Dutifully, Watson rose up upon hind legs and, pressing his front feet to the door, began to shake.

"What Watson doing?" Wei asked.

"Dispersing the mercury along a long thin tube inside

the lock." She looked to Ian. "Once I begin the process, I'll have only one chance. If the tube tips and the mercury pools, a chemical reaction will dissolve the pins."

He set down her reticule and moved closer. "Tell me what to do."

"On my word, *slowly* depress the plunger on the tube while I hold a number of lock picks in place."

"Ready."

She took a deep breath, then carefully inserted the copper coil into the key hole and readied the alkisorcyn. Reaching into her bodice, deep inside her corset, she pulled forth two highly-specialized lock picks. Ones she rarely used. Wind blew upon her bare fingers, stiffening them as she slid her picks past the copper tubing, probing, searching for the quartz tumblers.

There.

"Now," she told Ian, letting the cold fix her fingers in place. "Slowly and steadily."

The gel oozed inward, solidifying. When she was certain her picks would hold, she released them and turned her attention to Captain Jack's specialized dial. She pressed her ear to the vibrating door and made a few fine adjustments, waiting for the faint... *click.*

The glass level shattered, and she grabbed the handle, pushing the door open.

"Most impressive, Olivia." Ian's eyes flashed with admiration.

Beaming, she picked up her reticule and stepped inside.

Perhaps a future as a field agent wasn't outside the realm of possibility.

The ground floor of the mill was dim. Ian withdrew the bioluminescent decilamp from one of the many pockets hidden inside his waistcoat and gave it a good shake. The microorganisms, re-energized, demonstrated their approval by casting a green-blue glow into the room.

He directed the beam of light at the axel of the water wheel, an axel that extended inward from the outside water wheel to run parallel to the floor. An axel that connected to— She let out a low whistle. "A three phase generator."

This was the power source for Warrick's alternating current—and an alternating current was an oscillating one.

"An easy, inexpensive way to generate electricity," Ian said.

Warrick had disconnected the water wheel's axel from the many gears that once turned the millstone, grinding wheat into flour. Instead, the power generated by the water wheel had been re-directed into creating electricity.

A thick metal ring—a large magnet—was attached to the end of the axel. It spun in a blur of gray. Quite motionless inside this ring was a gear-like disc. Coil upon coil of copper wire wound about the disc.

"Ingenious," Olivia said. "How many wraps did he use?"

Ian bent to examine the disc. "At least forty."

Wei's brow wrinkled. "They use *this* to make electricity?"

"Yes," Olivia said. "It's a way of taking mechanical energy—the rushing water over the wheel—and turning it into electricity." She pointed. "The magnet spinning about the copper wire generates an electric current. The more wire wraps, the more electricity."

"What's impressive is the huge amount of wire used." Ian shook his head slowly. "The time it must have taken to wrap the disc…"

"What's this?" Wei pointed.

"Don't touch!" they both yelled at once.

Wei jumped several feet backward, hands in the air.

Using the torch's light, Ian traced the wires that extended outward from the disc's center to wrap about a tube, a tube constructed of two wine barrels placed end to end. Yet more copper wire—a vast length of it—enveloped the barrels.

A wide board, a kind of platform, was suspended inside the tube. The perfect length and width for one guardsman, for one patient to lie upon.

"A half-inch thick wire wrap!" Ian exclaimed.

Wei tipped her head, considering the crude yet clever arrangement of wood, metal, and wire. "They power… a tube?"

"It's an electromagnet," Olivia said.

"When its magnetic fields oscillate, the electrical forces will imitate physical stress which, according to Wolff's law, will in turn stimulate bone growth." Ian pressed a quick kiss to her lips and yanked Warrick's papers from his waistcoat. "Now I just need to calculate the exact dosage of arsenic and the length of exposure to the oscillating magnetic field."

Wei rolled her eyes. "I go inspect building." She wandered off.

Ian spread out the notes upon a rough workbench containing a rudimentary assortment of laboratory equipment. Propping the bioluminescent torch beside him, he ran his finger over Warrick's scribblings, over the mathematical formulas and Greek letters that filled the page. There was a wild, feverish look in his eyes as his mind wrestled with the problem, on the verge of forcing Warrick's notes to surrender their final secrets.

"Mendeleev's 1871 periodic table places arsenic in the same group, the same column as antimony," Ian muttered under his breath. "It explains the chemical properties they share. From that I can conclude that if his cells bind phosphate to arsenic, and the cells' metabolic activity is accelerated, then the dosage..." He dug a pencil from his waistcoat and began to scratch upon the pages.

Lost in calculations, he no longer registered her presence.

Turning her back on him, she paced the perimeter of the room, pretending to examine the boards nailed to a window set high upon the wall. In truth, she sought the dull beam of light that struggled through a narrow crack between planks. With a quick glance over her shoulder, she tugged Mr. Black's note from her bodice. Unfolding it, she squinted to read.

Found signal yesterday. Almost killed investigating creatures in woods. Beware Russian Agent Katerina

*Dyatlova. Local Roma stand ready to assist across
border. Situation report received. Require update.*

Gypsies? That was Mr. Black's plan, to transport them
from Germany into France by caravan? She'd hoped to read
the dirigible was repaired and waiting. Clockwork horses
could never outrun the count, not if he was mounted on a
pteryform. She bit back her frustration. Rolling the note into
a tiny ball, she popped it in her mouth and swallowed. The
ink was bitter, but without a fire close by, there was no other
option.

An update. How was she supposed to accomplish that?
With one acousticotransmitter in Ian's pocket and the other
in the castle kitchens, she had no way to contact Mr. Black
save to send Wei out into the streets. She closed her eyes and
tried to think logically.

"That's it." Ian slapped a hand on the table. "I have the
exact numbers to effect a cure."

"A cure?" Wei jumped from the rafters and ran to his
side.

"The two elements, arsenic and antimony, have a
number of similar properties, allowing both of them to bind
to phosphorus in bone matrix." Ian raised a finger. "If a
patient consumes arsenic—instead of antimony—while the
bones grow extremely rapidly, the concentration of the
poison will rise in the altered osteoblasts, causing them to
die," he smiled, "curing the individual of bone cancer." Ian
aimed the light at the wire wrapped barrels. "The alternating
current surging through the wires of this tube creates an

oscillating magnetic field that imitates physical stress to the bone, inducing new growth."

"Forcing the cells to accumulate the arsenic," Olivia finished. "This will cure Elizabeth?"

"Yes." Ian's voice was euphoric. "A cure for anyone who received transplants of Warrick's cells."

"We shove people inside?" Wei asked. "On the board?"

"We do," he said, eyes flashing with excitement. "Time for our first patient. Can you sneak out and find Stephan? Ask him to bring us a guardsman, one willing to defy the count in order to save his own life."

"Yes!" Wei darted away.

"How many can we cure with the single vial of arsenic we possess?" Olivia asked.

"Four," Ian answered. "Perhaps five." He drew her into his arms. "But it will take hours of work. Each patient is going to need four separate treatments lasting two hours each."

"Days, weeks." Olivia pressed her face against Ian's chest. Wrapped in his strong arms, she felt safe. "Months. The guardsmen will grow wise to the rockets, and with Katherine under our bed..."

"Tension will soar in the castle." He lifted her chin with a finger. Concern flooded his eyes. "You should leave—now —with Black. Take the osforare apparatus. I don't wish to be remembered as one who betrayed his country."

"But... I thought..." she sputtered. "How?"

Reaching into his waistcoat, he pulled forth the acousti-cotransmitter. The green light pulsed. "I turned it on before we left the castle. This is how he found you on the bridge." He tried to press the listening device into her hand.

Olivia tucked her hands beneath her arms. "No."

"You've said yourself, over and over, that you're not a spy. This is your best chance to escape. I've worked with Black before. He's a good agent. He'll keep you safe."

"No. I won't leave you. If I turn up missing, the count will take out his anger on you, on Elizabeth, and he'll hunt for me, with Zheng at his side."

"He won't find you, not if you're already aloft—"

She shook her head. "The escape dirigible is not airworthy yet. Mr. Black's current exit plan involves ground transportation via gypsy caravan. We need to make a coordinated exit. All of us at the same time."

Ian opened his mouth to argue—

Tap. Tap. Tap.

He slid his knife from its sheath.

The mill door cracked open, and two dark eyes peered upward—Wei.

Ian swung the door open, and a young guardsman stumbled in. A wary hope filled his eyes. "Wei says you can cure me?"

CHAPTER THIRTY-ONE

Once Ian dosed the guardsman with arsenic, stretched him out upon the board and slid him inside the pulsing solenoid tube, there wasn't much to do but watch and wait. For quite some time, worried the arsenic might kill rather than cure, he monitored pulse, breathing rate, lip color—but though the man was weak, his condition didn't worsen.

Thank the aether.

Earlier, he'd forced the acousticotransmitter into Olivia's hand. She'd given him a cold shoulder and moved to a distant corner to speak into the device, filling Black in on the latest developments. He watched her now, wondering how to convince her that she must leave.

Safe. His aching heart needed her safe. She caught his stare, frowned, and turned away.

Likely she informed Black that their exit from Germany must be delayed. Black wouldn't agree. He would insist she cease this unauthorized mission and return to British shores. Any minute now, he would knock upon the door and carry Olivia away against her will. Ian would help him, but not before he had some answers, beginning with the Duke of Avesbury's role in this mess.

For falling in love with the daughter of the Duke of Avesbury had certainly deepened his predicament. He would miss her, his unexpected and originally unwanted stowaway. Which made returning to London victorious more important now than ever, for only marriage would ease the pressure inside his hollow chest.

How could he have known his approach to hunting for a wife had been entirely wrong? All that time he ought to have been searching for a would-be spy. He smiled sadly. Yet he'd walked right past her—repeatedly—dismissive of her fluttering fan, her silly giggles and batting eyelashes.

There had to be a way to win her hand.

How could he convince her father to agree to his suit? After he'd accused the duke of complicity in the Warrick affair, of knowing about the inhumane experiments proposed, of providing laboratory space, supplies and funding to allow such a trial to proceed. Of heading the Committee for the Exploration of Anthropomorphic Peculiarities.

Doubt gnawed at his stomach.

In his mind, Ian could see the duke still. He'd stood, silent, behind that massive wooden desk in his study, hands clasped behind his back, his eyes burning holes into his skull.

Not a single syllable had passed the man's lips as Ian turned in his TTX pistol.

Despite Black's insistence, he saw no future for himself as an agent.

But perhaps—if he managed to escape and return to London—he might still work with the Queen's agents. Warrick's cells, this solenoid, he would see destroyed. It was too dangerous and too labor intensive. Cell implantation followed by constant treatment with arsenic and magnetic fields wasn't a feasible technique. It would be all too easy for a soldier in the field to miss a treatment and suffer a horrible death.

Ian's device and his transforming solution, however, had much to offer the Crown. Agents had a tendency to break many, many bones—all but the three comprising the inner ear. Those, they crushed. If human trials proved successful, they would need him, for agents would require hands-on training to use the osforare apparatus in the repair of a broken bone.

And, to date, the punch card was only designed to fix the ulna and radius, the forearm. The Babbage programming would need further development to address an additional two hundred and four bones. For that project, Ian would need the assistance of a Rankine engineer. One in particular came to mind.

But, assuming he didn't end his days in prison, there were Olivia's own aspirations to consider. Would she risk her career for him? Or insist upon continuing to Italy to marry this Italian baron in the hopes of becoming a young widow?

Ian glanced at his pocket watch. Soon they would be missed. With luck, he could slip back into the castle and make his way to the laboratory. Once there, he would claim Katherine had escorted him. *She* certainly wouldn't be contradicting him.

Flipping a switch, he cut power to the solenoid. "That's two hours." He helped the guardsman slide from the board that suspended him inside the barrels. Already, he seemed steadier upon his feet, and a touch of color had returned to his face.

Olivia left her corner to join them.

"How do you feel?" he asked the guardsman. She repeated his question in German.

The man spread his arms out. Wiggled his fingers. Bent at the waist, at the knees and answered. Olivia translated. "Strange. Am I cured?"

"No," Ian replied. "Not yet. You'll need at least three more sessions in the solenoid, maybe more. Wei will find you for your next treatment."

A slow smile spread across the guardsman's face as he pressed a palm to his heart. *"Vielen Dank." Many Thanks.* The guardsman left the mill, his step a little lighter.

Once Olivia was safely away and all of Warrick's residual cells destroyed, Ian would announce the discovery of a cure to the count. He would point to a crabbed note in the corner of Warrick's notes—scratched there by Ian himself—about the solenoid in the mill, and treatments for all the guardsmen would commence.

Then it would be time for him to plan his escape.

Watson blinked, curled up into a ball, and rolled toward Olivia.

"Eeee," Wei screeched, rushing down the stairs. "Count. He outside! Many, many guardsmen here. Mill surrounded!"

Ian swore under his breath. "Go upstairs," he ordered Wei, drawing the knife he'd stolen from Katherine. "Hide beneath empty grain sacks. Go with her, Olivia. Call for backup into that acousticotransmitter."

"Not an option." She held up the device. The green light that had glowed so readily just hours ago was faint and pulsing. Nearly dead.

What good was Black if he could not rescue a single, solitary woman waving a beacon inside a two-hour time frame?

"Go!" he yelled. "Grab your reticule and hide!"

"I won't—"

"You're not a spy," he snapped. "Do as I say."

Clutching her reticule, Olivia ran up the steps, and not a moment too soon.

Ian drew his blade as the door slammed open. Five guardsmen surrounded him, all pointing knives in his direction.

He froze.

Zheng strode through the door, chin held high. He examined the water-wheel generator and the wine-barrel solenoid without the slightest sign of interest, then turned his steely gaze upon Ian. "A dagger," he commented. "Of Russian make and model. Curious." His voice was scornful. "Drop it. Kick it away."

"His allegiances are immaterial." Count Eberwin strode

through the door. "Let him keep it." The count's eyes locked with Ian's. "But if he makes one move, kill him."

"A bad idea," Ian said. "For I've discovered the method by which the osteoblastoma—the bone cancer—can be cured." More than a few feet shifted uncertainly. A number of guardsmen possessing obvious tumor growths upon their mandibles appeared to understand English. Might his announcement cause dissension among the ranks?

Good.

Out of the corner of his eyes—for he didn't dare move an inch—Ian watched as the count circled the room, examining the generator, the solenoid. He stopped before Ian. "So. Does it work, this device?"

"Electromagnet," Ian corrected. "Yes, it does. With a carefully controlled dosage of arsenic and repeated exposure to the magnetic field, I believe most of your guardsmen can be cured."

"Arsenic? That is a poison, not a cure."

"In small doses..." Ian explained how he'd untangled Warrick's remedy.

"Progress at last. Though you defied my direct orders." The count waved his hand. "However, with Doktor Warrick's demise, I must alter my plans to remove your head from its shoulders."

"Against my advice," Zheng added.

"A stay of execution, if you will. Which brings us to the matter of my missing wife." The count looked at Ian, shaking his head. "Who, I am told, is Russian." He curled his lip. "Russians. Always the Russians causing trouble. I go through great effort to marry a British noblewoman with a dowry of the most interesting pteryformes and what do I get? A Russian pretending to be one."

"Countess Katherine?" Ian asked, feigning innocence. "I've met her family, spoken with her father..." All true. He too had been deceived. Deceived, in fact, by nearly everyone in his life.

"A house in London. A manor in the countryside. A whole host of family and friends to complete the façade." The count pointed a finger at him. "Your country, it is infiltrated with any number of spies. But I digress. Russians. We were speaking of them."

Ian held his tongue.

"No?" The count narrowed his eyes. "You have nothing to add? Zheng informs me Warrick and my wife were about to abscond with *my* cells. You too, perhaps, had travel plans?"

"I've no intention of traveling to Russia," Ian said.

"Good. Now. On to the next item. The osforare apparatus is missing. Where is it?" The count fell silent, waiting for an answer.

When Ian did not provide one, the count's gaze turned predatory. "No ready answer? Do you know where it is? Or are you too surprised to learn of its disappearance? For the countess, before her disappearance, mentioned something disturbing about your wife."

Icy fingers walked up Ian's spine, vertebrae by vertebrae.

"It took me some time to place the name." The count

clasped his hands behind his back. "You neglected to inform me that she is a member of the Ravensdale family."

"My wife's maiden name is Stonewythe," Ian insisted.

"Lies!" the count bellowed. "She is a British spy." His nostrils flared. "Everywhere I turn, betrayal. So, tell me, did you escort a British spy into my home?"

"No." He'd escorted a would-be spy.

Zheng finished searching the ground floor of the mill. "Not here," he said and placed a foot on the first stair, but the count lifted a hand. Zheng paused.

"Will Zheng find Lady Olivia Ravensdale upstairs?" An unspoken threat hung in the air.

Ian stared back at the count, hoping she had ignored his instructions to hide. He hoped she and Wei had found a way to slip unnoticed from the mill house. He prayed that even now, Black hustled Olivia away into the distance, leaving a trail impossible to follow.

"No answer?" The count's eyes bulged.

"She is not a spy," Ian ground out. "Ladies of the *ton* do not function as spies." They worked as societal liaisons. Though a ghastly marital arrangement, it was at least voluntary.

"Forgive me if I do not take your word." He waved at Zheng. "Search upstairs!"

"No need," Olivia said.

Heads swiveled. Ian's heart stopped. She stood at the top of the stairs, back straight and head held high. Air rushed from his lungs, his alveoli collapsing, one after the other, even as his heart pounded, demanding more oxygen.

"I have what you're looking for right here." Olivia lifted her reticule. A guardsman quickly relieved her of the burden.

The count sketched a courtly bow. "Lady Olivia Ravensdale."

She curtsied. "Finding our guardsmen asleep at their post and the rest of the castle seemingly under a sleeping spell, we brought it with us, following a lead Warrick provided before his untimely end." She waved a hand at the solenoid. "If you have been betrayed, it was not by me or my husband."

The guardsman holding her reticule drew forth the bundle and unwrapped it carefully, revealing the osforare apparatus.

The count's expression softened. "As I've yet to find evidence of your betrayal, I will hold my judgment in abeyance." He crooked a finger. "Come here."

Olivia's gaze flickered to Ian's. He wanted her nowhere near the count, but there was little choice. Given the black mood of the man, any misstep could cost them their lives. No choice but to obey. He gave her a pained nod.

She crossed the room to stand before Count Eberwin. "Please, allow us to continue our work here. We will correct Warrick's errors and heal your guardsmen. With the past behind us, we can move forward."

The count stroked his beard. "The programming for the apparatus is complete?"

"I've made much progress," she answered. "The punch card to heal a broken arm is complete."

The count raised an eyebrow at Ian. "And the transformative reagent?"

"Nearly ready," Ian hedged.

"Excellent." The count turned back to Olivia and held out a hand. "I must insist we return to the castle until my wife is located."

"But shouldn't treatment begin immediately?" She glanced at Ian, at the guards who still surrounded him, blades at the ready.

"It should," the count agreed. "Their time grows short. Your husband will see to things here. You have other uses."

None of which Ian cared to contemplate. "My work will suffer without her assistance," he protested.

"I doubt that very much, Lord Rathsburn. In fact, I will do all that is in my power to see that your work gathers speed. Your hand, Lady Olivia," the count insisted.

She placed shaking fingers upon the count's outstretched palm.

In one smooth motion, the count gripped her elbow with his free hand at the same time bringing up his knee. There was a loud snap as her forearm broke across his thigh as if it were a mere twig.

Olivia's scream of pain tore through Ian's chest, making his blood run cold.

"No!" Ian lunged. Hands grabbed him from all angles, restraining him. Knives pressed into his flesh and warm blood trickled down his neck.

Cradling her broken arm, Olivia collapsed to the ground, keening and white-faced.

Ian's heart pounded, every muscle tensed—every fiber of his being needed to be at her side, but no matter how he struggled, there was no escaping the five men who held him fast.

Zheng plucked the dagger from his hand.

As Olivia's sobs faded to pained whimpers, the count addressed Ian. "You will *prove* your loyalty and your ability. Prepare your potion. I will hold the apparatus." His lips stretched into a predatory smile. "You may treat your wife's broken arm the way you once planned to treat those of British spies—or you will not treat her at all."

"She needs immediate medical care," Ian pleaded, ready to do anything the count asked of him if it would save her. Olivia's anguished cries had flayed him raw. "The bones, they need to be set."

"Then you had best work fast." The count snapped his fingers. "Bring her."

CHAPTER THIRTY-TWO

O LIVIA DREAMED THAT tiny, monstrous spiders clawed from inside her arm, inside the bone itself, desperately trying to dig their way free. She twisted against the weight of the sheets above her, resenting their efforts to bind her to the cloud-soft mattress below. A pea soup fog wrapped about her mind, refusing to retreat no matter how she batted at it. But she needed to get up, needed to focus, needed to flee.

"No, no. Please don't move," a familiar voice penetrated the haze. A gentle hand pressed down upon her shoulder. "You'll only make it worse. Trust me, I know."

Elizabeth.

With great effort, Olivia pried open her leaden eyelids. The room swam and she struggled to focus. She was in the turret room. Lying on Elizabeth's bed. *Behind* the bars.

Elizabeth bent over her, pressing the rim of a glass bottle to her lips. "Here. Take a bit more."

"No." She pushed away the laudanum with the one arm that didn't pulse with pain. Her other arm lay at her side, bound to a wooden slat with strips of white cloth. Its position wasn't quite natural. "Tell me. What happened?"

"I set it as best I could while you were unconscious from the pain," Elizabeth said. "Not an uncommon reaction, particularly with multiple breaks."

"Multiple?"

"There are two bones in your forearm, the radius and the ulna. Both are broken. I was told that Ian would be along later to see to your arm, but it's been several hours…"

Olivia turned her head on the pillow. An oil lamp burned on the bedside table. The light shining through the window carried an orange cast to it. Sunset. An entire day, lost.

Time was passing quickly, too quickly, and she was helpless to assist. She pressed her good hand to her chest. Not entirely helpless, then. She wore a dressing robe, but only her outer gown had been removed. She still wore her corset.

Perhaps, when the pain faded a bit…

"I'm certain Ian will arrive soon," Elizabeth reassured her with forced optimism as she drew a chair up beside the bed. "As to *how* it was broken, I was hoping you would tell me."

"The count…" Olivia began, watching Elizabeth's eyes grow ever wider as she recounted recent events. A tale of Russians, arsenic and a three phase generator.

"Warrick is dead by Zheng's hand?" Shock and relief washed over Elizabeth's face.

Olivia nodded, happy to finally offer her a small comfort, but the very motion sent pain throbbing through her arm. No more moving.

"I can be cured?" There was amazement in Elizabeth's voice.

"Yes," Olivia said. Presuming the count allowed it.

"John intended to keep me bound to him." Elizabeth frowned. "A never-ending cycle. A bone breaks, he transplants new cells, and when I have healed—presumably before bone cancer develops—a dose of arsenic and time in his magnetic tube to eliminate any rogue cells."

"Such is my understanding," Olivia said. "Though Ian would take me to task for leaving out the details."

A brief smile crossed Elizabeth's face. "A tale that brings us back to your broken arm. The count is a violent man, but there is usually method to his madness. Why break it?"

"For spite. Because he believes me to be a spy." To think she'd once viewed this all as a grand adventure. "Because he wishes to force Ian to deploy the osforare apparatus using his transformative reagent. Unlike Warrick's cells, Ian's solution directly transforms the osteoblasts, the mature cells that build bone. These cells do not divide or migrate about. They will stay in place, focusing solely upon their task. Then they die. No bone cancer will develop."

If they worked as designed. No human trials had been conducted. But the rats he'd studied, well, they'd been fine. Small comfort that.

The procedure involved was at the forefront of her mind. The osforare apparatus with its one hundred needles was a device best described as one of torture—and she knew *precisely* how it functioned.

She closed her eyes as the room swam, focusing on the tiny, monstrous spiders that had resumed their escape attempt, and told herself the procedure couldn't be any worse that what she already endured.

"So you are?" Elizabeth asked in a hushed voice. "A spy?"

No. "Not really," she whispered. Not the kind they required. Not the kind with technologies and weapons and an endless knowledge of how to evade detection and capture. Obviously.

But Ian, he was. Or he had been.

A thought floated to mind. "Is Steam Matilda here?"

"Yes," Elizabeth answered.

"Talk to her," Olivia breathed. "Whisper into her ear everything that has happened—will happen—to me. Tell her of your procedure and of anything that has changed since."

"Why?"

But she couldn't answer. The room spun again as a wave of pain overtook her arm. Far more than bone felt damaged. There were any number of muscle, nerve and blood vessels inside that could have torn.

Elizabeth bent over her once more, again urging Olivia to sip from the bottle of laudanum. This time she didn't argue.

OLIVIA WASN'T sure how much time passed before a cool breeze blew into their cell, but she recognized the lilting voice and the patter of feet. "Wei," she whispered and pried open her eyes.

The girl stared through the bars with wide, worried eyes. "This bad. Very bad. Watson delivered your message to Black. Then returned."

"Black?" Elizabeth asked.

"His name is Mr. Black. He's a real spy," Olivia said. While speaking into the acousticotransmitter, she'd told him about their flight plan. When the transmitter's battery failed, when the count had stormed the mill, they'd lowered Watson from a window to the cobblestone street, sending him to intercept Mr. Black.

At the time, her broken arm was an unforeseen complication.

Wei frowned. "We have problem. Black says Russian airship sailing in our direction. They maybe come for countess. Black says no waiting. We need to leave. Tomorrow night at full dark."

"Tomorrow?" Olivia jerked in alarm, sending starbursts of pain through her bad arm. It was too soon. They would have no choice but to risk pitting gypsy evasive maneuvers against the count's overhead tracking techniques. She did not like their odds.

"I have wings, but with broken arm, you cannot fly." Wei shook her head. "Black hear most of what count do through other transmitter."

"Other transmitter?" Elizabeth asked.

"In Steam Matilda, in her ear. I installed it a few days ago so that no one would find it."

"I spoke to her as you instructed, Olivia." Elizabeth looked impressed. "So, at the moment you cannot fly. Let's hide the wings, nonetheless. My brother's contraption may yet solve our problems. We need to be ready for any opportunities that present themselves. Whenever they may occur. Push the wings through the bars."

After stashing one set of wings beneath the bed, Elizabeth strapped the second set of wings onto her back and turned toward Wei. "Teach me."

Olivia watched the gliding lesson, such as one could take place, what with Elizabeth able to leap off nothing taller than the bedside chair. Many steps Wei made look effortless, but were in fact quite complicated. Strapping the wings to the wrist, locking the struts, techniques for catching the air, turning, spiraling and very, very explicit instructions as to how to land.

Her head swam with the complexity of it all.

Elizabeth sighed as she took off the second set of wings and slid them beneath the bed. "Gliding sounds grand."

"Wei, can your nightingale carry messages?" Olivia asked.

"Tiny ones. Wrap on ankle." She pulled the bird from inside her padded jacket, demonstrating how to attach a thin strip of paper.

"Send word when the acousticotransmitter in Steam Matilda dies," Olivia said. "The battery. Only a few hours of power are left. Soon your bird will be our only way to communicate."

Wei nodded and tucked the bird away.

Sounds of an argument filtered through the door. Several men drew near. Olivia's stomach twisted into a hard knot. It seemed a potentially historic moment of scientific experimentation approached.

Darting for the window, Wei hung from the ledge only long enough to slide her arms into the wrist straps of her wings and close the window. There was a flash of canvas and wood, and the girl was gone.

The door opened and Zheng strode inside. Without comment, he crossed to their cell and unlocked the barred door, swinging it wide. Ian stepped into the turret room, bearing a tarnished, silver tea tray. On its surface rested a number of small bottles, cotton swabs, a syringe filled with a strange reddish fluid and the osforare apparatus, its needles gleaming like eager teeth in the lamp light. It looked hungry. Overly eager to bite into flesh and blood.

The count stopped by the door, a deadly blade clenched in his fist.

The count wielding a weapon? *This* was a first for her eyes. He might hunt, but the rest of the time, he'd been content to allow his guardsmen and Zheng to do the dirty work.

No longer.

Swallowing, Olivia concentrated on fisting her good hand and tensing her thighs, willing herself to remain conscious.

Ian set the tray down upon the small table inside Elizabeth's cell and clasped his sister in his arms. "How are you? How is Olivia?"

"I'm fine," Elizabeth said. "Aside from being held prisoner. But your wife, she's not doing well at all. I'm certain there is tissue damage."

Carefully, Ian lowered himself to sit by her side. He smoothed the hair away from her face and kissed her forehead.

"Mr. Black says we must leave," she murmured. "Tomorrow. Dusk."

"No whispering," Zheng ordered.

"I need to examine your arm," Ian said, raising his voice and casting Zheng a dark look. "It's going to hurt."

Unwrapping the cloth strips from the wooden slats, he poked and prodded, asking her to flex and extend her fingers, her wrist. "Broken, both bones. But the soft tissue damage is mostly bruising. We can proceed." He stared into her eyes, his gaze both searching and apologetic. "If the patient is willing."

"She consents," the count barked. "Or Zheng removes three more heads, and I begin the search for a new, more cooperative scientist."

"Two birds in a cage, what's the alternative?" she answered Ian, hoping he understood.

"I see." Disapproval tightened his voice. "Well, you certainly won't be spreading your wings any time soon. The rats healed quickly, but it still took two days for the bones to knit."

"Enough," the count growled. "Proceed."

"Elizabeth did a passing job straightening your arm, but it is tricky with two bones at once. When the procedure is complete, I'll fine tune the alignment."

Ian tipped a bottle of ethanol onto a cotton swab and wiped her forearm with the cold liquid. While it evaporated, he used a syringe to fill the glass reservoirs—the chambers connected to the India rubber tubing—of the osforare apparatus. Finally, he lifted the device into position, clamping the two jaw-like halves about her arm.

Her head felt unnaturally buoyant, as if all the air in the room had suddenly been replaced with hydrogen. "I don't think I'm going to last long."

"Stay with me a moment longer." Ian flicked open the programming slot. "Can you confirm this is the correct card?"

"Yes." Her voice was barely audible. Her breath came in short pants and her heart fluttered like a mouse cornered by a cat.

"Then there's no more need for you to remain conscious. In fact, it's better if you sleep, I'd rather not risk letting any movement disrupt its operation." He lifted a bottle of ether, pouring a small amount onto a cotton cloth, waiting for permission.

"Please," she begged, holding his gaze as her body began to tremble. "No memories."

"This will work," he promised.

There was the sweet smell of ether, then blessed oblivion.

CHAPTER THIRTY-THREE

Hands tied behind his back, Ian was marched back to his bedchamber at knife point. A knife the count himself held. Confidence in his subjects had eroded, much like the mortar holding up his decaying castle. Still, they were accompanied by five guardsmen.

The count had finally managed to force him to do the very thing he condemned: experiment upon a non-consenting subject, for Olivia had been given little choice.

Testing his work upon her had filled his stomach with lead. To see the procedure carried out required precision, accuracy and steady hands, and finding Olivia feverish in that drafty tower room had induced a rage that banded itself about his chest, tightening, crushing his ribs. He'd felt anything but clinical.

As Olivia drifted into a drugged—and thankfully, pain-less—sleep, he'd walled off his anger, brick by brick, until he could no longer sense its presence. Then, and only then, had he begun.

Though the procedure had gone perfectly, the osforare apparatus functioning exactly as he'd envisioned, the moment it was over, misgivings rushed back, flapping about his mind like vampire bats, draining his confidence.

So many variables were unaccounted for, the results uncertain. Had he used enough fluid? Transformed sufficient cells within the periosteum? Would Olivia's innate defense mechanisms accept the transformed cells, or mount an immune response and throw her into a delirium of fever?

On the experimental ward at Lister Hospital, Olivia would have been monitored around the clock by a team of trained professionals. Here he relied solely upon his sister. Her extensive experience with bone healing was small consolation.

The bones of a healthy individual took weeks to knit, and he—Olivia, Elizabeth, Wei—needed to leave this castle immediately. Olivia's cover was blown. Black skulked in the shadows, his own agenda unclear. And Elizabeth had murmured in his ear that a Russian airship was expected. When their agent and assets failed to appear, would there be yet more spies to contend with? If Zheng brought the Chinese government into play... then what? An international incident precipitated by the desire to possess indestructible soldiers? All with his research at the heart of the matter.

No. It was time to leave. Before Olivia and Elizabeth took it into their heads to glide from their seven-story tower. He'd received *that* message, glimpsed the wood and canvas beneath the bed. An insane plan he prayed they would not need to enact.

To that end, he needed to retrieve a particular object. He could not leave the device behind, couldn't risk the chance a chemist might analyze the residue left within its glass reservoirs. "Send the osforare apparatus to my room and I will continue to refine its function," he said. *Anywhere but here in Germany.*

"*Nein.* I think not," the count replied. "All further work will be supervised by either myself or Zheng." He jabbed Ian in the back. "How long to cure my guardsmen?"

"All of them cannot be saved," Ian said. "Those who show superficial signs of bone cancer, it's too late for them. Their cancer is too far advanced. Only those Warrick treated these past two or three months have any hope of surviving." He paused. "How many, exactly, fit that criteria?"

The count fell silent, leaving nothing but the sound of footsteps on stone as they climbed up the curving stairs. "About fifty."

"Twelve men can be treated each day. At four treatments per guardsman..." Ian did the mathematics in his head. "If the solenoid is run twenty-four hours a day, they could all be treated in thirty-three days." Assuming nothing broke.

They'd reached the end of the hall. Two guardsmen stood at attention.

"If he escapes," the count told them. "Your lives are forfeit."

"Please. Allow me to work," Ian pled. "I can do nothing here."

"Exactly," the count replied, shoving him through the door into the bedchamber, locking it.

The key ring he'd lifted from Katherine's person lay hidden in the mill. He was going nowhere for some time. Still, he had plans.

He stood quietly. Waiting. Pushing all emotion aside. Long, silent minutes passed. Finally, convinced no one else would be joining him, he crossed the room to the bed and pried the end panel free. Wrapping a hand about Katherine's collar, he dragged the woman as far as the axon thrall band allowed. He located his syringe, the antidote to the crinlozyme, and found her vein. Again, he waited.

Five minutes. Ten. He frowned. She should be awake. He glanced at the vial. Had he used enough of the—

There was a crack to the back of his ankles, and his legs were swept out from beneath him. He landed hard upon his rear.

"Murmph!" Katherine cried through her gag as a blue arc of electricity stalled her escape attempts. She tumbled back toward the bed, her legs lashing out from beneath her dusty skirts.

Ian rolled away, avoiding a second blow of her steel-reinforced boots, this time aimed at his spine. He hopped to his feet as she slammed the heel of her boot onto the floorboards. With a click, a blade shot out from the toe. He stared down into her dark eyes that glinted with threats, daring him to come closer.

"You will not be leaving for Russia," he said.

She would not be leaving on the approaching airship, carrying away all she knew. There was a chance she'd withheld his name—and Olivia's—from her superiors, intent upon presenting them and their work as her own discovery. Perhaps he was merely clinging to a fraying hope of suppressing his sojourn here in Germany, but he had every intention of returning to Britain—to stand before the duke's massive oak desk—with enough data to keep the man occupied with Russians for a decade.

Determining the location of the long sought-after Russian biotechnology laboratory was his first priority. It was known to be underground and east of Moscow, but in a country so vast, so cold, ground searches had yet to reveal the slightest trace of the facility.

Ian would then collect the names of sleeper agents. Katherine herself had numerous friends and family in London, a well-established life among the *ton*. He'd met her purported mother, sisters, a brother. He'd asked her *father* for her hand in marriage. Not a soul had so much as mentioned a German connection, making all of them suspect. Tugging at the threads of their lives might unravel an entire web of conspiracy, for who knew how many husbands she had tucked away.

And there were always the pteryformes to discuss.

Her eyes narrowed. Her foot shifted, glinting in the light. His mistake, missing that final blade.

"Yes," he said. "I'm aware you will not speak willingly. We'll skip the games." He pulled a syringe and a vial of lyophilized veritasium from his waistcoat. Converting drugs into powder form made them lighter to transport and extended shelf life.

Screwing the steel needle onto the tip of the syringe, Ian crossed to the wash stand and filled the syringe to the five centiliter mark with water. To rehydrate the veritasium powder, he pushed the needle through the rubber stopper of the vial and injected the water. White powder swirled in the current, disappearing as it dissolved. Reversing the plunger, he drew one fifth, a mere centiliter, of the truth serum into the syringe.

He faced his captive. "We've enough, Katherine, for several extended conversations."

Even with both her arms and legs bound, her eyes blazed with defiance.

"I realize you have no intention of letting me close enough to administer my truth serum, but it merely adds an extra step." From his pocket, Ian plucked the dart she had fired at Wei. "Remember this?"

The poison chamber was empty now, but he easily refilled it with veritasium from the syringe. He tested the weight of the dart in his hand. A garbled noise came from Katherine's throat.

"I understand your frustration. Quite a different game from the one I learned in the local pub, but..." He feinted to the right, then—as she rolled left—took aim and threw. The dart punctured her upper back, skewering her trapezius.

Katherine howled her displeasure through the silk-ruffled gag.

"Bit of a pinch?" he mocked.

In vain, she bucked and rolled, trying to dislodge the dart. Gradually, one muscle after the other succumbed, and she lay still. Not quite immobile, but rather like a young lord deep—very deep—in his cups. She would be able to form words. Her speech would be slurred and thankfully muffled, but intelligible.

Stepping onto her ankle, he bent to extract the blade that protruded from the toe of her boot. He tucked it into a concealed panel sewn into the lapel of his coat. Only then did he pluck the dart free, roll her over and yank the gag from her mouth. "Let's start with your name. Your *real* name. Tell me."

Her eyes blazed with defiance, but words tumbled forth. "Katerina Dyatlova."

"Now, Katerina, satisfy my curiosity," he began, tugging her into a sitting position and propping her back against the wall. "How many husbands do you have?"

She fought the veritasium, but the most she managed was to lift her chin at a defiant angle. "Four still live."

Four separate dowries had been paid. Perhaps more. The assets backing her deception were astonishing. "Where?"

"France. Denmark. Austria. Italy."

"Tell me their names."

Her nostrils flared as she recited the names of four minor, but influential individuals. Ian memorized them, a peace offering for the duke.

"An excellent beginning," he said. "We'll return to your

so-called family and friends in London later. When is the flyby?"

"Midnight."

"Tonight?"

"Tomorrow."

Ian fought the urge to swear. Time ran extremely short. If the Russians entered the arena in force, there would be little he could control. "Tell me the location of the Russian biotechnology research facility, Kadskoye. The one to which you so generously offered to escort me and my wife. Is it directly east of Moscow?"

Her head rocked back and forth. Her jaw clenched, her face contorting with the effort of keeping her mouth shut. "No."

"Southeast of Moscow?"

"No."

"The frozen icebox that is the northeast, then?"

"Yes."

Ian crouched directly in front of her. She twisted her head away. He gripped her chin, forcing her to face him again. "Give me its exact location. Latitude and longitude."

Katerina's body vibrated with frustration. An eye twitched.

Ian reached for the syringe. An additional centiliter of veritasium forced the numbers past her lips. "Excellent." This information alone would save him. "Tell me the names of the scientists you—and others—have *collected* for Russia. Begin with British citizens."

Defiance laced her voice, but Katerina produced name

after name. Ian sat back upon his heels, listening in amazement and concern. He recognized almost none of the names, but they hailed from all over the globe. A team of agents would be required to systematically investigate each individual, to analyze the implications of such an intellectual stockpile.

As his detachment slipped, he ran a hand over his face. Katerina couldn't be allowed her freedom; she would sound the alarm. Yet coldly eliminating her was undesirable; she was a wellspring of information. She needed to be dragged to British soil and interrogated with more finesse than he could manage. Once her sins were delineated, she could pay the penalty for her crimes.

"Who introduced you to Warrick?" He wanted the name of the man who sat on the shadow board, whose desire to seek out humans who were "other" put both individuals and his country at risk.

Clamping her lips shut, she shook her head.

Ian glanced at the window. Where the hell was Black? With only enough crinlozyme to immobilize her for six days, he needed—

The lock clicked, and the door slammed open.

Though guardsmen stood behind him, the count himself was poised upon the threshold. He raised a crossbow, pointing a steel-tipped arrow directly at Katerina's chest.

His brow furrowed and his nostrils flared. "How disappointing to find you in another man's bedchamber," he growled. "Our entire marriage, nothing but a convenient fabrication to pry into the affairs of the German empire. And now you have moved on to British undertakings. How easily you maneuver from one man to the next, manipulating all to your advantage. Yet it simplifies everything." He squinted, taking aim.

"Don't!" Heart pounding, Ian stepped in front of her. Stupid of him. The self-absorbed count rarely made rational decisions and rage glittered in his eyes.

The crossbow lowered. "You defend her?"

"I do not. But swift and cold revenge gains you nothing." Ian stepped forward. "I do not advocate mercy, but before you dispatch her like a rabid animal, might I suggest a dispassionate interrogation? Her secrets have value."

"Secrets? Russia? I don't understand." Katerina's voice trembled and a fat, glistening tear rolled down her cheek. "I came to visit *Frau* Rathsburn. What's going on, Otto? I have no secrets. Why has *Herr* Rathsburn done this to me?" She held out her ankle showing him the thrall band clamped about it. "Is he Russian? I've told him nothing." Her voice took on a more hysterical note. "I know nothing to tell!"

Already her speech was clearer, her ability to lie restored. A surprising and impressive tolerance to veritasium.

"You might start by asking about her most recent visit to London," Ian suggested.

"London?" The count eyed his wife.

A torrent of pleading German poured forth, and the count pursed his lips, considering.

Ian swore. "Do you not see what she's done? What she's doing? Don't let her win."

Had this entire project been orchestrated by Katerina, by the Russians, right from the start? Why not? How better to fund research than to access her enemies' resources? Discover those most easily manipulated, then bring them together. Disgruntled British scientists. Lofty German ambitions. The dark corner of a primeval forest. Watch and wait. Transport to Kadskoye only those experiments that meet with success. Terminate all others.

"We—my wife and I—will discuss this elsewhere." The count shoved the crossbow into the arms of a guardsman and barked a series of orders.

A guardsman with bulging tumors aimed a voltaic prod, gesturing at Ian to back up. Hands in the air, he did so. A second guardsman unlocked the axon thrall band about Katherine's ankle, and the count swept his deceitful, polygamous wife into his arms and marched from the room.

Ian very much doubted both of them would survive the night. If he were pressed, he would lay odds on Katerina.

CHAPTER THIRTY-FOUR

THE FIRST TIME OLIVIA woke in agony. Every inch of her skin burned, and her bones felt as if they were being forged from iron. Elizabeth held a cool compress to her forehead and murmured comforting words while pressing the bottle of laudanum to her lips.

The second time she woke she was damp with sweat, but the flames had retreated. Only the flesh and bone of her forearm felt molten. She let Elizabeth spoon clear broth—laced with antimony—into her mouth.

"Ian promises it will speed the healing process," Elizabeth said.

By dawn, when she woke for the fifth or sixth time, the pain only smoldered, deep inside her arm, like the coals of a dying fire.

Elizabeth helped her into a sitting position, insisting Olivia consume the entire bowl of antimony broth that Steam Matilda had brought.

Setting aside the spoon, she looked down at her broken arm set in a gypsum plaster cast that encased both her wrist and her elbow. She wiggled her fingers and was pleased to find them all in working order. Sore, but not overly so.

"How does it feel?" Elizabeth asked.

"It aches something fierce, but nothing like it did last night." Her voice was hoarse but, for the first time in what felt like a short forever, her mind was clear. "Is it normal to feel as if your bones are melting when they knit back together?"

"Not exactly. They throb and pulse with pain. But melt?" Elizabeth shook her head.

"It felt as though someone shoved my arm inside a forge before hammering it back in shape," Olivia said. "Now, it is as if the iron has begun to cool."

"Odd."

They both stared at her arm for a moment, wondering what the transformed osteoblasts had done. Were doing. Might do in the future. But there was no point in worrying about what might happen if there was to be no future.

"You've been speaking to Steam Matilda?" Olivia asked, breaking the silence.

"Whispering in her left ear as instructed." Elizabeth glanced toward the window. "No sign of Wei's bird yet, but the window is closed."

As such, there was no way of knowing what was going on outside. Olivia swung her feet over the edge of the bed.

"They changed the lock." Elizabeth reached out and lifted a heavy padlock hanging from a chain securing the door of their cage. "They said you were a British spy and confiscated the contents of your reticule, took every last hairpin..."

"But I still wear my corset." Olivia stood and wobbled her way over to the barred door. She bent to examine the padlock.

"Your corset?" Elizabeth repeated. "How—"

"Lock picks instead of steel stays," she answered. Renewed hope lit Elizabeth's face. "Most men don't suspect a woman. Of those who do, their eyes tend to skim over the corset itself and focus instead upon what it supports."

A slow grin spread across Elizabeth's face. "It seems my brother married... a truly unusual woman."

Olivia dropped her eyes to the lock and let the lie stand. Ian's offer for her hand was too new, a fragile, precious thing she clutched tightly to her chest and had yet to let herself fully examine. "Pfft. It's a basic Scheldner. Only three pins. Will you bring the chair?" Her legs wobbled and her head spun. Likely it was mere dehydration. "And perhaps some more water."

Settling herself before the iron door, Olivia reached inside her dressing gown and extracted two picks, somewhat grateful the count had broken her left arm and not her right. She contorted herself into a number of odd and uncomfortable positions, shifting this way and that, trying to accommodate the cast that immobilized her arm at a strange angle. She needed her left hand to hold the rake pick.

Heaving a sigh of frustration, Olivia dragged the chair closer to the lock and knelt upon the seat. She could do this.

A few adjustments later, her left hand slipped the rake pick into place.

"There we go. A few tweaks..." She slid a hook pick in beside the first, both feeling and listening for the pins. One. Two. Three. She had them. There was a faint *click*, and the deadbolt fell away. As a precaution, she gave the rake pick an extra twist, breaking off a small piece of metal inside the lock's mechanism. No one would use this lock again. Or the pick.

Elizabeth clapped her hands. "Have I mentioned how thrilled I am to have a sister such as you?

Sister. Olivia opened her mouth, then closed it again, unwilling to disabuse her of the truth. Soon. She would tell her soon. The minute they were safe.

"Can you teach me to do that?" Elizabeth continued. "Another day, of course."

"Another day," she promised, forcing a smile and wondering if that day would ever materialize.

They crept across the turret room, careful not to alert the guard standing outside the door. Elizabeth grasped the latch, pushed the window open. Together, they leaned out and stared down into the river valley.

Olivia's heart gave a massive thud. The big moment was coming. And soon. She would have to do it. Jump. Wei's exit strategy had turned into their only option. The alternative, becoming the count's pawn, was unacceptable.

"Look!" Elizabeth pointed.

Upon the riverbank beside the *Sky Dragon*, a tiny figure dressed in red waved her arms.

Wei.

The girl bent, then flung an object into the sky. One that grew larger as the nightingale's wings struggled against rising and swirling air currents, fluttering ever closer to the tower window.

Dark, gray clouds hung low in the sky. Threatening a storm. Olivia's heart skipped a beat. Snow flurries. Icy gusts. What might extreme weather conditions do to their wings? She pulled herself back inside and leaned against the cold, stone wall. She could have sworn the floor shifted beneath her.

"Seven stories," she breathed, pressing her good hand against her pounding heart. "And that's not even accounting for the height of the rock the castle stands upon."

Elizabeth placed a hand upon her shoulder. "A spy afraid of heights?" She lifted an eyebrow.

"I'm not much of a spy," Olivia confessed. "My duties have, until now, never extended much beyond lock picking and household eavesdropping—or programming a steambot to do so."

The nightingale swooped into the room, searching for a perch and settling upon the back of a chair. A long strip of paper was tightly wound about its ankle. She uncoiled the note and recognized Mr. Black's handwriting at once.

"Passed by mill," she read aloud. "Guardsmen agitated due to treatment delay. Something to do with the count's wife."

"What!" Elizabeth exclaimed. "I thought you said Katerina was unconscious and hidden under your bed?"

"She is. Was." She swallowed. Had Katerina managed to escape? Had she been discovered? Or perhaps Ian had turned her over as a gesture of goodwill to pacify the count. If so, given the count's state of mind, how long would he allow his wife to live? "I suppose we ought to be grateful he is not occupied with Ian. Or us."

Elizabeth nodded. "There's that."

But such a reprieve was temporary. When the Russians arrived—depending upon the value they placed upon Katerina—there might yet be more Russian agents swarming the castle. If that were to occur... She shook her head and frowned. No matter what path those thoughts ran down, none of them reached a promising conclusion. All the more reason to hasten their departure.

She turned back to the note. "Attempts to contact Rathsburn have failed. Window open, but no response beyond scraps of silk tied to bird's leg."

She looked up into Elizabeth's worried face. "Likely he has nothing with which to write. We gagged Katerina with strips of her petticoats. That must be his way of signaling her escape."

Elizabeth gave a tight nod.

"Rescue plan initiates at dusk. Fly one hour after full dark for green campfire in woods," she finished. Her pulse jumped. She'd insisted she could do this, leap from a tower window and glide to the ground. Soon she would have to match her actions to her words.

"Green?"

"A beacon of sorts, I presume," Olivia answered.

"Fly. How fast did my brother say his transformed cells would mend bones?"

She frowned at her arm. There was no more pain. Only a faint soreness. "I've little choice. We'll wait a few hours, then the cast will have to come off."

CHAPTER THIRTY-FIVE

"Rescue begins at dusk." Ian glared at the terse note from Black. Not a single word about how Olivia or his sister fared. Or if the two women really intended to glide from the turret room. Was it possible the procedure had been a terrific success? Or would their jump be one of desperation? Worry dropped like leaden ball into his stomach. He'd seen the wings beneath Elizabeth's bed, taken note that Olivia still wore her corset, its lock picks in situ. All was in place for their mad and dramatic leap.

Rescue. Alone, he could manage escape without assistance, though it would be difficult, but with Olivia and Elizabeth locked away in a tower, outside assistance was required. Particularly once they had feet on the ground. A large group headed toward the border would be suspicious, but in the company of gypsies, they might have a chance.

The count had posted numerous guardsmen outside the door, and one held the voltaic prod. The only reasonable path of escape was via the window. A window out of which he'd spent the better part of the daylight hours watching a riderless pteryform circle and storm clouds gather on the horizon—all while tying strips of the bedsheets together. When dusk arrived, he would need to descend quickly, before the guardsmen who patrolled below spotted him.

Midnight tonight.

All choice had been removed. With the cure discovered and the Russians en route, it was time to leave. Only one thing troubled him. Without the osforare apparatus in his possession and returned to British shores, he would be branded a traitor. Unless the duke took pity and deigned to accept his information about the Russians in trade.

An ache gnawed inside his empty chest; he missed Olivia. How to win her hand? Perhaps if her father accepted his sincere apologies, he could arrange for her career to accelerate... Would the duke permit them to work within the Queen's agents as a team?

The hours crawled past, until at last the sun slowly disappeared behind the surrounding hills, and the orange-gold rays of sunset began to fade. Nearly time.

He tied his makeshift rope to the bedpost and was flexing his fingers when the window opened and Wei slipped inside.

Her face and hands were covered in gray paint, her hair stuffed beneath an equally gray skull cap. Even her clothes were gray—adult-sized clothing, the arms and legs of which had been inexpertly hacked off, shortened for a girl of her size. Castle camouflage.

"It's as if a gargoyle detached itself from the castle down-spout and crawled inside," he said.

She grinned, far from insulted. "That the idea!" Hopping to the floor, she began to spin, turning a pirouette and unwinding a thin braided metal cord wrapped about her waist.

He recognized the cording. "Black outfitted you."

"Black has most interesting toys." Idolization gleamed in her eyes. The metal cording pooled upon the floor as she turned. "This he call Rapunzel cord. Except you go down, not up. Only one hundred feet. You drop last twenty. Black say not to break ankle."

"Mmm," Ian answered. He might resent Black's interference, but a swift and sure descent was preferable to one that was the visual equivalent of waving a white flag. He replaced the bedsheet rope with the cord and accepted the belt harness and geared winch from Wei with as much gratitude as he could muster. "No weapons?" he asked.

"Black said you ask. He say you want weapon, come down. He has daggers to spare."

"Not a pistol?" Ian grumbled.

"He say you ask that too. Say you not spy anymore. Say you good with blades and needles and potions. Stick to that." Wei climbed onto the window seat and threw open the window. "Come! We go now," she said. "You slide. I jump. We run for forest. Then princess and spy follow."

The image of canvas and wood beneath his sister's bed flashed to mind. "Olivia?" Ian said. "Is it safe for her to glide?"

"Yes. Princess talk all day to someone called Steam Matilda." Wei looked up at him in awe. "You fixed her arm. She take cast off. Bone all healed."

Could it be? In less than forty-eight hours the transformed cells had repaired her broken arm. His body straightened as if all the emptiness inside his chest filled with aether. "It's still a risk," he worried aloud. "Why not take the Rapunzel cord to them?"

Wei rolled her eyes. "*Because* they have wings. Come. Black worried. He say a Russian storm frigate approaches."

"A *storm frigate*?" He swore. Katerina's flyby involved a storm frigate, the largest and most dangerous of all Russian airships.

Clapping a hand to her mouth, Wei giggled at the descriptive phrases that erupted from his mouth.

But it was no laughing matter.

The outer hulls of Russian state storm frigates were super cooled, enough so that when they passed through clouds, it began to snow, obscuring the ship's position and blinding their enemies. Storm frigates also carried weapons and—presumably—many, many Russian agents.

Yet Katerina's departure had been described as a flyby. He'd hoped the airship would do exactly that. Fly by.

But to send a storm frigate for her? A chill settled in his bones. Katerina must be more important than he'd presumed. If she failed to board with her "cargo", would the airship pause, weigh anchor? Would black-garbed Russian agents drop ropes from the sky and slither to the ground?

Either way, Ian was in no position to resist them, not

trapped in this room. He climbed to the window's edge and flung the Rapunzel cord out, watching as it unfurled. Not a single guardsman so much as turned his head. With a *snick*, Ian hooked the geared winch to his belt and then to the cord. He pulled on his leather gloves and took hold of the thin metal line.

"Let's go," he said. Trusting to the engineering skills of those employed by the Rankine Institute, he stepped off the window ledge.

"Time to go." Elizabeth stood at the window, adjusting her wings. "An hour has passed since the sun disappeared behind the hills."

Olivia paced across the floorboards, flexing and extending her arm. An arm that had been badly broken some thirty-six hours ago. It was still sore and tender to the touch, but there really was no choice. None at all.

The nightingale had fluttered back and forth all day, carrying gliding tips from Wei and more detailed instructions as to where to land. A final note written in Mr. Black's hand instructed them not to delay. A Russian storm frigate had been spotted flying in their direction, and the resultant storm was expected to begin shortly after dark. Already winds had begun to pick up.

"I see a green light in the distance," Elizabeth called.

"Are you sure?" she asked, wiping her damp palms on her skirts. "Absolutely certain?"

Her stomach hurt and, though she'd been sipping antimony-laced bone broth—careful not to ingest too much at once—she felt as though she might lose what little liquid she'd swallowed. It was impossible to say if it was the antimony or anxiety. Either way, she didn't seem to be able to muster the intestinal fortitude to spread her wings and leap from their window. She was certain she would slam into the face of the castle wall on her very first turn, then crash to the ground, battered and broken beyond all repair.

She had a mental image of nearly every bone in her body shattering. Only one indestructible, silver-boned, antimony-reinforced forearm would lie upon the cobblestones intact.

When she'd agreed to glide to the ground from a height of over one hundred feet, she'd thought Ian would be at her side, ready to... Do what exactly? Kiss her before shoving her off the edge? No. This was a solo event. One took to the air a solitary individual. Voluntarily.

Elizabeth turned and fixed Olivia with a stare. "If you don't jump, my brother will refuse to leave."

She was right. Ian would come for her, risking his very life. Mr. Black would call for French and British backup. More Russian airships would arrive. Tumor-ridden guardsmen would die defending an insane count. British agents would be caught in the crossfire. Secret and valuable biotechnology representing years of effort and thousands of pounds would be exposed, lost to the hands of enemies.

Pressing a hand to her forehead, she swallowed. "Yes, of course. Ian wouldn't want me to cause an international incident."

"What?" Elizabeth exclaimed. "No. He would come for you, for his wife, for the woman he loves."

She froze. Love. Was it possible that Ian could want her for herself? He *had* proposed. She'd been so certain that it was merely a gentlemanly compulsion. That she'd been ruined. That he needed a wife. That her programming skills were valuable. That marrying her would prevent a charge of treason, force her father to reinstate him as a Queen's agent and ensure his laboratory work continued without interruption.

But what if Elizabeth was right? What if Ian loved her? *Me.*

Was another future possible? One that didn't involve prowling about her own home, suffering the attentions of a dishonorable husband so that she might pry into his unscrupulous activities? Waiting—perhaps indefinitely—for her husband to die before she could begin to truly experience life? Deep inside her belly, a fledgling hope stretched its wings, but didn't quite dare take flight.

Olivia didn't wish to leave the Queen's service, not exactly. Yet blindly marrying some loathsome target chosen for her was no longer acceptable, and fieldwork wasn't as appealing as she'd once believed. Perhaps she might serve her country in other ways...

But if she didn't jump, she'd never have the chance to find out.

She stiffened her spine, slid her wrists into the wing braces and nodded. If Elizabeth could fling herself into the air, so could she. "You first," she said.

Rolling her eyes, Elizabeth climbed onto the window ledge. "Remember. Ten seconds after me. You *must* jump. Mr. Black has been very clear about the narrow window of opportunity we will have to disappear if we are spotted before guardsmen swarm the forest."

"Yes, yes. Yes. I *will* jump." Olivia moved to stand directly behind her. "If I don't survive, be certain to tell Ian—"

She stopped herself. Voicing it out loud would make it irrevocable. She needed time to think, to analyze this madness. So did Ian. The circumstances of the last few days... could she trust her heart? Her instincts?

"Tell him yourself," Elizabeth said. Then she jumped.

"Wait!" Olivia yelled. But of course it was too late.

She climbed into the window, grateful for the numbing cold of the winter wind that buffeted her face and blew her skirts against her legs. Heart in her throat, she watched Elizabeth. In graceful arcs, she swooped and turned, spiraling toward the ground with incredible elegance, as if she'd always been meant to fly.

Maybe this wasn't as difficult as she imagined.

Three. Two. One.

Olivia spread her wings, locked them straight and—resisting the impulse to squeeze her eyes shut—jumped.

Icy wind snapped the canvas tight, yanking against the wooden struts, straining every muscle in her arm, in her chest. She struggled to make the first turn, narrowly avoiding an outstretched and snarling rainspout. On her second turn, her left wingtip scraped against the stone of a balcony, jarring her sore arm.

Too close.

A cry from the ramparts reached her ears, but she could not spare a moment's glance. Not with the bitter wind rushing over her, stabbing through her flimsy dressing gown, tangling her hair, and scraping away the protective tears that seeped from her eyes. Unlike Elizabeth who seemed part bird, she was meant to keep her feet on solid earth.

Straining against the wind, she pulled with her right arm, angling her body, trying to correct her course and largely succeeding. She soared over the River Kerzen, aiming for the green fire that burned in a clearing in the deep and darkening woods where, presumably, Mr. Black and a score of gypsies waited, ready to whisk them swiftly and secretly toward France.

In the distance, Elizabeth disappeared behind the trees. Olivia had no doubt she'd land with grace and beauty.

Whoosh.

What was that? Olivia turned her head. A mistake.

She faltered. Corrected course. But not before she'd seen a solitary archer astride a pteryform taking careful aim. The count?

Whoosh. A steel-tipped arrow rushed past Olivia. The next tore through her skirts. The one that followed a moment later pierced her left wing. She struggled to compensate, pulling with everything she had, desperately trying to reach the designated landing site where she could see waiting caravans—

Whoosh. Another arrow through her left wing. A ripping sound as the canvas tore. One minute the air held her aloft, the next minute it withdrew its support, and she topped sideways, plunging toward the trees below her all the while desperately flapping her one remaining wing to no avail.

Clawing branches rushed up at her, eager to snatch her from the air. The first few spindly branches scratched at her ankles, but none managed to maintain their grip as she crashed through the canopy, smashing and banging into a blur of branches of increasing size—

She jerked to a stop. Her pounding heart leapt into her throat, then dove toward her knees as her predicament registered. Some ten feet from the ground, a branch refused to release her, holding on tightly to the tattered canvas and wood and wire of her left wing. For a moment she hung there by her recently healed arm and whimpered in pain for said arm no longer felt wholly intact.

She kicked, feet flailing until finally her boots made contact with the trunk. She kicked again, reaching with her good arm to catch a nearby branch. She pulled and tugged and twisted, but the remnants of her wings thwarted her movement. Finally, she resorted to swinging her legs like a clock pendulum, gathering momentum until at last she was able to swing her legs over a sturdy branch.

"Help!" she called, looking up at the tangled mess in which her throbbing arm was enmeshed. Quite the pickle, this, hanging from a tree branch upside-down, blood rushing to her head. Bark dug into the skin of her fingers as muscles and tendons burned, a not-so-subtle warning that her grip was failing.

"Olivia!"

Ian. Thank goodness. "Here! I'm over here!" She wanted to weep with relief as he emerged from the now-dark woods and climbed the tree. Then he was beside her, pulling her upright and kissing her as if he'd thought her lost forever. Indeed, it had been close. She returned his kiss with equal fervor.

Far below them, Wei giggled, her laughter accompanied by a sound she recognized as Mr. Black clearing his throat.

Ian pulled away and, knife in hand, sliced through the canvas that held her prisoner. "Let's get you down. You've a border to cross."

Her chest grew tight. "*We* have a border to cross," she insisted. But even before he spoke the words aloud, she knew. He was going back to the castle. Without her. This nightmare wasn't over.

CHAPTER THIRTY-SIX

SNOWFLAKES DRIFTED lazily through the air, landing upon the long, dark-gold fringe of Olivia's eyelashes. Her deep blue eyes looked up at him, both fearful and accusing, as the canvas gave way and he pulled her against his side. When her feet found purchase on the branches below them, he pressed a kiss into the tangle of her windblown curls. "I'm sorry, Olivia, but I have to go back."

Watching through the spyglass Black had handed him, his heart had slammed against his sternum as first Elizabeth then Olivia leapt from the castle tower.

"When I saw the arrow slice through your wing—" Ian's throat closed at the memory. She'd jumped. She'd flown. And soon she would be safe. He would make certain of it. "Go with Black, with Elizabeth and Wei to the border."

She buried her face into the crook of his neck. "I'd rather come with you."

"No." Not an option. "As soon as I find the osforare apparatus—"

Thud. An arrow struck the tree trunk beside them, missing Ian's shoulder by mere inches. *Thwack.* Another ripped another hole through Olivia's already tattered skirts.

He leapt from the tree, landing hard upon the ground—Olivia in his arms—as everyone yelled at once.

"Overhead!" Black called. "Man on a pteryform."

"The count!" Wei cried.

"He's circling back!" Elizabeth screamed.

A dark, flapping shadow blotted out the moonlight as they ran through the woods, tripping and stumbling over tree roots, running for the cover of a rocky outcropping that seemed all too distant and all too meager a shelter.

The creature dropped from the sky cutting off their escape. It reared back on its hind legs, sulfurous eyes blazing and sharp beak snapping, as the count lifted his crossbow and took aim.

Ian shoved Olivia onto her feet, pushing her toward his sister and Wei who'd had the presence of mind to hide behind a tree. Black was nowhere to be seen. He threw his hands in the air. "Let them go," he yelled, "and I'll come without a fight."

The crossbow lowered an inch. "*Frau* Rathsburn?"

"Completely healed," he said, stepping forward from the shelter of the trees. "So strong she flew from your castle, crashed into the trees and still, her arm did not break."

"Excellent." The count's eyes lit with a predatory gleam. "Run, *Frau* Rathsburn, *Fräulein* Elizabeth," he called, raising his arm and taking aim. It seemed there would be no negotiations. "The Kaiser's chemists will analyze the residue in the device, puzzle out its composition. You are no longer necessary, but neither can I simply allow you to leave. Word of this success cannot spread before our army reaches your shore."

Ian was reaching for the handle of the dagger when a dark shadow—Black—stepped from the forest and a gleam of silver spun through the air. The count bellowed as Black's knife plunged into his thigh, but it did not slow him. He swung the crossbow toward Black, and an arrow whistled. This time it was Black who yelled, falling backward upon the ground clutching his shoulder.

Ian flung his dagger, but he was not familiar with the balance of the Russian knife and, though it sliced across the count's biceps drawing blood, the count managed to hang on to his weapon. The answering arrow sent in Ian's direction went wide. A small victory.

The women screamed, but not in terror. A volley of rocks flew at the count, at the pteryform. A small nightingale launched into the air, pecking and scratching at the count's head. As the count swatted at the bird, as the creature clawed the ground, its long, sinuous neck stretching out to hiss a fog of sulfur, Ian ran to Black. He dragged him into the relative shelter of the forest, searching out the arrow. "How bad?"

"Bad enough." The words emerged through gritted teeth as the agent pressed a weapon into Ian's hands. "Pistol's gone. Use my throwing knife."

"I give you but one chance, *Herr* Rathsburn," the count yelled, "to turn around and die facing me like a man."

Black gripped Ian's arm. "He has dismounted and stands ten paces behind you. Though his aim is true, his arm begins to shake. Don't miss."

Understood.

Ian tested the weight of the knife, gripping it lightly between his fingers. Crouching upon the balls of his feet, he shifted, sighting over his shoulder. In a single movement, he spun, flinging the knife into the count's arm.

The crossbow clattered to the ground as the count sank to his knees, blood staining the snow that coated the forest floor. He pulled a dagger from his hip. "We're not yet done, *Herr* Rathsburn. Try to finish me. Try."

But the count was no longer Ian's greatest concern. The pteryform, hissing and spitting, was advancing upon the women, talons lifted, beak snapping. He clapped his hands and yelled, drawing the creature's attention. With the hand signals Katerina had used during their ill-fated balloon ride, Ian gave the pteryform a new target: the count.

Confused, the pteryform turned away from the women. Its feet crunched over snow-covered leaves to approach its master. Nostrils flaring it bent over the count, dragging in the scent of his blood.

"No!" the count cried, "I am your master!" With his hands, he issued a new series of orders.

Tame or wild?

The creature let out a low, resonating moan that made

Ian's blood run cold. Tail lashing, the creature leapt upon the count, gripping him in its talons.

Pulling Black to his feet, he slung the man's arm over his shoulder. If this creature chose to make a meal of the count, he did not care to bear witness. Or to be the second course. As he dragged Black into the trees toward the wide-eyed women, the pteryform gave a final roar and launched itself into the air, lifting the count into the snowy night sky.

Wei ran to Black. Though unshed tears welled in her eyes, she announced, "When you are healed, you will teach me this knife trick."

"Maybe. When you are much older," Black said, ruffling her hair with his good arm. Those two had bonded quickly.

Elizabeth pressed a fist to her mouth, and Olivia stared at him with wide, blinking eyes. "Did it just—? Is it going to—?"

"We need to hurry," Ian said. He did not wish to discuss what the creature may or may not do with the count. They had greater concerns. Katerina might still live. More pteryformes might yet still take to the night's sky. And—somewhere—Zheng and the guardsmen prowled.

At the encampment, only two caravans—one man and one woman tending each—remained beside the smoldering remains of the strange green fire. Olivia approached the gypsies, speaking in halting Romani and presumably arranging for medical supplies.

The man brought Black a stool and held him steady, while the woman coaxed the fire back to life, heating the flat of a knife in the flames. Elizabeth turned away and covered her ears. It was a brutal few minutes, yanking the arrow from

Black's shoulder, cauterizing the wound, bandaging it tightly, and still this misadventure was far from over.

While Black caught his breath, he pointed the blue-green light of his decilamp at Olivia. "Your arm," he said. "Tell me."

She recounted a story of searing pain while Ian subjected her arm to a complete examination, poking and prodding, flexing and twisting. Though bruises discolored her skin, though the surrounding soft tissue was swollen, the bones—as he'd bragged to the count—appeared fully healed. "Amazing," he murmured. She had survived the first stage of treatment, but given his work was still in experimental stages, she would need to be monitored. Closely. Carefully.

Something Olivia said jarred him from these new concerns. He looked up to find everyone looking at him expectantly.

"Repeat that please."

"Katerina." Olivia's eyes narrowed. "What did you learn?"

"Much. But the count paid me a surprise visit. He interrupted my interrogation and dragged her away to conduct his own."

Black cleared his throat. "Any spy so deeply entrenched as to evade our suspicions is resourceful and capable of improvisation."

"If you both think she's free to roam the castle," Olivia said. "That means—"

"She's preparing to take the apparatus—with its biochemical residues—to Russia." He should have allowed the count to shoot her the moment he'd walked into the room.

A gong sounded in the distance. Two strikes. A pause. Then two more strikes. Wei's eyes were two round saucers. "Uncle is preparing to launch *Sky Dragon*. Is bell for all hands on deck. If leather bird took count's body back to castle and Uncle finds, he will be angry. He will not want countess to win."

True, Zheng had an over-developed sense of personal honor. "One of them will have the osforare apparatus," he said. "Our window of time to retrieve it grows short." He slid his hand down Olivia's bare arm, catching at her fingers. Time for him to leave her, to return to the castle and retrieve his device. Without it, they could have no future—and he could not leave the secret to unbreakable soldiers in the hands of the Russians or the Chinese.

Black stared at their entwined fingers.

Ian dropped her hand and stood. He'd proposed, but she'd yet to answer. He had no official claim. "The snow is picking up. Everyone to the caravans. The gypsies won't appreciate leading their clockwork horses in a blizzard. Best to move out of range of the storm frigate. Head for the border." He yanked Black to his feet. "I'll join you as soon as I can."

Black nodded. Words were unnecessary. Retrieve the technology and Ian would be allowed to return to his prior life. With the information he'd collected and the device in hand, the duke would forgive all past mistakes.

"You can't be serious," Olivia cried.

"There has to be another way," Elizabeth added.

With dark, sad eyes, Wei handed him a sack. Red Chinese characters adorned its surface. "I find this in Uncle's cabin. This yours, yes?"

"Yes." His shoulders released a knot. "Thank you." It would be a relief to work with familiar blades. He dug the knives from the bag, slipping them back into place, strapping his sword upon his hip. Finally, he felt balanced. One last mission, fully armed. Almost. Ian eyed the rough, stained bandage wrapped around Black's shoulder. Nor had he missed the man's slight limp, a reminder of his recent encounter with Katerina's pteryformes. There'd be no taking him to the castle as backup. "I don't suppose you have another TTX pistol?"

Black twisted his lips. "Much as I would like to see you reinstated, Rathsburn, that Russian spy relieved me of my only pistol and all my cartridges."

"I'm going with you," Olivia stood, her eyes flashing defiance.

"No," Ian said. "You're not."

"Certainly not in a torn dressing gown?" Black's eyebrows rose. "You'd freeze to death. As the storm frigate approaches, visibility during the resulting snowfall will drop precipitously."

"Then give me your coat." Olivia said. "I can help. I'm an agent."

"Not that kind of agent," Ian reminded her. He was rewarded with a narrow-eyed glare.

Black held up a hand. "Such was not the mission. If you

do not return to your mother's side post haste, Lady Olivia, there's no hope you ever will be. You broke protocol. Disobeyed direct orders."

Elizabeth piped up in her defense. "That's Lady Rathsburn to you, Mr. Black."

"Oh?" Black's eyebrows rose. "Is it now?"

Olivia lifted her chin. "I improvised, as any good agent would do. Lord Rathsburn was abandoning ship. Traveling out of range. I was able to assist you from the inside by stowing away upon his airship then later posing as his wife."

"Posing?" Elizabeth gaped. "You're not truly married?"

Glancing from Olivia to Ian, Black threw his head back and laughed. The next words that burst from his lips were in an unfamiliar language. Not that a translation was necessary.

"He has proposed." Olivia's face flamed as she jabbed Black in the chest with an index finger. "No more such comments about the man I love."

The man she loved. His heart flipped in his chest, then slammed against his rib cage, pounding in triumph. Pulling her to his side, he brushed a finger over the side of her face and whispered, "You have my heart as well."

An entire future stretched before them, but only if he could pry the osforare apparatus from Katerina's hands. Bone deep, he *knew* she possessed it. That Zheng would attempt to claim it for his own.

"Enough," Black said. "Time to act. We need to depart, as does Rathsburn." He handed Ian a compass and rattled off a number of coordinates. "That's the border crossing. We can wait a few hours, no more."

Ian nodded. He took a step backward, turning toward the woods.

"I'm coming with you." Olivia wrapped a hand around his arm.

"You can't," Ian said. "Katerina views you as a prize to be won, and she would not hesitate to use you against me." He pried her hand free. "Besides, as you yourself pointed out, you're not trained in weaponry or self-defense of any kind."

Olivia drew breath, preparing to argue. He stopped her with a kiss.

Sliding his hands into her tangled hair, he cupped the base of her skull, pouring forth the love he felt for this amazing woman. He wanted his future to include more than endless hours in a windowless laboratory. But before he could beg her to be his wife, there was one last loose end to tie up.

He pulled away and stared into her eyes. "It's better if I go alone. Please. See my sister, Wei, and yourself safe. All I need do is retrieve the apparatus. A simple task," he lied. "In and out. I'll meet you at the border crossing."

Kissing her forehead, and then his sister's, he turned and stalked off into the woods, ignoring their cries of outrage.

CHAPTER THIRTY-SEVEN

Mr. Black grabbed Olivia by the elbow, muttering in Romani, as he spun her toward the waiting caravan where the gypsy man held the reins. As the gypsy woman lifted the lantern and climbed inside, helping Elizabeth up the curved steps, she waved at Olivia to hurry.

She yanked her arm away. "What did you just say?"

"Get in," Mr. Black begged. "Please. Snow accumulates and my leg aches."

"No." She refused to climb inside. "Repeat that. Slowly and clearly and in English."

"You understood me well enough. The duke thought you would balk at following Rathsburn, even though you believe your heart set on working in the field. The duchess claimed you had more sense than to disobey direct orders." He tweaked her nose and grinned. "I alone knew that you would not prove impervious to the charms of a handsome young doctor. The Ravensdale clan... all of you so headstrong."

"This was a test?" She planted her hands on her hips. "My parents expected me to fail?"

"Your father *expected* to challenge your preconceived notions of fieldwork," Mr. Black said. "Your mother *expected* to provide you with an incentive to marry that Italian baron. The duchess worried you were about to rebel." His voice grew sing-song. "'Provide my daughter with a touch of intrigue. If she thinks she might someday become a field agent, she will go through with the wedding.'"

Olivia blinked. "She never intended to let me..."

"Work in the field?" Mr. Black shook his head. "No. She hoped with time and children your interest would fade. Always she underestimates her daughters, and this is how I end up camping among my people in freezing conditions." He sighed. "Italy was too much to hope for."

"I see." She bit out. She was never to be a field agent, never to be trusted with her own mission. She blinked back the tears that welled in her eyes. All her studies, all her training and still she was deemed fit only to retrieve information from a safe distance.

"Oh, for aether's sake." Mr. Black rolled his eyes. "Dry your eyes. If you'd not stowed away on his dirigible, slipping acousticotransmitters hither and yon, we might have lost Rathsburn and his technology to any number of foreign powers. No one foresaw the involvement of Russia or China." He paused. "And I expected him to have more time."

"You want him to succeed," she said. A dark cloud lifted. If anyone could sway the duke in Ian's favor, it was Mr. Black, his right hand man.

Mr. Black threw his hands in the air. "Of course. This is his chance to right an old wrong, to allow him to stop Warrick and retrieve his sister. Calmly. Quietly. Discreetly."

"You mean he's not to be charged with treason?" Aghast, her jaw fell open.

"Oh, should he fail, he'll be charged," Mr. Black said. "But if he retrieves that device, if he returns to Britain successful, no charges will be pressed. Instead, he'll be commended and promoted."

"If." Olivia swallowed. But if he failed... She glanced at her arm. "Did you not hear? I'm the one who was responsible for developing the programming for the device, for punching the cards that allows the instrument to function. I need to go help him."

A string of colorful Romani curses fell from the agent's lips. "No. We need to leave while the iron hooves of the clockwork horses and the wheels of the caravans can still move through the deepening snow."

She drew breath to argue further, but he held up a finger. "As to your involvement in programming the device, I heard nothing, and I advise you never to mention it again." He glanced over his shoulder into the woods. "Particularly if Rathsburn fails to return."

With that, Mr. Black turned his back on her, favoring one leg as he walked to the other caravan. Wei reached out to help him as he struggled up onto its seat. She ought to be

ANNE RENWICK

wrapped in a blanket and tucked inside, but the girl had a clear case of hero worship and would not be separated from him. He lifted the reins of the mechanical horse and raised his eyebrows.

Olivia glanced at the woods.

"No," Black yelled. "You'll only be taken captive and used against him."

If she didn't freeze to death first.

Blinking back frustrated tears, she jerked her chin in a nod and climbed the stairs, ignoring Elizabeth's concerned questions and the gypsy woman's considering gaze. Before she even had time to sit, the vehicle lurched into motion—rattling and rumbling through the forest over tree roots and stray rocks.

She landed on her rump with a thud. Drawing her knees to her chest, she tipped her head back against the wall of the caravan and studied the lamp that swung overhead. Was this how her adventure ended? Hauled home like a sack of potatoes while Ian took the final risk?

"Is there more than one kind of Queen's agent?" Elizabeth asked.

She was so tired of that question, regardless of its form. She ought not answer, but what did it matter? She was done with fieldwork, done with the Queen's agents. "I am—was—a societal liaison. Trained to marry a title, to monitor his illegal activities and report them to the Crown."

"Is that why you followed my brother?"

"Yes." She sighed. "No. Against all training, I attempted

to assist him. But by programming that device of his, by enabling the count to demand its use, I merely increased his odds of life in prison." So many lives might shatter if it fell into the wrong hands, and Ian would have every reason to regret ever meeting her. Yet here she sat, completely useless while the man she loved risked everything. Her chest felt heavy. Hollow. Was it possible for a heart to break? Because something deep inside was cracking, crumbling. "If he does not succeed, both of us are ruined."

The gypsy woman lifted her dark eyes to pierce Olivia with a fierce gaze. "You love him?" she asked in Romani.

"I do."

"Then you go."

The gypsy was right. Could Olivia fight? Not with weapons, perhaps, but she could do her best to stop Katerina's departure. She pulled herself to her feet, steadying herself against a wooden strut. She could not quit now, not at the mission's most critical point. "Are there clothes I can wear?"

"Yes." With a triumphant grin, the gypsy bent and threw open the lid of a trunk, rummaged through its contents and shoved a plain blue shirtwaist and a pair of dark knee-breeches into Olivia's arms. "Mr. Black is not always right," the gypsy said, still speaking in Romani. "Go help your love."

"What did she say?" Elizabeth asked. "What's going on?"

"I'm going after your brother." She would not sit idly while he walked back into that hornet's nest.

427

"Can you help him if you're not a full agent?"

"I don't know, but I have to try. If—when—that ptery-form drops the dead count at Katerina's feet, a chaotic power struggle could erupt."

She pulled on the shirtwaist, then the soft, worn breeches. They fit like a second skin, flaring at her hips, curving in at her thighs, buckling just beneath her knees and allowing a marvelous freedom of movement. Men had so many advantages. She took the leather boots handed to her, ones that rose above the knee and laced up the back. More clothing landed at her feet.

"I refuse to be treated like an incompetent." Olivia buttoned a leather vest, belted on a green velvet jacket. "Ian fails, and he's given a second chance. Me? I was barely allowed a first chance." Heat flooded her words, each scalding a bitter path across her tongue. "Years of training and I had to throw a fit to win the smallest of concessions. Then, because I haven't been properly briefed, I take the tiniest misstep in the interest of helping my country, and I'm to be chastised for failing to follow instructions to the exact letter?" She threw a hand in the air. "A male agent, he's admired for his resourcefulness, but aether forbid a woman takes initiative."

She would go back to the castle and help finish what she'd started. If they succeeded, she would not continue to work as a societal liaison on a determined path to widow-hood. She could do more than program household steambots to bake cream cakes and listen at doors. Perhaps she would begin by following her sister's example and storm the all-male citadel that was the Rankine Institute to demand they inscribe her legal name upon the diploma she'd rightfully earned.

All of *ton* society would think her stark, raving mad. She no longer cared.

Elizabeth pressed Wei's small zoetomatic bird into her hand. "Send a message back if..."

Olivia took the nightingale and tucked it into her coat pocket, the beginnings of a plan forming in her mind. She twisted her hair into a tight knot at the base of her skull, securing it with a handful of hairpins. "Have you any weapons on board?"

The gypsy woman nodded and pointed at a small trunk, an unremarkable brass-bound trunk. "That belongs to Mr. Black."

"Mr. Black?" Then it was anything but ordinary.

She skimmed her fingers over the metal strips, pressing at regular intervals, searching for the section that would yield to her touch. There. Between two commonplace rivets, the brass band slid to the side, exposing a sunken rotor. Not a particularly complex lock, but she'd trained to open these by sound. Listening for faint clicks on a wagon rumbling through the woods...

"Four. Six. Two. Five," the gypsy said.

"Mr. Black let you—"

"Let." The gypsy sniffed. "No. But I too am *just* a woman. A woman who has eyes that see around corners. Take whatever you want. I say nothing."

Olivia dialed in the numbers, and the trunk's lid hissed

open. It didn't hold much. She pawed through clothing, papers, various objects whose purpose gave her pause—she really ought to be more afraid of Mr. Black—and then her hand fell upon a pair of bioactive nocturnal goggles. She stared for a second in awe. So they *did* exist. She had heard whispers.

With such goggles, she could have been Ian's lookout. Anger seeped in, replacing indignity. Would be.

She hung them about her neck and dug deeper into Mr. Black's trunk.

The Roost. Katerina's trained pteryform could easily carry her—and the apparatus—from the castle to the storm frigate. Katerina would be heading there. Ian and Zheng would be in pursuit. Anything could happen.

The most direct route to The Roost was straight up. Olivia snatched up a set of mechanical climbing dragon claws. Scaling the castle walls with bare hands and boots was impossible, but with these... She shoved them into a sack and tied the bag to her belt with shaking hands. Looking up would surely be better than looking down. It would have to be.

Pulling on a dark, woolen cap to hide the bright beacon that was her hair, she swung an equally dark cape about her shoulders.

Elizabeth's mouth hung open as she stared at Olivia. "Are you certain you're not *that* kind of agent?"

She was tonight. She *had* to be. "Stay with Mr. Black," Olivia said. "He's the best of the Queen's agents. Do whatever he tells you. I'll see your brother safe."

And with that promise, she turned and leapt from the wagon.

CHAPTER THIRTY-EIGHT

L IGHT BLAZED FROM a castle window—the very window from which Ian had climbed out of mere hours ago. Katerina's silhouette filled the frame. A clear beacon. A reminder that she not only wished to deliver his technology to Russia, she also wished to deliver *him* to Russia.

He stopped in the shadow of the castle's stone wall. He'd lost much time and the advantage of surprise by rushing deep into the forest behind Wei, convinced Olivia and Elizabeth would both break their necks leaping from a seven-story window.

Squinting at the night sky, he searched for the Russian storm frigate through the driving snow. Nothing yet. But the mercury had dropped by several degrees and in the sky, a pteryform soared, flapping its great, leathery black wings, drawn by the increasing cold and awaiting its mistress' signal.

The snow swirled about him as one patrolling guardsmen greeted another, each clapping the other upon the shoulder with a smile. Though Ian could not understand the words, one guardsman pointed to the tumor upon his mandible, speaking excitedly. It seemed word was out that a cure had been found.

The plan was to stop Katerina, press the osforare apparatus into Black's hands, and see Olivia and Elizabeth safe across the border. Then he would return to this small German village. He owed a debt to the men, to the families whose lives had been irrevocably altered by the invasive bone cells he'd helped to create. He would obliterate Warrick's legacy from their bodies, their bones. Only then could he return home.

Unless Katerina had her way.

Even without his cooperation, Russia could reverse engineer the osforare apparatus. Her chemists could deconstruct the biochemical residue and, given enough time, they might reproduce it. But he would do everything within his power to prevent a future where men with silver skeletons attacked Britain riding astride armored pteryformes.

British security, his honor and his future depended upon his success. Katerina Dyatlova had to be stopped, and he had until midnight. Less than an hour.

OLIVIA SHOVED the bioactive nocturnal goggles onto her forehead.

She'd made it. Barely. If not for said goggles, she would have lost her race to the many tree roots that had stretched out to trip her, or the branches that tore and ripped at her arms, each assault a reminder that she was woefully ill-prepared for this latest self-appointed mission.

Her fingers and toes and ears and nose were frost-nipped. Her legs ached and her lungs burned from the unaccustomed exertion. And she'd only just reached the base of the castle. Far overhead, a pteryform circled, still tracing a holding pattern. Katerina had yet to order the creature to its perch, to The Roost, and that meant Olivia was not too late. Excellent, for her plan depended upon being the first to arrive.

Breathless, she unfastened the sack at her waist and drew forth the dragon claws. She fitted the steel hind claws to the toes of her boots, yanking the leather buckles to secure them more tightly than was strictly necessary. Then she slid her hands into the fore claws. With thumb and forefinger, she twisted the dial on each foot, each hand. A low hum began, informing her ears that power surged through their inner workings.

Pushing the goggles into place with the backs of her hands, she tipped her head back, studying the stone wall that stretched into the night sky. The Roost lay ten stories above her. If Wei could manage with bare hands and feet, certainly it wasn't madness for her to undertake the task with mechanical assistance. Was it?

Olivia took several long breaths, attempting to calm the anxiety that roiled inside her, then gripped the stone with one hand. With a flick of her index finger, the claw locked into place, holding fast. Impressive. She lifted her other arm and grabbed another piece of the wall. One foot secured with a toe-tap, then the next. A twist of her wrist and the first claw released. She reached higher. Hands. Feet. Limb by limb, she scaled the wall.

FIVE STEPS UP the tower stairs, Ian froze at the faint creak of door hinges. Sword raised, back against the wall, he waited. Anyone wishing to reach The Roost would need to pass this way.

More than an hour remained until the scheduled flyby. Early yet for Katerina to have left whatever bolt hole in which she'd hidden, but he hoped the prowler was her. He'd rather complete this task quickly and head with all due speed to the French border.

Alas, the cold, fierce eyes that stared up at him were not hers. These two dark pools belonged to a mercenary chemical peddler. "The count has been murdered." Zheng's voice promised to inflict vengeance upon all involved.

"Imagine that," Ian answered, keeping his face blank. "By his wife?"

Zheng's eyes narrowed. "He was hunting you and yours. He rode out upon the back of his pteryform, but came back in its claws. The beast dropped him from the sky, shattering his skull upon the courtyard's cobblestones."

"That's not murder," Ian answered. "Merely a predator returning with prey."

"Is it?" Zheng tipped his head. "The creature showed no interest in consuming him, but there were several deep puncture wounds. He'd lost much blood."

"Have you seen pteryform claws? The razor edge of its beak?"

"Your unanticipated return to the castle suggests a man who knows his way around a multitude of blades played a role. Upon your arrival, I removed several throwing knives from your person."

"So you did." Was this an accusation? Ian fought to keep amusement from his face.

"But as you were taken captive, you betrayed no loyalty, and so we have no further argument between us." Zheng waved a hand toward the stairs. "A Russian airship approaches, and that monstrous beast circles overhead. It now answers to the countess. I am certain she intends to leave with your device."

"Were you unable to keep Katerina secure?"

Zheng hissed out several words in Chinese. "No. She is a slippery eel."

On that they agreed. "I intend to stop her."

"I will help." Zheng nodded. "It is good you have returned. Britain will have need of antimony. We will form a new alliance."

It was hard to keep the shock from his face. "A partnership? With a man who allows his niece to sample poisonous food items? Who does not object to deadly

437

experimentation upon young men or women? Who kills a man in anger knowing the answers that man holds might save lives?"

"You had his papers." Zheng's eyebrows drew together. "He killed your father."

"And would have died," Ian spat, "*after* sharing all his secrets." Not entirely true. Given the option, he would have preferred for Warrick to end his days in a dank, dark cell. He gripped the hilt of his sword tighter as Zheng slid his hands into his sleeves of his tunic and withdrew a matching pair of wide but short—no longer than his forearms—swords. "I would rather proceed with your cooperation, but I cannot allow the device to fall into the hands of the Russians. As you decline an alliance..."

That was all the warning Ian received before Zheng attacked, shouting as he charged up the stairs. Both knifes spun in his hands, slicing through the air.

Steel clanged against steel and stone as Ian focused upon defending his position, of deflecting the unfamiliar slashing and hacking motions in the narrow confines of the tower stairs.

Zheng's short blades—perfect for fighting in tight, close quarters—and his unusual blade work quickly cut through Ian's defenses. A slash, a stab, and blood welled on his arm. But not before he managed to draw Zheng's blood as well—his tunic gaped open and a trickle of blood ran down from a small cut at his neck.

With a growl, Zheng altered his grip. Ian modified his defense strategies, and the fight clamored on.

"Gentlemen," a voice interrupted from below. "Please. I must pass."

Katerina. For once a welcome distraction. Again, she wore riding attire, black leather from head to toe, layered with a fur hat and cloak. In her hand she held *his* metal case containing *his* osforare apparatus.

Zheng spun to face the new danger, but spread his arms wide to keep a blade pointed at both threats. "You need me, Lord Rathsburn." He threw the words over his shoulder. "Admit it. Together our countries can stop Russia's imperial aspirations."

He tried to imagine Queen Victoria agreeing to an alliance with the Chinese emperor. The woman deferred to no one, and she certainly wouldn't appreciate Ian negotiating on her behalf. Except...

"That case she holds," Ian said. "Without it Queen Victoria will refuse to receive us." Zheng's blade lowered a fraction. Ian stepped closer. "And the countess is a Russian spy who once plied her trade on British soil. What a gift you could present to the Queen."

"Turn around, Countess." Zheng pointed both blades in her direction. "Tonight we board my dirigible, not yours."

Ian raised his blade and smashed the hilt into the base of Zheng's skull. He crumpled against the wall. Pointing his sword at Katerina, Ian said, "Set down the case."

"I am not in the mood for an argument, Lord Raths-burn." Katerina straddled Zheng's unconscious form, pulled a knife from her boot and slit the man's throat. As blood gushed onto the floor, she wiped the blade on

Zheng's tunic. A kick with her booted foot sent him tumbling down the stairs, a gruesome trail of blood in his wake.

Great aether but this woman is cold.

"I regret ever suggesting to Otto that he invite a Chinaman into our home. That man was nothing but an impediment from the day he arrived, unnecessarily complicating everything with his irritating loyalty to my husband." She raised her eyebrows. "Have you finally made the sensible decision to accompany me? I *will* make it worth your while."

"Set my case and your weapon down, and I will let you pass." They both knew it for the lie it was. "Flybys are swift and fleeting."

"My pteryform will wait." She slid the blade back into her boot and lifted a pronged weapon from her hip. "Russia needs a scientist such as yourself. I'll ask once more. Will you join me?"

The weapon she pointed in his direction was oddly reminiscent of a salad fork. Uneasy at its benign appearance, he took a step backward and upward. "I'm afraid I must decline."

She did not follow. "Bigamy? Or a trip to Russia?"

"Both."

"Your loss." She aimed the strange weapon and fired. He threw himself against the wall, but in the confined space—

An intense pain radiated through his arm, twisting and spiraling down to his wrist, his hand, his fingers. Every muscle convulsed. His sword clattered to the ground. Ian stared at the gelatinous strand that stretched from his arm to her weapon. It glistened in the torch light like... a tentacle?

Fighting to draw breath through the pain, he bent, reaching for his weapon.

"Ah ah," Katerina warned as she advanced, pointing her weapon at his abdomen. "Leave the sword on the ground. The cnidoblast of the sea comb contains enough poison to paralyze a grown man. A direct hit to the diaphragm, and you *will* stop breathing. Olivia will arrive soon, and it would no doubt distress her to learn of your death."

"Olivia?" he breathed out.

"Oh, yes. The poor, misguided fool followed you. Stay where you are, cause me no more trouble, and I will let you live. Once I've extracted your secrets from the device and her bones, I will ransom her. The Duke of Avesbury will pay handsomely. I wonder what secrets he would be willing to part with to see his daughter safe."

"Olivia is gone," he insisted through gritted teeth, praying that this time she hadn't ignored Black's direct orders. "She *is* safe."

"Safe? The way she keeps running after you, meddling in your affairs?" Katerina laughed. "If she persists in this business, please see that she receives some proper training. Her external ascent of the tower leading to the docking platform is lacking in both subtlety and finesse."

"She's here? Upstairs?" he gasped. The pain slowly crept over his shoulder, tendrils reaching out toward his throat. *Please, no.* But when had Olivia ever taken the safe path?

"Mmm. The poison seems to be affecting your hearing." Katerina kicked his sword. The blade clattered and clanged, scraping down the steep stairs until it stopped with a dull *thud* against Zheng's body. She turned sideways to pass. "Yes. Olivia will soon reach The Roost. Goodbye, Ian. I wish you had agreed to accompany me. As it is, I'm afraid I must ensure you do not try to follow. Do keep up the good work. I look forward to stealing your next discovery." She shifted her hand and discharged her weapon again. This time in his thigh.

Ian howled, then cursed as the pain shot through his knee and threaded across his hip, coiling about his lumbar vertebrae. His spinal nerves screamed the pain all the way to his toes as his legs collapsed beneath him.

"Until next time." Katerina blew him a kiss, then ran up the stairs.

CHAPTER THIRTY-NINE

ALMOST THERE. The stone balcony was only some five more feet above her head.

She paused in her climb as that blasted pteryform soared past. The beast had plagued her during her entire ascent, relentlessly circling the castle, growing more agitated the closer Olivia grew to The Roost. She hoped the creature's presence meant Katerina—and Ian—were still within.

Her arms and legs ached. The dragon claws only enhanced grip. This activity was not at all suitable for a lady who spent most of her life attending one social event after another, let alone one who'd recently had an arm broken and healed.

Three feet. Two. One.

She brushed a good two inches of snow away from the balcony's edge, then swung a leg over the stone wall and rolled onto the ground with a whimper of relief. Not only did her body ache, but between the biting wind and the icy snow that had pelted her during the climb, she was frozen to the core.

Pushing her goggles onto her forehead with the back of her hand, she unbuckled the dragon claw from her right hand and reached deep into her pocket to drag the nightingale forth. She tossed him into the air and watched him flutter about as he settled upon a metal downspout, before wearily shoving herself onto her feet.

"Stop right there," said Katerina. She was dressed entirely in form-fitting black leather and fur. The outfit was arresting, but even more so was the strange weapon she pointed at Olivia. In her other hand was the osforare case. Where was Ian?

"Hand over the case and tell me the name of the man who introduced you to Warrick," Olivia demanded, as if it would be that easy to convince a Russian spy to do her bidding. "Then I will let you go."

"You are quite adorable, Olivia," Katerina smirked. "No wonder Lord Rathsburn was so thoroughly charmed. So much so that he has declined to accompany me to Russia. You will go in his stead."

Her stomach turned. As she feared, Katerina must have waylaid Ian for he'd never agree to such a plan. "What did you do to him?"

"He's alive. As per my orders. No wasting a brilliant mind, not when he might still be recruited. Particularly with you to entice him, all round curves and golden curls." Katerina tipped her head. "You've been very useful. Distracting the lord, the count. Wei and Zheng. Programming the osforare apparatus. You could be more than a biological specimen, more than a hostage. I could mentor you. In Russia, the tsar does not let beauty blind him to a woman's abilities. To marry or not, it would be your choice."

"No, thank you." She would not betray her country or her newfound love.

The wind reached a furious pitch, blowing Katerina's hair into a wild tangle about her head. Far, far above several pteryformes flew toward a wide, dark shadow that took shape midst the driving snow. The Russian storm frigate calling them home?

The pteryform that had been circling the castle opened its beak and let out an ear-splitting screech. From the dark clouds above, it dove toward them, its wings beating against the night. She squinted as the beast soared past. A saddle was strapped to its back, a harness wound about its head and leather reins flapped in the wind.

"Her name is Sofia," Katerina said. "Yes, I see you eyeing my winged daughter. Not everyone can ride a pteryform. If they sense weakness, any weakness, they simply turn their head, pluck you from their back, and drop you to the rocks below. While we are airborne, hold tightly to my waist."

"I'm not—"

"Yes, you are. You will go with me, peacefully." Katerina narrowed her eyes. "If you do not climb onto Sofia behind me, you will force me to violence. Take a close look. This weapon I'm holding? Comb jellyfish poison. Even Ian was unable to fight off its effects and collapsed upon the stairs. You, on the other hand, might fall off a balcony. After which Sofia and I will swoop to the ground and sever your arm at the shoulder joint. I have been assured that a fresh bone or two will satisfy my scientists' requirements. Understand?"

Blood drained from her head, leaving her dizzy. She understood Katerina all too well. She swallowed and nodded. Time was short. Her mind raced, searching for a solution.

"Good," Katerina said. "Now, take off that ridiculous claw, it's time to leave."

As the pteryform circled back around, Katerina holstered her weapon and raised her arm in the air, making a fist of her hand. The pteryform screeched again, beating back with its wings, altering its direction. It stretched out a leg with sharp talons to grip the iron bar mounted to the stone balcony. It folded its leathery wings and swung its head toward Katerina expectantly.

She hoisted herself onto the balcony and reached for the reins.

It was now or never.

Whistling the tune Wei had used against the count, she sent the nightingale in Katerina's direction. It was only a tiny bird pecking the Russian spy's head, beating its small wings about her eyes, but it provided just enough distraction.

Katerina turned her head, hunching against the unexpected annoyance, and Olivia dove for the metal case, slamming into Katerina's side as she ripped it from her hands. The Russian spy lost her footing on the icy railing and fell over the side of the balcony with a scream of frustration. Dangling from the leather reins attached to the pteryform, she yanked her weapon from its holster and pointed it at Olivia.

"Give it back," Katerina demanded.

Oliva held the case over the railing. "If you shoot me, I'll drop it. *I* can build another, but you will need more than my arm to reconstruct it. Now, tell me the name of the man who introduced you to Warrick." Her father traded in information, and Olivia would have several demands upon her return. Assuming she survived the next few moments.

Katerina swung a foot over the railing, hooking it with the crook of her knee. She was coming back for the case.

The pteryform screamed with displeasure, throwing its head from side to side.

Olivia grabbed Katerina's ankle with the dragon claw, flicking her index finger to ensure a tight, unbreakable grip. Then she shoved her backward, holding the Russian in the air, slung between the reins attached to the pteryform and her claw. "I want a name!" Olivia yelled. She *needed* to know. "Tell me!"

"No." Katerina's jaw jutted in defiance.

With a roar of frustration, Olivia flung the metal case at the pteryform's head. She missed, but managed to strike the creature's shoulder. As the case tumbled to the rocks below, the pteryform flung its head backward and spread its wings, launching from The Roost, ripping the leather strap from Katerina's grip.

Olivia held on with all her strength, her feet skidding

across the icy balcony and slamming into the stone banister as Katerina fell backward, downward to slam against the castle wall. The sudden stop all but yanked Olivia's shoulder from its socket, and the muscles of her thighs strained to keep her from toppling over the railing.

It would be so easy, so very easy, to flick her wrist and send the Russian tumbling to her death. Instead, she reached with her free hand to grab the woman's other boot.

Far above, a shrill blast sounded.

"Let me go!" Katerina howled, kicking at her.

"Are you insane?"

"I said, let me go!" and the woman fired the odd weapon she held.

Olivia screamed as a flash of burning pain sliced through her shoulder. Every muscle spasmed in her arm, rendering it useless. But her arm was still attached to Katerina's boot and with every kick, she slid further over the balcony.

"Don't be a fool," Katerina yelled. "You'll fall with me. Let go!"

"I can't," Olivia yelled back.

"Hang on!" Ian called behind her. Then he was there, dragging Katerina upward and onto the balcony. But the Russian would have none of it; she lashed out, kicking at the hands and arms that held her ankle even as he drew her close to the balustrade.

"I CAN'T MOVE MY ARM," Olivia yelled.

Fighting through the intense pain, Ian had crawled, step by step toward her voice, arriving in time to see the silvery-white strand lash out and wrap itself about her limb.

"I have Katerina," he yelled. "I'm going to release the dragon claw. Ready?"

Olivia bobbed her head.

Holding tight to Katerina's ankle, he slid his hand down her arm, to her wrist and flicked the claw free. The sudden release of tension sent her staggering backward to sag against the castle wall.

She was safer there, away from the ledge.

Overhead the pteryform beat its wings, circling, crying her displeasure.

He turned his attention to Katerina. "You want me to let go?" Ian bellowed into the wind that pelted icy snow at his face. "I'll let go." His fingers were growing numb; if the spy wanted to be dropped to her death, he would cheerfully oblige. "But first answer her. Give me the name."

Katerina twisted and kicked.

"Last chance!" If he went through the effort of hauling her in, he would make good and certain she landed in a British prison.

"Darby," Katerina yelled. "Now let me go!"

He released her ankle—and stared in amazement as Katerina tumbled though the air only to land on the outstretched wing of her pteryform. She scrambled onto the creature's back and into the saddle, taking up the reins as if this were a much-practiced move. Probably, it was. The air cracked with the powerful beats of the beast's wings, and they disappeared into the swirling snow of the storm.

He turned. Olivia was gasping for breath, hand pressed to her throat. Rushing to her side as fast as his still-anesthetized leg would allow, he lifted her with his good arm and dragged her into the relative warmth of the tower room.

"Can't... breathe..." she wheezed.

"It's the jellyfish poison," Ian said. He ripped the tentacle fragments from her neck, flinging them aside. The muscles of her throat were constricting, cutting her off from air. He reached into his waistcoat pocket and dragged out his vial of veritasium. Part muscle relaxant, it should work. Except he had no syringe. "Stay with me."

He dragged her against his chest and snapped the vial's narrow class neck. Using its sharp edges, he made deep scratches into the skin of her throat and trickled the veritasium into the bleeding cuts. "Keep breathing, Olivia," he commanded her as her breathing took on a particularly strident tone.

With horrible rasping sounds that almost stopped his heart, Olivia dragged in a breath. Then another. And another. He pressed his lips against her hair, waiting. Agony tore through him at the thought that he might lose her. There would be no recovering from such a blow.

Finally, her breaths began to come easier.

"Zheng?" she wheezed against his chest.

Tightening his arms about her, he let go of a breath he'd not realized he was holding. "Dead," he answered. "It's just you, me and a number of terminally ill guardsmen we need to cure before we can leave Germany." No point in trying to convince her to leave without him. He'd wanted a strong, loyal woman, and he'd found her. He smiled. Rather, she'd found him. Now, it was up to him to find a way to keep her. "We'll head for the mill, as soon as we can manage the stairs."

CHAPTER FORTY

"DON'T BE RIDICULOUS," Mother chastised her nearly three weeks later over tea. Her needle plunged in and out of the silk fabric she held, her fingers gripping the embroidery hoop so tightly her knuckles were white. "I strongly advise you allow me to cancel Lord Rathsburn's afternoon audience with your father. You are being foolish. The best course of action is to marry Baron Volscini."

"Why?" Olivia asked. Her hand shook slightly as she sipped her tea.

"Why!" Mother threw her hoop aside and then her hands in the air. "You know why. Because... because..."

Life had moved in a bit of a blur after Ian had saved her in that tower. Holding each other up, they'd staggered down the stairs, past Zheng's body and through the kitchens into the courtyard. There they'd encountered dozens of guardsmen staring upward into the snowy night as the

Russian storm frigate passed overhead, their hunt for the traitorous countess brought to an infuriating end as she disappeared upon the back of a pteryform.

Hands raised, Olivia had called out to them in German. With her translation skills, they'd soon sorted things out, and an entire retinue of guardsmen had escorted them to the mill with unsurprising haste. The nightingale was dispatched with a message for Mr. Black and, before the sun could rise, the first of many guardsmen lay—dosed with arsenic—within the solenoid.

Mr. Black returned, negotiating with the Chinese for the return of all parts necessary to repair the escape dirigible, including a considerable amount of aether to re-inflate the balloon. She and Wei had climbed among the rocks at the castle's base, collecting what pieces they could find of the osforare apparatus, which amounted to not much. Elizabeth, when not inside the solenoid herself, acted as chaperone.

"Not married," she'd said, clucking her tongue. "We've had enough impropriety. Standards must be reinstated." Thereafter, Olivia and Ian had not been allowed a single moment alone.

Then word came that the heir to Burg Kerzen and its lands was en route.

Mr. Black insisted they depart. Ian objected. They compromised by recruiting and training a physician from a nearby village to complete the treatments. Though, had Warrick's victims not already shown great improvement, Ian would have refused to leave.

Exhausted, they'd boarded the repaired escape dirigible

to limp back to England. They'd landed in Dover where Mother had swept in, whisking Olivia away, subjecting her to a sharp tongue lashing the entire train ride back to London. In her absence, Baron Volscini had accepted Father's invitation to visit, and this evening there was to be a ball. Olivia was to be charmed and over the moon when the baron asked her for a third dance.

She objected. Vociferously.

"No," Olivia had told Mother. "I no longer wish to be a field agent. Or even a societal liaison. I want to be a programmer, one who is properly recognized."

"Don't be ridiculous," Mother had said, stabbing her needle into her embroidery and tossing it aside. "Women do not work as programmers, and the favors we exchanged to allow you to matriculate at the Rankine Institute need to be repaid. You will begin by marrying a gentleman approved by your Father."

This morning she'd nervously picked through her many gowns—all of which fit again following a prolonged diet consisting mostly of brown bread and broth—finally settling upon a pale blue afternoon dress. It matched her eyes perfectly and set off her golden hair and creamy complexion —and its golden brocade cincher nipped in her waist displaying two particular feminine assets to their best advantage.

There was only one gentleman occupying her mind.

But would Father approve of Lord Ian Stanton, Earl of Rathsburn? Unlikely. Not if Mother had any say.

The teacup rattled upon upon the saucer she held. She

loved him. Ian. And she did wish to marry. Ian. Only not as an obligation or as a means to finance the restoration of his crumbling estate.

She needed to speak with him. Privately. *Before* he spoke with Father. "I am of age," Olivia said. "I will marry if and when I choose. I *choose* not to marry Baron Volscini." She'd had an all too brief taste of love and wanted more. She would not settle. Not to appease her parents. Not to satisfy Ian's gentlemanly instincts.

"But the baron is eighty-three, wealthy, and powerful," Mother sputtered.

"And wrinkled and rheumatic and not likely to last another year." Olivia slammed her teacup down, splashing the dark liquid onto the pristine lace tablecloth that covered RT. He dinged and whirred his objections.

"Exactly." Mother fell back against her cushion. "A brief alliance with Baron Volscini will accelerate your advancement into the field by several years. We've been over this."

Olivia took a deep breath. "I know this comes as a shock to you, all my plans, tossed to the winds, but I never wished to be a societal liaison. It was a means to an end. As I no longer desire to become a field agent, it makes no sense to marry to satisfy anyone but myself."

"All that training, wasted," Mother objected.

"Oh, please," Olivia said, leaning forward on her seat. "You were never going to let me work in the field. Always you would have found some excuse."

Mother's jaw dropped.

"I could still work for the Queen. I could offer classes

in household technology and applied programming. Imagine the impact I could have upon national security if I were allowed to train all new female agents. A program that resembles a recipe for cream cakes or the instructions for a new way to knot a cravat, but is in fact hiding a..."

Why was she arguing her case before Mother? Sitting primly in the parlor, allowing herself to be relegated to the sidelines, waiting for the men to convene, to discuss her fate without any input from her?

Surging to her feet, Olivia stormed from the parlor, ignoring her mother's cries to see reason. She was done letting others arrange her future. She had a bird to send.

STROKING a hand down the smooth metal neck of a clockwork horse, a magnificent piece of gypsy craftsmanship, Ian struggled to wrap his mind around Black's words. "Say that again. The duke was hoping his daughter would break protocol?"

"He deemed Lady Olivia perfect for the task, a multilingual non-agent with lock picking and programming skills with aspirations of working in the field. Everyone but her mother hated to see her many talents—and charms—wasted on some ancient nobleman."

"You *expected* her to seduce me?" Ian gaped.

"Did she now?" Black sniggered. "As a gentleman, you should not have laid a finger on her."

True, though he couldn't regret what they'd shared. "I've offered her marriage."

"The duke is prepared to forgive all, should you arrive at your appointment with a special license and a *willing* bride. I expect a minister and a handful of witness will attend." Black climbed onto the horse's back, his mouth twisted with amusement. "Good luck."

"That's only two hours from now," Ian protested.

Black merely laughed as the clockwork horse trotted away.

Overhead a tiny bird appeared, flapping its wings. He plucked the nightingale from the air and unwrapped the narrow strip of paper banded about its ankle.

Follow me.

His head snapped up, searching Clockwork Corridor through the dense, sooty fog that had socked London in this past week. There. Across the street the feeble glow of a streetlamp illuminated a single golden curl escaping the confines of a heavy, hooded cloak.

Delicate fingers lifted the edge of the hood and two bright eyes flashed at him. With a sly smile, she turned and hurried down a dark alley. Alone.

His heart nearly stopped. This was no place for a lady. But then it gave a massive thud and raced in anticipation. *What is she up to?* He dashed over the cobblestones, chasing after her. A shadow moved at the end of the alleyway, turning the corner. A flip of her cloak, revealing a hem of blue silk.

Turning onto the intersecting street, he caught a glimpse of her booted ankles disappearing into a steam carriage. No driver sat at its wheel. His lips twitched. *An assignation?*

Body humming, he opened the door and climbed in. "Olivia?" he called into the dark space. Not a single light glimmered.

A hand grabbed him by his cravat, pulling him downward. Warm soft lips brushed his. "Kiss me," she whispered. "I've missed you so much."

He pushed the hood away, stabbing his fingers into her soft hair and happily obliged. He'd meant to keep it gentle, persuasive, but Olivia would have none of it. Her lips parted, inviting him inward. She wrapped her arms about his waist, sliding her hands beneath his coat, his waistcoat, clutching handfuls of his shirt and tugging it from his trousers.

It had been weeks. Two weeks and six days since he'd last kissed her. Longer still since that single night they'd shared a bed, and his entire body throbbed in anticipation of her touch, one particular part more than the others.

Panting, he pulled away. "Not here."

"Why not?" Olivia's fingers skimmed upward along the buttons of his waistcoat, loosening them.

He grabbed her arms, pressing them to her sides. "Not until we've settled things between us."

"Very well."

Her skirts rustled and there was a faint snapping sound. A soft, white-blue light began to glow, and he nearly changed his mind. She pushed her cloak from her shoulders, revealing the blue silk gown beneath. It was clear she'd dressed with his seduction in mind. Nothing improper, but the deeply cut neckline was more suited to an evening affair, and the tight cincher wrapped about her waist uplifted and showcased her beautiful, full breasts. Breasts she knew he greatly admired. Breasts he very much wished to touch again.

He sank onto the bench and groaned. "Not fair, Olivia."

Her laugh was self-satisfied and husky. "Let's settle things then. Quickly. I've not heard from you since we landed. Why?"

"Work," he answered.

It had been a busy week. Bioengineers excitedly labored in their laboratories studying armored pteryform tissue samples and attempting to reverse engineer the Russian tentacle. Agents exposed Russian spies burrowed so deeply into *ton* life that the damage to British security would take years to uncover and repair. Already Queen's agents were en route to Kadskoye. He wondered what—if anything—they would find.

"But everything goes well." Both her father and the Queen were satisfied with his accomplishments and a tacit agreement to forget any past transgressions was reached. "I've been reinstated as a Queen's agent and assigned to help infiltrate the Committee for the Exploration of Anthropomorphic Peculiarities."

"Good," she said. "They need to be stopped."

He reached into his coat pocket and held out a silver sphere upon his palm.

"Watson!" she cried, clutching the zoetomatic to her chest. "I thought he was lost in the village streets, stuck in a snowbank rusting away."

"He was found aboard the *Sky Dragon* in a corner of Wei's cabin," Ian said. "A crew member recalled Wei's fondness for the mechanical creature and included him along with her belongings. Watson only reached my hands this very morning."

"Thank you," she said and kissed his cheek. "Are Wei and Elizabeth getting along in the countryside?"

"They are, and asking about you." He paused. It was too soon to turn the conversation toward marriage. "What has filled your days?"

Her eyes narrowed. "Enduring my mother's diatribes blackening your name while listing, repeatedly, all the reasons I ought to consent to marry Baron Volscini. If I agree, the Queen will overlook my transgressions and allow me to continue on my former career path."

A thin sheet of ice crusted his heart. He swallowed, afraid to ask, afraid of the answer he might receive. "Is that what you want?"

"No." She dropped onto the bench beside him. "I want to work for the Rankine Institute, for the operations branch under my own name. Think of all I could teach future agents. Of the useful inventions with which I could provide them. I've a number of ideas of how to improve upon steambot programming and usage. How personal zoetomatics—"

He pressed a finger to her lips. "Allow me to support you in such endeavors. Marry me."

She frowned and looked away. "I never meant to trap you into actual marriage, Ian. It was all an elaborate charade, a game... until it wasn't." She took a deep breath. "I meant what I said. You needn't chain yourself to me out of a sense of obligation. *That* is why I needed to see you. Now, before you meet with my father, before he insists."

"No one is forcing me to marry you, Olivia. I *want* to marry you. It's true, before I saw behind the façade you presented to the world—that of a bubbly, empty-headed society miss—I would have passed on the opportunity to make your acquaintance."

"I waylaid you upon a railroad platform." Though she sounded dismayed, a corner of her mouth twitched.

"And snuck into my private chambers and stowed away. Though I suppose we'll have to alter that portion of the story when we tell it to our children."

Her blue eyes snapped to his, shining with love.

"Until I met you, I had no idea how alone I was," he continued. "You've filled an empty space in my heart I didn't know existed, and I've fallen in love." For once he didn't struggle to find the right words. "You're more than beautiful. You're intelligent, determined and... I watched you persevere through hardships and disasters and trauma that would have brought another person—man or woman—to their knees." He brushed a finger over her cheek. "*You* are the woman I want at my side. The *only* woman."

She pressed a hand to her heart. "You don't mind that I wish to use my engineering degree?"

"Mind? I insist. Publicly if you wish. Or secretly while continuing to assist the Queen's agents." Ian smiled broadly at the thought of her working by his side. "For if you agree not to tell your father, I would welcome your assistance hunting down those shadow board members."

"Occasional covert field maneuvers?" She returned his smile, lifting a hand to his jaw. "You *do* know the way to my heart."

"Then marry me. Say yes." He pulled her onto his lap and kissed the corner of her mouth, the edge of her jaw, the smooth column of her throat. "So we can combine business and pleasure."

"Yes," she said. "I love you and want to marry you and no one else."

"Today," he insisted. "By special license."

"As soon as possible," she agreed. "Now. Are things settled between us?" She squirmed against him. "Because I've arranged for us to have an entire carriage to ourselves, and I desperately wish to review several of your earlier lessons."

Raw desire surged through him at the thought of all they could manage in a carriage. "Review?" He pressed a hot, open-mouthed kiss against her neck as his hands roamed over the curves he'd been denied for days. "I thought to demonstrate more advanced material. If you'll climb astride..."

EPILOGUE

THREE WEEKS OF wedded bliss later, Olivia's first group of students—three girls placed in her care to learn the basics of zoetomatic programming—assembled around the end of a dining room table capable of seating sixteen. Strewn across the remaining surface area was a motley collection of scribbled notes and various clockwork mechanisms in different stages of construction.

"This is called an arithmetic logic unit," Olivia said. "It allows us to perform all four arithmetic operations."

A hand shot in the air. "And comparisons! And square roots!" Mildred had a tendency to shout out facts and figures as if she were answering a question even if one had yet to be asked.

"Exactly," Olivia said. "We will begin with these paper cards and punch a—"

Watson whistled, then spun in a circle before darting toward the door where Ian beckoned. She stood and smoothed her skirts, doing her best not to rush from the room and into his arms. It wouldn't do to let impressionable young minds witness anything improper. There was public behavior—she smiled—and there was private behavior.

"Girls, please attempt to punch cards that will allow Watson to calculate a simple mathematical operation," Olivia instructed. "I must speak with my husband."

"May we use the Franconian multipunch, Lady Rathsburn?" Anne inquired.

"Not yet," she replied, ignoring the manner in which Anne sagged in her chair and stuck out her bottom lip.

Wei rolled her eyes at the behavior of these upper class young ladies, but she was no angel. The gliding lessons she provided the other students ended, more often than not, in twisted ankles and scraped elbows.

Ian's shoulders were unusually stiff and tense, and her smile fell away as she followed him into the hallway. "What's wrong?"

He lifted a piece of paper, his face pinched with concern. "Our first assignment arrived. Elizabeth will supervise the girls. You need to pack a trunk."

She nodded. "Where to?"

"We're meeting Black in Glasgow. He needs me to vet a temporary undercover agent. If his skills are sound, he'll insert him into the laboratory of a scientist under suspicion of working for CEAP."

"It's true then?" Her eyes widened. "Selkies have been found off the coast of Scotland?"

Ian shook his head. "None have been spotted yet, but

that doesn't mean they're not there." A faint smile twitched his lips. "If it's excitement you're after, we can lurk about the rocky shores, peer out across beaches and stormy seas through a spyglass." His voice grew rough. "It'll be cold, but I promise to keep you warm."

"And my presence is necessary, why?" she asked, tracing the brocade pattern of his waistcoat, wanting to hear him speak his desire aloud.

"Your insight and expertise are always indispensable. But," he drew her close, sweeping his hands down her back as she melted against the warm planes and angles of his body, "I want you with me. I wouldn't be able to sleep without you."

She shivered in anticipation. "We scarcely sleep at all."

He pressed a kiss to the edge of her jaw. "Exactly."

ABOUT THE AUTHOR

Though ANNE RENWICK holds a Ph.D. in biology and greatly enjoyed tormenting the overburdened undergraduates who were her students, fiction has always been her first love. Today, she writes steampunk romance, placing a new kind of biotech in the hands of mad scientists, proper young ladies and determined villains.

Anne brings an unusual perspective to steampunk. A number of years spent locked inside the bowels of a biological research facility left her permanently altered. In her steampunk world, the Victorian fascination with all things anatomical led to a number of alarming biotechnological advances. Ones that the enemies of Britain would dearly love to possess.

www.AnneRenwick.com

instagram.com/anne_renwick
facebook.com/AnneRenwickAuthor
pinterest.com/AuthorAnneRenwick